# OREGON BRIDE

**DIVERSIONBOOKS**

To those brave souls who settled the American West, especially those who survived the hardships of the Oregon Trail. This book is dedicated to their spirit and determination and, more, to the women who bore that rugged journey in silent suffering.

## More from Rosanne Bittner

The Bride Series
*Tennessee Bride*
*Texas Bride*

Full Circle
Until Tomorrow

Diversion Books
A Division of Diversion Publishing Corp.
443 Park Avenue South, Suite 1008
New York, New York 10016
www.DiversionBooks.com

For more information, email info@diversionbooks.com

First Diversion Books edition May 2014.
Print ISBN: 978-1-62681-376-2
eBook ISBN: 978-1-62681-281-9

... Love much. There is no waste in freely giving;
More blessed is it, even, than to receive.
He who loves much alone finds life worth living:
Love on, through doubt and darkness; and believe
There is no thing which Love may not achieve...

—*Ella Wheeler Wilcox*

# One

## March, 1851 …

Marybeth MacKinder stood at a window of the cramped apartment she shared with her in-laws. She longed to breathe some fresh air, clean, sweet air like the kind she used to breathe in Ireland. But the beauty of Ireland, its rolling green hills and gentle, musical breezes were thousands of miles away. There was no sweet air to breathe in New York City; there was no green here, especially in March, when the melting snow turned rock hard and showed an ugly gray color, and the air outside was still far too cold for an open window. Besides, Marybeth's five-month-old son, Daniel, lay nearby, and she didn't want him to get a chill.

She watched horses and buggies clacking back and forth in the wet street, watched crowds of people going this way and that, women lifting their skirts to avoid the slush. No one was aware of Marybeth's particular predicament, and certainly none of them cared, especially not about an Irish Catholic. She wondered if every city in this land called America was as big and dirty and cold as New York. Mostly she wondered what it was like in Oregon, that strange land three thousand miles away where the MacKinders had decided to go.

Much as Marybeth disliked New York, she liked even less the idea of going into the "wilderness," as her father-in-law called it. At least in the cities in the east, there was help—doctors, food, housing. She strived to envision the sheer nothingness Murray "Mac" MacKinder had told them about just that morning. William Stone, a friend Murray had met at the ironworks where both men worked, was the one who had planted the idea in Murray's head to go west. He was the one who had been as far as a place called St. Louis and had told Marybeth's father-in-law about the opportunity that lay farther west.

"California has filled up fast," the man had told Mac, "what with all the fools who went rushing out there looking for gold. All the attention has been drawn away from Oregon over the last couple of years, and there is still some prime land left there for the pickings, I'm told. After taking what we got from Mexico, and the northwest territory from Great Britain, there can be nothing but good things in store for all the west, Mac. Manifest Destiny, they call it. We Americans are destined to own all the land between the Atlantic and the Pacific. A man would be crazy not to get in on the ground floor."

Stone had spoken with a great deal of authority, as he was prone to do. Marybeth doubted he always knew what he was talking about. He liked to sound important, but Marybeth suspected he had no idea what really lay out west and was just in it for the adventure, as a lot of men probably were. But now, with her husband dead, Mac needed to get away from things that reminded him of his oldest son.

"You're a farmer at heart, Mac, you've told me that," Stone had badgered. "You hate the stink and dirt of the city, and now that your son is dead, what's the use? To stay here means an early death, like Daniel, and continued ridicule from the Protestant bastards who are always insulting you. Religion makes no difference to me, mind you, and out in Oregon the air is clean and a man can own all the land he wants; and people are too busy getting settled and surviving to care about your religion."

Marybeth's eyes misted at the reference to Dan's early death. Her husband had died in a horrible accident at the ironworks, burned to death when he fell into a vat of hot metal. That had been just a little over three months ago, in December of 1850; baby Danny was only two months old at the time.

Marybeth felt sorry for the way her husband had died, but she could not help the relief she secretly felt at realizing the man could no longer abuse her. She could only pray God would forgive her for marrying a man she didn't love in the beginning, and learned to hate over the four and a half years they were married.

The MacKinder family had owned the land on which Marybeth's family worked, and Dan MacKinder and his brother John both had an eye for Marybeth from the time she was twelve years old. Both young men had frightened Marybeth with their big, brawny size and loud voices. They were blustery, bragging, drinking men who believed every woman had her place and that every woman they met desired them.

If it were not for the sudden death of Marybeth's father from a heart attack, Marybeth reasoned she would never have married Dan. But she and her mother had been left penniless and dependent, unable to pay the rent on their cottage and unable to put out enough work on the MacKinder farm to pay their way. It was then Dan had taken advantage of the situation, speaking words of love Marybeth had allowed herself to believe, telling her that if she married him, she would be a part of the family and her mother would be taken care of. It was for that reason alone Marybeth, only fifteen years old at the time, had married Dan in the spring of 1846, choosing Dan over John simply because he was at least slightly less frightening than his younger brother. She had convinced herself that for survival she could tolerate Dan MacKinder, and perhaps after a while she would learn to love him.

A lump rose in her throat as she watched a gentle rain begin to fall. It had rained nearly every day for the past two weeks, a cold rain that made one's joints ache. Now Marybeth wondered what it might be like to truly love a man. She had quickly learned it was impossible to love one like Dan MacKinder. He had wasted no time in taking advantage of his husbandly rights on their wedding night, and Marybeth had never since given herself to him openly and joyfully, had never felt loved nor known a moment's peace with the man. The only good thing that had come of their marriage was little baby Danny, all she had left now, her most precious possession.

How she wished her mother could see the baby. But her

mother had been buried before they left Ireland, a victim of the horrible potato famine that had killed so many thousands. The MacKinders had lost everything, and had used what little money they had left to come to America, landing in New York, the men taking jobs right away at the ironworks to build up a savings.

Life had been hard here, the pay at the ironworks minimal. The MacKinders had lived in near poverty, a startling contrast to the comfortable life they had once lived in Ireland. The worst part had been the ridicule and mud-slinging they had all suffered at the hands of prejudiced Protestants. Marybeth could not help wondering that if Mac and her brother-in-law, John, were more civil toward people themselves, perhaps they would have been better accepted. Their threatening size and bragging personalities only seemed to aggravate the situation.

The move to America had ultimately cost Dan MacKinder his life, and losing a son had brought bitter disillusionment to Murray MacKinder, making him even more belligerent. He was a farmer at heart. When Bill Stone began talking about Oregon and the wonderful climate and soil he had heard that land boasted, Mac decided that Oregon was the place to settle.

They would leave New York soon. Bill Stone would accompany them, since he "knew the way" to St. Louis. At St. Louis they would take a riverboat across a place called Missouri and at a place called Independence they planned to join a wagon train headed west. According to Stone, hundreds, perhaps thousands, would go west again this year. Marybeth wondered if some day there would be no one left in the east. In 1849, just two years after they arrived in New York, the ironworks had lost over half its employees because so many had run off to California to find gold. There had been a steady migration west ever since, but to Marybeth "the west" sounded like some mythical place that didn't really exist, a place where people went, only to disappear forever, and a place that would put her even farther away from her beloved Ireland, which she knew with an aching heart she would never see again.

Little Danny started to cry, interrupting Marybeth's thoughts. She walked over to her son and picked him up from the cradle, walking with him and patting his bottom. Her feelings over his father's death were mixed. She was sorry little Danny did not have a father, yet she would not have wanted her son to grow up with Dan MacKinder as a role model. Dan had been a loud, demanding, impatient man, who would have been a harsh father, and would have raised little Danny to be just like him, just as Mac had done with his sons. Marybeth wanted *her* son to be strong and brave and sure, but she wanted him to have compassion; to be quietly strong, not a braggart; to smile and know joy.

"Have you finished packing yet?"

Marybeth turned to see her mother-in-law, Ella MacKinder, standing in the doorway. She wished Ella could be like her own mother, who Marybeth missed more deeply every day. Ella's own marriage to Murray MacKinder had been arranged, and Marybeth wondered at how unhappy the woman had to be deep inside. It was that unhappiness that made it easier for Marybeth to forgive the woman's cool, stern attitude.

"Not yet," Marybeth answered the woman, cradling Danny in her arms. "Danny started fussing."

Ella marched into the room, her red hair graying, her lips seeming to be set permanently in a hard frown. Marybeth noticed two distinct wrinkles embedded above the woman's nose from always knitting her eyebrows together in displeasure and quiet acceptance of her fate.

"It won't hurt to let the boy cry once in a while," Ella said aloud to Marybeth. "He's five months old and knows how to get your attention. You're spoiling him. You know we need to finish packing. In two days we'll be in a house on wheels headed into God knows what. I'm sorry you have to trudge into the wilderness with us, Marybeth, but you certainly can't stay here, and little Danny belongs with us." The woman was folding blankets as she spoke. She faced Marybeth then. "You certainly can't be going out to try to find work with a baby to care for. We're taking good care of you and Danny, aren't we?"

Marybeth met the woman's icy blue eyes. "I never said anything about going out to find work or not going with you,

Ella. You and Mac have continued to give me and Danny shelter. I'm very grateful."

The woman sniffed, opening a dresser drawer and sorting out some clothes. "I should hope so. When we came over here, we never dreamed something would happen to Dan and we'd be left with a daughter-in-law and grandchild to support, let alone the filth of this city and the meager wages poor Mac and John bring home."

Marybeth's heart fell at the words. Ella MacKinder always had a talent for making her feel in the way, a bother and a burden, and it angered her. "You just said yourself I don't have much choice for now," she answered, laying Danny back in the cradle. "But as soon as I can find a way to be out from under your feet, you can be sure I will take advantage of it." She reasoned that the "meager" wages would go a lot farther if Mac and John didn't drink half of them away in the saloons on payday.

Ella felt a sudden fear at Marybeth's words, wondering why she always managed to say something cutting to Marybeth when she didn't really mean to. She wondered just when the bitterness had taken such a firm hold in her soul. She turned to look at her daughter-in-law.

"I didn't mean that the way it sounded," she said, an unfamiliar pleading in her voice. "I … enjoy having Danny with us. He's all that's left of my son."

*"But look how your son turned out,"* Marybeth wanted to shout at her. *"I don't want my baby to be like him. I don't want him to grow up under the influence of Mac and John."*

"I understand," Marybeth said aloud. There was no sense in telling the woman she did indeed intend to fend for herself some day. Somehow she would find a way. She was free of Dan now—free of his demanding rules, free from being his household and sexual slave, free from his shouting, free of his big fists. Her father-in-law and John were no different, but she didn't belong to them and they couldn't touch her. She was well aware that she had to get away from this family somehow, some day. She simply had to find the right time, and she had to be able to take care of herself and Danny when it happened.

She heard John come into the apartment then, yelling for supper.

"It will be ready in a bit," Ella called to her only remaining son.

The sound of John's voice made Marybeth's heart tighten with dread. John MacKinder had become her most pressing reason for being free of the MacKinder family. John was twenty-eight, and like Dan, he was a big man, standing six feet four inches, big-boned and hard-muscled, with very dark hair and eyes. At first glance most women would think him extremely handsome, just as Dan had been; but Marybeth had quickly learned to think of Dan as almost ugly because of his temper and egotistical manly pride. She felt the same way about John.

Since Dan's death, John had been watching her, declaring that because she had been his brother's wife, it was his responsibility to look out for her now. Marybeth didn't want him looking out for her. She knew what he really wanted. Now that Dan was dead, John had been giving sly hints that because of baby Danny Marybeth had a responsibility to stay in the family. Marybeth knew exactly what he meant. He wanted to take Dan's place. She knew that both Ella and Mac would whole-heartedly approve of such an arrangement and would encourage John, who would not be an easy man to deal with or to turn away.

Her only saving grace for the time being was that Dan had been dead only three months. It was far too soon for any man, even her husband's own brother, to make advances. Whenever John MacKinder even hinted at such a thing, Marybeth always reminded him to remember his brother was still practically fresh in his grave.

"Aren't you afraid to go to Oregon?" Marybeth asked her mother-in-law.

Ella shrugged. "There are a lot of things I've been afraid to do, but I did them anyway because it was expected of me. That's the way it is for a woman. She remembers her place and does what's expected. You remember that. I've seen a haughty streak in you sometimes, Marybeth MacKinder, a look of independence. That isn't good in a woman. It's sinful and unbecoming."

The woman held out an empty carpetbag. "You're a

MacKinder, Marybeth, and where the MacKinder men go, their women follow. I'm not afraid because Mac and John will take care of us, and Bill Stone knows what he's about. Mac says once we get to Oregon, we'll have the biggest farm west of the Mississippi River, wherever that is. Knowing my husband, he can probably do it. And you'll be a part of it. It will take a lot of hard work, but we can make it. Now fill this bag with clothes—practical ones. There will be no room for fancy things. We've got to sort out the least important items. Bill Stone says we've got to keep the wagons light, especially when we cross the mountains."

Marybeth did not argue the issue. Trying to reason with Ella MacKinder, or to carry on a decent conversation with her, was like talking to a stone. Her way was the MacKinder way and there was no room for discussing anything different. She took the bag from the woman and set it on her bed.

Ella watched Marybeth with irritation, both at herself and at her daughter-in-law. Ella was a short, stout, big-busted woman, who wished she could bring herself to be more open to Marybeth, but who often found herself resenting the younger woman's delicate beauty. Ella remembered a time when she was slender, when her hair was a shining red like Marybeth's, her figure trim, her blue eyes carrying a sparkle like Marybeth's green ones did.

Ella's resentment of her faded beauty had grown worse when she lost her son. She felt only anger toward her husband for convincing his sons and the rest of the family to come to America, where Dan had died. But her hidden anger toward her husband had begun many years before her son's death, almost from the moment they were married. She had never known a day's kindness, and she wondered where all the gentle, loving feelings she once possessed had gone.

Most of all Ella resented Marybeth for missing the same fate of an unhappy marriage. Dan's death had ended what Ella suspected was a loveless marriage. Marybeth was free now, and that both irritated and frightened Ella. Her own unhappiness had been eased somewhat by knowing her daughter-in-law suffered the same marital problems as she. But now Marybeth was shed of that unhappiness. Ella's biggest fear was that she could lose her grandson, the only sweet, happy being in the entire MacKinder family. If Marybeth found another man, she would take little Danny away.

The MacKinders were determined Marybeth should go to Oregon with them and stay within the MacKinder family. After all, she was Dan's wife, and her baby was a MacKinder. Ella worked hard at making sure Marybeth remembered that, since Marybeth had always had an air of independence about her, something that had irritated Dan and had brought her beatings she could have avoided.

Now that she was free of Dan, Ella was going to make sure Marybeth didn't get any ideas about leaving the family. She saw that Marybeth suffered proper feelings of obligation. Without the MacKinder family, Marybeth would be lost in this new land. After all, what was there here in New York for an Irish Catholic widow woman with a small baby? Marybeth's world had been this small apartment and this street and just a few streets beyond. She had not worked outside the home since arriving in America, and she and Dan had lived with the family ever since they married five years ago. They were points Ella harped on nearly every day.

The best insurance that Marybeth would stay with them was if the young woman would marry Danny's brother John, who the whole family, including Marybeth, knew had wanted to marry her clear back when Danny won the honors. John had remained angry for a long time after the marriage, not even speaking to his brother that first year.

"Do you think the mountains are like the ones in Ireland," Marybeth was asking.

"Much bigger, Bill says. Of course he hasn't even seen them himself. He's just going on what others have told him. I'm inclined to believe the man likes to exaggerate. But we'll see. We'll see."

Marybeth closed her eyes against the thought of the journey: wild Indians, disease, gigantic mountains to cross, mountains so high, that sometimes the snow never melted at their tops. She took some petticoats and underwear from her drawer and put them into the carpetbag, wondering how she was going to separate fancy from practical when she didn't own anything fancy in the first place.

"I just hope Danny doesn't get sick out there," she said to Ella. "There are no doctors like here in New York."

"There's no sense questioning or complaining," came the reply. "It's been decided and that's that. Danny is a healthy baby and you're a healthy mother. You'll both be just fine. When you're old and full of pains like I am, you'll have something to complain about, but even then you'll keep it to yourself because that's the proper way."

*"Is it really?"* Marybeth wanted to ask. *"Or is that just Murray MacKinder talking? Did you ever used to smile, Ella? Did you ever want to sing, long for some genuine affection? Have you ever known a day of tenderness from Murray MacKinder?"*

"I wasn't complaining," she told Ella aloud. "I was stating a simple fact. But I will say that I won't miss this city and its filthy air. Maybe at least when we get away from here the air will smell clean and sweet like Ireland. Do you ever miss it, Ella?"

The woman stopped her packing and straightened, staring at a wall. "Of course I miss it," she answered. "But we had to come here to survive. Lord knows we didn't know it would be this miserable. Maybe things will be better in Oregon." She cleared her throat, and Marybeth detected the woman was suddenly struggling not to cry. "I only wish Dan could have lived to go with us. We should have gone as soon as we got here." She sighed deeply. "They say Oregon is a lot like Ireland—lots of rolling, green hills. Do you suppose they're right, Marybeth?"

Marybeth frowned, surprised at the sudden show of feeling in the woman's voice. She realized Ella missed Ireland as much as she did. "I wouldn't know," she answered quietly. "I only pray they're right."

The woman resumed packing. "Well, we'll find out, won't we? Now finish your packing. We have a lot of other things to do. Mac and Bill Stone have gone to get the wagons. John will be driving yours." The woman turned to face her. "John's a good, strong young man like Dan was. Some day he'll make a fine replacement for Dan—a fine father for little Danny. I know you're mourning Dan right now, but when we reach Oregon, you'll understand how much you need a man, Marybeth; how much Danny needs a father. It's no good a woman being alone out there. You'll have all of us until we get there, and it will make things a lot simpler for the whole family if you let John take over for Dan in your life."

Marybeth felt her heart pounding with dread. "But ... I don't love John enough to marry him."

Ella looked startled at the remark. "Love?" She let out a little chitter. "Did you love Dan?"

Marybeth reddened. "I ... I married him, didn't I?"

"That is not what I asked you. And I already know the answer." Ella stepped closer. "You married him to help your mother. I know that. I knew it from the beginning." That said, she turned away, walking over to look down at Danny. "My marriage to Mac was arranged. I quickly learned love is just a frivolous and unnecessary ingredient to a woman's life, Marybeth. We can love our children, but it isn't necessary to love the men who bed us. We do our duty. Even for women who think they love their men before they marry them, it ends up the same way—a woman makes a home for a man, cooks for him, gives him sons. It's that simple. She does what is expected of a woman, what she was put on this earth to do. And I'll not have you shame this family by being too long a single woman, or deny my grandson his needs by raising him without a father. We both know the right thing you should do after a matter of time. And in the meantime, you watch yourself on this journey. You're a beautiful woman, Marybeth."

She returned to packing, her back to Marybeth. "I was not a bad-looking woman once myself. But beauty fades fast, young lady, and if a man marries you just for your looks, he's quickly disappointed. So don't be thinking about things like love. And don't be giving the eye to any strange men on this journey. You stay close to us and mind yourself. You're a MacKinder now. Dan may be dead, but that doesn't change your station with us.

You remember that, and you remember who is looking after you, putting food in your mouth."

Marybeth closed her eyes and turned away, realizing there was no sense expressing any of her personal feelings to the woman. Her miserable loneliness had only grown worse with every passing day, and she was almost in pain from a need to just sit down and cry. But she had to force back the tears. MacKinder women were not supposed to cry. It was a sign of weakness and displeasure. It was forbidden. Marybeth wondered when the last time was that Ella MacKinder had wept. Perhaps it was on her wedding night.

# Two

The rain poured down so hard that Marybeth wondered if God intended to break His promise that He would never again flood the Earth.

"Come on out, Marybeth," she heard John shout. "We need everybody to push!"

Marybeth pulled her wool, hooded cape around herself, praying little Danny would not get sick from the cold, wet weather. John helped lift her down from the wagon, his big hands more familiar with her body than necessary.

"Every man and woman on this wagon until we get through this muck," he shouted at her above the thunder.

John and Mac each took a wheel, while Bill Stone tugged at the mules from the front of the wagon and Marybeth and Ella pushed at the back. The men had got Bill Stone's wagon through the muddy hole of the road by themselves, but now the MacKinder wagon was stuck deep. Marybeth pushed with everything she had, her feet sinking almost to her knees. The wagon gave way and Marybeth fell forward into the muddy mire, holding back an urge to scream. So far the trip had been miserable. The weather had been cold and rainy most of the way, and they were only as far as a place called Ohio, about half way to St. Louis. Already Bill Stone was telling them that this was the easiest part of the journey; the real problems would come after they left Independence.

"At least here we hit a town every few miles," the man had told them over a campfire the night before. "But you'd better be sure to have plenty of supplies once we leave Independence. Supply stops are few and far between then."

Marybeth liked him less and less for getting all of them

into this, but Mac considered Stone his best friend since coming to America. Bill was an "American." He had been to the "great west." He knew where the opportunity lay in this country. He was not prejudiced against the Irish, and he actually seemed to look up to the MacKinder men, which Marybeth knew fed their great egos.

A strong hand grasped Marybeth's wrist and she felt herself being pulled from the mud. John MacKinder laughed at her.

"Aren't you a pretty sight now?" he said with the same robust Irish accent as the rest of the MacKinders.

"And I'll be thanking you not to pull my arm from its socket, John MacKinder," Marybeth answered with an equal Irish roll to her tongue.

John just laughed, pulling her close as though she belonged to him. "I like when you get angry, Marybeth. You get all pouty. What did my brother do with you when you got like that?"

Marybeth pushed him away. "It's none of your business." She trudged off to catch up with the wagon, and John MacKinder watched, wishing there was no such thing as a "proper mourning time." He didn't miss his brother at all. In fact, if Marybeth and his parents knew the truth…

He shook off his thoughts. Dan was gone, and that was fine with him. What more logical thing should Marybeth do than turn to John? He reasoned that after a time she would begin to need a man, *want* a man. When that happened, he would be more than ready.

Marybeth reached the wagons, shivering. Mac and Bill had pulled both wagons under a tall stand of pine trees, which gave only a little shelter from the rain. Marybeth longed for a hot bath; sometimes she even longed for the dreary little apartment back in New York. At least it was warm and dry.

"We'd best get inside the wagon and get into dry clothes," Ella told her, walking up beside Marybeth. "The men are hungry. All we can eat right now is some of those leftover biscuits from this morning."

Both women climbed inside Marybeth's wagon and quickly changed. Marybeth hung her wet muslin dress outside the wagon so it wouldn't drip all over things inside, but already a few blankets and other belongings were wet and muddy. She longed for warm, dry shoes, but as long as the ones she wore were already soaked, she decided to leave them on and keep her other pair intact. She winced at the squishy feeling inside them. She pulled on a black calico wrapper dress, having trouble with the arms when the material stuck against her damp skin. She wrapped a dry shawl around her shoulders, hanging her wet cape outside the wagon.

The rain continued to pour, and Marybeth checked little Danny, making sure none of his bedding was damp. Ella dug some biscuits out of a leather bag and called to her husband, who left a spot under a huge pine tree where all three men were huddled.

"Eat these biscuits for now," she told Mac.

The man took one from her and studied it, water dripping from his hat. "After all the work me and John and Bill have done this morning, us sitting out here in the cold rain—and you give us cold biscuits?" His blue eyes lit up in a rage.

Marybeth knew the look well. She had seen it many times in Dan's eyes, and often in John's. Murray MacKinder was just as big and dark as his sons, only graying at the temples, his belly beginning to sag. He liked his whiskey; Marybeth didn't know many Irishmen who didn't. But whiskey didn't seem to affect all of them the way it affected Mac and John; the way it had once affected Dan. Mac and John and Bill had been guzzling whiskey all morning "to keep their blood warm" while they trudged through the mud, and the alcohol was catching up with them.

Mac threw two of the biscuits to the ground and squished them into the mud. "You know we need more than this, woman!" he shouted to Ella.

"And how can I be expected to cook you a meal in that rain, and with no fire?" she asked.

Mac's eyes widened, and he reached up and grasped her hair at one side of her head, making her wince. Marybeth looked away, anger burning in her soul.

"Are you talking back to me, woman?"

"I'm only stating a fact, Mac," she answered. "I can't cook without a fire."

The man let go of her, giving her a little shove as he did so. "I don't want to hear any complaints about the inconvenience of this journey," he told her. "You'll have your fancy do-dads when we get to Oregon and get all that land. You'll have a place to cook, and maybe then you won't be talking back. Bill got some dry wood he's been carrying in his wagon and he'll get a fire going under that tree over there. When you see it burning good, you come out and cook us a proper meal." The man moved his eyes to Marybeth. "And you help. If we're going to feed you all the way to Oregon, you do your share around here."

"You know I've done just that so far," Marybeth said sharply. "I never meant to be a burden to any of you! And do you consider little Danny a burden also—your own grandchild?"

The man just glared at her, hating the way his daughter-in-law had of not only talking back but making sense. He didn't like women who knew how to think for themselves. Somehow they seemed a threat to his manhood. Women like Marybeth were nothing but a burden to a man. It seemed that since Dan's death, she had become more obstinate and independent, and he didn't like it one whit. "You go help your mother-in-law," he repeated.

"I'll help her—but because I *want* to help her and because she shouldn't have to go back out in the rain, not because you've ordered me to help."

MacKinder glared at her a moment before trudging back to the other two men. Bill had a fire going and the three men warmed their hands over it.

"Mother going to fix us some supper?" John asked his father.

Mac looked at his son, scowling. "She'll be along." He shook his head, looking back at the fire. "It will be a good thing when you marry that daughter-in-law of mine," he added. "She needs a man to put her in her place."

John only laughed. "Her big ideas will get her no place where we're going, Father."

"Me, I'm glad I have no women hanging around my neck,"

Bill Stone put in, lighting a thin cigar. He dipped his head and water ran off the brim of his hat. Stone was a short, pouchy man who always looked as though he needed a shave. He admired the MacKinder men, big, brawny, sure of themselves. Being Murray MacKinder's friend had made him feel more important back in New York. People were afraid of MacKinder. Now, to have these two big men looking to him to guide them to St. Louis only enhanced Stone's feeling of importance.

"Ah, my Ella is no problem," Mac told the man. "She knows her place. She gets a little spicy once in a while, but a good whack knocks it out of her. Marybeth could use a good wallop herself, but she'll come around, especially when she's got a man in her bed again. John will take care of that part of it before this trip is over, I don't doubt."

John watched Marybeth climb out of the wagon then. Sleeping in Bill Stone's wagon every night and thinking of Marybeth lying asleep in the other wagon was a source of torment for him. Every day he worked beside her, ate beside her; his hands were caloused from helping drive the team of mules that pulled his father's wagon, a wagon in which Marybeth often rode with Danny when it was feeding time. During the day they were almost like man and wife. But then would come the nights, the teasing, provocative nights—sleeping in separate wagons.

"Yes, Pa, you can be sure I'll take care of it," he answered, slugging down some more whiskey. All three men chuckled, waiting for their meal.

Every mile of the journey Marybeth feared for Danny. The weather remained miserable, as did Marybeth's spirits. Each mile took them all deeper into a muddy wilderness, and Marybeth felt more and more isolated, realizing little Danny was truly all she had and all she cared about. She could not imagine what she would do if anything happened to him.

All through Ohio and Illinois the canvas-topped wagons creaked and jolted their way along rough roads mucky with spring thaw. Marybeth began to wonder if her bones would ever again enjoy any warmth or if her feet would ever again know comfort. A combination of blisters and cold made walking a painful burden, but walk she did most of the time, for the animals were not to be overburdened with extra weight.

Sometimes Marybeth was sure the MacKinder men were more concerned for the mules than they were for their women, and she began to feel like little more than a plow horse herself, trudging on mile after mile, often carrying Danny in her arms or picking up firewood along the way, trying to keep clothes and bedding clean, helping with meals. There was always water to fetch, fires to make, clothes to be washed, small animals to be skinned and cooked. The chores were endless. She had never minded work, but she did mind being ordered about like a servant, with never a word of gratitude.

If this life bothered Ella, she refused to show it. There were days when Marybeth was sure Ella did not feel well, when the woman looked as though she was ready to drop. But she carried on silently, afraid to speak up for fear of offending her husband. Watching her, remembering the unhappy years of her own marriage, only made Marybeth more determined she would not marry John MacKinder and spend her whole life being little more than his slave. She began to wonder if Ella was right—that all men turned out the same, no matter how a marriage started. If that was true, Marybeth planned never to marry at all.

For now she could only be grateful for the difficult journey, for it kept everyone too busy and tired to talk about personal interests. April finally brought some warmth, but it also brought an unexpected heat wave to the Ilinois prairie, which awakened what seemed millions of insects. The men spent most of their time cursing at bites, and Marybeth spent most of her own time trying to keep mosquitoes and other pests off of Danny.

The first of May brought drier, more comfortable air to the land, and the MacKinders arrived in St. Louis just in time to join a line of at least seventy wagons lined up in front of the domed courthouse near the Mississippi River. Arriving at the bustling, rapidly growing frontier city helped ease Marybeth's concerns.

St. Louis was fascinating, much more pleasant than New

York, although many times smaller and much less developed. Most of its streets were still dirt, many of its buildings made of logs. The most beautiful and modern building was the courthouse, and while the MacKinders and Bill Stone met with other travelers to get information on what to do next, Ella stayed with the wagons and Marybeth walked with Danny in her arms, studying the great dome of the courthouse, led by curiosity through its doors.

Inside it was cool. She could hear the voices of hundreds of travelers echoing in a central room surrounded by a railing. She walked to the railing, leaning over and peering upward to a great, golden dome rising what seemed to her a hundred feet high. The walls of the dome and of several upper floors that circled it were painted with beautiful artwork. Marybeth stared in awe at the lovely structure, wondering what it would be like to climb the circular staircase past the several floors to the very highest platform and look down.

She looked around for the stairs, then walked over to the wrought iron steps and began ascending them. She shifted Danny to her right arm, her left arm aching from holding the growing baby boy. "Look at this, Danny," she told her son, kissing his forehead. "Isn't this a beautiful place? Bill Stone says this is where all the emigrants meet to go to Oregon and California. It's a long journey we have ahead of us, isn't it, child? But Mama will see that you get there safely. I'll not let anything happen to you."

She reached the first landing and stopped to catch her breath. "I only wish you could see Ireland some day, Danny boy, but I'm afraid that will never be. We're far, far away from your mama's homeland, and going farther still. This is a very big land, this America. I didn't know it would be this big. And Mama will make sure life is good for you once we get to Oregon."

She proceeded to the next landing and peered over the railing. "Would you look at that? See all the people down there?" She spotted Mac and John, more by their loud voices than by sight. She shook her head at the realization she could easily find them even in a crowd because they talked louder than anyone else there. "They don't even know we're watching them, Danny," she told the boy. She looked down at her son and kissed his cheek. "That John MacKinder will never be your father, Danny, I promise. I'll not be pushed into marrying a man I don't love again, even if it means Mama has to raise you alone."

She climbed to the top landing and looked down, the dome just above. Everyone looked so far away and unreal. How she wished she could stay under the shelter of the dome, stay in this beautiful, cool building and stay away from John MacKinder forever. She thought about staying right here in St. Louis, but she owned next to nothing, and she was a foreigner with a tiny baby to care for. She was not yet sure enough of herself to consider staying anywhere in this new country alone, and she thanked God for Danny, her only comfort, the only thing that kept her sane.

"Well, then, we'll be traveling with your train, my friend."

Marybeth could hear Mac's voice all the way to the top landing. She wondered if her father-in-law would chide her for being here, but she didn't much care. It was fun to be doing something daring without his knowledge, to be going against his wishes.

"We had better be getting back to the wagons," she told Danny. She smiled, bundling him back to her left arm. The baby cooed and smiled, reaching up and grasping at some of her long, red hair. Marybeth headed back down the stairs, being careful not to slip with the baby. Her high-button shoes were already getting worn and she realized with disappointment that she would probably have to start wearing her only other pair soon, wondering if they would take her all the way to Oregon. As far away as Bill Stone said Oregon was, she wondered if she would have to walk all the way. She could not imagine it, but the men had already talked about buying oxen, which were much sturdier than horse or mule for such a trip; still they talked about keeping the wagons light, which meant carrying passengers as little as possible.

"Oxen have to be driven by walking alongside them with a whip," Bill Stone had told them. "You don't use reins."

"Well, if we have to walk the whole way with the oxen, then the women will do the same. No favoritism in this family," Mac had put in. "Besides, MacKinder women are strong."

*They have to be*, Marybeth thought, her heart heavy. *A weak woman would never survive one year with a MacKinder man.* She often wondered just how long her own strength would hold out.

As she rounded another landing a man and woman were climbing the stairs, talking softly, laughing together. The man had his arm around the woman's waist, and the way they looked at each other brought an ache to Marybeth's heart. The woman acted as though she enjoyed being near him. Marybeth thought about Ella's warning that all men turn out the same eventually, that when a woman loses her beauty or after the man has got used to her, he looks at her only as someone to cook his meals and keep house for him. But the couple she watched now were surely in their late forties, perhaps early fifties, and the man looked at her so lovingly, that the woman's face glowed.

"Hello," the woman spoke up, catching Marybeth's eyes.

Marybeth reddened deeply, embarrassed at being caught staring. "How do you do," she answered.

"Oh, a baby! Let me see it. My own children are all grown."

Marybeth came closer, feeling nervous and foolish, but always happy to show off her son. She pulled the blanket away from Danny's face.

"What a fine baby! Is it a boy or a girl?" the woman asked.

"It's a boy. His name is Danny, after his father."

"Oh, such an accent," the man spoke up. "You're from Ireland, I can tell." He looked at her as though she were some kind of alien being from another world.

Marybeth nodded. "That I am," she answered, holding her chin up.

"Well, the boy's father must be very proud. That's a healthy-looking, handsome lad," the woman said, showing only kindness.

Marybeth smiled appreciatively. "Thank you. But ... the boy's father is dead."

The woman frowned. "Oh, I'm so sorry."

"It's quite all right. You didn't know." She looked at the

man. "My name is Marybeth MacKinder. I am going to Oregon with my husband's family. Are you two going west?"

His wife smiled and replied, "No, our family is here in St. Louis. We just come here to hand out information to other travelers and see if there is anything we can do for them. I'm Susan Rogers, and this is my husband Henry. Is there anything we can do for you or your family, Mrs. MacKinder?"

"Oh, no, I don't believe there is," Marybeth answered, wanting to scream out that she was afraid, that she needed a kind woman like Susan Rogers to talk to, needed help in getting away from the MacKinder family. But she saw the lingering prejudice in Mr. Rogers' eyes and knew there would be no help. "I must be getting back to the wagons. It's nice to have met you."

"And you, too, child. God bless you on your journey," Mrs. Rogers answered. "It won't be easy, but we're told Oregon is beautiful. We'll pray for you and your family."

Marybeth touched the crucifix she wore around her neck. "Thank you." She turned and walked down to the next landing, feeling suddenly more lonely than ever. If only Mac or John would look at her with the kindness she had seen in Henry Rogers' eyes when he looked at his wife, or if Ella would speak to her as softly and sweetly as Susan Rogers had…

She reached the ground floor and ducked back as the MacKinder men walked past her. She waited a moment, then walked around the corner, smack into a man who bumped her so hard she stumbled slightly. She felt a hand quickly grab her and a strong arm came around her to protect her and the baby from pitching forward. She hung on to Danny as the stranger helped her get her footing.

"I'm awful sorry, ma'am." The words were spoken in a strange drawl Marybeth had never heard before, and the voice was deep. Her own cheeks turned crimson. She looked up into the face of a young man who looked hardly older than she. He removed his hat, and his sandy hair tumbled in a cascade of waves that danced in every direction and hung down past his collar. His wide-set, dark eyes were warm and apologetic. "You all right?" he asked her.

Marybeth stepped back, blinking, momentarily confused. "I … I'm just fine. It is I who should be sorry. I wasn't looking where I was going."

He grinned, a bright, warm smile that almost startled her. He was perhaps six feet tall and broad-shouldered. She half expected to be berated for being so clumsy. She waited for the kind of shouting a MacKinder man would have embarrassed her with, but this man's voice remained calm and gentle as his eyes moved over her in a way that gave her a pleasant shiver. She felt suddenly awkward, embarrassed that she had left her slat bonnet behind and was bare-headed. "What kind of accent is that, ma'am?"

She felt her cheeks reddening again. "I … I'm Irish, and proud of it, I might add."

He gave her the same scrutinizing look that Henry Rogers had. "You might." He broke into another warm smile then. "That's a real pretty accent." His eyes fell to Danny. "I hope your baby is all right."

She patted Danny's bottom. "No damage, I'm sure."

The young man stepped a little closer and peeked at the child. "A boy?"

"Yes." Marybeth noticed John coming back toward the entrance to the courthouse then. "I must be going! I'm sorry I stumbled into you."

He grinned again, putting on his hat. "Well, I'm not." By the time he got the words out Marybeth was already out the door.

Joshua Rivers watched as a big, dark-haired man came up to the pretty red-haired woman he had just met. The man started yelling at her, obviously angry about something. Josh guessed the man was her husband; he grabbed the young woman's arm and half dragged her away. Although the young woman was a stranger to him, Josh felt a little surge of anger at the sight. He could see no reason for the harsh treatment.

He adjusted his hat and watched until the two of them were out of sight. He had heard about the Irish; gossip, mostly. He was not one to put much store in other peoples' opinions. He preferred to make up his own mind about everything; and he had learned the hard way how wrong it was to judge any man or woman by race, color, or creed. His own prejudice against the man his own sister loved had nearly cost the woman her life.

He reminded himself that was a long time ago, back in Texas. He missed home, but the past was past. He sighed and walked into the courthouse. His sister, Rachael, had told him about this place, and he wanted to see St. Louis for himself before he headed west.

He walked on legs slightly bowed from riding horses since he was old enough to walk. He looked up at the dome of the courthouse and breathed deeply, shaking his head at the wondrous structure. St. Louis was everything Rachael had told him it was, and he was half tempted to just stay here. He had been to a theater and to huge supply stores he never dreamed existed. There were schools here, one where Rachael herself had taught for a time. Some of the streets were bricked, and warehouses lined the shore of the Mississippi for what seemed a mile. Riverboats docked there by the hundreds. Just yesterday Josh had watched the brightly painted boats with their huge paddle wheels load up with emigrants headed up the Missouri to Independence.

From there they would head for Oregon, and that was where he was going. St. Louis was an interesting place, but Joshua Rivers was used to wide open spaces, and tragedies in his life had given him reason to start a new life in a new land. In just two days he would head home for a last good-bye to his sister and her family and be on his way.

He wondered if the red-haired woman from Ireland had settled in St. Louis, or if perhaps she, too, was an emigrant headed west. He shrugged, realizing it made little difference. Not only was she married and had a child, but she was Irish and probably Catholic, two things he knew little about. It wasn't that he'd look down on her for it. Some folks even said the Irish worked harder than most. But for himself, he'd had enough problems in life without getting involved with a foreigner. He'd likely never see her again anyway. Still, for some reason it bothered him that he hadn't even introduced himself or asked her name.

# Three

Cows bellowed, chickens squawked inside their cages, and oxen snorted. Marybeth stared in wonder at the menagerie that boarded the riverboat. She clung to Danny, watching with pity as black slaves jumped at orders from white men who directed them to lift boxes and other supplies that looked far too heavy for their bony, underfed bodies. She had heard about the use of slaves in the South, but until now she had not witnessed its practice. She watched one old black man hurry to obey an order, and she thought wryly how the slave reminded her of the way Ella jumped to Mac's orders.

The boat rocked as another passed it in the river. Considering the number of boats that sat at the docks, and many more that paddled up and down the river, Marybeth decided it was amazing that there were not a considerable number of accidents along the St. Louis riverfront. She held Danny protectively as several wagons were pushed on board, stored on the lowest deck with the animals. Most of the emigrants, including the MacKinders, would also stay on the lower deck, sleeping in their own wagons, unable to afford the comfortable cabins of the upper decks. But at least they could walk the main deck and watch the activity.

John and Mac shared a drink with a man dressed in a fringed shirt and pants that John had told Marybeth were made from deerskin. Marybeth listened to talk of snakes and deserts and poison water, and she shivered. The man in deerskin was some kind of scout; he had been west and could tell others what to expect. As far as Marybeth was concerned, there couldn't possibly be anything but terror and danger ahead.

"Ah, but Oregon—she's every bit as beautiful as people tell you," the man said then. "Greener than anything in the east, crowned with snow-capped mountains, her valleys rich with soil made for growing anything you want."

"Sounds good to me," Mac said with a hefty laugh.

It did sound pretty. But no matter how pretty it was, the fact remained they had to travel nearly two thousand more miles to get there; two thousand miles through snakes and desert, she was sure.

She continued watching more people board, some with animals and wagons, headed for the mysterious west; others with only a little baggage, perhaps just going to visit a relative. Two or three men in very fancy suits and ruffled shirts also boarded. Marybeth jumped when the ship's steam whistle blew twice, and little Danny began to cry. Marybeth rocked him in her arms and tried to soothe him, but when the whistle blew a third time Danny cried harder. Before she realized what was happening, John marched up to her and whisked the child out of her arms, holding him up high and laughing.

"And what are you crying about, boy?" he said in his booming voice. "A MacKinder shouldn't be afraid of a little whistle."

Marybeth watched in anger, irritated that he had taken the child from her arms without warning. Danny only cried harder, and Marybeth reached up for him. "Give him to me," she said.

John looked down at her, holding Danny so high that she couldn't reach him. "The boy has got to learn not to cry," he told her.

"The noise frightened him. He's only a baby, John. Now give him to me."

"I don't want a MacKinder to be crying."

"He's not your child, so don't worry about it. And if you'd learn to lower your own voice, it would help calm him. Isn't there anyone in the MacKinder family who knows how to speak softly?"

A gleam of anger filled John's eyes as he lowered Danny but held the baby away from Marybeth. "The boy *is* a MacKinder! He's my brother's son, and that makes him as much *my* son. You remember that, Marybeth." He shoved the baby into her arms. "And I'll thank you not to tell me how loud I can speak. A man's got to raise his voice if he's to be obeyed. Now you teach that boy not to be afraid of every little thing! Don't you be making a sissy of him."

John returned to Mac and the scout, who had walked farther away to join Bill Stone and two more bearded, buckskin-clad men. Marybeth held Danny close, patting his bottom until he quieted. She knew she would have to join Ella below soon, but she wanted to stay on the main deck as long as possible, enjoying the sights and sounds and excitement of all the movement as people boarded, so many that Marybeth was certain the riverboat couldn't possibly get up enough steam to make the paddle turn against so much weight.

Danny began sucking on his fist. Marybeth watched a few stragglers hurry on board. It was then she caught sight of him, the man she had run into at the courthouse. She remembered his red checkered shirt, and the shoulder-length hair that popped out carelessly from under his wide-brimmed hat. He had a cloth bag slung over his shoulders, and he led a buckskin horse up the plank and onto the boat.

Marybeth thought it strange that her heart pounded so hard at seeing him, and wondered why she was so excited that he had got on the same boat. She chided herself for being attracted to a complete stranger, yet she found herself suddenly reasoning that it was time to go below, secretly hoping she would see the man again. She shifted Danny in her arms and headed for the stairway to the lower deck.

Everything below was bedlam. Marybeth traced her way among animals and people, stepping over cow and horse dung, searching for the MacKinder wagon. A small child had opened a cage of chickens, letting them fly out. The squawking and mooing created turmoil as the chickens proceded to land on the backs of cows, startling them.

"Grab those chickens!" a man shouted. A woman walked up to the child and scolded him, and a chicken flapped past Marybeth, startling her as its wing brushed her face. She ducked and turned, putting a blanket over Danny's face to shield him from possible chicken claws. Several men scrambled to gather up the flighty birds, and Marybeth tried to get out of the way.

"Hello, there," she heard close by. She turned to see the young man from the courthouse. He held a chicken under his arm. "We meet again."

Marybeth felt her cheeks going hot at his wide, warm smile. "Yes. I was looking for our wagon."

"Things could get dangerous down here." The chicken he held began struggling and squawking, digging its claws into the young man's side. "Ouch!" He worked his hand down to grab the chicken around its legs, while he hung on to his horse and backpack with his other hand. He pulled the chicken away, holding it upside down by the legs while it clucked and flapped its wings. "You Jezebel!" he scolded. "I'm just trying to keep you from being stepped on or snatched up for a meal, and this is what you do to me."

Marybeth could not help smiling.

"Over here!" he called out then. "Come get this old hen before I pull off her feathers and roast her. I haven't eaten all day!"

An older man came running up, taking the hen from him. "Thanks, mister. That boy of mine is always getting into mischief."

"I think I remember my own father saying that about me," the young man answered, handing the chicken to its owner. He laughed, a wonderful, gentle laugh, Marybeth thought; not the loud, roaring laughter of a MacKinder—the kind that made people jump and babies cry. He looked at her then, pushing his hat back from his handsome face. "I'm sorry that I didn't introduce myself back there at the courthouse, ma'am. Name's Joshua Rivers. May I ask yours?"

"Marybeth MacKinder," she answered. Just those two words made his heart flutter, the music in her voice, the beautiful smile she gave him. Her eyes reminded him of fresh spring grass, her hair the color of the red rocks of Texas. It almost angered him that she attracted him so—a foreign woman with a husband and a baby!

"Well, Mrs. MacKinder, it's nice to see you again so soon.

Kind of a crazy coincidence, isn't it? Me, I always felt certain things have meaning—like running into you again—like there's some reason, you know?"

Marybeth was amazed at how relaxed he seemed to be, how easily he talked to her, as though he had known her for a long time. There was a sweet, homey quality about the man that made a person like him almost immediately.

"I ... I think I know what you mean, Mr. Rivers. However, I cannot imagine what the reason could be." She wanted to smile for him, wanted him to think she was pretty, wanted to stand there and talk with him forever. The realization of those thoughts startled her. She saw Ella headed toward her then, and she didn't care to have the wrath of John and Mac visited upon her for talking to a stranger. Surely that was bad enough, let alone the fact that she was supposed to still be in mourning. "I have to go now. Good luck on your journey, Mr. Rivers, wherever you are going."

"Wait a minute!" he cried. But she had turned and left quickly, not looking back. Josh watched her approach an older woman, then walk with her toward a wagon. The woman took the baby from Marybeth, and Josh guessed she was either a mother or mother-in-law. He realized that both times a family member had approached, Marybeth MacKinder had skittered away like a scared rabbit. He wondered what kind of family would cause her to be afraid to talk to others.

He sighed, leading his horse to a corner stall, where he paid a young boy to take care of it and his gear. The smell below was not pleasant. He headed up the stairs to fresh air, deciding to try to find the cabin he had rented. He glanced across a sea of animals and people to see the pretty Irish woman standing near the older woman. She climbed into the wagon then, and Josh realized she would be staying below.

*She deserves better*, he thought. She was so pretty, he could imagine her in a beautiful dress, walking elegantly down the fanciest street in St. Louis, going to the theaters, the best restaurants. She seemed made for better things than riding the lower deck of a riverboat, sharing her quarters with cattle and chickens.

*Jesus, Rivers, what's the matter with you*, he chastised himself. *It's none of your damn business!* He turned his thoughts to Oregon and his plans for his own future.

The night air rang with laughter and banjo music. Josh stood at the railing of the main deck, watching the way the moonlight danced on the water. He puffed a thin cigar, listening with irritation to the dark-haired man he had seen Marybeth go to back at the courthouse, the man Josh was sure must be her husband. He talked so loudly that Josh was certain everyone on the boat and most people on either shore could hear him. He was arm wrestling, and so far had challenged and beaten several men.

"The man who beats John MacKinder would have to be one hell of a man!" he bragged, laughing loudly.

Josh turned and watched as he took on another. Two other men stood behind him cheering him on. One of them looked a lot like John MacKinder, and Josh guessed he was the man's father. Apparently the older woman he had seen Marybeth go to earlier in the day was her mother-in-law. From the loud, overbearing attitude of the MacKinder men, Josh could understand Marybeth's skittish nature. It angered him that something so pretty and soft-spoken could be linked to such brutes as the MacKinders, and it angered him even more that he cared at all. For all he knew the young woman was very happy, but he had not seen joy in her eyes—only fear.

Again he was confused by the fact that it mattered to him if a foreign woman he didn't even know was happy. He turned away but could not ignore John MacKinder's bragging as he beat still another man. Josh clenched his right hand, flexing his muscles, telling himself it would be childish to go and challenge the man just to prove to himself he could do it. John MacKinder would probably tear his arm off. But then size didn't always mean anything. Josh was a well built man in his own right, but not as big as MacKinder.

Still, he knew he was a lot stronger even than he looked. And when he was angry sheer determination often took over and brought added strength, like the time his brother was captured by comancheros and Josh managed to ride for miles to get help, in spite of being badly wounded. *And what about that time the wagon fell on Pa and you lifted it up all by yourself*, he asked himself. He didn't doubt that the thought of John MacKinder bullying the pretty Marybeth would give him that little bit of added strength. MacKinder was a braggart who needed to be taught a lesson. Maybe it would shut his big mouth.

*You're a damn fool*, he told himself as he headed for the table where John MacKinder stood up, stretching his big arms and asking if anyone else wanted to find out who was the strongest man on the riverboat. "I'll take you on," Josh said aloud.

MacKinder turned to look at him, then grinned, putting out a big hand. Josh could tell the man didn't recognize him from the courthouse. He had only glanced at Josh for a moment, not allowing his image to register. Josh shook his hand as others cheered and placed new bets. MacKinder squeezed his hand firmly, warning Josh he didn't have a chance. Josh squeezed back.

"And what might your name be?" MacKinder asked.

"Joshua Rivers."

"John MacKinder, Mr. Rivers, an Irishman, through and through." The man took a swallow of whiskey from a bottle handed him by his father. He handed back the bottle and straddled an iron stool, motioning for Josh to sit down across from him. "Might as well get this over with," he told Josh, putting his elbow on the table.

Josh reached into his pants pocket and pulled out five dollars in paper money. "Not until I place a bet on myself." Everyone quieted as MacKinder glanced at the money. "You willing to bet against me, MacKinder? Two to one. I lose, I owe you twice what I laid there on the table—ten dollars. I win, you owe me five."

MacKinder's smile faded. He glanced back at his father. "There's not a man can beat you, John, you know that," the older man told him. "Go ahead and bet him. He looks strong, but he's not as big as you. Hell, you've beat bigger men."

John scowled at Josh. "What makes you think you can beat me?"

Josh shrugged, "I just think you're a loud-mouthed braggart full of hot air," he answered. "If you're afraid—"

"Afraid! A MacKinder?"

The crowd had fallen silent at Josh's insult, some of them stepping back. John clenched a fist and waved it in front of Joshua. "I'll break your wrist!" he threatened.

"Have you got the money to cover this bet or not?"

John stood up and dug into his pockets, dumping five dollars in coins onto the table. "I shouldn't have bothered," he growled. "I'll just be putting it back in my pocket."

Joshua said nothing. He simply glared at MacKinder, picturing the man blustering orders to Marybeth MacKinder, imaging him behaving in bed the same way he behaved out of bed—pushy, brutal, bragging. Again, it annoyed him that he had considered the thought at all, and he surmised that plain frustration at his own thoughts would give him added determination. After all, if John MacKinder weren't the bully he was, he wouldn't be forced to feel sorry for the man's wife and he could get her off his mind.

Everyone gathered around as Josh put his elbow on the table. MacKinder grasped his hand, and for a moment they gripped and regripped, each man trying to get the best hold while a buckskin-clad mountain man eyed their hands and wrists to judge whether the grip was proper.

The two men's eyes burned into each other, and Josh's jaw flexed in his anger and determination. This no longer had anything to do with the woman he had met earlier, the woman to whom he had no business giving a second thought. This had to do with the ancient need of men to challenge each other; the deep, primitive need to dominate, to show who was the strongest. It was no different from Bighorn sheep ramming heads to see which would lead the herd, or from ancient Indian rituals of manhood. Josh thought about the words of his half-Comanche brother-in-law; "The Indian believes a man can do whatever his spirit wills him to do."

The mountain man dropped his hand and the contest was on. Muscle strained against muscle, veins quickly expanding to show their blue pathways just under the skin. John MacKinder realized almost instantly that this Joshua Rivers was indeed stronger than he looked. The men around the table cheered and shouted, but their voices fell on deaf ears for Josh, who forced all his concentration on the man across from him. John MacKinder deserved to be taken down a notch or two, and he was, by God, going to do it.

For sixty seconds the men seemed evenly matched, each man managing to push the other only a little before being pushed back.

"No man ... beats ... a MacKinder," John growled through gritted teeth.

Josh said nothing, not wanting to waste an ounce of strength in even the slight effort of talking. John MacKinder was indeed a powerful man. He thought again of the pretty Marybeth, and anger at the thought brought forth one more surge of determined effort. He pushed MacKinder's arm down far enough that MacKinder lost his leverage. With one more grunt he touched MacKinder's hand to the table.

The crowd shouted almost in unison, and John MacKinder jumped up, tossing the table aside as though it were a match. The money went flying, and men scrambled to pick it up.

"You cheated!" John shouted at Josh.

"It was fair, and you know it. Everyone here watched."

"I've already wrestled ten men. The only reason you beat me is because I had already used up most of my strength. My arm was tired!"

"If your arm was tired, you should have said so and wrestled me another time. Quit looking for excuses, MacKinder. I beat you. It's that simple."

John lunged at Josh, taking a swing at him, but his father and three other men grabbed him as Josh ducked back. "Don't be shaming the MacKinder name by being a bad loser, son," Mac told John. "There will be another time."

John jerked away from their grasp, glaring at Josh. "You can bet there will be another time! I'm not letting it go at this, Rivers!"

Several men handed Josh his money. Josh shoved it into his pants pocket, grinning. "That's fine with me." He walked off into the darkness, then turned to watch MacKinder again shove his father off when he tried to lead him away. He grabbed the bottle of whiskey from his father and drank some down, then handed it back. "I'm going to sleep," he growled. "And by God this isn't over!"

"Let it go, John. You'll likely never see the man again anyway. Besides, you were right. Your arm was tired. Everybody knows you're the strongest man here. There's not a man among them brave enough to stand up to you."

Both men disappeared down the stairway that led to the lower deck, and Joshua was suddenly very sorry he had caused such turmoil. He only then realized that if John MacKinder was angered, he might take it out on his wife. But then he wondered which was worse—an angry John MacKinder, or one who was drunk and happy and eager for his woman. Either way, Marybeth MacKinder would have to lose. He took off his hat and whacked it against the railing in frustration.

Below Marybeth cuddled Danny closer inside her wagon when she heard John and Mac coming. "Goddamn cheat, that's what he is!" John raved.

"Hey, mister, be quiet," someone grumbled. "People are trying to sleep."

"I'll put you to sleep permanently if you don't mind your own business," John answered.

"You keep it up and we'll have you put off this boat, Irishman," someone else hollered. "You'll get the animals all stirred up."

Marybeth was glad to be inside the dark wagon instead of standing near John in daylight and suffering the embarrassment of being associated with him.

"You've got to quiet down, John," his father warned. "It was a one-time thing, something that will probably never happen again."

Marybeth frowned, wondering why John was so angry. She was sure he had been drinking and possibly gambling. Had someone cheated him at cards?

Ella stirred nearby. "Now what?" she muttered. She sat up, moving to peer out the back of the wagon. "What's going on, Mac?" she asked.

"Get on into the wagon and get some sleep," Mac was telling John as John climbed into the men's wagon.

"He'll pay for this! We'll meet again when my arm isn't tired."

"Sure you will." Mac walked up to the women's wagon, telling Ella to hand him his bedroll. "The boy got beat arm wrestling. The young man was pretty good size, but not as big as John. I couldn't believe my eyes."

"John? Why, he's never been beaten before, has he?"

"He sure hasn't." Mac took the bedroll while Marybeth listened in the darkness. "Lost five dollars to the bastard. We need that money, but we didn't dare put up a fuss. Too many men there to say it was fair."

"Well, was it?"

"Yes, I suppose it was. But John's arm was tired. He'd already wrestled several others. Then this fellow, Joshua Rivers, he called himself, steps up and challenges him two to one."

Marybeth's eyes widened, and she was glad no one could see her face. Joshua Rivers? He had beaten John MacKinder? She actually had to struggle not to laugh aloud. How she wished she could have been there to see it! John's shame would have been doubled if he knew she was watching. How wonderful that someone had knocked some of the wind out of John.

Why had he done it? Was he just one among a string of men who had been drinking and challenging John? Or did he have a more personal reason? She told herself that was a foolish thought. He couldn't have done it on her account. Surely he didn't get enough of a look at John at the courthouse to remember him. Maybe he had just connected the name. Did he know she felt trapped in this family, that John MacKinder was as much a bully within the family as he was outside it?

She said nothing to Ella as the woman settled back to sleep.

Did John know she had talked to Joshua Rivers earlier in the day? She prayed he did not, or he would make a scene. She realized that after tonight she would have to make a point *not* to talk to him if the opportunity arose. To her chagrin that thought disappointed her. Joshua Rivers had suddenly become an intriguing person, with his soft voice and funny drawl. She wanted to talk to him again; to find out where in America he came from that he talked different from people in New York. She didn't want to bring unnecessary trouble to a perfect stranger, but they would be on the riverboat several days, and she might run into him again. She would have to try to avoid him.

# Four

Marybeth spent nearly the entire journey along the Missouri on the smelly lower deck with Ella. The MacKinders were too poor to afford a cabin above; but both John and Mac insisted the main deck was not a fit place for the women even for daytime strolls, since that was where most of the gamblers and drinking men caroused. Marybeth wondered if that was where Joshua Rivers spent most of his time. Was he a drinker and a gambler? She doubted he did either with the gusto of John MacKinder and his father.

She could not get the stranger off her mind. She liked his Biblical name, liked his kind eyes and soft voice. She also found herself worrying about him, since all John talked about was "getting even" with Joshua Rivers.

In the evenings the riverboat stopped at designated locations, where steerage passengers could use outhouses and build fires for their one hot meal a day. At those times Marybeth would cautiously scan the riverboat, and once she spotted Rivers standing on an upper deck, watching her. She made it a point to act as though she didn't notice him, but she could feel his eyes on her. She wished she had worn a fancier dress; but the rugged journey did not allow pretty dresses. It was either her black calico wrap dress, or her gray cotton dress—which was coarsely woven and irritated her skin—or her blue muslin. She found herself choosing the blue muslin most of the time, since it had a fitted waist and was decently attractive in spite of being practical.

She wondered what a fool she must be to worry about what she wore. Joshua Rivers could disembark the boat at any time and be on his merry way, and she would never see him again. He could even be a married man. Yet she longed to put on her best dress, the yellow calico that fit her figure perfectly; longed to wear it and go and talk to the man who had so disturbed her thoughts. But that would be much too bold, and it would only bring trouble to both herself and Joshua Rivers.

"Don't you be burning the damn pork," John told her then, awakening her to reality. "That meat is precious. We'll be down to beans and biscuits before long and Bill says we can't always count on finding game out there."

Marybeth quickly turned the meat, feeling Josh Rivers' eyes on her family's camp.

"I'll say one thing," John grumbled. "That brother of mine must have been a saint putting up with your cooking."

Marybeth straightened up and turned to face him. "Well, you don't have a whole lot of choice, now, do you, John MacKinder? If it's so bad, why don't you let the family have one nice meal aboard the riverboat? You're ready enough to throw away your money on whiskey and bets on arm wrestling, but you won't let your own mother have one night off from bending over a fire."

John reddened with anger, stepping closer, aware that others camped nearby could hear. "You lower your voice, Marybeth," he hissed.

"I'll speak as loudly as I want. The way Bill Stone talks, the trip ahead of us is full of danger and hardship, and you said yourself there won't be much food. You could have afforded us one nice meal before we get off the riverboat. And if you don't like the way I cook, you don't have to eat it! I'm not making it just for you. I'm making it because the rest of us have to eat or starve to death! You make your own choice which *you* want to do!"

Someone nearby laughed, and John whirled to glare at him. The man instantly shut up. From where he stood, Josh could see there was some kind of confrontation between Marybeth and John MacKinder, but he couldn't hear what they were saying. He grinned when he saw Marybeth face the man, who dwarfed her. Her hands were on her hips and she was talking right back to him.

"You tell him, Mrs. MacKinder," he said quietly.

"You never talked to Dan that way," John growled

to Marybeth.

"I was a new wife. I did what I thought wives were *supposed* to do. And I'll remind you that you are *not* my husband; even if you were, I would expect to be treated a little better than the black slaves I have been watching since we first arrived in St. Louis!"

John grasped her arm, pulling her away from the rest of the camp. Back on the riverboat Josh watched, gripping the hand rail more tightly. He glanced at the elder MacKinders, neither of whom made a move to interfere.

"I'll remind you how you came to be in this family, Mrs. MacKinder. You owe us!"

"I've done my share, John MacKinder, and will continue to do so. But my situation in this family does not give you the right to order me around like a servant, or to embarrass me and the rest of the family in front of others."

"Let them stare and gossip. It's not their business."

"I'll not put up with it through the whole journey to Oregon! Or haven't you suffered enough shame from being beaten at arm wrestling? Maybe you *like* people laughing at you."

John's eyes narrowed with indignation. She smiled at the look of awkward embarrassment on his face. He clenched his fists. "Some day, woman, I will put you in your place. And when I am done with you, you won't be talking back to me again. You'll be reaching your arms around my neck and asking my forgiveness for forgetting your place."

He turned and left her, and Marybeth glanced at the riverboat. He was there, watching. Was it foolish to think that Josh Rivers might have stormed right off the boat and come to her aid if John had got rough with her? But she wouldn't want that. If something happened because of her, she would be devastated and humiliated. She turned back to their camp, to see John walking up to a nearby fire, glaring at a man who was sitting on a log staring at the MacKinder camp.

"What are you looking at?" John growled, fists clenched.

The man reddened. "Nothing, Irishman."

"You mind your own business! And say the word Irishman with more respect!" John stormed back to his own campfire and plunked down on a log. Marybeth returned to see Ella dishing out pork and potatoes.

"She doesn't deserve to eat our food," John told his mother, indicating Marybeth.

Ella cast him a look of disapproval. "She's got a baby still feeding at her breast. She'll eat." She looked at her husband, as though suddenly realizing she had better get his permission.

Mac nodded. He looked over at Marybeth. "Once the boy is weaned, there will be some decisions to make," he told her. He kept his voice low, but Marybeth detected the cold determination in it. "You'll have some respect for this family, Marybeth, and do what you know is right; if not, little Danny comes with us and you'll be left to fend for yourself. Whatever happens, our grandson is a MacKinder and he'll *stay* a MacKinder."

Marybeth took the plate of food offered by Ella, but she didn't feel hungry. She boldly held Mac's dark, determined eyes. She realized what he was telling her, and for the moment she decided not to create a worse scene than had already been created. A long journey lay ahead, and little Danny would feed at her breast through most of it. She told herself no one could take a child from its mother. But Murray MacKinder didn't care about rules. The only law for him was MacKinder law. If she wanted to keep her baby, she would have to remain a part of the MacKinder family.

She felt isolated, threatened. She wished this country were not all so new to her. If she had friends in this land, if she knew more about it, she could get away from the MacKinder web. More than that, she didn't have any money of her own; and with a new baby, it would be next to impossible to find work.

She took a couple of bites of the pork, suddenly thinking of Joshua Rivers again, realizing that she actually felt comforted when she thought of him.

She waited until John and Mac were both engrossed in their meals, then turned to look at the riverboat. Why was it so easy to spot him? Perhaps it was because she knew he would still be watching.

Everything was clamor and confusion when they disembarked at Independence. People came off first, then wagons and belongings, then cattle, horses, chickens and oxen. Horse traders and men with oxen were camped everywhere, ready to do business with the emigrants. John and Mac left the wagon and women on the bank of the river to do some trading, since Bill had already informed them the journey could not be made without oxen.

Marybeth watched the people who came off the boat, whole families, young couples, old people, little children. She did not miss the lonely looks on the faces of some of the women, and she realized that even if they were from America, the land into which they would travel would be just as foreign and frightening to them as it would be to her. Children ran about excitedly, for the moment little affected by the hardship and danger that lay ahead. For them it was a great adventure.

Her own heart pounded with a mixture of dread and anticipation. She realized that if she were making this journey with a more pleasant family situation, with a kind husband and dreams of making a home together in the place called Oregon, she would not dread this trip nearly so much. She told herself that at least she wasn't still in the city, that she was going to a land that was a lot like Ireland; but she was plagued with desperate thoughts of what she would do once the journey was over. How could she get out from under the viselike MacKinder grip on her and Danny without risking losing Danny and being left destitute? Whatever she chose to do, Mac and John would make it as difficult as possible.

She decided she could only take a day at a time. She still struggled with homesickness, and with missing her mother. She had no place else to turn now, and at least for the next several months the MacKinder men could not bully her too much. There would be too little privacy on such a journey. Her biggest problem would come when she reached Oregon.

A young couple walked by, looking very happy. Marybeth watched longingly as they passed her, the man's arm around the woman's waist. He was a big man, nearly as big as John, but with blond hair and very fair skin. The woman was small like

Marybeth, and looked about the same age. She looked up at her husband and said something in a language Marybeth did not understand. But she understood the look, and wondered what it must be like to be married to a good man, to truly want a man and enjoy being with him. She realized she had never held a look like that for Dan. She had tried; oh, how she had tried. She had wanted so much for it all to work. But love and passion were foreign words to MacKinder men.

She noticed Joshua Rivers then. He was mounted on his horse and rode slowly in her direction. Marybeth looked away, helping Ella tie a barrel of flour to the side of the wagon. She sensed the horse coming closer and could not resist turning to look when she knew he was close. He smiled and tipped his hat, but didn't say a word. Marybeth was grateful he realized that with Ella there he shouldn't speak to her. He rode off then, and Marybeth wondered if it was for good.

She returned to tying the barrel, then watched him once more, studying the broad, muscled shoulders and trying to envision him beating John MacKinder. The thought of it made her blood rush warmer and brought a pull to her insides no man had ever stirred in her. She glanced at Ella, who was diligently working to check the supplies, as ordered by Mac. She took a bucket from the side of the wagon then and walked to a well that had been dug for travelers to load up on a supply of fresh water before leaving for country where fresh water was scarce. She waited her turn in line, telling herself what a fool she was to be allowing her feelings to overtake her better sense. She looked around; Joshua Rivers was a considerable distance away now, heading north. She was surprised at the keen disappointment she felt at the realization he was apparently not heading west with the others after all. He was riding away!

One wagon train headed out the second morning Marybeth and others had made camp after disembarking the riverboat. They had been told that another had left three days earlier. There were eighteen wagons left along the riverbank. John and Mac had purchased four oxen, and Bill Stone two. Everyone had stocked up on supplies at Independence, according to instructions from an old mountain man who called himself Harley Webster, preferring the title "Cap," short for Captain.

Men from the remaining group of travelers had hired Cap, an experienced but aging scout and mountain man, to lead them west. He had brought along two scouts, one called simply Devon, and the other Trapper, a nickname derived from his real name of Jake Trapp. Both men looked fierce enough to give Marybeth the shivers, but Cap insisted they were excellent scouts. Devon had dark hair that hung well past his shoulders. He wore a cloth headband and a calico shirt, a weapons belt draped criss-cross over his chest.

"Man's got to be part Indian," someone had muttered.

Marybeth studied him curiously. She had heard of Indians in this country, but she had not seen one. They were supposedly a wild, uncivilized people who stole women and babies and killed white men. "Some can be bargained with," Bill Stone had said. "You never know with an Indian. Can't trust them, not for a second."

Marybeth wondered if they could trust Devon. Still, Cap seemed to trust him completely. The man called Trapper was a burly, bearded man who wore deerskin clothing like she had seen men wear on the the riverboat.

Marybeth helped pack three more sacks of flour, a hundred pounds of bacon, fifty pounds of coffee beans, two cases of whiskey, ten pounds of tea, a bushel of dried apples, kettles, a coffee mill, pickles, potatoes, three sacks of beans, yeast, salt, soap and several more necessary items. Ella and Marybeth cleaned out the wagon and repacked bedding and clothing, sewing more pockets into the inside canvas to hold small items like scissors to keep them within easy reach. They arranged tin cups, candles, fry pans, soap, weapons and ammunition in boxes and hung wooden pails on hooks at the sides of the wagons.

Water barrels were filled at the well, and Devon and Trapper instructed greenhorns on how to handle oxen. John and Mac learned quickly, big men who were good at shouting orders.

Marybeth thought how the animals fit the MacKinder men, big, clumsy oxen that knew nothing but brute force.

With much cursing and shouting at animals, whistles, mothers ordering children to be careful, chickens clucking and cattle mooing, the wagon train got underway May 10—nineteen wagons, including the cook wagon brought along for the captain and scouts; eighty-nine oxen; twenty mules; seventeen horses, either herded or tied to the backs of wagons. Twenty-five men would make the trip, including the scouts and Cap, and the man who would be in charge of the cook wagon for the scouts, Ben Stramm; nineteen women and twenty-eight children, three of them teenage boys who would be men before the journey was over.

Marybeth walked with Ella, the two women taking turns carrying Danny; Bill Stone, Mac and John took turns guiding the oxen that pulled their two wagons. Today they were fourth and fifth in line. Each day, according to Cap, they would move back a notch, the last wagon taking first place, so that all wagons were rotated daily, giving no one the advantage of being at the front of the line where they didn't have to put up with choking dust later in the journey; or with the deep muck that wagons ahead would churn up the first few weeks.

Most of the women walked, to keep wagons as light as possible. For the long journey, the animals would need all the relief they could get, and Marybeth usually rode inside the wagon only when she had to feed Danny.

On the third day of the journey, as Marybeth scanned the wide, green and gold expanse of land ahead of them, a chill moved through her at the realization that this was indeed a journey into a wilderness. For the moment she could not believe there were mountains ahead higher than she could ever imagine. Nor could she believe there was a place five or six months away called Oregon, a place Bill Stone had assured them he had heard was as green and beautiful and full of rolling hills and rich farmland as Ireland. She felt pulled and driven against her will, not wanting to do this, but having no choice.

She wanted to hand Danny to Ella to ease her aching arms,

but she knew Ella herself was in pain. All the women were already suffering from swollen feet and legs. It would take a lot more walking to break in muscles that were not accustomed to this much exercise. After a while Danny would begin to feel like an anvil. Marybeth noticed Mac was driving the oxen for the moment. That meant John was free to carry Danny for a while. She didn't like leaving the baby in the wagon. Danny was beginning to crawl, and between her fear of the baby crawling to the back of the wagon and somehow falling out; and the fear that a sudden jolt could cause something to fall on him, left Marybeth no choice but to keep the baby with her while she walked.

Much as she despised looking to John for any kind of help, Marybeth hurried over to where John walked. "I can't carry Danny any longer, John, and your mother is in pain, I can tell. Would you take him for a while again?"

John looked down at her. "On top of having a sassy mouth, you aren't much on strength, are you?" He took Danny from her and perched the boy on his arm. Danny stared at the man with wide eyes that were a pretty green like his mother's. "Don't you cry on me, boy," John warned. He looked back at Marybeth. "I'm doing this for my brother, and because this boy is a MacKinder. I'm not doing it for you."

Marybeth looked straight ahead. "I hardly thought that you would." Other than having John carry Danny once in a while, Marybeth had refused to speak to him since the argument along the river, and the embarrassment and humiliation it had caused her. It was bad enough that they were talked about because they were Irish, but John and Mac only made things worse by their actions and attitude. Still, to her irritation, Marybeth realized that to survive this journey, she would have to keep things civil between herself and John. Much as she disliked the man, his strength could not be denied, nor the fact that she might need to rely on that strength now and then. She summoned all her courage and humbleness before speaking again.

"I'm sorry about the argument back at the river," she told him. "I do my best and do more than my share. You cannot say that I don't. I cannot abide being ordered about, but I realize everyone is anxious and upset. We have left a lot behind us, John, and we cannot be sure what lies ahead. Tempers are short."

They walked on in silence a while longer. "A woman has her place, and you seem to have forgotten that since my brother died, Marybeth MacKinder."

Marybeth's heart felt like lead. There was no getting through to the man, no hope of reaching some kind of compassion and understanding. "You brought it on yourself with your shouting and carrying on, drawing attention to us. I have told you before that if you would learn to speak softly—"

"Be still! Go back with my mother where you belong."

Marybeth closed her eyes and turned away. She tried to reason that if she could learn to love John MacKinder and become his wife, he would be kinder and gentler to her. But she knew better, and it was difficult to even like the man, let alone love him. She wondered if she should have taken the risk of staying behind alone in New York, or perhaps in St. Louis.

She put a hand to her aching chest, again wondering how she could get free of this family. It was obvious it could not be done while they were on this journey. It would all have to wait until they reached Oregon. Perhaps by then she would know some of these people well enough that one of these families could help her.

"Hello!" someone called out.

Marybeth turned to see the young woman heading toward her whom she had seen back at Independence walking with her husband and looking so happy. She noticed the woman's wagon was two wagons behind the MacKinder wagons. It was easy to spot, because the woman's huge, blond-haired husband could be seen guiding the oxen. Marybeth waited as the petite, dark-haired woman approached her, dressed in a plain brown cotton dress.

"Already I can see we must all quickly make friends, for friends will be sorely needed out here, No?" the woman was saying, putting out her hand. "I am Delores Svensson."

Marybeth took her hand and squeezed it lightly. "I am Marybeth MacKinder. And I agree about needing friends." She watched the young woman warily. "We are from Ireland. We settled in New York for a while, but we did not like it there." She watched for the usual animosity but noticed none.

Delores smiled, her dark eyes sparkling from beneath her slat bonnet. "My husband, Aaron, and I have come from Indiana, where we were married not long ago," the woman told Marybeth with a sing-song accent. "We are originally from Sweden. How long have you been married, Marybeth?"

Marybeth walked on sore feet. "I was married a little over four years. My husband was killed in an accident at the factory where he worked only a few months ago."

"Oh, I am so sorry! And you so young! Oh, you poor thing! I would want to die if anything happened to my Aaron."

Marybeth felt a piercing pain at the words. How could she explain her own husband's death had been tragic only as far as no one deserving to die so violently; but in terms of how it had affected her personally, she felt no painful loss. How she wished she did! How she wished she could have just once felt about Dan the way this woman seemed to feel about her own husband. Apparently it really was true that some husbands and wives truly loved each other. Her mother and father had seemed happy. And this woman literally bubbled with love.

"It was last December," she told Delores.

"I am so sorry to know. We thought you were married to the big man who drives your team."

"He's my brother-in-law, John MacKinder. We farmed potatoes back in Ireland, until they were wiped out by disease. Now John and his father hope to return to farming in Oregon."

"Ah, yes, that is what my Aaron and I will do." Delores folded her arms rather nervously then. "I must tell you, I think I am glad John MacKinder is not your husband. He seems, well, not a very kind or patient man."

Marybeth smiled, taking an immediate liking to Delores, sensing the young woman's sincere concern. "It doesn't take much observing to figure that out," she told her.

"I'm very sorry. I must seem very nosy. But, thinking he was perhaps your husband, I thought—well, Aaron and I thought, that perhaps you needed a woman friend. This will be a long and difficult journey. I just wanted you to know you are welcome to come and visit at our campfire any time. I love my Aaron, but on a trip like this the men will have to stick together to keep animals tended and wagons repaired and the like; and we women have our work cut out for us. I can see already there will be none of the pleasantries of home—few baths, no fancy clothes, little chance to make ourselves pretty. Perhaps if we form friendships and share our troubles it will take away some of the hardship. Some of the other women and I will hold a little worship service in the morning, if you would like to join us. Who is the older woman with you?"

"That's my mother-in-law, Ella."

"Bring her along, and the menfolk, if they will come."

"I doubt that. And Ella won't come if my father-in-law doesn't want her to go."

"What if they don't want *you* to go?"

Marybeth put a hand to the crucifix around her neck. "They cannot keep me from worship." She looked at Delores. "I should tell you I am Catholic."

Delores smiled. "It makes no difference what faith you are. We are all of different faiths. What matters is to have a chance to worship and keep up our spirits." She tucked a strand of hair under her cap. "Already I am wishing I could set a nice table, wishing for some privacy and solitude."

Marybeth sighed. "Yes. We all wish for those things."

"When we reach Oregon, then things will be better. We'll have real homes again. I will pray that you find yourself a fine husband, Marybeth."

Marybeth felt a pain in her heart. Again she wondered what she would do when she reached Oregon. Settle with the MacKinders? She had already lived with them longer than she thought she could bear. But she might not have any choice.

"Yes," she answered, thinking again of Joshua Rivers and wondering why he kept invading her thoughts at odd moments. "Do pray for me, Delores." She looked at the young woman, a lump rising in her throat. "I'll be at your worship service in the morning."

# Five

The looks on the women's faces was the same—quiet resignation to a situation most of them hated; an aching loneliness, a longing for home, for loved ones left behind. Some wept as they sang hymns, realizing they would most likely never again see mothers and fathers, sisters and brothers. They followed their men faithfully into a land that was frightening, now leading a life crude and miserable compared to the homes they had left, whether log cabins or sturdy brick.

Marybeth's greatest fear was that Danny would get sick and there would be no help. There was a chill in the air this morning, and she had left the baby behind with John with orders to watch Danny closely. "You should not be going to that worship," he had told her angrily. "We are Catholic."

"You cannot tell me how and when to worship," she had answered, wondering how a man could talk about his religion and behave the way John did. She had looked at Ella, pleading with the woman to come along, sure she wanted to go. But Ella looked at Mac, and he had frowned and shook his head. Ella stayed at the wagon.

"I'll watch Danny for you. John has work to do," she told Marybeth.

Marybeth left, realizing she would have ended up like Ella if Dan had lived. In order to enjoy some kind of peace, she would have had to jump at Dan's commands and suffer his brutality the rest of her life, for her religion would never have allowed a divorce, and she would never have considered it. She couldn't help thinking of Dan's death as almost a blessing, and the thought brought on an unbearable guilt. She quietly prayed for forgiveness.

A woman Marybeth now knew to be Florence Gentry began reading from the Bible. Her youngest son, Toby, was the playful curly-headed six-year-old boy who had created the confusion with the chickens on the riverboat. It was obvious he was full of mischief, and this morning he wiggled and scratched restlessly as he stood beside his eleven-year-old brother, Billy, and eight-year-old sister, Melinda. Samuel Gentry stood behind his son, big hands on his shoulders warning him to stay put.

The Gentrys seemed happy, and Marybeth longed for that kind of solid family, with a strong, but gentle and supportive husband. Some of the couples were obviously happy, like the Gentrys and Delores and Aaron Svensson. She envied another woman, Bess Peters, who not only had two children—Andy, thirteen, and Lilly, ten—but also had her mother along. Marybeth still missed her own mother almost as though she had died only yesterday. Bess's husband, Al, was a short, stocky man with a stem look to him, a man who was obeyed by gently spoken commands that carried with them a message of love, rather than the loud, passionless orders John and Mac barked to her and Ella.

Another couple, Wilma and Cedrick Sleiter, were childless. They were perhaps in their late forties. Cedrick's hair was balding; Wilma, a heavy woman, had a good share of gray sprinkled into her auburn hair. The Sleiters were also from Indiana. Delores had told Marybeth about them, since Delores and Aaron had traveled to Independence with both the Sleiters and Peters. The Sleiters had lost a twenty-two-year-old son, James, just a year ago, their only child. Wilma Sleiter was still not over the loss, and they had come west to get away from familiar places and things. At least Cedrick had thought it would be better for her, but Wilma had not wanted to leave.

Marybeth watched the woman as another hymn was sung. There were circles around her eyes, and a visible agony that tore at Maybeth's heart. She could not imagine anything worse than losing an only child, and a lump rose in her throat at the thought of losing little Danny. There had been little love shared between herself and the boy's father, but that had no affect on her feelings for her baby. He was the most precious thing in her life.

Every woman from the wagon train except Ella was at the worship service, as well as most husbands. The scouts, as usual, were nowhere to be seen; and Marybeth wondered if they even believed in a God. Cap and the cook were at the cook wagon going over some kind of map. Children were coughing and fidgeting, and another prayer was offered.

Marybeth took her rosary from a pocket of her dress and quietly whispered three Hail Marys. A few people turned to glance at her, but most just looked away again. Marybeth sensed that on such a journey, how a person worshipped mattered little. For the duration of the journey they would all have one thing in common—survival. They all needed God and the hope their various religions brought them. They had even broken away from the firm conviction that only a man should lead a worship service. Most of the men along were too bashful, too busy, or couldn't read well enough to take that responsibility, and it was the women who had insisted on worship, and who conducted the same. The only man who participated in leading some of the prayers and songs was a Raymond Cornwall, who had been a deacon at his Baptist church back in Pennsylvania and was the closest thing they had to a real preacher.

Cornwall began reading from the Bible. "Who's that coming?" Marybeth heard someone say quietly as the man read. She glanced in the direction of the woman's eyes, and her heart seemed to skip a beat. A man wearing deerskin shirt and riding a buckskin-colored horse was approaching. She thought she recognized the horse, but because of the Indian-style shirt and the way the sun behind him cast his face in shadow, she could not be sure who the rider was. He led his horse around the outside of the crowd, realizing they were at worship, and Marybeth noticed he also led two grayish-white pack horses, both of them with spotted rumps, a breed she had never seen before. When he got a little closer, she saw who it was, and she quickly turned away, her heart pounding wildly.

Joshua Rivers! She told herself it was foolish and sinful . to be so happy he was here. What difference did it make? He was just another traveler. And yet she was glad to see he had come alone. Surely he had no family, a man traveling alone to Oregon. With shaking hands she continued praying with her rosary beads, and to her surprise her eyes teared with absolute joy.

"Would you look at that?" Bill Stone spoke up, rising from digging stones out of an ox's hoof. Mac and John both looked up from the axle they were greasing to see Joshua Rivers ride past them, leading two pack horses.

"What in God's name is that bastard doing here?" John grumbled.

Joshua looked in their direction slowing his horse for a moment in surprise. Then he nodded, grinning wryly at John, who stood and stared at him as he headed for the cook wagon.

"You don't suppose that sonofabitch is going to be traveling with this train, do you?" John asked Mac.

"Looks that way to me."

Bill Stone grinned to himself, thinking how interesting the tedious journey could become with Joshua Rivers and John MacKinder thrown together.

Josh rode up to the cook wagon.

"You Harley Webster?" He was speaking to the buckskin-clad, bearded man who looked too old for such a venture. The man turned.

"Yes, sir, but everyone calls me Cap," the man answered, reaching up to shake Josh's hand. Josh took his hand and dismounted.

"Joshua Rivers. My brother-in-law, Brand Selby, said to look for you." They released hands. "Brand said he sold some horses to you a year or so back, in Independence. He's part Indian and good friends of a scout called Devon, who told him you're the best at leading folks west."

"Well, I don't know about that, but any friend of Devon's or any relative of Brand Selby is welcome on my wagon train," Cap told him.

Josh grinned. "I was told back at Independence you and

Devon both had already left with a wagon train. I was there a few days ago myself, but I went home for a last good-bye to my family and I missed you. Been riding hard to catch up ever since. I'm headed for Oregon myself, but it's dangerous country out there for a man alone."

"That it is. You a single man then?"

"Yes, sir. I'd be glad to offer my services in any way I can. I'm a pretty good shot; be glad to hunt for you, and I'm packing the latest in repeating rifles."

"Well, we can use a man who will keep us in meat. My scouts are out now, checking the trail ahead. They do some hunting, but that's not their primary duty. An extra man is welcome. You look like you can take care of yourself."

Josh nodded. "Been doing it for years."

"Those are mighty fine looking Appaloosas you have there," Ben Stramm spoke up. He reached out his hand. "I'm the cook—Ben Stramm."

Josh shook his hand. "Thanks. My brother-in-law raises Appaloosas. He's one of the best—half Comanche. You know how Indians are at breeding horses."

Ben's eyebrows shot up in surprise. "They're about the best. But I'm surprised your own brother-in-law is Indian."

"It's a long story."

"You must know a little about Indians then. You might come in handy farther along on the trial."

Joshua smiled then. "I mostly know about Comanche. I'm not real familiar with the tribes of the northern plains. But I'm told they don't make much fuss; mostly poke their noses around to trade. They haven't figured out yet that this invasion of whites is going to get worse. The Comanche figured it out a long time ago. They've been at war with the whites in Texas for years."

"That where you're from?" Cap asked. "I thought I recognized that Texas drawl."

Joshua sobered, a terrible loneliness coming into his eyes. "Lived here all my life, up till about six years ago. That's another long story. You don't mind then if I join you?"

"Not when you're a healthy young man who can help us

out; you have a tent or something?"

"Yes, sir. I didn't want to be encumbered with a wagon. A tent is good enough."

"Well, then, tie your horses and have some coffee with us. Most of the people from the train are attending a worship service. If you're from Texas, you're pretty familiar with the West and its dangers. That's a big help, too. I'll bet you've had your share of drought, snakes, cactus, dust storms and the like."

Joshua grinned, already wondering why in God's name the MacKinders had to be a part of this wagon train. He told himself he should move on right now, but he had specifically wanted to travel with Webster and Devon. "Texas has all those things and even more wonderful attributes," he answered.

They all laughed and Cap handed Josh a tin cup full of coffee. "Well, most of these folks do have some surprises ahead," he said. "It's the women I always feel sorry for. I haven't led one of these trains yet without seeing some woman go just about crazy. They lose children, husbands, mothers—leave behind fine homes. I have to admire most of them. They're only here because their men-folk have big dreams about owning lots of land and being their own masters. Trouble is, once Oregon and places like that get settled enough, the people there will find out they have the same problems, rules and restrictions, taxes and such as they had back home. But who am I to tell them they're crazy to leave behind loved ones and comfortable homes and farms? It's their choice. All I can do is try to get them there safely, and I'll tell you, most of these people know precious little about what they're in for and how to survive out here."

Josh nodded. "I can imagine." He thought again of Marybeth, then shook the thought away. He was a man headed for Oregon to carve his own destiny in a new land. The fact that the MacKinders happened to be on the same wagon train was just an inconvenience, nothing more.

He watched then as the little prayer meeting in the distance broke up. Families headed back to their wagons, and he saw John MacKinder headed toward the cook wagon, his face dark with rage, his hand clutching a hammer. Josh sighed with irritation as he boldly held John's nearly black eyes with his own soft brown ones.

"What is this man doing here?" John barked at Cap.

Cap frowned, folding his arms. "What's it to you, Irishman?"

"I don't like him! He's a troublemaker."

A few people wandered in the direction of the voices, unable to avoid hearing John MacKinder. Marybeth's heart sank and she felt her cheeks going hot with embarrassment when she, too, heard John shouting near the cook wagon.

"What's that big Irishman grumping about now?" someone muttered. "I wish someone would shut him up."

Marybeth's eyes filled with tears. She had no doubt what the argument was about.

"Well, so far on this trip, the only troublemaker I've seen is *you*, MacKinder," Cap was saying. "This man just got here, and he's single and able to hunt for us. He wants to go along and I'm letting him. What's he done that leads you to believe he's a troublemaker?"

John's breathing came out in snorts that reminded Marybeth of a bull. "He just is, that's all! You'll find out! You'll regret letting him come along."

"Mr. MacKinder is just upset because I beat him in an honest match of arm wrestling," Josh told Cap, all the while smiling and watching John. "It was a couple weeks back, on the riverboat to Independence."

John's face turned a deeper red.

"You call that troublemaking?" Cap asked John.

John just glared at Josh. "He cheated," he told Cap. "He knew my arm was tired." He held up a fist. "Nobody beats John MacKinder, you hear?"

Cap just grinned and shook his head, stroking his beard. "All you had to do was save the challenge for when your arm was rested. If you chose to go ahead, then I'd say it was your loss, MacKinder." He lost his smile then, stepping between John and Josh. "Now you listen to me, Irishman. I can tell already this is a good man. You need him, if you want to keep your family fed. Right now I'd say *you're* the biggest troublemaker on this trip, and you'll follow my orders and hold that temper of yours, or you'll find yourself at the back of this train every day—or better yet, I'll kick you clean out and you can either travel alone or wait for another wagon train to come by! If you want to take that kind of chance with two women and a baby along, that's your decision."

John looked right over the man's head at Joshua. "You stay away from me and my family, Rivers, you hear?"

"I've got no reason to be coming around your wagon. But I do have a right to join this wagon train. You mind your business, MacKinder, and I'll mind mine."

John gripped the hammer as though he would like to use it on Josh, then whirled and stormed away. People moved out of his way, some staring after him and shaking their heads. Marybeth hung on the edge of the crowd, feeling a strange but pleasant stirring at the way Joshua Rivers had stood up to John. How she wished again she could have seen the arm wrestling contest.

"This here is Joshua Rivers," Cap told the others, "originally from Texas. Don't know much more about him except that his brother-in-law is a fine man and a good friend of Devon's. He seems pleasant enough, he's single and can hunt for us." He looked at Josh, as the crowd of on-lookers dispersed. "As long as you hunt for us, Ben here will cook for you," Cap told Josh then. "Welcome to our little group—not so little, actually. We've got roughly seventy-five people along, almost half of them children—nineteen wagons, almost ninety oxen, twenty or so horses, and a small herd of cattle, not to mention chickens."

"Sounds like you've got your work cut out for you," Josh replied.

"Now you know why I appreciate an extra hand. Though you might regret this, Josh."

Josh glanced at Marybeth, who lingered at a distance. She reddened at being caught staring at him and immediately turned and walked away. "And you might be right," he said almost absently. "I might regret picking this train to travel with."

Cap followed his eyes. "I wouldn't be lingering my gaze on that one, Josh. She's a MacKinder. Couldn't be you came along because of *her*, could it? Is there something more between you and MacKinder I don't know about?"

Josh looked at the grizzly old man. "No. I'm just a man headed for Oregon, Cap. I had no idea the MacKinders were along, and I sure as hell don't go around messing with other men's wives."

He handed his empty coffee cup to Webster.

"Wives? Marybeth MacKinder is a widow," Cap answered him.

Josh turned, taking some tobacco from his supplies. "You mean she's not married to John MacKinder?" He struggled not to seem too interested when he asked the question.

"Nope. That big ape is her brother-in-law. The older ones are her in-laws, and the man they travel with is just a friend."

Josh rolled some tobacco into a piece of paper and licked it, then stuck it in his mouth and lit it. "I'll be damned. When I saw the whole family on the riverboat, I thought she was married to MacKinder."

Cap touched his arm and Josh turned to look down at him. "I want no trouble on this train, Josh. You understand me?"

Josh puffed on the crude cigarette. "You'll get none from me. I don't start trouble, Cap; but if somebody brings it to me, I finish the job."

"Those MacKinders, they're a tight family; don't do much socializing. John MacKinder has a grizzly bear's temperament. Stay away from them."

Josh tipped his hat. "I'll do just that. In fact, if you'll tend to my pack horses, I'll ride out right now ahead of the train and do some hunting."

Cap nodded. "Good idea. Welcome aboard, Josh."

Joshua mounted up, untying his pack horses. "Thanks, Cap." He gave the old man a wink and rode off, inwardly disturbed at the frustrating realization that Marybeth MacKinder was a free woman.

The wagons rolled on with monotonous squeaks and groans, inching up tall, grassy hills, jolting over an occasional rock, pressing pretty wildflowers under heavy oxen hooves and iron-rimmed wheels. Marybeth tried to ease her pained feet and legs and her aching back from carrying Danny by picking flowers and sticking them around the wagon or into a buttonhole of her dress. She began sharing Danny with Ella again, but felt guilty whenever she let the older woman carry him. Ella had grown even more silent, and Marybeth guessed she was in pain and simply quietly putting up with it. She told Ella she should ride in one of the wagons once in a while, but the woman refused. "I'll walk like the others," she told Marybeth. "I'll not be a burden."

One of the Gentry children had taken sick, and her constant coughing upset Marybeth, whose fear of Danny getting sick had not subsided. The Gentry wagon was just behind the MacKinders, and Marybeth walked with Florence Gentry, reassuring the woman that eight-year-old Melinda would be fine.

Every day Delores Svensson joined them, and a close friendship was beginning to form among the three women. Marybeth wished Ella would join them, but she walked alone. Mac didn't like his wife socializing too much. Marybeth knew it was because he was afraid she might get ideas of independence, might begin to realize she didn't have to live the way she had been living.

Marybeth was determined that the MacKinder men would not hinder her own need to have friends, and she treasured the time she got to spend with Delores and Florence, who seemed to accept her the way she was, Irish, Catholic, and a widow. A few others shunned her, but their common travails made most of them friendly and receptive. Her heart ached at Florence's worry over her little girl. They were beginning to pass graves now, almost daily. Some were fine, stone-covered graves, with wooden crosses bearing names still in place. Some were already overgrown, their markers lying on the ground; still others had been dug up. Whether it was by Indians or wolves, no one could know for certain, and the sight of the graves made Marybeth shiver with dread and hold Danny closer.

"That was fine rabbit we ate last night, thanks to that Mr. Rivers," Delores spoke up as they walked.

Josh had been with the wagon train for ten days now. Marybeth shifted Danny to another arm. She didn't reply. Every night Josh had come back to camp with rabbits, wild turkey or grouse, handing out food to someone different every night. But he avoided the MacKinder wagon, and she knew why. She hated John for it, for her stomach literally ached to taste some fresh meat instead of the daily boiled peas and beans.

"Mr. Rivers is a good hunter. I'm glad he came along," Delores added. She glanced at Marybeth and offered to take the baby from her. Marybeth obliged. Danny was growing heavier every day. "You should let the baby ride in the wagon," she told Marybeth.

"I'm afraid to leave him in there alone, and John and Mac won't let me or Ella ride in the wagons. Cap says the less weight the better."

"That doesn't mean you can't ride once in a while for the baby's sake," Florence put in. "And for your own back. Those men are impossible."

Marybeth reddened, saying nothing.

"I'm sorry, Marybeth. I had no right saying that."

"It's all right. I happen to agree with you."

Delores turned and noticed the hint of tears in Marybeth's eyes. "You told me once that your husband was just like his brother. Whenever I think of it, I am so grateful for my Aaron and how good he is to me. Forgive me for saying it, but your marriage must have been unhappy. I am sorry for you. You should think about taking another man, Marybeth. It isn't good to be alone, with a baby and all."

"I can't think about another man right now. John would be furious, and when he is riled, he can be a vicious man. He's a good fighter. I've told you, John intends for me to stay in this family. I'll not try to do anything about that until we get to Oregon."

"He can't make you—"

"And who is going to go up against him? I can only do so

much, Delores."

"Well, there's a long journey ahead, and I feel sorry for you having to go through it with that family," Delores said.

"We do what we have to do," Marybeth answered. She took Danny from her. "I'd better go ahead and walk with Ella for a while."

"I'm sorry if I upset you," Delores told her.

"No, you did not." How could she tell them she had already thought about another man, a man she could never have. She hurried to catch up with her own wagon. To her surprise and relief Mac offered to take Danny. "Ah, he's a MacKinder, all right," he said, bouncing Danny and exclaiming about how big he was getting. "He'll be as big or bigger than his father." He suddenly scowled at Marybeth. "You're spending too much time with those other women, Marybeth. You'd be best to walk with Ella and keep her company."

"I need their friendship. And I think Ella does, too. You should let her walk with us."

"And let you and those others plant ideas in her head? You're getting more independent every day, Marybeth, and I do not like it, nor do I appreciate it. Why do you continue to embarrass and shame us?"

"*Shame* you? What on Earth have I done to shame you?"

"Talking back, like you're doing right now. Maybe you won't listen to John, but you'll by God listen to me. If you insist on continuing to turn away from your own family, you'll be doing it alone. My grandson belongs with us and that is where he will stay. If you don't want to be left behind, you'll stop gabbing with those women back there and stay here where you belong."

Marybeth stopped walking and grabbed Mac's arm. "Give me my child," she demanded, her voice low but menacing.

"You heard what I said, Marybeth."

"I'll not turn into a frightened prune like Ella," she seethed. "Nor will I stand for you threatening to take my child from me! If you want to be a grandfather to your grandson, you'll think twice about trying to take him from me, Murray MacKinder!"

The man shoved Danny back into her arms. "That boy is

*family*, woman; all that is left of my dead son. But *you* are *not* family! And apparently you don't *want* to be. I'm tired of your ungratefulness, and if it keeps up, I'll make good on those threats, even if it means separating from this train and taking Danny off with us. No one here is going to bother interfering with that. They're all too busy with their own problems to stick their noses into *ours*! You're *Irish*, Marybeth! You will make life a lot easier for yourself if you stick to your own kind!"

Marybeth glowered at him. "I've come along with you because I had no choice, but you have no right dictating my life. I have no intention of keeping Danny from you and John and Ella, but I will have to eventually if you don't start treating me like a human being."

"And just where would you go? Would you shame yourself by forcing your company on one of the other families, people who have enough problems of their own? Would you go begging to them? I'm telling you how it will be, Marybeth. You will stay with us for this journey because you have no choice. And when we reach Oregon, you will have mourned Danny long enough. You will do the right thing by marrying John and you'll settle down into your proper place!"

The man stormed away. Others, including Delores and Florence, had caught up while Mac and Marybeth argued. Some had stared, but Delores and Florence had looked away. Marybeth knew they could hear, and her humiliation knew no bounds. She stood there with Danny, feeling helpless, as the rest of the wagon train passed her. Dust rolled around her, and she turned her back to it, tears stinging her eyes. For a brief moment she considered walking in the opposite direction, just heading out over the plains and walking to nowhere—anyplace away from the MacKinders.

It was then she saw him riding toward her—Josh Rivers. An antelope bounced on the back of his pack horse. She stood there and watched, feeling literally lifted by his warm smile as he approached. Josh noticed the pain in her face, saw the lingering tears in her eyes. He rode closer, looking from Marybeth to the wagon train that passed her.

"You all right, Mrs. MacKinder?"

"Yes, I … I just got tired and stopped walking for a while."

Josh's eyes moved over her in a way that made Marybeth's blood run warm. "I'd be glad to give you a ride forward."

"There's no need. I'll catch up."

He noticed her hitching the baby to her other arm, noticed she limped slightly. He realized that after a while even a baby would begin to feel like a fifty-pound flour sack to such a small woman. It irritated him that the MacKinder men didn't let her ride in the wagon once in a while, or at least rig up a better way of carrying the baby.

"Please, ma'am, let me help you."

"No!" She looked at him with nothing less than fear in her eyes. "Please, please go away, Mr. Rivers, before people see us talking. *Please!*"

He rode closer again. "I'll go—this time. But if you think I'm afraid of John MacKinder or his father, I'm not. And neither should you be, ma'am. You're free to make your own choices."

"And I choose not to make trouble."

He rode very close and leaned down, pulling his hat lower on his forehead. "Suit yourself. Good-day, ma'am. I'll bring some meat by your camp tonight."

He rode forward. "Please don't," she called out to him. But he only waved and kept riding. Marybeth watched after him, touched by his charm and concern, upset at his brashness, yet finding it intriguing. She admired him for obviously holding no fear for John MacKinder. Most men shyed away from him. But Josh Rivers intended to walk right into his camp tonight and offer some meat. Marybeth put a hand to her heart at the thought of it. Josh Rivers was interested in her, she was sure. But she realized the tragedy that could bring him. She wanted nothing more than to welcome him into her life, but reason, and concern for his own well being, told her that could never be.

# Six

"We'll reach the Platte River soon," Bill Stone spoke up. "Cap says we'll have to cross it several times. We'll follow it clean into Wyoming, so at least we'll be near water most of the way."

"Good. The women can keep things a little cleaner then," Mac answered. He eyed Marybeth, the warning still there in his dark eyes. She glared back at him but said nothing. Inside she felt frantic. Could he really find a way to take Danny away from her if she tried to leave the family? She knew she would get no help from Ella, and she was too proud and too embarrassed to go asking any of the others to help her. Not only did they indeed have their own problems, but she was not about to visit the MacKinder wrath on any of them.

"We eating those damn biscuits and boiled peas again?" John asked.

"We'll have potatoes tomorrow," Ella answered. "I'm trying to preserve them. All of you should eat a dried apple. The captain said it will help prevent scurvy—something about teeth falling out."

Marybeth moved farther into the shadows, opening her dress and covering herself with a blanket to feed Danny. Mosquitoes buzzed around her, but the blanket helped keep them off the baby. She wondered how many more nights she could stand the insects without going insane.

Crickets sang loudly. Somewhere in the distance a child was crying and his mother was scolding. Ella dumped some dried peas into a pot of water and suddenly someone loomed into the light of their fire. It was Josh Rivers. He held a rabbit in each hand.

"Evening, folks," he said casually.

ROSANNE BITTNER

"What in the name of the Saints do you want," John sneered.

"I thought you might like some meat tonight. Everybody gets their turn."

"We don't need your handouts," John growled.

"It's not a handout. I'm hunting for everyone. The rest of you have enough to do. Each one does his share on a venture like this. My job is to provide meat. If you don't want it, I'll take it to Ben. I'm hungry, and I don't intend to stand here all night forcing it on an ungrateful bastard like you."

"You think you're the great hunter, do you? Does that make you the better man?"

"John, don't be such a fool!" Marybeth spoke the words from the shadows. Josh looked in her direction and could just make her out. She had a blanket over herself and he realized she was feeding her baby. He was instantly irritated at the rush of unwanted desire the sight stirred in him, and he looked away. "We need the meat," she added, "Not two minutes ago you were complaining that we'd be eating peas again. I'm hungry for a piece of meat, and now here we have some for the taking! Are you going to let your stupid pride keep us hungry?"

John rose, clenching his fists. "You keep your thoughts to yourself in front of others, woman!"

"She's right," Ella spoke up, surprising all of them. She looked at her husband with a mixture of fright, apology and pleading in her eyes. "I'd like to cook the rabbit, Mac. I'm as tired of peas as everyone else."

Mac watched her for a moment, then looked up at Josh. "Leave the rabbits, as long as we all understand it's your duty. We won't be accepting favors or feel we have to be grateful to the likes of you. Like you say, everybody gets his turn."

Josh looked at the man with contempt in his eyes. He laid the rabbits in front of Ella, quickly surmising the poor woman's situation. "You want me to help you skin them, ma'am?"

Ella looked at him as though shocked by the offer.

"She can do it herself," Mac grumbled.

"I didn't ask you," Josh answered, his growing anger evident in his voice. He looked back at Ella.

"I ... I can do it just fine," she told him.

Josh sighed and rose.

"We've got something to settle between us," John told him then. "I hope you don't think it's ended, Rivers. I won't make trouble for Cap while we're on this trip, but when we reach Oregon, you'll find out you were just very lucky that night on the riverboat."

Josh met his eyes boldly. "You might be a man in size and looks, MacKinder; but on the inside you're about as mature as a six-year-old kid."

John stepped toward him, but Mac barked an order to stay put. "You'll get us banned from the wagon train," he said. "Let it go for now, son. Your time will come."

John stood glowering at Josh like a raging bull. "That it will," he seethed.

Josh just shook his head and turned away.

"Mr. Rivers," Marybeth called out.

He stopped and turned. "The rest of this family can be rude and ungrateful if they choose," she told him from the shadows, "but I refuse to compromise my own ethics. Thank you very much for the meat. Please bring us more whenever you can."

Josh turned away again. "Glad too oblige, ma'am." He walked off into the night.

"You never quit, do you?" Mac growled at Marybeth. He looked at his wife. "When that rabbit is cooked, don't you be giving any of it to Miss High and Mighty over there. She can eat the peas!"

Marybeth looked at him in wide-eyed astonishment. "I'll remind you I'm feeding your grandson. If I don't have enough nourishment, he doesn't get enough either."

"You're looking healthy enough. A couple more days without meat won't make any difference. Maybe after this you'll learn to stop talking out of place. I'm damn tired of it."

Marybeth rose and climbed into the wagon, not wanting the man to see her tears. She held Danny close, whispering that somehow, some day, she would get him away from the rest of the family. She cried until she fell asleep, then was awakened by the savory aroma of roasting rabbit. Her stomach growled and ached with hunger. Walking all day long, as well as doing heavy chores and breast-feeding a baby left her with a bigger appetite than normal. She wanted desperately to eat, but she was determined she would not sit and eat peas while the rest of them chomped on rabbit.

She felt around inside the wagon for the gunny sack that held more biscuits. She pulled one out and chewed on it, hardly able to swallow because it was so dry. She choked it down, then took a dried apple from the bushel basket that held them. She ate that, then sat back, the tears wanting to come again. She thought about Joshua Rivers, how he had offered to clean the rabbits for Ella. He was so gentle and thoughtful. His woman would never go hungry or neglected. She would not want for affection and attention. She would never know fear. She realized then that she was picturing herself as that woman, and she also realized what a foolish thought it was.

She laid Danny into the feather mattress and sat back, trying to relieve her lingering hunger by thinking about other things. She decided it was useless and wrong to think about Josh Rivers. She turned her thoughts to Ireland, beautiful, green Ireland. Oh, how she missed it! She prayed that others with the wagon train wouldn't judge all Irish people by the MacKinders. She missed her father's raucous good humor, his twinkling eyes and immense affection. But he had been dead for a long time, and her mother was gone, too. Since joining the MacKinder family, all the joy had gone out of her life, wiped away on her wedding night.

Without realizing it her thoughts turned again to Josh Rivers. How would he have treated a frightened young virgin on her wedding night? With great care and affection, she had no doubt. Maybe that first night he wouldn't even touch her.

She sighed, listening to John and Mac complain about everything they could think of. She knew they were drinking by now. Mac laughed about Marybeth refusing to eat anything. "If she wants to be that stupid, let her starve," he grumbled.

"She'll come around soon enough," John put in.

"I'm going to sleep," Bill Stone said.

"I think I'll do the same," John said.

The men's voices quieted, and for several minutes Marybeth could hear Ella cleaning up. She left Danny sleeping inside the wagon and climbed out to help the woman, but Ella motioned for her to get back inside. Marybeth frowned with confusion. She sat down inside the wagon, and a moment later Ella handed her a plate and a tin cup of coffee. "Not for you," she told her. "But you've got to stay healthy for Danny's sake."

Marybeth took the plate, which held peas and two pieces of rabbit. "Thank you, Ella," she whispered.

"I told you, it's for Danny."

Marybeth didn't argue with the woman, nor did she believe her. In everything she did she refused to go against her husband. Marybeth knew that to give her the food was enough disobedience for one night. To admit Marybeth deserved the food was going too far.

Marybeth bit into the tender meat and chewed slowly. "And thank you, Josh Rivers," she said softly.

The days turned hot, and the nights were miserable with mosquitoes. Spring rains turned the ground to mush, and Marybeth's shoes and the hem of her dress were caked with mud. Not a day went by that wagons did not become mired in it, and for once the MacKinder men were useful. Though they helped reluctantly, at Cap's orders, they put their backs to other wagons that became bogged down. Aaron Svensson also did his share of pushing and pulling, as did Josh Rivers.

John MacKinder seemed to understand for the moment that this was no time for arguing. The first order of business was survival. He helped push out wagons, and he grudgingly accepted meat from Josh Rivers, but never thanked him for it. Only Marybeth bothered to thank him, in spite of Mac's insistence she not be allowed to eat any of the meat as long as she continued to disobey his order not to speak to Josh Rivers.

Neither Mac nor John realized that one night Josh

remained in the shadows watching their camp. With seething anger he heard Mac order his wife to give Marybeth no meat. How he longed to walk right into their camp and take Marybeth away from there; still, how did he know how she would react? After all, no matter how she was treated, the MacKinders were still her family.

Josh spent the next three days away from the wagon train, so angry he knew he didn't dare remain anywhere near Marybeth MacKinder. He hunted from dawn to dark, still finding it hard to sleep at night, his thoughts filled with fantasies about carrying Marybeth away from the MacKinders. He hardly knew her, yet he felt close to her, drawn to her. He hated the helpless feeling of wanting to protect her and being unable to do anything about it, and at the same time he chastised himself for having any feelings at all. He tried to concentrate on Oregon, and his plans for building his own empire there. Maybe Brand and Rachael and his younger brother, Luke, would join him someday.

He returned to the wagon train just before it reached the Platte. On his pack horses he carried two antelope, three rabbits and a wild turkey, everything already gutted to avoid spoiling. He spent the rest of the afternoon after he returned skinning and dividing up the meat, passing it out among the travelers in small enough portions that it would be eaten or smoked right away, since there was no way to preserve the meat in the hot weather.

When he came to the MacKinder camp, he stood holding the hind quarter of an antelope wrapped in its own skin. John and Mac looked up at him from their whiskey bottles, while Marybeth and Ella put more wood on the fire. Bill Stone backed away, noticing the look of hatred in Josh Rivers' eyes, and Marybeth slowly rose, noticing herself that he looked different this time.

"Well, man, what are you standing there for," Mac asked, rising. "What have you got for us this time?"

Josh glanced at Marybeth. "How are you tonight, Mrs. MacKinder?"

Marybeth frowned in curiosity at the way he posed the question. The sun had not yet set, and nearby campers could not help seeing and hearing the confrontation. Delores watched and listened closely, realizing something was wrong and hoping it would not mean trouble for Marybeth.

"I ... I'm fine," Marybeth answered.

"Oh? I thought maybe you were feeling a little weak." Josh turned his eyes to Mac. "From lack of food."

Marybeth's eyes widened, and she felt her face reddening.

"What is that remark supposed to mean?" Mac sneered.

"It means that if you keep refusing your daughter-in-law any of this meat, Mr. MacKinder, this is the last meat you'll get from me. And I'll make sure neither one of the scouts or Cook or Cap or anybody else gives meat to the MacKinder men." He kept his voice raised so that several people overheard. "Now people know, MacKinder, and they'll be watching your camp. They're not going to have much respect for men who keep their women half starved just because they choose to be decent and civil to others. You're walking a thin line, MacKinder. People are fed up with the way you behave, and this is the last straw." He walked closer and plunked the meat into Mac's arms. "Enjoy your supper!"

Josh turned and left, and Marybeth stared after him, loving him, admiring his courage, wanting to run after him and thank him. Others stared a moment longer, until Mac turned on them and asked what they were looking at. Marybeth glanced at Delores, who gave her a soft smile.

"Well, you've gone and done it now, haven't you," Mac asked, stepping closer to Marybeth. "I suppose you went and told those gossiping women friends of yours about the meat!"

"I didn't tell anyone."

"How did he know then?"

"How would I know? Maybe he was standing near the camp one night and heard."

"Which means that sonofabitch has been sneaking around our camp at night. Why? Is there something going on I don't know about, Marybeth? You'd better not shame this family!"

Marybeth was so embarrassed her cheeks felt on fire. "How dare you suggest such a thing! I hardly know the man!"

"Ah, but you would like to. You think I haven't seen the look in your eyes when he brings the meat?"

She glanced at John, who rose, glaring at her. She looked back at her father-in-law. "If I look differently at Josh Rivers, it's because he's a decent, kind man who treats other people with respect," she answered boldly. "That is something I've never seen from MacKinder men!" She grabbed the meat from Mac. "Now go do your chores while Ella and I prepare the meat!"

Mac looked around, realizing others could still see and hear. He leaned closer, lowering his voice. "You think you're so high and mighty. You remember what I said about Danny!" He stormed off, picking up a whiskey bottle on the way.

John just watched her as she turned to Ella with the meat and removed a butcher knife from a crate of utensils tied to the side of the wagon. She felt John's eyes boring into her, knew what his reaction would be if he guessed for one minute that she might be interested in Josh Rivers. He finally turned and walked away, and Marybeth breathed a sigh of relief, inwardly grateful to Josh Rivers for sticking up for her. How she wished she could tell him in person, talk to him, get to know him better.

"Why do you keep Mac all stirred up?" Ella asked her then, angrily taking the knife from her. "All he does is take it out on me."

"I haven't done one thing wrong, and you know it. Must we give up all our principals because of the MacKinder tempers, Ella? There is a softer, kinder side to life. Maybe you can't see it any more, but I'll not lose sight of it. It has to do with love, Ella. That's what is missing in this family. I'll not raise Danny in such an atmosphere."

Ella looked at her, alarm in her eyes. "What is that supposed to mean?"

"You know very well what it means. I'll not have Danny turning into a John MacKinder, bragging and hating and bullying his way through life, incapable of compassion, void of feeling. That's what you allowed him and Dan both to become, because of the way you have always bowed to Mac. It won't be that way for me! Somehow I'll protect Danny from all that!"

Ella studied the tears in her eyes. "Do you think I didn't feel that way once? Do you think I didn't have dreams once? Sometimes you get into situations that you know will never change, Marybeth, so you make the best of them. You accept what is and you go on."

"Well, I'm not married to this family! I *was* married to Dan and he's dead." She saw Ella flinch at the statement. "I'm sorry, Ella, but I'm only saying that you had less of a choice. Mac is your husband, and if Dan had lived, I suppose I would have given up one day just like you did. But now I don't have to. I'm only standing up for what is right, and if that makes Mac angry, there is nothing I can do about it. It's his problem, not mine."

Ella sighed, blinking back her own tears'. "Get the fire going better. We've got to cook this meat."

Marybeth watched her a moment, realizing then that even if Ella wanted to agree with her, she didn't dare. With all the years of pent-up emotions behind her, the woman would probably go mad if she let go of her feelings now. It was easier for her if she remained hard and refused to face the truth.

The wagon train reached the Platte River, and the water was a welcome sight, but also frightening. The river was swollen from spring rains, and anyone could see that crossing it would not be easy or safe. Trapper and Devon rode up to Cap, whose own mount was a mule as big as a horse. The two scouts indicated the best place to cross. Both of them were soaked, so they had obviously ridden across themselves to find the most shallow spot, and that with the firmest bottom.

Cap motioned for the first wagon to go across. It belonged to a man and wife by the name of Stuart and Rebecca Ellerbee and their five children, the oldest fourteen and the youngest six. Marybeth watched Josh Rivers ride up to their wagon and offer to take two of the children across on his horse. The two scouts would take the remaining three so they would not have to be inside the wagon.

The three men carried the children across, all five of them

clinging fearfully to the men as the water swirled to the horses' saddles. Their mother watched anxiously, clasping her hands when her children reached the other side safely. Josh came back for the woman, and Stu Ellerbee headed his wagon and team into the river while Josh took his wife to the other side.

The Ellerbee wagon bogged down slightly midstream, and Josh and the scouts rode back into the river to help goad the oxen into trying harder. The wagon finally made it.

Bill Stone's wagon was next; then came the MacKinder wagon. Josh rode up to their wagon, water running off his clothes and horse. He had left his gear on the opposite bank so it would have a chance to dry out. "The scouts and I will take the women and baby across," he told Mac. "You and your son keep those oxen in line. If you veer too far one way or another, you'll soak everything in the wagon. The path the first two wagons took is the most shallow."

"We don't need orders from you," John told him. "And you'll not be taking Marybeth with you."

Ella had already been helped onto Devon's horse, and the savage-looking scout headed toward the river. "Devon already has your mother, and Trapper is headed back to get the Gentry children. Don't stand there arguing and holding up the train," Josh told John. "We have a lot of wagons to get across that river. Just do what you're told, MacKinder."

Josh reached down and told Marybeth to hand Danny up to him. She obeyed, feeling safe and confident. He took his foot from the left stirrup and told Marybeth to pull herself up in front of him. "Hold on to the baby and I'll hold on to both of you," he told her.

John watched with seething rage as Marybeth seemed to gladly obey. She sat sideways as Josh scooted back slightly so she could hook one leg around his saddle horn. She took Danny, refusing to meet Josh's eyes, desperately afraid of what she would feel being so close to him. She clung to Danny as Josh Rivers' arm came around her waist.

"Hold Danny as high as you can," he told her. "We'll see if we can keep him from getting wet. Don't be afraid."

"I'm not," she answered. *Not with you*, she wanted to add.

Josh headed into the river, and Marybeth felt the cold waters swirl around her dress and lower legs. She clung tightly to Danny, and Josh pressed his arm more tightly around her, as though to assure her not to be afraid. But she sensed it meant more than that. It was like a signal that he would watch out for her.

Josh breathed deeply of the scent of her auburn hair. Beneath his arm he felt a slender waist, and he longed to move his arm up and cup one of her full breasts in his hand, to touch her neck with his lips, to taste her mouth.

"You getting your fair share of meat?" he asked when they were half way across.

"Yes," she answered, speaking up because of the rushing waters.

"You tell me if you aren't," he told her. "Don't worry about John or Mac, understand?"

Marybeth didn't answer. Her heart pounded wildly at the feel of his strong arm around her, at the wonderful warm rush of passion that moved through her as she leaned against his powerful chest. So close! He was so close. If she dared turn her head, his face would be inches from her own, close enough for their lips to touch. Was it wrong to feel this way about a near stranger, especially when she was still nursing a baby and that baby's father had been in his grave only six months? Never in her life had any man made her feel this way before. This was the way a woman was supposed to feel about a man, and she greatly envied Delores. Surely this was how Delores felt about Aaron. She thought how wonderful it must be to be proud of a husband instead of embarrassed and ashamed; to want a man rather than to be afraid of him and dread his very presence.

They rode up onto the opposite bank, but Josh did not release her right away. "Marybeth," he said softly. "Look at me."

She felt as though fire was searing her insides. She hesitantly turned her head, and his gentle brown eyes held her own. "Don't let them destroy your spirit," he told her. Their eyes held a moment longer, and it was torture for both of them to refrain from letting their lips touch. How she longed to know what it would be like; and how he longed to show her how a woman was supposed to be treated. He had already figured that if she was married to John MacKinder's brother, her life must have been hell.

Marybeth looked away and Josh helped her climb down, his hand inadvertently brushing across a breast as he lowered her. Marybeth felt faint at the unexpected touch, and she refused to look up at him. He turned his horse and rode back across the river.

Marybeth joined Ella and watched as John and Mac cursed and shouted at their oxen until their wagon was across.

Next came Samuel and Florence Gentry, their three children already brought over by the scouts; then came Delores and Aaron Svensson, then Al and Bess Peters. Josh rode Bess's ageing mother across, and the scouts brought the Peters' two children. Then came Wilma and Cedrick Sleiter, but their wagon suddenly bogged down dangerously low. Several men waded into the river to push and pull at wagon and oxen, but the wagon seemed to be mired in the mucky river bottom.

"It's too heavy," Marybeth heard Cap shouting. "What's she got in there?"

Marybeth watched Wilma walk closer to the river's edge as the men talked. Wilma put a hand to her chest as her husband climbed inside the wagon.

"Well, get rid of them," she heard Cap shout.

"No," Wilma said quietly.

Minutes later a huge oak chest of drawers was hauled out of the wagon. Several men carried it to a deeper spot in the river and dropped it there.

"No!" Wilma screamed. "Cedrick, don't do it!"

Next came a heavy headboard for a bed, and its wooden frame.

"Oh, my God, no! It's all I have left of him! All I have left of James!" The woman waded into the river, screaming at her husband and the other men.

"Somebody get that woman out of the river!" Cap shouted.

"Cedrick, James made that for us! We can't leave it behind!"

"We've got no choice, Wilma!" the man shouted to his wife. Even from a distance Marybeth could see tears in the man's eyes. "We'll never make the river crossings, let alone get over the mountains."

"Damn you! Damn you to hell!" she screamed, while others watched in silence, sick with pity for Cedrick Sleiter. "Our son is dead and you take me away from his grave! Now you throw away the beautiful furniture he made us! Don't do it, Cedrick! I won't go on without that furniture!"

Josh rode over to the woman and tried to coax her out of the river, but she refused. He finally dismounted and grabbed her from behind, keeping a tight hold on her arms as he dragged her back to higher ground. She kicked and screamed about her dead son, then broke into bitter sobbing. Marybeth handed Danny to Ella and hurried over with Delores and Florence to try to comfort the woman, while Josh kept hold of her until her husband got their wagon out of its muddy bed. With the elimination of the heavy oak furniture, the oxen easily pulled it the rest of the way across.

"You don't need that furniture to remember your son," Josh tried to tell the woman. "Hell, ma'am, I lost a whole ranch—home, furniture, everything I owned to my name, and a brother to outlaws down in Texas. Before that my Ma and Pa passed away. I reckon' everybody here has suffered some kind of loss. But we've got our memories. I don't have anything left of the only home I ever knew, and nothing left that belonged to my brother."

There seemed to be no consoling the woman. Marybeth and the other women tried to comfort her as best they could, and Marybeth longed to ask Josh Rivers about his family in Texas. Her heart ached at his story, and she wanted so much to know more about him. What family did he have left? Why had he joined the wagon train so late?

Cedrick Sleiter came to his wife's side then, and Josh carefully let go of her. Others backed away as Cedrick tried to hold the woman, but she pushed at him wildly, telling him not to touch her. She stumbled farther away from the others and knelt beside a rock, bending her head and weeping bitterly, crying her dead son's name over and over. Marybeth couldn't help feeling sorry for her husband, who watched with a look of unbearable grief and helplessness. She looked at Josh, seeing personal tragedy in his own eyes. She had so many questions, but knew there would be no opportunity to get them answered.

Josh sighed deeply and returned to his horse, riding back across the river. Marybeth returned to Ella, and Mac and John were standing with her by then.

"Why can't you ever stay where you belong," John asked Marybeth.

"The poor woman needed to know someone cared," Marybeth answered, taking Danny from his grandmother.

"If she was my woman I'd knock some sense into her and tell her to quit making such a scene," Mac grumbled. "Cedrick Sleiter must feel like a damn fool."

Marybeth stared at him in disbelief, never ceasing to be surprised by his callousness. She looked at Ella, who just turned away. "We'd better see what got wet inside the wagon," she told Marybeth.

# Seven

The wagon train moved deeper into Nebraska Territory, crossing the river twice more but at places so shallow people remained in their wagons. One man who was traveling with two other men developed a tooth ache that turned into an infection. His horrible screams of pain sent chills down peoples' backs. Cap tried to remove the tooth, but the man wouldn't let anyone touch him. Four days later he died. It was the first burial for the wagon train, and although the man had been a complete stranger to her, Marybeth could not help weeping over the memory of the man's terrible suffering, and again she feared for Danny.

Since crossing the river, Wilma Sleiter had spoken to no one, including her husband. No one knew quite what to do for the woman. Many tried to get her to talk, but no one succeeded, and every night the whole camp could hear her screaming at her husband not to come inside the wagon. "You wanted to make this hellish trip! You can sleep outside with the snakes and the ants!"

Marybeth didn't know who to feel the most sorry for, Wilma or Cedrick. Poor Cedrick was totally grief-stricken, and he had been seen crying more than once. The only benefit of the situation was that it helped ease Marybeth's own agony. She told herself that no matter how bad things might seem, there was always someone else whose situation was worse. At least she had her Danny. Poor Wilma Sleiter had no one, and had been forced to give up the most precious gift her dead son had given her.

Others began unloading other precious items along the way, furniture, clocks, even heavy china. Every night Cap had walked among the wagons preaching that the lighter they could make them, the better, before they reached the Rockies.

People were beginning to understand just how long a journey this was going to be, and how precious were their mules and oxen. Never in their lives had any of them seen such wide open spaces, such an endless horizon. Something that looked a mile away ended up being ten miles away. At times there were no markers at all, just a nothingness that gave one the anxious feeling that this was all there would ever be, that there were no more trees, no mountains, no life of any kind ahead, that the mysterious Oregon would never be found. But the rutted trail left by those who had gone before was a sign that there was indeed something ahead, something that had induced thousands of others to go before them.

For the two years preceeding their journey, tens of thousands had traveled this way in response to the cry of gold. John and Dan had considered heading west then, but Mac insisted they should stick to their jobs, something that was guaranteed. "Most of those fools will find nothing," he had preached. "We will save our money and buy some farmland some day."

Now they would buy the farmland, but Marybeth wondered if Mac ever felt guilty for not letting Dan go early to California. If he had, Dan would still be alive. Did Mac ever think about it, ever feel sorry for anything, ever weep over losing Dan? She had never seen him show any kind of emotion, and his sons had been taught to behave the same way.

They continued to pass graves. Not a day went by that they weren't shown the cruel reminders of just how difficult this trip could be. The heat and humidity had become intense, and there was little talk among the travelers. Women opened the top buttons of their dresses and wore fewer petticoats. Marybeth tied her hair behind her neck with a ribbon to get it away from her face, and she wore her slat bonnet to keep the sun off her head and face. Children fussed, including Danny, who Marybeth had been forced to put inside the wagon in the afternoons. It was simply too hot to carry him. She walked behind the wagon to be near him, dodging dung from the oxen and fanning away dust.

The MacKinder wagons had moved to the rear. By the time the rest of the wagons had passed over the trail, ruts already worn into the prairie grass by the thousands who had gone before were now only raw, dry dirt. Every night Marybeth relished going to the river and rinsing dust from her face and arms. She wondered if she would ever look or feel pretty again, and she worried about Danny, who fussed constantly because of a heat rash. Everyone began to wonder if there was such a thing as wind or cool rain in this land, and if the entire trip would be this miserable.

Florence Gentry was in great pain from a turned ankle, which had swollen to the point she could not wear a shoe. She was forced to ride inside her wagon, which was actually more miserable than walking. The heat under the canvas was intense, and the constant bouncing and jolting had made her sick to her stomach. Marybeth missed Delores and Florence both, since their wagons were toward the front of the line. After several days they finally moved to take their turns at the rear, and Delores began walking with Marybeth again, both of them joking about the dust and dung. It seemed the only way to bear their misery without going mad was to find whatever humor they could in their situation.

John and Mac both scowled at their banter and laughter. They had given up trying to tell Marybeth she could not visit with her new friends, but Mac still held the warning look that Marybeth read well. She said nothing to Delores about his threats, and she refused to talk about Josh Rivers, for fear John would hear. But she longed to tell Delores what he had told her at the river, how it had felt to have his strong arm around her. She wanted to ask Delores how it felt to truly love and want a man ... Yet it all seemed so foolish, for she hardly knew Josh Rivers.

Still, above all the hardships, Marybeth's little island of peace came only when she thought about Josh. Not even talking with Delores could bring her the warm, happy feeling she got when she remembered how Josh had pressed her close, how his eyes had held her own. She actually found herself worrying about him, riding out alone every day in the awful heat to hunt. Cap had said they could run into Indians any time now, that they were deep into Pawnee and Cheyenne country. Marybeth could not help wondering if Josh would ride away some day and never come back. The thought of it brought a surprising panic and sorrow to her soul.

But every night, to her secret relief, he returned to the camp. Lately game had been scarce, and he often came back empty-handed. The travelers reverted to beans and peas, dried apples and for those who had some left, jerked meat.

After three weeks of sweltering misery and faces and arms dotted with red bumps from mosquito bites, relief from the heat came fast and furious when dark clouds loomed on the western horizon, spitting white lightening and rumbling a warning. A cold wind came up in an instant, stinging humans and animals with sharp sleet. In moments Josh and Devon were riding up and down the line of wagons, warning everyone to get out of their wagons and head back to a small dip in the ground they had passed just minutes earlier.

Marybeth grabbed Danny and ran. Josh rode past her, carrying Tilly James, Bess Peters' mother, on his horse. He stopped beside Marybeth. "Hand the baby to me," he told her. Marybeth obeyed, not sure what was happening but realizing the orders wouldn't have been given without good cause. Josh took Danny and told Marybeth to keep running.

"What the hell is the hurry?" Mac grumbled. He caught up to Marybeth, dragging Ella with him. "It's only a storm."

"Tornado … someone said," Ella panted. "We've read … about them … remember? Terrible wind."

Devon rode by carrying Florence Gentry on his horse. Her ankle was still too painful for her to walk, let alone run. John ran up beside them and they all headed for the dip in the earth that was no more than twenty feet wide. Old Tillie James waited there with Danny, and Marybeth took the boy from her, obeying orders from Josh and Devon to kneel down and put heads down. Mothers and fathers covered their children. Marybeth wondered where the other scout, Trapper, was, but knew he was a man experienced in these things and could take care of himself. She wanted to thank Josh for taking the baby, and it seemed for a moment none of it was necessary after all.

The chilly wind and sleet stopped, and everything grew suddenly so silent it almost hurt Marybeth's ears. The air hung eerily heavy and the sky seemed almost green. Those unfamiliar with such weather thought perhaps the storm was over, but again the wind picked up, this time with more power. Marybeth ducked her head again when dirt stung her eyes, and she heard a great roaring sound like nothing she had ever heard in her life. Dirt swirled so fast she could feel it ripping across her back, felt it grinding against her neck and seeping its way under her bonnet. Danny remained quiet, as though realizing something was not quite right and he must not cry and cause a distraction. Marybeth held him against her breast protectively, shivering with fear.

In the distance she heard a crashing sound. Oxen bellowed, cattle mooed and horses whinnied. Nearby she could hear a woman crying. It sounded like Wilma Sleiter. The woman had wept so often that everyone was familiar with the sound, and most had grown so used to it that they had managed to ignore it or else be brought down to Wilma Sleiter's despair.

A few children also cried, and for the next minute, which seemed more like an hour to the emigrants, a wind black with soil roared past them with a mighty force. Suddenly it was calm, and a light drizzle began to fall. People slowly raised their heads. Marybeth was almost afraid to look, but most of the wagons seemed to be intact. Clods of dirt and branches from distant cottonwood trees along the river lay strewn everywhere, along with debris from two partially destroyed wagons.

"Oh, Sam, our wagon!" Marybeth heard Florence Gentry cry out.

They all began to rise. Marybeth stepped away from Danny and shook dirt from her hair and dress, removing her bonnet to shake it out also. She picked up Danny and walked slowly back toward the MacKinder wagons, relieved to see the canvas was slightly ripped but there was no other damage.

"The cattle will be scattered everywhere," she heard Cap saying. "Some of you men who brought horses along go help round them up. But keep track of each other. We don't want anybody gettin' lost."

Sam helped a weeping Florence walk to their partially destroyed wagon, and another couple with two children were hurrying toward their wagon, which lay in splinters. Cap was shouting orders to those who had not suffered any loss to help those who had. Marybeth headed for the Gentry wagon.

"Where are you going, girl," Mac asked her.

"I'm going to help Florence," she answered.

"She'll get all the help she needs."

Marybeth glowered at him. "I'm going to help her," she repeated. She turned and walked away. Josh rode up to her then, asking if she was all right.

"Get the hell away from Marybeth!" John shouted so loudly that all heads turned. "The storm is over now, Rivers. You don't need to be talking to her."

Marybeth wished she could dig a hole and climb into it. A deep anger rose in Joshua's eyes, and he rode toward John, his whole body flexing with a desire to light into the man. "It's my job to check on everyone, MacKinder!"

"And I see who you checked on first," John growled.

The heat and filth had heightened tempers, and Josh started to dismount. "Josh!" Cap shouted from a few feet away. Josh looked at him and caught the warning look in the man's eyes. "Let it be!" Josh moved back into his saddle. "Get on to your wagon, MacKinder," Cap ordered.

Marybeth, tears streaking her dirty face, walked quickly toward the Gentry wagon, her humiliation knowing no bounds.

"Look out there," Cap was saying to Josh.

Josh followed the man's gaze to see an odd black movement on the horizon. "Buffalo," he muttered.

"Badly needed meat. We'll be held up here a while, Josh, picking up the mess, rounding up cattle, mending wagons. You and Devon go on out there and get us a good supply of meat. You *have* hunted buffalo before, haven't you?"

Josh realized the diversion could not have come at a better time. It would help keep his mind off John MacKinder; more important, it would help him stop thinking about Marybeth. "With a Comanche for a brother-in-law? Yeah, I've hunted buffalo. I was taught by the best."

"Then get going. I don't doubt Trapper is already out there."

Josh looked down at the man. "We need to talk, Cap."

"Save it till you get back, after you've cooled down. Just get out there and bring down a couple of those shaggy bison."

Josh nodded and rode off, and Cap hurried to give aid to those who needed it. He couldn't help feeling sorry for Marybeth MacKinder himself, but a man in his position had to stay neutral. His job was to get these people to Oregon, nothing more. How they conducted their lives on the way or after they got there was not his affair, and he wished Josh Rivers could stay out of it himself; but a pretty, red-headed Irish woman had got under the man's skin. Cap hit his hat against his leg in frustration.

Cleanup was a major project. Marybeth's heart ached for Florence, whose job was made more difficult because of her ankle. Delores and several other women and their husbands came to help, picking up belongings that had been scattered so far that some of the men had to ride several miles back to find some of it. A good share of the Gentry clothing and utensils were recovered, but only three of their dozen chickens. Aaron Svensson helped little six-year-old Toby build a cage for them out of what could be found of the old cage. Little Toby cried over the lost chickens, his mop of curly hair hanging in damp ringlets about his face as the heat returned after only two days of cooler weather.

"I didn't mean to let them go on the boat, Pa," Toby sniffled, sure he was being punished by God for the trick he had played on the riverboat.

"It just happened, Toby," Sam told his son. "It's got nothing to do with you letting the chickens go. You just be a little man and help me and your ma get things back in order."

"But we ain't got a wagon," Toby said as he studied what was left of the chickens inside their new cage.

Marybeth sat with Delores at the Gentry campfire, helping wash some of the dishes that had been retrieved caked with mud. She wished she could offer one of the MacKinder wagons, but she already knew what Mac would think of that.

"Several others have offered to put us up until we get to Fort Laramie where we can get another wagon," Sam told the boy. "We'll just have to split up for the next few weeks, son. Nobody has enough room for all of us to share their wagon. But we'll always be together at the night campfire, that I promise."

Marybeth envied the love within the Gentry family, the way Sam Gentry was constantly reassuring Florence and the children that everything would work out all right. Mac and John would be steaming around finding a way to blame what had happened on the women, ordering them to get things straightened up, complaining about the inconvenience.

She looked out at the horizon. Josh was out there somewhere. She had watched in wonder and awe as the great herd of buffalo had passed the wagon train, Josh, Devon and Trapper riding very slowly beside the great shaggy beasts. Never had Marybeth or any of the others seen the monsters of the plains, and everyone stared with their hearts in their throats, realizing how easily they could destroy everything in their path if alarmed and stampeded. They had no doubt the destruction would have been worse than what the tornado had done. The closeness of the wagon train to the herd was the very reason Josh and the scouts had not shot at them when they first discovered them. They had very gently coaxed the buffalo to move farther east, causing them to amble slowly in the direction of the wagon train and past it, all of them moving in one continuous line.

It seemed to take hours for the magnificent animals to move past the frightened and wary travelers. But all waited patiently, since Cap had explained that most buffalo could outrun a horse, and all knew that if the great animals were spooked, it could mean many deaths.

Cap had told them that unless stampeded, buffalo nearly always travel in single file. When they had passed, the bison, some of which, Cap explained, could weigh more than two thousand pounds, had worn a ditch nearly a foot deep into the soft earth. Cap warned the travelers that between this place and the Rocky Mountains, they would have to watch for such ditches, which could break a wagon axle or an ox's leg; and also watch for buffalo wallows, holes in the earth where fighting buffalo had pawed the ground until a hole as much as eight feet in diameter and eighteen inches deep was created.

"The loser finds the wallow is his grave; the winner lays in it and soothes his wounds," Cap told them. "Sometimes the holes are made when a buffalo decides to roll on the ground and scratch. These here prairies will be dotted with wallows all along the way now. Once that hole is made, grass don't generally grow there any more. Sometimes they collect rain water, which can be helpful when we leave the river, but we'll be followin' the Platte most of the way."

Marybeth worried about Josh. He was out there somewhere now, chasing the dangerous buffalo. His horse could run into one of those buffalo wallows and stumble; Josh Rivers could be seriously hurt, maybe killed. Cap had told them many Indians had died hunting the beast, which was the mainstay of their existence. Someone had told her they heard Josh had a Comanche brother-in-law who had taught him how to hunt the beasts. The thought only enhanced her curiosity about the man. How she wished they could talk to each other, but she decided in her own heart she could never allow it even if the opportunity arose.

After two days of repairs to the damaged wagons, Cap got the train rolling again. Florence and her family stored what was left of their belongings in the Svenssons' wagon and the wagon of a family by the name of Rogers, and they began taking turns spreading the family out every night to sleep in or under other peoples' wagons, something that upset Florence greatly. She took her predicament as humiliating, even though it could not have been helped. Her ankle was still not healed, and against Mac's wishes, Marybeth often walked along behind whatever wagon Florence was riding in each day in order to keep the woman company, since poor Florence was almost constantly close to tears because she felt she was a burden to the others.

The tension around the MacKinder camp each night was almost more than Marybeth could bear at times. Ever since Josh had stopped to speak to her after the tornado, John slammed things around and deliberately made messes that would cause more work for her and Ella. "Maybe if you're kept busy you'll mind your ways and not shame this family," he told her once. Mac continued his threatening ways, even more angry with her for spending what he considered too much time helping others and not enough helping her own mother-in-law. Ella hardly spoke to her any more, often giving her extra chores as a kind of punishment for being the cause of extra work.

It was two weeks before Joshua returned with Devon and Trapper. "Had so much meat, we had to dry some of it and smoke the rest," she heard Josh telling Cap as the old man walked along with their horses, greeting them happily.

"I figured that's what took you so long," Cap replied. "Everybody will be glad to get some of that meat. Supplies are gettin' low. Be glad when we get to Laramie. And I'm glad to have my scouts back. Devon, you and Trapper restock your supplies and rest up here tonight, then get back to the trail ahead."

"There are several more groups of wagons behind us," Marybeth heard Josh say as they headed up to the cook wagon, their pack horses loaded down with meat. She knew better than to look at him. She tended to the cook fire, feeling both Mac's and John's eyes on her, neither of them aware that she felt like crying at the sight of Josh Rivers. She said a secret prayer of thankfulness that he was all right.

After a little while Marybeth finally stole a look to see Josh and Devon had stretched two buffalo hides across the sides of the cook wagon to dry. Bill Stone had noticed the same and commented that Devon must want to use the skins for blankets or maybe for trade.

"Indians use every part of the buffalo, they say; couldn't survive without them." He grinned. "The way I look at it, we do a good job of killing off the buffalo, we take care of our Indian problems. Those devils have been getting pretty rowdy, I hear.

The more the west is settled, the less room they're going to have to be roaming about."

Marybeth hated the way he tried to speak with such authority, as though he knew about all things. She also hated the way he watched her lately as though he were keeping an eye on her. She wondered if Mac had told him to watch her.

"I don't much care one way or another about Indians. I know nothing about them," Mac put in. "I just want to get to Oregon. They say there is not much problem with them there."

"Mostly Chinook and Nez-Perce," Bill said, lighting a pipe. "I've been studying up on these Indians. They say the ones out in Oregon are mostly friendly, but not too awful clean—and they'll rob you blind if you need ferryin' across a river or anything like that. You gotta' stay away from their women, though, or you'll be crawlin' with bugs!" The man laughed heartily, and John and Mac both joined in. Marybeth was embarrassed, and Ella simply tended the fire, acting as though she had not heard a thing.

Marybeth heard Danny start to cry, and she walked to the back of the wagon and took the baby out. "I'm going to feed him," she told Ella, moving to the outside of the circle of wagons where no one could see her. She unbuttoned her dress, deciding she would have to try giving Danny more solid food. It was simply too difficult to breast-feed on the trail, where there was seldom any place to sit down in private except the inside of the wagon, which half the time was too hot. Besides that, her milk seemed to be decreasing. Danny never seemed able to get quite enough.

She took her breast from her dress and undergarment and Danny found his nourishment. It was so warm she hung the blanket she normally used to cover herself over the wagon wheel. She looked down at her little son. "You're my only joy, Danny," she told him softly. She looked around for a crate to sit on, but suddenly John came around the side of the wagon, his eyes falling on her exposed breast before she had a chance to cover herself.

Marybeth's eyes widened and she grabbed the blanket, while John only grinned. "How dare you!" she cried. He stepped closer.

"Not so loud, little woman. You don't want everyone to know what I have just seen."

"Go away and leave me alone!"

He came close to her then, backing her against the wagon and putting a hand on either side of her as though to pen her in. "And maybe you were hoping Josh Rivers would come by and get an eyeful, were you?"

Marybeth shot him a look of rage. "You have no excuse for a remark like that! Why do you insist on taunting me and upsetting me? If you *do* have any desire to make me a part of this family again, how can you think that you could ever win me over by treating me the way you have?"

To her shock and devastation he ripped away the blanket and pushed a finger against Danny's mouth to make him stop sucking so that her nipple was exposed. Marybeth yanked the baby up close over her breast, and Danny started crying at being refused his food. "You get away from me or I will scream and humiliate you in front of the whole wagon train!" Marybeth told him through gritted teeth.

John grasped her arms. "I don't have to win you over, as you put it, Marybeth. And I treat you the way I do because I want you to understand a woman's place. You're going to be my wife some day, woman. That is the only future you have to think about, so you get other men out of your head, and you quit thinking about being a free woman, because you're *not* free! My father has told you, and now *I'm* telling you! And I'm not so sure I want to wait until we get to Oregon. Bill Stone says people think nothing of quick marriages out here. Women shouldn't be making this trip single—it's too hard on the men, and it's too hard on *me!*"

He bent down to try to kiss her, but Marybeth bit his lip. He jerked back, refusing to cry out for fear of drawing stares. In the next moment a huge hand slammed across her face, hard enough to make her ears ring and to make her almost lose her balance. She felt him grab her hair then, and he jerked her head back. "If I had hit you as hard as I could, I would probably *kill* you,

Marybeth. But I don't want to do that. All I want to do is make you understand your place. I'll hit you harder next time if I have to! Are you starting to understand now? Are you going to straighten up and be a MacKinder woman?"

Marybeth struggled against tears, refusing to cry in front of him. All she could feel at the moment was rage, and she met John MacKinder's eyes. "You could be such a handsome man, John MacKinder, if you weren't so ugly on the inside!" she spat at him. "And my last name might be MacKinder, but I'll never be the kind of MacKinder woman *you* want me to be! And if you raise a hand to me again I'll scream so loud every person on this wagon train will come running and see the kind of *coward* big, bad John MacKinder really is!"

He stood towering over her, fists clenched, his breathing coming in heavy pants. "This isn't the end of it," he told her. He returned to the campfire, and a moment later Marybeth could hear him laughing as though nothing had happened. It was only then that she shivered and broke into tears. She knelt down and picked up the blanket, devastated that he had looked at her. She covered herself and walked farther away from the wagon, sitting down on a lone, flat rock and putting Danny back to her breast, hoping the ordeal with John hadn't upset her so much that her milk wouldn't come.

She brushed at Danny's tears, then at her own, wincing with the ache at the side of her face and wondering if it would turn into a bruise. How would she explain it? But chances were that everyone would know it was one of the MacKinder men who put it there. They would know what brutes they truly were; but they would also wonder what had caused one of them to hit her. Would they think she had done something shameful?

"Marybeth?"

She looked up to see Delores approaching, then looked away again.

"Marybeth, why are you sitting way out here?"

"I just ... wanted some privacy. Please go away, Delores."

Delores frowned, coming closer. "What happened, Marybeth?"

"Nothing. I told you I just want to be alone."

"I don't believe you." The woman knelt in front of her and Marybeth met her eyes, watching Delores's widen with shock. "Marybeth! Who did that to you?"

"Is there a bruise?"

"More red and white, but turning a little purple." Delores's dark eyes blazed. "Did that big ox John do that?" Marybeth looked down at Danny again. "Yes."

"But why?"

"MacKinder men don't need a reason. Now you know why I don't seem to be in deep mourning for Danny's father, sinful as that might be."

Delores reached out and stroked her hair. "It isn't sinful at all. No one would blame you for not missing a husband who would do this to you. I can't imagine Aaron doing such a thing. Why I … I would just want to die if he did."

"Aaron is a good man. There were times when I wondered if there really was such a thing, but I've seen it among most of the men on this wagon train." She looked at Delores with tear-filled eyes. "Please go, Delores, before they see you talking to me. It will just make Mac try harder to keep us apart, and I don't want to lose your friendship. Go and help poor Florence with the children."

"Will you be all right?"

"Yes, I'll be fine."

Delores rose, sighing. "It's shameful, that's what. How can John MacKinder call himself a man?"

"He thinks something like this makes him *more* manly. Please, please go, Delores."

"All right. But you come to me if you need me."

"I will."

Marybeth watched the soft blue cotton of the young woman's dress as she left her. She wanted to scream for her to stay, but she feared a confrontation between John and Aaron over Delores's "nosing in," as John would call it. Something moved then to her right, and she turned to see Josh Rivers sitting on his horse several yards away, watching her. For a panicky moment she thought he was going to ride up to her and talk to her, but instead he rode to the Svensson wagon, stopping to talk to Delores.

Marybeth felt new tears come when she realized why he must have gone to Delores. He must want to know why Marybeth was sitting off alone. He turned his horse and watched her for a moment, then rode off. Marybeth, too angry and hurt to return to the MacKinder campfire right away, sat where she was until after dark, wishing she would never have to go back. But out here there was no place to turn. She simply had to go on.

She heard the soft footsteps then of a horse at a gentle trot. It came up behind her, and she rose, looking up in the moonlight into the face of Josh Rivers. "That will never happen again," he told her. "John MacKinder might try to kill me for it, and I might be the biggest fool ever born, but I'll never let him hit you again."

It was all he said. He rode off, leaving her standing there feeling suddenly comforted and protected. She returned to her wagon and laid Danny inside. He had fallen fast asleep. She straightened her dress and found her hairbrush, running it through her hair. She walked to the side of the wagon and splashed water from a barrel onto her face, then patted it dry, wincing when she touched her left cheek. She turned and sat down at the campfire, glancing at Ella, who got a strange look on her face when she saw Marybeth.

Marybeth looked at her proudly. She had made up her mind that John MacKinder could beat her to a pulp if he wanted. She was not going to cower to him or let him get away with anything.

"Your big, strong, brave son hit me, just because he doesn't want me to have other friends," she told Ella. "That was really very brave of him, don't you think? MacKinder men do have a way of proving their manhood. It isn't just any man who would take on a hundred and ten pound woman with a baby in her arms."

John stood up, gripping his whiskey bottle and glaring at her, looking like a bull ready to charge.

"Go ahead, John, show everyone what a man you are,"

Marybeth goaded him.

John turned so red Marybeth thought he might have a stroke. "You damn bitch!" he hissed. He turned and walked off, and Marybeth just stared after him. She proceeded to help Ella scrub and repack the supper dishes. Every day seemed an endless ritual of packing, unpacking, cooking and packing again.

She was not aware that Josh Rivers was close by in the darkness. *One hell of a woman*, Josh thought before walking off to his own tent. He longed to possess her, to have her vent her fiery passions in his bed. His thoughts and plans for Oregon had suddenly come to include Marybeth MacKinder.

And still he hardly knew her.

# Eight

Marybeth wore her bonnet in spite of cloudy skies. It helped hide the bruise on her cheek. She vowed John MacKinder would never get her alone again, and a growing fear was building inside her that he would decide to "show" her in a more violent, humiliating way that she belonged to him. He was a man who enjoyed women and who had gone a long time now without one, and what John MacKinder wanted, he usually took. She stayed at the campfire every night until he had gone to sleep, and she never wandered anywhere alone. She spent her days walking with others, helping Florence Gentry or walking with Delores.

Delores said nothing more about Marybeth's bruise, but her heart ached for Marybeth and she and Aaron wished they could help. But Aaron was hesitant to interfere, as were others. The fact remained Marybeth's problem was a family affair, and few cared to challenge the hot-tempered MacKinders.

"You heard Cap," Aaron argued quietly one night inside the wagon. "We can't be making trouble, Delores. It's risky enough you befriending her like you have, her being Irish *and* Catholic, but I'd not stop you from that. You're a good woman with a big heart. That's what I love about you. I agree Marybeth MacKinder is a fine woman in her own right, and I don't judge her for her religion. It's just that not everyone on this train thinks it's right to get involved."

Every night when she lay in Aaron's arms, and when they very quietly made love, Delores could not help wondering how lonely and afraid Marybeth must be, and at prayer services she prayed that somehow Josh Rivers would find a way to do something about the situation. She would not forget the anger on his face the day he rode up to her and asked why Marybeth was sitting off alone. It was so obvious the handsome young man from Texas was enamored with Marybeth MacKinder, and Delores could not help imagining what a beautiful couple they would make.

"Josh Rivers won't let this continue, Aaron," she said to him quietly. "I can see it in his eyes. I never realized until two nights ago, when he asked me why Marybeth was sitting off alone, that he truly seems to care about her."

"Yah, I can see it, too," he answered with his strong Swedish accent. "The day that man and John MacKinder come together will be a sorry one indeed. I am not so sure for which man, but I fear it would be Joshua Rivers who would be sorry." He sighed deeply. "Many the times have been that I have thought of giving MacKinder what is coming to him myself. A man can only stand by and do nothing for so long. I do not want you to think I am a coward or that I do not care. I *do* care about Marybeth."

"I know that." She kissed him. "And you are just as big as that brute, John MacKinder, and I know you would do just fine if you were to stand up to him."

"Perhaps. But I am not a fighting man, Delores, and that John MacKinder has been in fights before. Experience and a mean temper can make a big difference."

She hugged him. "That's part of what I love about you. You're so big and strong, Aaron Svensson, but you never brag about it or go around trying to prove you're stronger than someone else like that John MacKinder does; and I know that if it ever came to having to protect me, you would fight a man twice your size."

He laughed lightly. "We will hope that I will never have to prove that." He pulled a light blanket over their heads against mosquitoes. "I would much rather prove I am a man in other ways," he told her then, pushing up her gown.

They came to another river crossing. The river was much shallower, but Cap still insisted the wagons cross only where the scouts indicated they should cross. Again, the MacKinder wagons had taken their turn at the rear of the wagon train, a lonely spot for Marybeth, away from Delores and far from the cook wagon, the only place where she managed an occasional glimpse of Josh Rivers.

John walked back from the river, where he had gone to check things out and to splash some of the welcome water on his face. He paced impatiently. "That river is as shallow as a creek," he grumbled. "Why do we have to cross in single line? It takes forever this way."

"Cap says that's how we gotta do it," Bill spoke up.

"And who says he's always right?" John looked at his father. "I know the man is right about most things, Pa, but the oxen are restless for a drink, and besides, the sooner we cross, the sooner the women can do the wash and prepare the noon meal."

"Eating is just about all you think about, isn't it, John," Bill joked.

John glanced at Marybeth and grinned. "No, it's not *all* I think about." All three men laughed, and Marybeth went to the wagon to change Danny's diaper.

"Let's just take the damn wagon across, Pa," John was saying. "Cap won't do anything about it. Others can follow us and we'll be saving a lot of time."

Mac shrugged. "Why not? If we make it, others can follow. It could mean making a few extra miles. The sooner we get to that Fort Laramie, the better. Cap says there's supplies there, and whiskey."

"We should do what Cap says and wait our turn," Marybeth spoke up.

"It's not for a woman to decide," Mac told her. "Don't be sticking your nose into men's business."

Marybeth took Danny from the wagon, hating Mac more than she ever had before. His only remark when he saw the bruise on her face was that it was about time she learned her place. "When you marry John, he'll tame you down soon enough," he had told her. "Then you'll behave like a proper daughter-in-law."

The day was refreshingly cool, and Marybeth wrapped a blanket around Danny. "If you're going to cross against orders,

I'm not going to be inside the wagon when you do it," she told them.

Mac ordered Ella to get into the wagon, and John whipped at the oxen, shouting at them to get moving. Mac walked beside him as the wagon creaked and groaned. Oxen and wagon moved out around the others, and Bill whistled and cracked a whip at his own oxen, following the MacKinder wagon. The wagons passed Marybeth, who decided to lag behind. She didn't want to be present and suffer the embarrassment the rest of the MacKinders and Bill Stone would experience when they were reprimanded for falling out of place in line and disobeying orders.

She watched as they passed the other wagons and headed for the river. In the distance she could see Josh Rivers riding toward them. She held her breath as she watched him shouting at John and Mac. As she came closer she caught the words "damn fool," spoken by Josh.

"I'm tired of taking orders from the likes of you, Rivers," she heard John shouting. "You can't always be telling us what to do. That river is plenty shallow and we're taking the wagons across."

"It's shallow, but some places are more dangerous than others. There are rocks in the river, and places where a wagon can sink so deep nothing can get it out."

"And you know everything there is to know, right? That makes you a big man, does it?"

"I'm only telling you what Devon has told us. He knows this river like the back of his hand. But you've insisted on making a total fool of yourself this whole trip, so go ahead and do it again!"

"We'll get across just fine, and when we do, others can follow and we'll be saving a lot of time. Cap's an old man who gets a little *too* careful," John yelled back.

Other wagons began moving out of line, several others agreeing with John, even though most disliked him intensely. The weather and boredom, mishaps and fatigue had begun to do their dirty work on tempers and patience. Others were anxious to get to the water, and even more anxious to get to Fort Laramie. They began lining up behind John, and John proudly drove the oxen into the river, feeling like the victor, deciding he was becoming just as experienced at these things as Josh Rivers thought he was. He was sick and tired of being made to look the lesser man just because he had never been in such country before; also, he was tired of Josh Rivers looking like the great hero just because he was a good hunter.

*Give me a horse and musket, and I'd do just as well*, he thought as he headed into the refreshing water.

The oxen balked a little and he whipped and shouted at them. Josh rode up to Devon and Cap. "What should we do?" he asked.

Devon just grinned. "Let him go. You will enjoy it."

Half way across the oxen seemed to stumble. Their eyes grew wide with frantic fear as their hooves slid off smooth rocks and their feet sank into a quicksand-like river bed. Instantly they struggled to get free, lurching forward and dragging the wagon against a huge hidden boulder, bringing the left front wheel up and over the rock so that the center of the wagon came crashing down against it, cracking the bed. John shouted at the oxen to calm down, but they kept charging ahead, even though the rear wheel had become embedded in the soft bottom and could not be pulled up and over the rock. The oxen strained until the rear wheel snapped away from its hub, breaking spokes and cracking the rear axle. Finally the oxen, with a mixture of fear and their mighty strength, strained so hard at the yoke that they snapped the tongue from the rest of the wagon and made it to shore dragging the tongue behind them, leaving the badly damaged wagon behind, still in the river.

Several men hurriedly brought the shaken oxen under control, and John stood in the river, cursing with such vehemence that mothers tried to cover their children's ears. In spite of the gravity of the situation, Marybeth could not help the laughter that rose inside of her and came out in full force. It felt good to laugh, especially to laugh at John MacKinder. For the moment it didn't matter that the wagon was buried and broken. All that mattered was that John MacKinder had lost again.

She realized then that others around her were also laughing, and she glanced at Josh Rivers, who looked back at her and grinned. Mac was helping Ella out of the wagon, and the woman waded back to shore while Bill Stone waded back in with Mac to check the damage and try to figure out how to get the wagon out of the water. Cap rode to the sight on his mule, ordering those who had got out of line to get back where they belonged.

"This is what happens when my orders are disobeyed!" he shouted. He rode the mule part way into the river. "MacKinder, I ought to kick you off this train! It's gonna take the better part of four or five days to repair that damn wagon, I can tell that from here! We ain't waitin' that long. You can just sit here and fix that wagon and catch up. We're goin' on without you, you damn fool!"

"I'll catch up sooner than you think," John shouted back, raising his fist. "This is Josh Rivers' fault! He nodded toward this section of the river like it would be all right."

"And you're a damn liar!" Cap turned to Devon. "Help the rest of them across. We'll make noon camp on the other side and then we're going on without the MacKinders. They can catch up." He shouted across the river. "Some of you men on the other side see if you can help MacKinder get that wagon out."

While John and Mac were busy cursing and tugging at their wagon, Josh rode back to Marybeth, who was still laughing. He grinned and looked down at her. "You don't seem very upset."

"I can't help it. John MacKinder always has to learn things the hard way. I enjoy seeing him make such a grand fool of himself. It serves him right."

Josh detected the bitterness and hatred in the remark, in spite of her lingering laughter.

"The only bad thing about it is Mac's going to leave them behind to repair the wagon. They'll have to catch up. Between repairing the wagon and making up for time, it could be six to ten days before they reach the wagon train again, maybe longer."

Marybeth's smile faded. She looked up at him, suddenly looking like a beautiful, vulnerable young girl to Josh. "You mean—we'd stay behind—alone?"

He nodded, noticing a growing panic in her eyes.

She hugged Danny closer. "Wouldn't that be dangerous? We could be attacked by Indians or ... or starve to death. Anything could happen!"

"Another wagon train would probably come by in a week or two."

"But ... I don't *want* to be with another wagon train. I want to stay with this one ... with Delores ... with—" She looked up at him. "*With you*," she wanted to say.

He could read it in her eyes, sensed she only felt safe when he was around. "I'll go talk to Cap. Maybe we can figure something out. I'll try to convince him that because of the baby you shouldn't be left behind."

Her eyes shone with gratefulness. "Talk to Delores. She'd let me stay with her, I know she would. Cap might be more agreeable if he knew I had willing help."

He nodded. "Good idea."

"John and Mac—they might not allow it."

"After what they pulled today? They'll have to go along with Cap or suffer the wrath of most people on this wagon train. You wait right here."

Her eyes showed their gratefulness. "Thank you."

Their eyes held and he gave her a wink. "All in a day's work, ma'am."

He turned his horse and she watched him ride up to Cap. He dismounted and seemed to be arguing with the man, but she could not hear what was being said.

"You think I don't know why you want her to go ahead with the rest of us," Cap was saying. "You're lookin' for big trouble, Josh Rivers, the kind I told you to stay out of when I first hired you on."

"It isn't for me, Cap. She's afraid of John MacKinder. He put that bruise on her face. My God, Cap, if she's left behind alone with them, that man might force himself on her. How is she going to fend off a man that size? You know how crazy a man can get out in a wilderness like this, and you know Mac

MacKinder or Bill Stone wouldn't do a thing about it! Besides, she's got a baby. That could be your excuse for insisting she be allowed to go on."

Cap looked him over. "I know how a single man can lose control out here, all right. That what *you've* got in mind?"

Josh sighed mightily. "Damn it, Cap, I didn't plan on any of this. I've been wanting to talk to you about it, but I haven't had the chance. Right now I'm not asking for my sake, Cap. It's for *her!*"

Cap scratched his head. "What would she do? Walk? Sleep out in the open with a little baby?"

"Delores Svensson would let her ride with them. I haven't asked her yet, but I know she would. She's become a good friend to Marybeth."

"Marybeth? What happened to Mrs. MacKinder?"

Josh closed his eyes and sighed again. "Cap, please."

The old man grinned a little. "All right. But it's against my better judgment."

"Thank you, Cap. And be sure to make it look like your idea—your order. Leave me out of it. I'll ride across river and talk to Delores,"

Marybeth watched Cap nod, saw the two men shake hands. She breathed a sigh of relief and kissed Danny's head, and she prayed there would be no big problems over the decision. Six to ten days away from the MacKinders! It would be like being let out of prison! How she relished the thought of it. She walked up to the edge of the river and watched as several men tied a team of mules to what was left of the wagon tongue. Several more men lifted the back of the wagon and shoved while the mules pulled, and after a lot more cursing and shouting and one man suffering a badly pinched hand, they managed to get the wagon to the other side, where its broken bed sagged sadly and its left rear corner hung nearly to the ground. A few others carried out what was left of the broken wheel.

"I've got a spare wheel," Marybeth heard Bill Stone telling Mac. "You can use that. I'll stay behind and help you, Mac."

Mac shouted for Ella and Marybeth to wait until Bill could

bring his own wagon across and come across with him. Marybeth waited, watching with a pounding heart when Cap crossed the river and rode up to talk with Mac and John.

"Never!" she heard John shout. "She stays with us!" His big, booming voice was easy to hear.

"... baby!" she heard Cap say more calmly. She couldn't catch all his words, but she heard something about Indians and food. "What kind of men let pride get in the way of the safety of women!"

John looked around, realizing others were staring. "All right," she heard him bark. "But my mother stays with us. We've got to have a woman to cook for us. With one less mouth to feed, our food should last."

"I'll give you some extra meat rations," she heard Cap tell them. "Get some of your sister-in-law's and the baby's things out of the wagon. She'll be riding with the Svenssons until you catch up."

Marybeth could not imagine why John had suddenly agreed, except that he probably knew that Cap meant business, and if he argued any further and lost, it would make him look bad. He had made enough of a fool of himself for one day. Whatever his reason, Marybeth had not known such joy in years.

The long line of wagons finally got across, and Marybeth climbed into Bill Stone's wagon with Ella and they crossed the river. Marybeth had to struggle not to show her joy at the prospect of leaving the MacKinders behind, even Ella.

"You'll have to take everything out of that wagon," Cap was telling Mac. "You can't fix it with all that weight in it."

The man rode up to Marybeth and told her to take out what she needed. Marybeth handed Danny to Ella and walked to the MacKinder wagon on shaking legs, still afraid John would change his mind. But John and Mac were both too involved in inspecting the sagging wagon bed to pay her any attention. She quickly grabbed some clothes and toiletries, the bucket for Danny's diapers, and more clothes for the baby. She set them outside, then returned inside the wagon to get some blankets. When she turned to leave, she found John standing at the back of the wagon. He climbed part way inside where he couldn't be seen by everyone and grasped her hair painfully.

"Real happy about this new arrangement, aren't you?"

Marybeth winced. "I'm only obeying orders. Do you think I like the idea of putting someone else out because of your stupidity?"

He suddenly kissed her, savagely pressing her lips against her teeth. Marybeth tried to get away from the kiss, but he held her head too tightly. With so many people around, he knew she would not make too much of a fuss. He finally released the kiss, keeping a tight hold of her hair. "That was just to make sure you know where you belong, Mrs. MacKinder; and to remind you you'd better not do something to shame yourself and this family! If I hear you went anywhere near that Joshua Rivers, I'll kill him with my bare hands, and you know I can do it! You understand what I'm telling you?"

"I understand you're a pompous fool!" She watched his eyes blaze with a desire to hit her, but he didn't dare do it right now. She smiled. "Your arrogance caused the destruction of our wagon and some of our belongings, John MacKinder. And it just might cost you more than that some day! If you make trouble for anyone who has helped us on this journey, including Joshua Rivers, I just might take a gun and kill you myself, no matter what others might do to me for it! It would be worth it to keep Danny from growing up under your influence!"

"Ah, and aren't you brave when others are about? We both know you don't have it in your soft little heart to do such a thing. You've got no choice but to belong to me eventually, Marybeth, and I'll kill anyone who gets in the way of that. I wanted you much worse than Dan ever did, and I've waited too many years already. It wasn't fair, him getting to marry you just because he was the oldest. Do you know what torture it was for me knowing he had you in his bed? You should have been *mine*, and you *will* be—soon! You remember that, and if you don't want to be the cause of Joshua Rivers' death, you stay clear of him while we're away from this wagon train!"

"I've got no reason or desire to be near the man. But I also don't have to take your orders. I've told you that, and I mean it. Threaten me all you want, John MacKinder! I will *never* marry you! And I will *never* bow to your orders."

He only grinned, pulling her hair so hard she was sure it would come out. "I have to say, I like your spirit, Marybeth. It will be a great challenge conquering it."

He let go of her hair and Marybeth quickly climbed out of the wagon with the blankets, shivering inside at the knowledge she truly was helpless against him, but refusing to let him see her fear. She opened a blanket and threw hers and Danny's belongings inside it, telling herself not to worry about what she would do when the MacKinders returned. The only thing she could do now was take advantage of the peace the next several days would bring her.

She picked up the blanket full of belongings and walked to the Svensson wagon, saying nothing to Mac before she left. She faced Delores with tear-filled eyes, and the young woman walked up and hugged her.

"Oh, it will be so nice for us, won't it, Marybeth, especially for you?"

Marybeth swallowed back tears. "You don't mind then? I mean, you and Aaron haven't been married long—"

"It's only for a few days. Aaron would never refuse. Oh, Marybeth, many are the times he has wanted to give John MacKinder a piece of his mind and a taste of his fist. He just doesn't want to make trouble for Cap. I was so happy when Joshua Rivers told us Cap was going to ask us to take you along. We didn't hesitate for one minute saying yes."

Marybeth sniffed back tears. "Thank you, Delores." She pulled away from the woman and looked up at Aaron. "Thank you, Aaron. The baby and I won't eat too much, and I'll be sure John and Mac pay you something."

Aaron shook his head. "Pay is not necessary. We are glad to do it."

Marybeth saw the somewhat worried look in the man's eyes. She hated having to put anyone out, but she knew what would happen to her if she stayed behind. "I'll go and get Danny from

Ella." She left, her natural pride wounded at having to turn to others for help. She went to get Danny from Ella, who handed him over with a look of stern disapproval on her face, then marched to the MacKinder wagon.

Marybeth hugged Danny close, feeling as though a mountain had been removed from her shoulders, in spite of having to infringe on Delores and Aaron's privacy. For the first time since she could even remember, for a few days there would be no MacKinders in her life.

# Nine

"Cap?" Josh approached the cook wagon, where Cap sat at the campfire. The old man looked up at him.

"I already know what you want to say, Josh. You're lettin' your feelin's for that MacKinder woman run away with you."

Josh sighed, sitting down across the campfire from him. The air was filled with the sound of crickets, and a mosquito buzzed near Josh's ear. He slapped it away, thinking how loud the slap sounded in the dark, quiet night. Most of the emigrants were already bedded down, and the whole camp was unusually quiet.

"I didn't lie about why I wanted her to stay with the train," Josh told Cap. "You know as well as I what John MacKinder would have done to her once they were alone."

"I know. I also know the trouble that's brewing. I know you ain't gonna let this chance to get to know her better slip away from you. I was a hot-blooded young man myself once, you know."

Josh grinned, taking out a thin cigar and lighting it. "You ever do something totally stupid and risky over a female?"

Cap chuckled. "More than once. But in this situation, considerin' the MacKinders' tempers, it could be dangerous, not just to you and the woman, but to others. You can't tell what men like that will do."

"I promise to do my best to keep it from getting out of hand."

"With the woman, or with her relatives?"

Josh laughed and puffed on the cigar for a moment. "Both, I guess." They talked softly because of the quiet night. "I give you my word, Cap. If things get too bad, I'll do whatever needs to be done, including leaving the train if necessary."

"My bet is if anybody ends up leaving the train, it will be the MacKinders, not you. All I can say, Josh, is that from my position, I have to be fair, no matter what my feelin's. If you start somethin', you're the one who goes. If they start it—same thing. Lord knows I can't stop you from what your heart and other parts of your body are pinin' after. But you understand my own problem."

"I understand. I'm sorry, Cap. I didn't plan on any of this."

"I know that. Just go easy and stay alert. I happen to like you."

Josh grinned and rose. "I consider that a compliment. I think I'll turn in."

Cap nodded. "Maybe I should wish you good luck. You'll need it."

"Thanks."

Cap watched him walk into the darkness. He shook his head. "Damn fool," he muttered. He stared at the flames, thinking how they resembled Marybeth MacKinder's flaming red hair, and the MacKinders' fiery tempers. There wasn't a man along who didn't recognize Marybeth's beauty, but Cap knew that beautiful women could mean trouble. "Never fails," he muttered. "This ought to be one hell of a trip, as if it hasn't been already."

"What are you grumblin' about now," Trapper asked, approaching from the darkness.

Cap snickered. "Love ... and whatever it is that makes a man do crazy things for a woman."

"You in love, Cap?"

The old man laughed again. "No, sir. I'm too old for that kind of trouble."

"Josh Rivers, huh?"

Cap stared off toward Josh's tent. "Yeah." He shook his head and stirred the fire. "I think I've got my work cut out for me on this one, Trapper."

The wagon train followed the river more closely for the next three days, and whenever they could, Marybeth and other women set up a screen of blankets along the bank so they could bathe. It felt wonderful to feel clean and to wash hair and clothes. Little Danny loved the water, a refreshing break from the heavy heat that had returned.

Never had Marybeth felt happier or more lighthearted. Even Danny seemed more contented without the MacKinders around. He slept better and smiled more, and Marybeth could not remember the last time she visited so much or laughed so often. She knew that in only a few days she would have to return to her former drudgery, but she would take advantage of every splendid, free moment until then.

For the first three days after leaving the MacKinders at the river, Josh Rivers had been gone on another hunting expedition. Marybeth was grateful for his intervention on her behalf, but she knew the problems he would have if John or Mac realized her going on ahead was Josh's doing. Part of her wanted to be able to be with him, to talk to him and ask him all the questions she had wondered about, but another part of her prayed he would not come near her.

Still, she could not help remembering the concern in his eyes the day he had told her the MacKinders would have to stay behind. The realization that he apparently did not want John to touch her made her feel special. It was a wonderful feeling knowing someone cared about her. When Josh rode into camp in the late afternoon with a deer draped across his pack horse, she realized it was the first time she welcomed the sight of a man, foolish as her feelings might be.

The sun formed a magnificent golden-red sunset, creating red linings around scattered, blue-tinted clouds as it settled behind huge bluffs in the distance. Marybeth put Danny to sleep inside the Svensson wagon and sat at campfire with Delores and Aaron, watching the sun disappear, bringing to life the countless thousands of insects that started their nightly singing. This night was cooler, and the mosquitoes didn't seem quite so bad. Marybeth went to the wagon and removed her bonnet, brushing out her hair and humming an Irish song. She wrapped a shawl around herself and walked back to the campfire, looking out toward the river.

"You seem so much happier, Marybeth," Delores told her. "I know it sounds sinful, but sometimes I wish those MacKinder men would never come back."

"I don't even want to think about it. I just want to take advantage of this wonderful feeling of being who I want to be and doing what I want to do."

Delores walked closer and gave her a light hug. "I'll keep an eye on Danny. It will give me practice."

"Practice?"

Delores smiled. "I think I am going to have a baby."

"Oh, Delores, that's wonderful!" Marybeth suddenly frowned. "At least I think it is. But … they say the worst is ahead of us—getting over the mountains and all. Aren't you a little bit afraid, being with child way out here in the middle of nowhere?"

"A little. But my Aaron is with me. And there are plenty of women along. Besides, we will be in Oregon before I have the baby."

"I pray we will be." She looked past Delores to see Aaron had left the campfire for the moment. "What does Aaron think of it?"

"Oh, he is very happy. I hope I can give him many children. We will need them to help on the big farm we will build in Oregon."

"You look so happy. I'm glad for you, Delores. You are so lucky to have such a good man. I cannot tell you how much it means to me that you agreed to take me along with you. But I feel so bad interfering in your lives this way."

"I am glad to do it. You can stay with us the rest of the trip if necessary, Marybeth."

"Oh, no, I would never allow it. Just these few days will give me the strength I will need for the rest of the journey. I will be fine until we get to Oregon. Then somehow I will find a way to take care of myself and be free of John and Mac."

"You can always count on us."

"I know I can. Thank you so much, Delores." Marybeth breathed deeply of the fresh night air. "It is such a nice night. I think I will walk down by the river for a little while. I won't be long."

"Be careful, Marybeth. We are not supposed to go off alone."

"It isn't far, and it feels so good to just do what I want."

Delores smiled sadly. "Yes, I suppose it does. Go on with you then, but stay within calling distance."

Marybeth smiled and walked off into the darkness toward the river. She tried to imagine sharing the wonderful news of having a baby with a man who would consider his wife nothing less than a saint for giving him a child. Dan's only comment had been "It's about time." And how sweet and pleasurable it must have been for Delores to share herself with Aaron and get pregnant by him. She wondered if she would ever know that kind of joy with a man.

She looked up at the stars, feeling suddenly insignificant under the magnificent sky. Its blackness was so full of twinkling lights that some of them seemed to run together. How she wished she could reach one, could take Danny and fly off to some new planet where only kind, happy people existed; where there was an atmosphere of love and joy; where a woman was free to be whoever she wanted to be and never had to answer to people like the MacKinders.

She walked through soft grass to the edge of the river. A bright moon made it glitter, and she knelt beside it, reaching out and touching the water. She felt almost like a little girl again, able to enjoy simple things, to laugh if she felt like it. She felt like dancing or running. She wanted to be pretty, to feel like a woman instead of an old, unappreciated work horse. Most of all, she wished she would never again have to listen to shouting and bragging and growled orders, or fear physical abuse.

"Didn't Cap warn you women not to wander off alone?"

Marybeth gasped and jumped up from the river's edge, startled by the voice. Her frightened heart pounded at first from the unexpected intruder, then beat even faster when she realized it was Joshua Rivers. She put a hand to her chest as he walked closer, and she prayed he couldn't hear the beating, for it was so strong it almost hurt.

"I ... I forgot. I wanted to ... be alone."

"Feels good, doesn't it?"

"What?"

"Being away from the MacKinder men."

He stepped even closer, and in the moonlight he seemed taller, broader, more handsome than ever. She caught the provocative scent of leather and man. She stepped back a little. "It wasn't that."

"Of course it was."

She swallowed. She had half wanted this, yet now she feared those thoughts would show, that she would seem too forward—more than that, she feared for Josh Rivers.

"I thank you, Josh Rivers, for ... for making Cap convince John and Mac that I be allowed to go on. But that doesn't mean I have to share personal thoughts with you."

"You already have. You were the one who begged me to see what I could do about letting you stay with the train. I know what John MacKinder did to you, Marybeth, and I don't intend to let you be alone with him even once on the rest of this journey."

She turned away, confused, grateful. "It isn't your duty to see about such things. I can take care of my own problems, Mr. Rivers. And I ... I don't recall telling you you could call me by my first name."

"You didn't. It just seemed natural. I'm sorry. I'll keep it in mind, *Mrs.* MacKinder."

She sighed and smiled a little, turning to face him. "Marybeth is fine."

"And you call me Josh."

She studied his eyes in the moonlight and suddenly envisioned him going up against John MacKinder. Such a fine, respectable, handsome man he was. Did he really have any idea what talking to her alone like this could mean for him? "You shouldn't be here. I mean—*we* shouldn't be here like this."

"Like what? We're just two people talking."

The vision of John beating on the man became suddenly much too vivid. "You know what I mean. Please, leave me alone. That's why I came out here—to be alone."

"Is it? You want to talk to me as badly as I want to talk to you, Marybeth—not want, but *need* to talk to you."

She turned and walked away from him. "I'm a widow in mourning. I shouldn't be seen alone with any man."

"In mourning? You were married to John MacKinder's brother. Do you think I don't know the kind of man your husband must have been? What I can't understand is how someone as sweet and gentle as you ended up with a man like that."

"It isn't your business." She realized how horribly guilty she would feel if Joshua Rivers suffered John MacKinder's wrath because of her. Perhaps if she was rude to him, he would go away. And yet another side of her wanted so much for him to stay. He was right. Deep inside she *had* hoped he would find her here alone, and yet that was so foolish! "And I am in mourning."

She heard him sigh, felt him coming closer again. Suddenly gentle hands were on her shoulders, and she could not bring herself to pull away. Yet she knew that if she turned around this moment, she would fall into his strong arms and make a complete fool of herself.

"Marybeth, you're trembling like a frightened kitten. What are you so afraid of? No one knows we're here, and the MacKinder men are nowhere around."

She finally stepped away. "Someone might come and see us. It wouldn't look right. And they might say something to John or Mac."

"You can't live your whole life being afraid of those bastards. Pardon the word, but that's what they are. And if you're worried about me, don't be. I'm not the least bit afraid of either of them."

"Well, you should be. I've seen John MacKinder fight. He nearly killed a man back in Ireland. He is well known there for his skill with his fists."

"And he uses them on defenseless women. He might be strong, Marybeth, but he's no man in my book, and *any* man can be beaten. I proved that when I arm wrestled him. I didn't do it to show off or brag like MacKinder. I only did it because the bastard needed to be put in his place, and by God, if it needs doing again, I'll do it—with fists or any other way he chooses." He came closer again. "I want to talk to you, Marybeth, get to know you better. Let's not waste the few precious days we have. I've wanted to really talk to you ever since that day you ran into me at the courthouse back in St. Louis. Don't you believe in fate, Marybeth—in destiny?"

"Destiny? You mean ... you and me? I don't understand why you seem so interested in me, Mr. Riv—I mean, Josh. You don't know anything about me!"

"I know you're Marybeth MacKinder. I know your husband is dead and you have a beautiful baby boy. I know you feel trapped into a life with people you hate and that you must feel very alone and afraid—that you must miss Ireland very much. I know you're a young widow headed for Oregon, and you're the most beautiful woman I've ever set eyes on. You're sweet and a good mother, and you're strong, able to take whatever life hands to you. And I know you deserve much better than what has been handed to you the last few years."

She smiled nervously, glad it was too dark for him to see her face redden. His insight into her life was unnerving. His deep awareness of another's feelings made him seem so much more man than John MacKinder could ever hope to be. This brash young man from a place called Texas confused her, created feelings deep inside she had never felt for any man, certainly not for Dan. Were they the same feelings Delores had for Aaron? She had wanted this moment, yet now she felt awkward and inexperienced. She knew little about men, especially American men. What did Josh Rivers expect of her? Did he really care, or was he making fun of her? Surely he was sincere. He had already stuck his neck out for her more than once.

*The most beautiful woman I've ever set eyes on.* She touched the fading blue muslin dress she wore, thinking how plain she must look. Yet he had told her she was beautiful. No MacKinder man had ever told her that. But just the thought of John and Mac brought back the heavy weight of their threats and abuse so that even in their absence she felt watched.

"Please do go away," she told Josh. "I just want to be alone for a while. I don't want any trouble."

"I'm used to trouble. Down in Texas I faced the deaths of my parents; struggled with drought, flooding, tornadoes, Indians, Comancheros; everything I owned was destroyed, my brother murdered in front of my eyes—and I have a brother-in-law who is half Comanche. Believe me, I've had my own share of troubles, Marybeth."

She wanted to run, knew that would be the best thing to do. As though he sensed her thought, he touched her arm, and a startlingly warm sensation pulled at her insides. "I've faced a lot worse things than John MacKinder, Marybeth. And right now the man isn't here. He won't be for days. We need to talk as much as we can while we have the chance. You know I'm right."

She closed her eyes and sighed deeply. "I am Catholic, and Irish. Some people do not think much of either."

"I don't judge people by their background. I learned the hard way about that. And down in Texas there are a lot of Catholic missions. Most Mexicans are Catholic so I'm not completely unfamiliar with the religion; and as far as I'm concerned, religion is a personal thing anyway. It doesn't have much to do with a person's worth."

She struggled to find another excuse for not talking alone, her feelings and desires torn. "Delores ... will wonder what happened to me. She'll send Aaron looking for me."

"I already stopped by the Svensson wagon. If anyone asks about you, Delores will tell them you're asleep in the wagon."

She looked up at him in surprise. "You *told* Delores you were coming out here? What will she think?"

"When are you going to stop worrying about things like that? Besides, Delores is your friend. She'll understand."

"Oh, I don't know! I should go back."

He held her arm more tightly. "Marybeth, when are you going to start being your own woman? I've seen you come so close, when you take your stand against the MacKinder men.

Don't let other people dictate your life for you. You're too intelligent and proud for that."

She looked up into his eyes, and the soft, night air hung silent for a few provocative seconds. It suddenly seemed as though they were the only two people in the whole world. And he was right. No one but Delores knew they were here, and much as she thought it was wrong, she *wanted* to be here with Josh Rivers. "All right. I will stay for a few minutes."

She could see his bright smile in the moonlight. "Good. So tell me. It *does* feel good to be away from them, doesn't it?"

She smiled too, in resignation. "Yes." She studied his eyes, which softly glittered in the moonlight. "I hope you know not all Irishmen are like John and Mac. The Irish are a fun-loving, big-hearted people; good people, Josh. They are hard workers. Mac is just … he's a little soured from the potato famine. They lost so much. Everyone did. It was devastating. Back in Ireland, the MacKinders were once well off. In that respect I have to feel sorry for what happened to them."

"Is that why you came to America?"

She walked away from him and he stood behind her. "Yes. My father had died, and my mother lost his farm. We were destitute. The MacKinders farmed next to us. We moved onto their farm and worked for them, but the potatoes got diseased and the MacKinders couldn't keep their help. Dan and John both had always been after me to marry me." She swallowed back tears at the thought of Ireland and her mother. "We were desperate, hungry. At the time the MacKinders had some money left, and Dan MacKinder convinced me how much better off my mother would be if I would marry him. We'd both be taken care of. If I hadn't married him, my mother and I would have had to leave, and we had no place else to go. By marrying a MacKinder we became part of the family."

"So you married him for your mother's sake?"

She wrapped her shawl closer. "Yes. I was fifteen. I lied to my mother and told her I loved Dan, so she wouldn't feel responsible for my unhappiness. I tried hard to hide it from her. I never liked the MacKinder boys much, but Dan promised me a good life. I was foolish enough to think if a woman married a man, she would surely learn to love him. But I found out—"

She stopped, shivering at the thought of her wedding night. "I didn't know he would turn out to be so brutal. I knew they were a bragging, loud-mouthed lot; but I didn't understand … about…" She was embarrassed to finish. "You were right. There is little difference between John and Dan."

Josh listened with a silent rage building in his soul at the thought of Dan MacKinder bullying a young Marybeth. He had no doubt the man had used a fist on her more than once, just as John MacKinder had done. "Why do you stay with them, Marybeth?"

She shrugged. "I have no other choice for now. Dan died only six months ago. I was a foreigner in a land I knew little about, with a new baby to care for. The MacKinders are all I have, such as they are. In a place like New York, Irish families have to stick together. Most Protestants there hate us. We can't help coming here poor. It was because of the famine." She sighed. "At any rate, when Mac decided to go to Oregon, I had no choice but to come with them. I couldn't stay behind in a place like New York City, with a baby to care for, no skills, no work, surrounded by all that prejudice. But I've decided that when I get to Oregon, I'll find a way to be on my own." Her chest tightened at the thought of trying to get away from the MacKinders. "It won't be easy. John and Mac think I should stay in the family. Mac has already threatened to take Danny away from me if I don't stay with them and marry John. As you well know he has no use for what he calls independent women. But I will never again marry for any reason but love. I will find a way to provide for Danny."

She felt Josh step closer, felt a surge of excitement rush through her when he spoke softly. "MacKinder can't take Danny from you. No law would allow that."

"Law? Out here? He knows I'll be more helpless to do anything about it in a land where men can do as they wish."

"There *is* law in Oregon. I've heard they've already set up a court system and—"

She laughed lightly. "Josh, for MacKinder men there is only one form of law—their own."

He touched her shoulders again. "There's something a lot stronger than the MacKinders, Marybeth. It's called faith—faith in what is right. And behind that faith is a love stronger than anything that might come up against it: a mother's love for her child. Love can conquer a lot of things. I learned that when my sister fell in love with a man who was half Comanche. They went through hell to hang on to that love, and they made it."

She turned to face him. "I never knew men could have such grand thoughts. You're a very unusual man, Josh Rivers. And you've already made me tell you more than I should have about myself." She smiled. "You're an easy man to talk to. But you don't say much about your own life. Isn't Texas awfully far from here?"

"A few hundred miles south of Hell, which is a few more hundred miles south of here."

"You make it sound like very rough country."

Even in the moonlight she could see the sorrow come into his eyes. "It is, but it's also beautiful—big, open, endless land, the biggest state in the Union; a wild, restless place full of thorns and thick-skinned critters, wild Indians and dust and hot sun. It can be all green one day, and dried up into brown nothingness the next. It's a land you hate to love and love to hate. And it's a land I reckon I'll never go back to."

The way he spoke the words made her almost want to cry. "You sound like you miss it the way I miss Ireland."

He smiled sadly. "I suppose I do. What is Ireland like?"

"It's very beautiful. Unlike your Texas, it's always green—an emerald green, with rolling hills and—" She swallowed back a lump in her throat. "My parents are both buried there. Not long after I married Dan, the disease in the potatoes grew worse, and even the MacKinders lost everything. Mother got sick and died. I guess wherever we are, the land can be kind to us, or cruel. But we still love it. Like you, I will never see my homeland again." She turned and met his eyes. "Does your sister still live in Texas?"

"No. We all left together; moved up near Independence.

That's where I was before I left to join the wagon train—saying a last good-bye to Rachael, that's her name. I meant to go to Oregon a long time ago, but Brand—that's her husband, Brand Selby—he needed help getting a horse ranch started, and my younger brother, Luke, wasn't quite old enough yet to help in the ways I could. Then Rachael got pregnant, and I felt like I should stay around to see the baby—and then she got pregnant again—so I stayed around for *that* baby." He laughed lightly and Marybeth blushed. "Then I told her I thought she was just having babies to keep me around and if I didn't leave she'd have more than they could ever take care of. I took a trip to St. Louis just to see what a big city was like. Rachael went to school there. She's a school teacher, but she quit doing that for a while because of the babies. At any rate, I spotted you at the courthouse—and then on the riverboat. I figured you were headed for Oregon, but I had no idea you'd be on this particular wagon train. I chose it because I knew and trusted Devon, and I had heard Cap was damn good at what he does."

She tried to digest all he had just told her. It had all come out so easily, as though they were old and dear friends, sharing memories that hurt, each explaining to the other how they came to be on the trail to Oregon—how they reached this precious moment, standing here together beside the Platte River in the middle of Nebraska Territory. All at once the world seemed amazingly small to Marybeth, and she suddenly understood his comment about destiny. Were they both destined to come to this moment?

Afraid he would read her thoughts, she turned away. "I should get back to the wagon. We've been out here too long, Josh."

"Not long enough. Tell me you'll meet with me again, Marybeth—every night that I'm in camp we'll meet someplace. I've already talked to Cap—you know how he feels about trouble. I promised not to make any, but I also told him that didn't mean I'd stay away from you while the MacKinders were absent."

Her cheeks felt hot at the meaning of the words. "I don't know. Everything is so new and strange to me. All I ever knew of this country was New York, until we left to come here. It's like my whole life has been turned upside down, starting from when I married Dan. I feel so lost sometimes. The only sure and real thing for me is my baby." She turned and faced him. "How do I know it's right to be meeting you alone? I am not even sure *why* I would be doing it."

"I think you do know why. We both know there is something between us that can't be ignored, Marybeth. When my sister was first attracted to Brand Selby, I couldn't understand then why she'd want to get mixed up with a half-breed. She said there was just something there that she couldn't explain and couldn't ignore. Sometimes these things just happen."

Marybeth stiffened. "Are you comparing me to a half-breed Indian? Is my nationality that strange to you?"

"Of course not! I didn't mean that at all! I'm attracted to you, Marybeth, and I can't stand seeing you abused."

The humiliation of being talked about by most people on the train, of Josh Rivers knowing what her personal life was like, brought angry tears to her eyes. "I do not want your sympathy, Joshua Rivers! I am not a poor abused soul who needs your help, and if that is the attraction I hold for you, that is not a very good reason to get to know each other better!"

She started to walk past him, and he grabbed her arm. "It's not just that, and you know it!" She felt the power in his grip, but felt none of the fear she would have felt if John had grabbed her the same way. There was a gentleness in his hand, and his closeness made her feel weak. She remembered the day at the river, when his arm had brushed across her breast as he lowered her from his horse. She wondered if he remembered, wondered how it would feel to let Josh Rivers touch her breasts out of desire.

Desire. Yes, that was what she felt at this moment. She realized that for the first time in her life she truly desired a man, and it almost terrified her. She had known Dan MacKinder most of her life but had never desired him. She knew this man hardly at all, yet she wanted him more than she had ever wanted anything, and none of her arguments against seeing him seemed to work.

"Your personal life has nothing to do with how I feel," he was telling her. "It makes me damn angry, yes; but I'd stand up to anybody who abused a woman or a child. It wouldn't mean I'd have special feelings for that woman. All I know is that day I saw you at the courthouse, I couldn't forget your face, and that was before I knew anything about your problems with the MacKinders, or about your background or religion or anything else! Say you'll meet me again, Marybeth."

Her eyes teared. "I ... I don't want anything ... to happen to you," she answered, her voice shaking.

He rubbed a thumb gently over her arm. "Is *that* what's really bothering you? Nothing is going to happen to me, Marybeth. I've been taking care of myself for a long time now. Just say you'll meet me again. You let me worry about the consequences."

She sighed resignedly. Wrong as it seemed, and logical as her arguments were, she could not tell him no. "I'll take another walk tomorrow night, after everything is settled down."

He released his hold. "Good. I'll watch for you."

She looked up at him, and their eyes held a moment longer. Marybeth felt as though she was falling into a bottomless pit, and she was pulling Josh Rivers in with her.

"You just let me handle things," he added.

She felt nearly faint at his provocative closeness. "I have to go," she told him quickly. She hurried away, afraid if she stayed a moment longer she would make a fool of herself; wondering if she would be wrong to meet him as she had promised. She reached the Svensson campfire, and Aaron looked up at her from where he sat on a crate drinking coffee. He smiled gently, and Marybeth wondered if he could tell how red her face must be.

"Delores is inside the wagon," he said.

She glanced at the wagon and back to Aaron. "I'm sorry about ... I mean, I would gladly sleep under the wagon if you would rather be inside."

He shook his head, still grinning. "We are just fine. I would not think of making a woman sleep on the ground. Besides, Delores is waiting to talk to you. She is full of questions." He gave her a wink and Marybeth hurried to the wagon, her heart as light and excited as any young girl in love for the first time.

Was that what this was? Love? She didn't dare let herself think such a thing. It wasn't possible—not this easily; not this suddenly! Yet no one made her feel more happy and secure than Josh Rivers. Right or wrong, she would meet him again, as often as she could before she had to face the reality of the MacKinder hold on her.

# Ten

The gunshot startled Marybeth awake. Delores rose at almost the same time, the two women looking at each other in the brightly moonlit wagon.

"What was that?" Delores asked.

"I think it was a gunshot."

"What time is it?"

"I don't know. It must be very late."

They heard footsteps. "What was that?" someone else asked farther away.

"Are you women all right?" Aaron stood at the back of the wagon.

"Yes," Delores answered him. "What is happening?"

"I don't know. I'll go check. You two stay right here."

There came another gunshot then, and Marybeth bent down and drew Danny close, feeling an awful dread. "What could it be this time of night?"

"Heaven knows."

The two women drew closer, waiting with pounding hearts for several long, silent seconds.

"Oh, dear God!" they heard a woman scream then, followed by dreadful sobbing.

"Holy Jesus," someone else exclaimed.

"Somebody get Cap!" another voice yelled.

"Don't touch the bodies," a man ordered. "Wait for Cap." It sounded like Josh's voice, and Marybeth breathed a sigh of relief that whatever had happened, he had not been hurt. They heard footsteps returning toward their wagon. A moment later Aaron stood there again.

"Aaron, what happened," Delores asked anxiously.

The man sighed deeply, hesitating. "Delores," he said finally, his voice strained. "You do not hate me for bringing you out here, do you?"

"Aaron! I could never hate you. Why do you ask such a thing?"

The man swallowed. "It is Mrs. Sleiter," he said quietly. "She—killed her husband—and then herself."

Delores gasped, and Marybeth's eyes widened. "Dear Lord, none of us realized just how depressed the woman had become," Marybeth said in a near whisper. She hugged Danny closer, realizing how much more she would hate the MacKinders if her baby died on this journey. She would also want to die, but suicide was a mortal sin for a Catholic. She knew she could never go that far, and somehow she knew that buried deep within her was a profound strength that would help her through such a horror. She could only pray she would never have to put that kind of strength to a test.

They could hear other gasps and exclamations now; more women crying. A few children started to cry, frightened by the sounds of gunfire and the women crying.

"Some of you men wrap the bodies so the children won't have to see them in the morning," Marybeth heard Cap ordering. "Put them inside the Sleiter wagon for now. We'll have a funeral come sunup, but I'm afraid we can't be taking too long. We've got to keep going."

"Are you all right, Delores?" Aaron asked her.

The woman wiped at her eyes. "I think so. Oh, Aaron, how awful!" She moved to the back of the wagon, and the man reached up and embraced her. Marybeth longed to also be held right now, to feel warm protection from the horrors of the journey and what awaited her once she had to rejoin the MacKinders. The murder-suicide seemed to bring into focus the unpredictability of peoples' behavior under such strenuous conditions, and again she realized how violent John would be if he knew she was meeting Josh alone. Would he be crazy enough to try to kill Josh? Out here there was no real law, and this wilderness did something to a man—and to a woman.

Aaron left to help with the bodies. "Oh, Marybeth, what a tragedy," Delores sobbed. "It makes me afraid."

"Everyone on this wagon train is a little bit afraid. And we have a long way to go. Just be glad you have Aaron and you can draw from his strength. All that matters is that you have a good man who loves you. He'll get you to Oregon, Delores."

Delores lay back down against her pillow. "And Josh Rivers will get *you* there safely."

Marybeth laid Danny back down gently. The little boy had not even awakened. "Don't say it that way, Delores," she said quietly, lying down beside her son. "I only talked to him once. I'm not even sure how I feel about him."

"Yes, you are. I saw it in your face when you came back tonight. You feel about him like I felt about Aaron when first we met. I knew then and there that we would always be together."

Marybeth smiled at the Swedish woman's odd accent that made her end sentences with an upswing in her voice, making everything sound like a question. She sighed deeply, realizing that just thinking about Josh helped relax her, gave her a comforting feeling of safety against horrors like what had just happened to poor Mrs. Sleiter. "You shouldn't call him 'my' Joshua."

"He *will* be your Joshua."

Marybeth said nothing. Inwardly she liked the sound of it. *My Joshua.* Had Wilma Sleiter once felt this way about her husband, or had she perhaps never truly loved him? It seemed sometimes the line between love and hate could be so thin. On a journey like this one, love either grew stronger, or turned to bitter hatred, and old hates only got worse.

"Poor woman," Delores said quietly. "Poor, poor woman."

"Yes. Throwing out her dead son's furniture seemed to make something snap inside of her. But I think her husband must have suffered more than she did. He must have felt so alone, so guilty."

"Who can know what is going through a person's mind?"

"Marybeth." She heard the name spoken softly outside. She sat up, pulling a blanket around herself, recognizing Josh's voice. "Yes?"

He stepped to the back of the wagon. "Are you all right?"

She moved toward the gate. "I am just fine."

He lit a thin cigar, using the light of the flint to study her lovely face and the way her hair tumbled around it. "I'm just sorry I didn't see it coming."

Marybeth was amazed that he seemed to half blame himself. The MacKinder men would only have fumed about the woman's weakness and stupidity. She could just hear Mac saying "Good riddance—a woman with no backbone to support her husband isn't worth having around anyway. It's just too bad she took a good man with her." There would have been no sympathy; no compassion.

"Any one of us should have seen it," she told Josh, "most of us sooner than you. You were gone hunting most of the time. The rest of us tried to console her after they took the furniture off her wagon. After a while, we just gave up. She wouldn't even speak to her own husband."

Josh met her eyes, taking the cigar from his mouth. "She wasn't ready for a trip like this. Her husband thought he was doing what was best for her, but he was wrong, poor soul." He sighed, pushing his hat farther back on his head. "I'll see you in the morning at the funeral."

"Yes," she answered, surprised and touched that he had come to check on her.

He left her then, heading for the cook wagon, where Cap was settling back into his bedroll. The Sleiter bodies were wrapped and lying inside their wagon, and people returned to their bedrolls. Joshua thought how odd it was—life and death seeming to walk hand in hand. Two people lay in tragic death, and life went on. He knelt down near Cap.

"What about the Sleiter wagon?" he asked, taking a puff on the cigar.

"What about it?" Cap answered.

Josh shrugged. "What will you do with it?"

Cap eyed him curiously in the moonlight. "Probably split up the belongings among the others—try to find out if there are relatives who should be notified—break up the wagon for firewood. What the hell do you care?"

Joshua sat down, leaning against a wagon wheel. "I want it. I want the wagon and most of the supplies inside it. I'll pay for it. You can send the money to relatives, if there are any."

Cap frowned. "What do you want with a wagon?"

"I'm not sure yet. I might ... need it."

"For what?"

"Jesus, Cap, what do you care as long as I pay for it?"

"Two reasons. One is, I need you to hunt. You can't hunt and drive oxen at the same time."

"I'll find somebody to drive them. There are a couple of older boys along who would probably jump at the chance to make some money and have something to do to relieve their boredom."

"All right. The other reason is I think you want it for that MacKinder woman. You're up to something, Joshua Rivers, and it smells real bad. We've already had one tragedy on this wagon train. I aim to keep such things to a minimum. I already told you that."

"And I already told you I can take care of it. Trust me."

"I trust my own instincts above everything else, and they tell me you're a young stud with his eye on the prettiest filly out of the herd. You just remember that with wild horses, a lot of times a male has to fight another male for control of the herd. You might be after only one mare, but the other stud is going to fight just as viciously for her as he would a whole herd."

Joshua grinned. "You didn't have to put it so crudely, Cap."

"Crude or not, you get my meaning."

Joshua smoked quietly for a moment. "She's a free woman, and I'm a free man. I can't say this minute what will happen, but I'm going to pursue it because there is nothing I can do to stop myself. Like I told you before, all I wanted to do when I joined up was get to Oregon, start a ranch of my own, regain what I lost down in Texas. I didn't plan on meeting someone like Marybeth on the way."

Cap laughed lightly. "Ain't many men who plan something like that."

Josh grinned himself then. "Well, if there's too much of a ruckus over this, I'll leave the train. I said it before, and I mean it. Whether I leave with or without Marybeth MacKinder depends on what happens between now and when the MacKinder men catch up."

"You're diggin' a mighty deep hole for yourself, Josh. There won't be no climbin' out once you fall into it. Just don't get buried alive."

Josh took another puff of the cigar, envisioning again the way Marybeth had looked at the back of the wagon. How he wanted to tangle his hands in that beautiful hair! He rose and stamped out the cigar. "I can't let any man bully me out of what I want, Cap. And even if Marybeth doesn't want me, I can't let them force her into a life of unhappiness. Somebody has to help her." He headed toward his tent. "I guess I'll try to sleep. It won't be easy after what we've seen tonight."

Cap settled back against a saddle. "I've seen it happen before. Folks come out here with big dreams, knowin' nothin' about what they're headed into until it's too late to turn back. It's sad. All I can do is keep the rest of them goin'. But somethin' like tonight—it never gets any easier on a man. You'd think I'd get kind of hardened to it, you know? But I don't. They're good folks. It's too bad."

"It sure is." Josh started to walk away, then stopped and turned. "The Gentrys," he said to Cap.

"What?"

"The Gentrys can use the Sleiter wagon until we get to Fort Laramie. If I don't need a wagon by then, they'll have one for the rest of the trip. If I do, they can get one at Fort Laramie. Either way, I've got a driver between here and the fort at least. And the Gentrys can all be together again as a family. It's a good excuse to keep the wagon without involving me."

"Well, you're right there. Good idea, Josh, but what do you mean if you don't need a wagon by then? You figurin' on comin' up with a family in the next two weeks?"

"You never know, Cap. Stranger things have happened out here."

Somewhere in the distance an owl hooted, and the night creatures went on about their business, animals and insects unperterbed by the wild, unpredictable land that had just claimed two lives by a loneliness so intense they could not survive it. But women like Marybeth *could* survive the worst life had to offer. Her strength was part of what attracted him to her. He realized she was the perfect kind of woman for this land, strong, proud, determined. He realized it wasn't just her beauty, or her predicament that had drawn him to her. It was the whole, wonderful woman that she was.

The funeral was the saddest Marybeth had ever attended. None that she could remember, not even her mother's death, or Dan's horrible death, carried with them this kind of tragedy. She could still hear Wilma Sleiter's pitiful sobbing after the furniture was set off her wagon; could see the vacant stare in the woman's eyes those last few days before she held a gun to her sleeping husband's head and pulled the trigger, then turned it against her own head.

Marybeth prayed over her rosary as Raymond Cornwall read from the Bible. "Now I say, brethren, that flesh and blood cannot inherit the kingdom of God; neither doth corruption inherit incorruption. Behold, I show you a mystery; We shall not all sleep, but we shall all be changed. In a moment, in the twinkling of an eye, at the last trump: for the trumpet shall sound and the dead shall be raised incorruptible, and we shall be changed."

Cornwall knew his Bible well and had done some lay preaching. He had gradually become the leader of the emigrants' religious services, and some had turned to the man for spiritual guidance.

Josh watched Marybeth move the beads in her hand, admiring her faith and the strength she must draw from it. He knew that some of those with the train thought the Catholic religion somehow wrong or odd, even threatening; but as far as he was concerned, a person had a right to worship any way he or she chose. He thought about some of the beautiful missions in Texas and realized the Catholic religion had always fascinated him, although he understood little about it.

The last few years spent with Brand Selby had helped him understand that God could be many things to many people. To the Comanche and other Indians he was a Great Spirit that lived in the animals, the trees, the earth, the sun—in essence, earth was God, a bear was God, the sun was God. Josh had come to believe the same, but he kept his religious thoughts to himself. Such things were personal, and he was glad that at least on this journey the others along seemed for the most part tolerant of Marybeth's faith, and most had stopped staring when she prayed over her beads.

"Death is swallowed up in victory," Cornwall read. "O death, where is thy sting? O grave, where is thy victory? The sting of death is sin; and the strength of sin is the law. Thanks be to God, which giveth us the victory through our Lord Jesus Christ."

The man raised his head to look at the quiet, somber group of travelers. "Let us learn from this, brothers and sisters, how much we need each other, how we must not turn our heads and hearts from those who suffer silently just because we have our own problems. The problems of each one of us here become the problems of all of us. Who knows if any of us could have prevented this tragedy? We can only go on from here and hope such a thing will not happen again. Wilma Sleiter is with her son now. She is happier than she ever could have been here with us. Surely God will welcome her, understanding her tortured heart, her bitter grief. Surely our forgiving Father will understand why Wilma Sleiter took a life before she took her own. If we mortals can understand the love and loneliness behind what she did, who are we to say God will not understand? Let us sing."

The man began singing "In The Sweet Bye and Bye." Josh stood silent, as did Marybeth. He was sure she wanted to join in the singing, but she probably didn't know most Protestant hymns. "We shall meet on that beautiful shore…" He watched Delores move closer to Marybeth and put an arm around her as she sang loudly, helping Marybeth learn the words. He liked Delores. She and her husband both were generous people with good hearts. So were the Gentrys. Their eight-year-old daughter had stayed at the Svensson wagon with Danny so that Marybeth could pray over her rosary beads at the funeral. Florence and Samuel Gentry had been touchingly grateful to have a wagon to use so that their family could all be together again, although no one rejoiced over the circumstances that had left an empty wagon.

The funeral ended, and although it seemed almost sacreligious, people hurried back to their wagons. Too much time had already been lost. Life went on, and people loaded up, ready to leave the two lonely graves behind.

"I'm so glad you have a wagon now," Marybeth told Florence. "And all the supplies inside it."

"Well, we won't keep everything. Cap is going to try to find out if there are any relatives back in Indiana, where the Sleiters came from. He'll try to find a wagon train or other travelers to go back to them and pay them for the wagon and the things we keep. Actually, Josh Rivers will be paying for the wagon itself. We'll just pay for the food and utensils, things like that. We'll have to buy another wagon at Fort Laramie."

Marybeth frowned and stopped walking. "Josh Rivers? Why would he pay for the wagon?"

Florence smiled at the way Marybeth's eyes always lit up at the mention of the man's name. She glanced at Delores. as though the two women shared a lovely secret. "Didn't you know?" Florence asked Marybeth. "Oh, that's right. You weren't with me when Cap first discussed our using the wagon. I told Delores later, but I never told you. Cap said to keep it quiet. Josh Rivers asked Cap to keep the wagon. He wants it for himself, but he's offered to let us use it until we reach Fort Laramie."

Marybeth dropped her rosary beads into a pocket on the skirt of her dress. Today she wore the black calico because of the burial. "Why would Josh Rivers want to be burdened with a wagon? He's gone hunting half the time."

Delores arched her eyebrows. "Who knows? Maybe he thinks he'll be needing one sometime in the future." Their eyes held, Delores's dancing with good humor. Marybeth suddenly reddened, realizing what they were thinking.

"That's ridiculous!"

Delores and Florence both laughed lightly as Florence left the other two to go to the Sleiter wagon. "I don't think it's ridiculous at all," Delores told Marybeth. "I think Josh Rivers is just a cautious man who plans ahead."

"And I think he is a foolish man who is going to be burdened with a wagon he won't need. Once John and Mac rejoin us, I'll no longer be able to even talk to the man, let alone ... well, what you're implying—you know what I mean."

"All I know is you have to stop letting those men dictate your life, Marybeth. They have no hold—on you *or* your heart."

"Well it seems to me there are others who are ready to take over for the MacKinders and try to tell me what to do with my life. As you keep saying, Delores, it is *my* decision. And I am too confused right now to make any decisions that will affect the rest of my life. I certainly won't be making any decisions at all until I reach Oregon."

"But you'll still meet with Josh tonight, won't you?"

"I don't know ... I suppose. My heart is so heavy right now from the funeral, I cannot think about anything else."

Melinda Gentry climbed down from the wagon. "Danny is sleeping, Mrs. MacKinder."

"Thank you, Melly. Your mother is waiting for you at the Sleiter wagon."

Melinda frowned, wrinkling up her freckled face. "Do you think it's okay to use dead peoples' wagon?"

Marybeth put an arm around the girl's slender shoulders. "Of course it is all right," she told the girl. "The Sleiters would have wanted your family to use it. You can help your mother pack away Mrs. Sleiter's things to be sent back home. You must be very careful with everything, as though Mrs. Sleiter was still alive and you were helping her pack them."

"Yes, ma'am."

Melinda left, and Marybeth peeked into the wagon to make sure Danny was all right. "Let's ride up on the seat while Danny is sleeping," Delores told her. "You can watch him better that way."

"Are you sure it's all right? The extra weight?"

"Aaron said we should take a break today and rest our feet and legs. Cap said the trail today will be very flat and not so much of a burden on the oxen; after that we will be gradually climbing toward the mountains and will have to do more walking."

They climbed onto the seat of the wagon, and Marybeth noticed the hem of her dress was becoming tattered from constantly being dragged over prairie grass and wildflowers and rocks. She wondered if she would have one decent dress left when she arrived in Oregon. She sat down and looked at the horizon ahead as Aaron shouted and coaxed the oxen into motion. She refused to look back at the graves of Wilma and Cedrick Sleiter, but she could see them in her mind, and her heart ached at their tragic story. How sad that Wilma could not at least have been buried next to her son, whose death had been the cause of her own. She wondered if the river waters had already destroyed the beautiful handmade, oak furniture the young man had made for his mother.

# Eleven

The night was blessed with a gentle, summer breeze that helped keep insects away. Marybeth, her heart beating with a mixture of anticipation and worry that she was doing the wrong thing, walked blindly into the darkness outside the circle of wagons, trusting that she was in no danger. Josh Rivers would be watching.

"I'm glad you came," he spoke up from somewhere in the darkness.

She turned at the sound of the voice, seeing only the glowing end of his thin cigar. Clouds covered the moon, and there was the smell of rain in the air. She could make out his form as he came closer and took her arm. "Over here." She let him guide her toward the river, down into a thick grove of cottonwood trees, where he lit a lantern. He held it up to her face and grinned. "You're awful pretty when you're looking all scared like that. Only thing is, I'm not sure what you're scared of. Surely not *me*!"

She felt a delicious flutter inside at being so close to him again, and she wondered if any man could be more handsome than Josh Rivers. "No, not you. I'm just ... so afraid this is wrong."

He waved her off and turned to sit down on a blanket he had spread out on the ground. "If you really believed it was wrong, you wouldn't be here. Sit down, Marybeth."

She watched him warily. They were alone here in the darkness, and he had brought a blanket. Was it proper to sit down beside him? She watched his eyes move over her, and suddenly she felt self-conscious in the yellow dress she had worn, her best calico. It fit her form beautifully and was one of the few dresses that still had its hemline intact.

"That sure is a pretty dress," he told her. "But it wouldn't be so pretty without you in it." She had worn it just for him, but now that he realized it, she was embarrassed.

"Thank you," she answered, her face reddening. She stood stiffly looking down at him, feeling a sudden compulsion to run. He must have sensed it, because he reached up and took hold of her hand.

"Come on, Marybeth, sit down. We've both waited all day for this." He gently pulled, and she sat down, keeping as many inches between them as she could and still be on the blanket. He squeezed her hand gently before letting go. "How's your boy," he asked.

"So far he's fine, but I worry so much about him—all those graves we pass every day. Others have told me stories they have heard about sickness on such journeys. Some of the graves we've seen are so small. Burying the Sleiters today didn't help any." She looked at her lap. "Danny is all I have. And he's such a good baby. He's most of the reason I intend to some day get away from the MacKinders. I don't want him to grow up under their influence and be like them."

"With a proud mother who stands up for what is right and fair, he won't be. You're a strong woman, Marybeth. I've told you that before. You just have to realize you don't have to do anything you don't want to do—including staying with the MacKinders."

She met his eyes. "You make it sound so easy."

"It *is* easy. Once you get to Oregon, you could find all kinds of things to do to get by on your own, and there are plenty of people along who would gladly help you. For Danny's sake if not for your own, you've got to break away from them, Marybeth."

She sighed deeply. "I know. But you have no idea how determined MacKinder men can be."

He puffed the cigar quietly for a moment. "I think I can guess." He laughed lightly. "How old are you, Marybeth?"

"I am twenty." She looked at him, the same question in her eyes.

"Twenty-six," he said. She wondered as she studied the

beautifully formed lips and straight nose, the gentle, wide-set brown eyes, how many women this charming, soft-spoken man had wooed and coaxed into his bed. She tore her eyes from his, afraid he would know what she was thinking. Most of all she couldn't help wondering what it would be like to have a man like Josh Rivers make love to her. It was a thought she had struggled to avoid, had told herself was wrong, but there it was, stabbing painfully at her insides. How she longed to know if it could really be enjoyable being with a man.

"Tell me more about Texas," she said presently. "You said you saw your brother killed. Can you talk about it?"

"Oh, that's a long story. The shortened version is a man I thought was a friend, a Texas Ranger, had a real yen for my sister, Rachael. Rachael was probably the prettiest woman . in Texas, but she didn't care a bit for the Ranger. Nobody knew the man was double dealing with comancheros—those are what we call the worst of outlaws down in Texas—men who steal women and sell them in Mexico, sell guns to Indians, that kind of thing. Anyway, the Ranger had my ranch raided by comancheros made up to look like Comanche Indians. They burned my house and murdered my brother Matt—chopped him up like a side of beef."

Marybeth shuddered, her heart going out to him. She met his eyes and saw that his own were watery. "How awful! I'm so sorry."

He sighed deeply, puffing on the cigar again. "Yeah." Lingering hatred was evident in his voice. "Apparently the Ranger thought if he got rid of Rachael's brothers, she'd be more dependent, more eager to marry him. The comancheros rode off with my youngest brother Luke as a captive, figured to sell him as a slave for some rich Mexican. They left me for dead." He smoked quietly again. "But I damn well wasn't dead. I rode all the way into Austin with an arrow in my side. But I had made a real big mistake, Marybeth, and ever since, I've told myself never to judge a man by his race or appearance. That's why I understand when you say not to judge all the Irish by the MacKinders. Besides, you're Irish, and look how nice you are."

She frowned, meeting his eyes. "What happened?"

He leaned back, resting on one elbow. "Well, I didn't know then that the Ranger had planned the whole thing. I thought he was a friend. I knew my sister had secretly been seeing Brand Selby—the Comanche half-breed. You've got to understand that in Texas the word Comanche fans the fire of bitter hatred, ten times worse than any hatred you have ever felt. I'd had some pretty tough words with my sister over it—mainly because I knew the ridicule she'd suffer for loving an Indian, the names people would call her and all. She was too pretty and gentle and intelligent for that. I'm afraid I was as prejudiced as everybody else. She'd told me she wanted to marry Brand, and I treated them both pretty bad. After the raid, I figured Brand had done it out of revenge; I thought the raiders were Comanche. I went to town and said so, and everybody went after Brand Selby. The Ranger was so angry when he heard about Rachael and Brand, he had Rachael kidnapped and planned to sell her to the com-ancheros, but not till after he got what he wanted out of her first."

Marybeth reddened and looked away. "How awful!"

"Yeah, well the worst part was that it was really my fault for judging Brand Selby. I rode out and found Brand, and with his nose for tracking, we found the comanchero camp. With the help of a couple young Comanche men, we raided it and killed most of them, got Luke back, and Rachael. I thank God we got there before the Ranger could do what he intended to do with her. We brought him in. He was hanged for dealing with murdering comancheros. Rachael and Brand got married."

He sat up again, staring out into the darkness. "After that, there were just too many bad memories in Texas for us, even though we had grown up there. Ma and Pa settled there after leaving Tennessee when Rachael and I were just babies. My pa was raised by Cherokee Indians. They called him River Joe, the white Indian." He shook his head. "He sure loved my ma. That's another long story—how they got together." He looked at Marybeth. "They went up against some pretty tough odds, Marybeth—nearly lost their lives, some of the same problems

Brand and Rachael faced because they loved each other. I learned a lot from those two, and from remembering what my folks went through. I guess if love isn't strong enough to survive the big challenges, it's not worth pursuing at all."

She watched his eyes, realizing he was talking about her own situation. Was he saying he loved her? Was he willing to face John MacKinder to win her hand? She dropped her eyes, studying a ruffle on her dress. "I've never known that kind of love," she told him. "I never really loved Dan and he didn't love me. I was just … something pretty that he wanted to own. I didn't understand that at first, I was so young. But it didn't take long to figure it out." She breathed deeply and put on a smile. "Well, it sounds like you at least patched things up with the man your sister loved. You all left Texas then?"

He nodded. "Brand's a good man, one of the finest I know. He got to know my sister because she was a school teacher and he wanted to learn to read and write. He had never had the opportunity. He knew there was no hope of surviving the Indian way any longer, so he took up ranching. Heck, he can read and write and do math as good as any man now. We all came up to Kansas and Brand started a ranch outside of Independence, Missouri, on the Kansas side. Does a good business selling horses and cattle to emigrants. I told you the rest. I always intended to go on, but I wanted to help Brand and Rachael get a good start first." He shook his head. "I sure do miss Texas, though."

"I wish I could see it some day."

He met her eyes and smiled. "And I'd like to see Ireland. But we'll both be lucky to make it to Oregon for now."

She returned the smile. "I will be satisfied with that myself." Their eyes held, and she was more awe-struck than ever, realizing how strong and brave he must be—nearly dying from the comanchero attack but finding the strength to go on and hunt down the men who had captured his sister and brother. Yes, Josh Rivers could take care of himself. She began to feel more confident that maybe she really could find a way to get away from the MacKinders, that Josh meant it when he hinted he could help her. But a gun battle with comancheros was not the same as a one on one fist fight with John MacKinder. "I would like to have met your sister and her husband. I cannot imagine an Indian being educated and civilized."

"Oh, there are plenty. But, believe me, the ones who don't have a white man's education are pretty wise in their own right. Whites underestimate the Indians' cleverness—and no better fighters exist than the Indians. They can out-ride and out-smart the best soldiers, and they're damn smart businessmen when it comes to trading."

He leaned back on his elbow again. "Sometimes you can deal with them, and sometimes you can't. I guarantee, the more the Plains Indians realize the white man is here to stay and not just passing through, the more hard-nosed they're going to get, and the harder they'll be to deal with. We already have to watch the livestock. The Indians figure anything out here is theirs for the taking. They love to steal horses and cattle. To them it's nothing more than war games. Warriors who come back with stolen horses are honored. Their way of life is as ingrained as our own, yet whites come along and expect them to change overnight, when they've lived this way for hundreds, probably thousands of years."

She listened, lost in him. Everything he said spoke of compassion, a willingness to understand; it described a man who was concerned with much more than his own personal wants and needs. He was concerned about others, even men as uncivilized as the Indians. He actually *wanted* to understand them, instead of just labeling them as worthless dogs the way most whites labeled them.

"You are an unusual man, Joshua Rivers."

He met her eyes. This time it was he who looked a little embarrassed. "I've really overdone it, haven't I? I've been sitting here talking a blue streak, talking about things you probably don't care anything about." He shook his head. "I swear I don't usually talk so much. Mostly I'm pretty quiet. Something about being around you—I don't know. I just feel like you'd understand what I'm trying to say. Out here a man gets awful lonesome.

Sometimes it just feels good to unload."

"Unload?" She frowned and Josh laughed lightly.

"That means to say things out—get them off your chest instead of holding them inside." He turned to face her, leaning closer. "You keep too much inside, Marybeth. I've watched you silently carrying the load the MacKinders push onto you. You don't have to do that. And I'm here to tell you that you can share the hurt with me—that I'll help you if you want to get away from them."

It was a wonderful thought. Was it really possible to be free of them? "Why?" she asked Josh.

"Partly because I don't like to see people abused. And partly because—" He hesitated. "Because I think you're special. You're a woman with the kind of spirit it takes to survive out here. You would never fall apart like Wilma Sleiter. You've got courage, and a person can push you only so far. I just don't want somebody like John or his father to slowly destroy that spirit and that courage."

He searched her eyes, as with his hand he again gently touched her face. Marybeth sat spellbound, wanting to run, but wanting more to stay. There was fire in his fingers. "More than all that," he told her, "you're just plain and simply more woman than I ever met before. I'll say it out, Marybeth. When I get to Oregon, I plan to have my own spread, to build a ranch again like what I had in Texas. And it's going to take a hell of a strong-willed woman to help me do that. I'm not saying I know right now you're that woman. I know it's too soon. I'm just saying ... I've never met somebody who fit everything I'd want in a woman, and who made me feel on fire on top of it."

He leaned closer, and she felt frozen in time. She did not resist when his lips gently touched her mouth. His tongue lightly tasted her lips, forced them apart in a kiss that grew deeper, expressing the passion that surged inside the man. Never had Marybeth been kissed so tenderly, or with such desire and appreciation. And never had she parted her lips willingly, feeling a terrible desire to move her own tongue along a man's mouth as she found herself doing now. Her response only drew out his own desire, and he continued to kiss her, moving an arm around her and laying her back, his broad, solid chest crushing against her breasts as he let out a little groan, his kiss growing more savage. Even when he became more aggressive, Marybeth felt none of the fear or revulsion she had felt when Dan MacKinder had savaged her in their marriage bed. Still, she suddenly realized how permissive she had been. What would he think of her!

She pushed at him lightly, finally turning her face away. "Don't, Josh."

She could feel his tension, felt his warm, sweet breath on her neck as he breathed out a long sigh of frustration. He lightly kissed her neck and a rush of ecstasy swept through her so that she quickly sat up, afraid of what one more kiss would do to her. She pushed some hair back from her face as he sat up behind her, touching her shoulders.

"I never should have let you do that," she told him.

"Why not? How else are we going to know if what we feel between us is real?"

"I have never said how I feel."

"You don't have to. I can see it in your eyes. I felt it in your kiss." He moved her hair to the side and leaned down to kiss the back of her neck, sending shivers through her.

"Please don't do that, Josh."

He merely smiled, reaching around her, his strong arm just above her breasts. He pulled her against him and she leaned back against his shoulder. Suddenly the tears came, unexpected, unwanted. He held her tightly from behind. "I suddenly ... so want to ... believe you," she wept. "Please don't make a fool of me, Josh. Please—don't lie to me."

He kissed her hair. "Marybeth, I'm not lying. Why in hell do you think I bought the Sleiter wagon? I bought it for the day when you decide to get away from the MacKinders and go it alone. It would be easy to find someone to drive for you. Nobody on this train would let the MacKinder men bring you harm while we're on the trail, and you could settle with one of the other families when you got to Oregon. But that's not all I was thinking, Marybeth. I was thinking that maybe, before this journey is over—maybe you and I would need that wagon together. I can't say anything for sure right now, and I know you can't either. But I do know you're on my mind practically all the time. That has to mean something. So does the fact that you came back out tonight, and you let me kiss you."

She brushed at her tears and pulled away from him, rising. "I had better go back."

Josh stood up, looking down at her. "You aren't angry with me for that kiss, are you?"

She searched his dark eyes, eyes that awakened passions raging within her that Dan had never aroused. "No," she answered quietly. "But I can't think when I am this close to you."

He smiled the warm, moving smile that made her feel weak. "Good. I don't *want* you to think when we're close. I don't want you to do anything but be happy and forget about all your troubles."

"I also have to do what is wise and proper, which means giving a lot of thought to some of the things you have told me."

He leaned down and kissed her cheek. "Then you go back and do all the thinking you want, but promise me you'll meet me again tomorrow. And if we still feel this—this attraction, this good feeling we have around each other, I'm going to talk to you and share meals with you and hold your baby boy all I want. We're going to be open about this, Marybeth, and let everybody know we're good friends—maybe more than friends. Things like this happen fast out here, Marybeth. People understand that. I'm not going to sneak around about it, and I don't care if the MacKinder men find out. They might as well, because their presence isn't going to change anything."

He saw the fear and dread come into her eyes at the mention of their return. "Quit being afraid of them, Marybeth." He moved an arm around her back and crushed her against him, a sudden power and determination in the movement. She could feel his anger and realized that when challenged, this man could be just as volatile and fierce as John MacKinder. Maybe he was more of a match for John than she realized. Yet she dreaded the thought of ever having to find out.

"Quit being afraid," he repeated. He grasped her hair and pulled her head back gently, picturing her head thrown back this way in ecstasy while he made love to her. He brought his mouth down over hers, kissing her savagely this time, pushing his tongue deep as though to hint at another invasion he would one day make on her. She whimpered in an awakened ecstasy that made her cheeks burn and her insides ache.

The kiss became more tender then as he slowly released her mouth. She could feel him trembling just as much as she was. "Jesus, I'm sorry," he told her. He reluctantly let go of her. "Go on back, Marybeth."

She put her fingers to her mouth, her whole body trembling. She turned and fled, amazed at the feelings he had stirred in her, shocked at the fact that she had discovered she actually wanted a man to touch her. For a brief moment she had wanted the thrill of feeling her body naked against his own, the ecstasy of taking him inside her. She had never had such desires before. When Dan had made love to her, it had only brought pain and degradation. It was always done with deliberate force, whether she wanted him or not. She had felt like an instrument for his pleasure, but had never considered taking pleasure in return. Josh Rivers had awakened pleasure in her soul. Yes, that was it. Pleasure. Was it sinful to take pleasure in a man? Surely not. Surely that was what real love was all about. She had no doubt Delores took pleasure in Aaron.

She reached the wagon and climbed inside. A lantern was still lit as Delores sat brushing her hair and Danny lay sleeping in a corner. Delores looked at her and Marybeth touched her lips again, wondering if she looked any different, wondering if Delores knew.

"Is everything all right?" Delores asked. "You look—" She broke into a smile. "Marybeth, you look absolutely beautiful, so—so happy!" She moved closer. "You aren't going to *cry*, are you?"

Marybeth's lip quivered. Never had she felt this terribly confused, this afraid for someone else's well being; never had she suddenly cared so much for another human being except her own parents and little Danny. It hit her with sudden reality how much Josh Rivers had come to mean to her, and the feeling frightened her.

"Oh, Delores," she said, looking wide-eyed at her. "I think I love him," she whispered. Her eyes filled with tears.

Delores smiled, shaking her head. "That isn't something to cry about, Marybeth. You should be happy!"

"I know, but I'm so afraid … for him, not for me. He's so—so brash and sure. He thinks it will be so easy."

"Not easy, Marybeth." Delores put down her brush. "And he is a man who I think has seen his share of trouble. He knows it won't be easy. But love can see people through some very difficult things. I am sure that is what he is saying. Marybeth, did he say he *loves* you?"

She shook her head, taking a handkerchief from a pocket of the yellow dress and dabbing at her eyes. "He didn't use the word, but he's thinking it, and he knows *I'm* thinking it. It's just … so sudden."

"Is it really? We've been on the trail for weeks, Marybeth. We've suffered through a lot of things together already. And you met him clear back in St. Louis, talked to him on the riverboat."

"But we didn't *really* talk—I mean, not like the last two nights. It just doesn't seem logical, Delores."

Delores only smiled. "Love is never very logical. I don't think it is supposed to be. I knew I loved Aaron the first day I met him. I know it sounds perfectly ridiculous, but it's true."

Marybeth put a hand to her head. "Oh, Delores, what am I going to do when John and Mac catch up? *What am I going to do?* I know what is happening is going to make terrible trouble, yet I can't seem to put a stop to it. I don't *want* to stop it." She met the woman's eyes. "He even thinks that if nothing comes of our relationship, I should still get away from John and Mac. Delores, he bought that wagon for *me*, so that I would have my own wagon when I decide to leave the MacKinders. I don't think I can do it! What if they try to take Danny from me! And what would they do to anyone who tried to help me—especially to Josh if they find out he's behind it all!"

"Is Josh worried about it?"

"He isn't the least bit afraid."

"Then neither should you be. No one is going to let those men hurt you or take Danny—or hurt Josh Rivers. The MacKinders can't take on the whole wagon train, Marybeth."

Marybeth shook her head. "It won't be like that. Not everyone would help. And out of those who *are* against John and Mac, how many-would really stand behind me if they were challenged by John MacKinder? You know how he can be. *I* know, better than all of you."

"All I know is that if God means for you and Josh Rivers to be together, you *will* be. And you have five or six days yet before they get here. Make good use of them, Marybeth. Don't you give up the fight. You think of Danny."

Marybeth looked over at her son. "That's what Josh said. I should do it for Danny if I cannot do it for myself,"

"And he is right."

Marybeth moved closer to her son, leaning down and kissing his soft cheek. "He *is* right." She studied her little boy, her heart pounding from the realization of what she must do, and from the lingering ecstasy of Josh Rivers' kiss.

# Twelve

The land finally began to change, from flat and monotonous to gradual swells that looked deceptively flat until the oxen began to snort and pant from the constant climbing. Marybeth's own heart pounded with the effort of walking, and when she looked back, she could see for what seemed miles and was amazed at how high they were. Far off to the north there was a continuous line of hills so high they could almost be considered mountains. She wondered if they were the mountains Cap and the scouts had talked about. If so, they had lied about how big they were. Ireland had much higher hills in places.

After the first unexpected incline, the wagon train descended again for nearly the same distance, giving man and animal a small break. But then would come another swell, longer and higher than the last, and Marybeth began to realize they were going to be climbing constantly now. Surely that meant there *were* mountains ahead, much bigger than any she had seen yet. She longed for the change of scenery.

Grasshoppers seemed to be everywhere, and the bottom half of her skirt was peppered with them. She gave up trying to swat them away and decided to just let them have a free ride. At least she didn't have to carry Danny all the time. The Gentry children took turns watching the baby, either inside the Svensson wagon or sometimes inside the wagon Josh had purchased to let them use. Little Danny was nearly nine months old now and to Marybeth's relief he was breast feeding less, only three times a day. She realized she might have to reduce that to twice a day, since she seemed to keep running out of milk. But she worried about feeding him solid food, afraid some of it would make him sick. But just that morning one of the other families, who had a milk cow along, had offered to let her have whatever milk she needed. Her heart was warmed by the offer, and she felt more accepted every day.

Still, all that really mattered was how Josh Rivers felt about her. She had not seen him all day. He had ridden off to hunt, and she realized that in the few short hours since she had seen him the night before, she actually missed him.

The thought surprised her, but also made her happy. Suddenly there was someone special in her life, and her future didn't seem so dark. She realized he was right, that she had to live her own life away from the MacKinders, and his support gave her the extra courage she needed to do just that. She could only pray that courage would remain strong when she again looked into the eyes of John MacKinder.

The afternoon turned hot and muggy, and Marybeth put Danny into the Svensson wagon because little Toby Gentry felt sick. No one thought much about it at first, until by evening the boy was vomiting frequently and shaking with chills and fever. By the time the sun disappeared behind the western horizon, the child was badly dehydrated and groaning with pain all through his body. When Marybeth went to Josh's wagon, where the boy lay, she was shocked by the dark circles under Florence Gentry's eyes and the look of horror on her face.

"Go away, Marybeth," she told her. "Cap says he thinks it's cholera."

Marybeth felt her blood run cold. Cholera was more dreaded by travelers than all the other dangers they faced on such a journey. The word was like a death knell to Marybeth. Little Toby had helped watch Danny that morning. Not only did her heart ache for poor Florence, who had already lost most of her belongings in the tornado, but now her little boy could die— let alone the fact that her other two children, and even Florence herself or Samuel, could get the dreaded disease. Worse for Marybeth, Danny could catch it. Everyone knew that cholera was very contagious.

"Oh, Florence," was all she managed to say, her eyes brimming.

"Go and keep an eye on Danny," the woman told her, her voice cold and dull. "I pray to God the baby doesn't get it. To watch your own child suffer is the worst horror a mother can experience. I would feel responsible if Danny gets sick."

Marybeth stepped closer to the wagon but did not climb inside. "It wouldn't be your fault. How can any of us know how something like this gets started?"

Florence breathed deeply for self-control, and Marybeth heard Toby groan. "Cap says it might have been the river water. Toby swam in it a couple of days ago—kept dunking under it and must have swallowed some. Cap says not to drink any river water unless you boil it first."

Marybeth reached up to grasp the woman's hand, but Florence drew away. "Go on now, Marybeth. Cap says we have to pull the wagon away from the others and wait a day or two before going on to see if anyone else gets sick. Please tell Josh Rivers I'm sorry. The wagon might have to be burned."

Marybeth felt almost dizzy from the shock of it. She turned away, half stumbling back to the Svensson wagon. She climbed inside and grabbed up Danny, hugging him close and telling Delores the awful news.

"Delores, Danny was around Toby this morning," Marybeth said, the words sounding like a death sentence. Delores met her eyes, and she saw the terror in Marybeth's. "I could face anything but losing Danny," Marybeth told her. "I would marry John MacKinder and live with him the rest of my life, if it meant saving Danny. I would give up my own life."

Delores touched her arm. "We just have to pray that by some miracle he doesn't get it. You have to have faith, Marybeth."

Marybeth hugged Danny close and burst into tears. "Nothing has gone right in my life," she cried. "How can I expect to be spared this? If Danny gets sick, I hope I do, too. If he dies, I want to die."

Delores watched her helplessly, wishing she knew the right things to say. She put a hand to her belly, where she was sure Aaron's son grew. Would she get sick, too? After all, she had helped watch Danny. If she got sick but didn't die, would the disease kill her baby? She had never heard of anyone having cholera and surviving.

Outside she heard Cap calling a meeting. She knew what it would be about, and she stayed in the wagon with Marybeth. She heard a rider come in and guessed it must be Josh Rivers. Moments later she heard weeping, and then a wagon clattered away. Poor Florence would have to suffer through the next couple of days alone, watching Toby die—possibly more than one child—and there would be no one there to comfort her.

"Could have been the river water," she heard Cap saying. People mumbled, and someone started crying. "Might have had something to do with the chickens," Cap said then. "Who can say? Sam Gentry is going to kill the chickens and burn them."

Neither Marybeth nor Delores could believe the things they were hearing. "We'll stay here a couple of days and wait to see if anybody else comes down with it. Everybody try to keep your children in and around your own wagon—no mixin' company for a while. Anybody has a member of the family get sick, you drop behind and stay far to the back of the train when we do ride out until you're sure you're clean. I expect you can keep the wagon, as long as you burn everything that had anything to do with the sick person—bedding, towels, clothes, utensils—everything. Understood? And stay away from river water for drinking. If you run out of fresh water, boil river water before you use it. A doctor in San Francisco told me that sometimes helps. He's seen this among the miners."

There were quiet murmers and more weeping. Then the camp grew strangely quiet. Usually children romped about; here and there a man would play a tune on a harmonica or a fiddle; people visited back and forth. But there were none of those sounds this night.

Marybeth told herself she had to be strong now, for Danny's sake. In the back of her mind she realized this holdup meant another dread: Mac and John would catch up with them sooner.

"Marybeth?"

She turned to see Josh standing at the back of the wagon. "Go away!" she cried. "Toby Gentry helped watch Danny this morning."

He frowned and climbed into the wagon. "*Go away!*" Marybeth told him again.

"I won't. Do you think I don't realize what you're suffering right now? I've seen cholera down in Texas, Marybeth. I've been around it before and I'm not going to let it scare me off from being with you when you need me."

"I had better go outside and talk to Aaron about this," Delores told Marybeth, touching her arm. "We will pray for Danny, Marybeth."

"Pray for yourselves," Marybeth whispered. "I'm sorry, Delores. If I hadn't stayed with you—"

"Don't speak nonsense," the woman answered. "How could any of us have known?" She patted Marybeth's arm and climbed out of the wagon. Marybeth felt a strong arm come around her shoulders.

"Oh, I wish you would stay away from us," she entreated Joshua. "Cholera can kill anyone. It doesn't matter how strong you are."

Josh rubbed her shoulder. "Let me see Danny. I've never even got a good look at him up close. Hell, it might be important for the boy to get to know me, you know."

She looked at him with tear-filled eyes. "How can you do this? My baby could be carrying the disease. If you get close to him—"

He only grinned, reaching through her arms and taking Danny from her. He spoke softly to the boy, and Danny smiled, kicking and reaching up to grab Josh's nose. Josh laughed and set the boy on his feet, helping him stand on fat, strong legs. "He's going to be big—a real MacKinder, in size, at least. Let's hope he's not a MacKinder in personality." He met her eyes and saw her devastation. Josh pulled the boy close against him and took Marybeth's hand. "Look, you still breast feed him, don't you?"

She reddened at the words and looked at her lap. "I ... yes ... but lately I seem to—I can only feed him twice a day."

"Well, it's not a solid proven fact, but I've heard that while babies are breast feeding, they're a lot less likely to get certain diseases because of something or other in the mother's milk. There is nothing much healthier than a baby while he's still on his mother's milk. I'll bet this kid has never had so much as a sniffle or a cough, has he?"

She looked at him with hope in her eyes. "He hasn't … is that true?"

He wasn't sure it was true at all, but if it gave her hope, that was all that mattered. "Sure it's true. Why would I tell you if it wasn't? My sister's babies never had one sick day while they were still breast-feeding."

Her eyes misted. "Oh, Josh, if anything happens to Danny, I want to die, too! I'm so scared. No MacKinder ever frightened me like this frightens me!"

He smiled for her. "You're both going to be all right. After all, I already told you there was a reason you ran into me at that courthouse. Somebody means for us to be together. How can that happen if you and the boy go and die on me?"

She smiled through her tears. "You're always so sure of things you can't even control."

He put an arm around her shoulders again. "Well, us Texans have a way of thinking nothing can get the better of us. There aren't many more stubborn than people south of the Red River; and there aren't many who have suffered through more hardships. Out here we climb one mountain at a time. Right now the mountain is cholera. When we've made it over that one, there is the MacKinder mountain to tackle. We'll take care of that one, too, and then there will be the *real* mountains to get across. And somewhere out there in Oregon there is a pretty valley called the Willamette. When we reach that, there won't be any more mountains to climb, Marybeth."

She rested her head against his shoulder and hugged both Josh and the baby, crying. "Oh, hold me, Josh. I know it seems wrong and bold, but just hold me and don't let go!"

Danny reached out and patted at her face, saying, "Mama."

"There's nothing wrong with needing to be held once in a while," Josh answered, gladly keeping his arm around her.

For two days they waited. The first morning they saw a fire in the distance and knew little Toby must have died. The Gentrys were burning the boy's belongings. Marybeth ached to go to poor Florence and comfort her, for she was still haunted by the memory of Wilma Sleiter killing herself.

"Florence Gentry is a lot stronger than that," Josh told her.

She wondered if she could have gotten through the ordeal without him. He stayed with her almost constantly, telling humorous stories about Texas around the Svensson campfire, keeping up their spirits. Every time Marybeth fed Danny, she remembered what Josh told her and clung to that hope, praying her milk would not dry up completely. Josh's reference to the breast feedings had created a feeling of intimacy between them. It struck Marybeth that she felt as natural near Josh Rivers as though he had always been here, as though Danny belonged to him. When Danny was awake, Josh played with him, and the boy responded to him in a way he had never responded to either his uncle or his grandfather.

Seven more families were struck down with the disease. After two days Cap got the wagon train moving again, and all eight affected wagons dropped behind. Every night the rest of them could smell the smoke from burning belongings, and to their horror they noticed the Gentrys again made a fire. To ease Marybeth's anxiety, Josh rode back to their camp, keeping his distance as he yelled out to Sam Gentry, asking if they had lost someone else. He rode back to Marybeth, sorrow in his dark eyes. "Melinda," was all he said.

"Oh, dear God," Delores gasped.

Marybeth closed her eyes and fell into Josh's arms. "She was only eight years old," she wept. "How can a woman stand to lose even one child, let alone two? Oh, Josh, all those little graves! Poor little Toby and Melinda!"

"Death is just part of the circle of life, Marybeth," he told her softly. "That's one thing I learned from my brother-in-law."

Marybeth prayed almost constantly over her rosary beads, and she realized Josh seemed to accept her religion without question. He even asked her once to say a "Hail Mary," for him.

"Not for cholera," he told her, "but for the day I face down John MacKinder." He gave her a wink then, and she realized he was just trying to keep her mind off of the dreaded disease and the awful deaths.

After five days the lagging wagons began to catch up with the rest of the train. No one else came down with the disease, much to Marybeth's great relief, and she offered thanks to God.

But the toll had been devastating—nine children, two women and two men. One couple lost all four children. Devastated, their eyes blank and sunken, they turned their wagon and headed back east. Two men were left alone, losing their wives to the disease; one of those men was left with only three of his five children, the other with one child that had managed to evade the disease. Two women were left with no husbands and four children between them to raise alone in an unfamiliar land. Other men took turns helping drive the women's wagons for them and looking out for them.

For the next few days, it was common to hear someone sobbing as they walked, even men, whose dreams of settling in Oregon with wife and children were shattered, men who felt guilty for bringing their families west. Everyone teamed up and drew closer, helping those who had lost so much.

The Gentrys rejoined the train with only their eleven-year-old son, Billy. Josh's wagon was stripped nearly bare, most of the belongings inside it burned. Again the Gentrys had practically nothing but the clothes on their backs, and again they had to accept help from others. There was no longer a cage full of clucking chickens to joke and complain about. The chickens and little Toby, who had loved them, were all gone.

Marybeth and Delores did what they could to comfort Florence, but nothing could be said or done that could relieve the sorrow. Only time could help heal the woman's grieving heart, and Marybeth knew it would never completely heal. She would be forever haunted by the sight of two small graves left behind, never to be visited again, graves that would likely be lost to the elements eventually, made oblivious by time and nature.

Although Josh had spent considerable time with Marybeth,

they had had very little time alone. When it looked as though the epidemic was over, Josh went off hunting again, and it was not until the seventh night after cholera first struck that he managed to get Marybeth away alone, taking her hand after supper and insisting she take a walk with him. She was still hesitant to leave Danny, but Josh convinced her she no longer had to worry about him getting the disease.

The nights had begun to get a little cooler, and Marybeth wrapped a shawl around her shoulders. Josh wore his buckskin jacket, and to Marybeth he seemed even more handsome than ever in it. He seemed to fit this land, as if he were born into it, and knew it well. He walked with his arm around her, and she let him. It seemed so natural now. She was not afraid or hesitant when he guided her into the darkness where others couldn't see them.

"I guess you were right about a mother's milk," she told him. "Danny seems to be fine."

He grinned. "Well, to tell you the truth, that was a lot of hogwash. I just wanted to keep you from worrying so much."

She turned and faced him in the moonlight. "Josh Rivers! How am I going to know now when to believe you? I have a feeling half those wild stories you told us about Texas aren't true either!"

He laughed lightly. "Well, they kept you entertained, didn't they?" He drew her close against him. "Here is one thing that *is* true, Marybeth MacKinder. There is no doubt left in my mind that I love you."

She watched his eyes, feeling suddenly weak. "Oh, Josh, it's so sudden," she said softly.

"Is it? We've both felt drawn to each other from the beginning. I love you, Marybeth, and if we make it to Oregon, I want you to marry me. I want you to promise me you'll think about it between now and then."

"Josh, I—"

He put his fingers to her lips. "I know how hard this trip has been for you—and I know the turmoil you're feeling over losing a husband you never loved and wanting to get away from the MacKinders. I don't expect an answer right now. I just need to know you'll think about it."

"You know I will," she whispered.

He leaned down and met her lips, drawing her tight against himself. She reached up round his neck, and the kiss lingered long and deep, fires of desire burning in their souls. He moved a hand over her bottom, pressing her against his hardness and groaning with the want of her, and Marybeth knew in that moment that she could give herself to this man with none of the dread and humiliation she had felt with Dan. Josh would make her feel beautiful, wanted, the epitome of woman. He would take her gently and appreciate what she gave him, and she would take in return, take and take and take.

He left her mouth and moved his lips to her neck, and she whispered his name over and over.

"I want you, Marybeth," he groaned. "I never wanted any woman this much. I want you with me forever, to protect you, provide for you, have you give me sons as strong and healthy as Danny. I'd love Danny like my own. We could be so happy."

She pressed her hand against his chest, feeling his strength. "I know that I love you, too, Josh. But ... I want to be sure I am not just clinging to you because of my unhappiness. I don't want to use you to get away from John. I want what I feel to be real."

"It is real. You'll know that by the time we get to Oregon. I just don't know if I can wait that long to make you mine."

His words, his strength, his gentleness made her body ache with desire and her head swim with indecision. It seemed too soon, yet so right. She hadn't known him for very long, yet being with him came so naturally. Letting him be intimate with her came so easily.

"I'll think very hard about it, Josh. I don't know if I can wait either, but I must be sure. Sometimes I feel like I don't even know who I am any more. I feel so lost and confused."

"All you have to know is how you feel about me, how good it feels to be together, how fate seemed to make our paths cross. I'm as sure of this as I'm sure the sun will rise tomorrow. But I'm willing to give you some time."

She sighed deeply, gently pulling away from him, afraid of her own responses to his touch. She turned and walked a little bit away from him.

"Oh, Josh, thank you for understanding why I can't say yes this very moment. That is part of what I love about you—your tolerance and compassion."

He walked up behind her, putting his hands on her shoulders. "I'm not guaranteeing how far that tolerance will go. Out here a man's needs get pretty strong."

She reached up and put a hand over his own. "Soon we will have something to distract us from these ... desires. John and Mac—they could show up any day now," she said quietly.

He sighed deeply. "How well I know. What do you intend to do, Marybeth? If you want to stay away from them from here on, you know I'll help you, and so will Delores and Aaron. After we reach Fort Laramie and the Gentrys get another wagon, you can use mine."

She leaned back against his chest, and he wrapped his arms around her pressing them across her breasts as though she already belonged to him. "I think at first I had better rejoin them, just until we reach Fort Laramie and we know the Gentrys have another wagon. I will tell them I intend to continue on my own. It has to come from me, not from you or Cap or anyone else."

His grip tightened. "I don't like it. I don't want you around John."

She put a hand on his powerful forearm. "I can handle John MacKinder. I've done it before. The man is capable of doing a lot of foolish things in front of others, but he wouldn't want to be known as a ... a man who *forces* women, and that is what it would be if he tried to prove I belong to him."

She could feel him tremble with rage at the suggestion. "I'd kill him," he said flatly. She knew that he meant every word of it.

"I don't want that kind of trouble, Josh. It will be all right. Give me some time to try to work it out peacefully first."

"They don't know the meaning of the word peaceful. John has already struck you once. What will he do when you tell him you don't want to travel with them?"

"Nothing, as long as I stay within sight of others."

"You be sure you do that. And you come to me the minute you need help. I've said it before, and I'll say it again. I'm not afraid of John MacKinder."

He leaned down and kissed her temple. She leaned her head back and he bent his head around and met her lips. She whimpered when his hand circled over her belly, and he moved his other hand gently across her breasts, lingering there, lightly squeezing the full breast in his big hand. The kiss grew deeper as his tongue searched her mouth and his hand moved to her other breast. She grasped his wrist then, pulling his hand away and kissing his palm. "You aren't allowing me much room to think," she said, her words a near gasp.

"Maybe I don't want you to think. I just want you to feel and react and be the woman you've never been."

She grasped his hand in both her own and held it against her chest. "I want the same thing. But I just can't allow my feelings to rule over reason right now, Josh. Promise me ... promise me that if for some reason nothing should come of this ... you won't think the worse of me."

"You know me better than that by now. If something did happen to end this, how could I think the worse of you? I love you. Nothing will change that." He turned her to face him now, holding her against him. "I love your fiery red hair, your eyes green as prairie grass in spring, your pride and courage. I need to touch you, and you need to be touched. We both need a lot more than that, and we'll have it, Marybeth. You'll see. You just remember to be strong when the MacKinders return—not for me or for you, but for Danny. I'll stay away at first, but I'll by God be watching. If John MacKinder lays one finger on you, it will be my problem then, not yours."

"Oh, Josh, be careful," she whispered. "I love you so. I would die if something happened to you because of me."

Their lips met once more, then Marybeth pulled away. She searched his eyes in the moonlight, thinking what a wonderful, brave, brash man he was. She suddenly shuddered with the realization of just how dangerous it was for him to love her.

It seemed so unfair that she couldn't enjoy this newfound happiness because of the MacKinders. Her heart tightened at the thought of how John MacKinder would react if he knew she was in love with Josh Rivers, that the man had kissed her and held her and had been intimate with her.

"Josh, I … if I should decide it isn't right—"

He grasped her arms firmly. "You *know* it's right! Don't let the thought of John MacKinder keep you from following your heart, Marybeth. Trust me."

She closed her eyes and clung to him. "I know you would try, but—"

"No buts, Marybeth. We're going to be together, and no MacKinder can separate us."

She gently pulled away. "I want so much to believe that. Just promise me you will stay away at first. Let me try it my way."

"I'll do it, but only until we get to Fort Laramie."

She turned away, not trusting her desires, not daring to spend one more minute alone with him. "We had better go back now."

They reluctantly returned to the wagons, their eyes holding in love and understanding before Josh left her. Marybeth slept restlessly that night, in near pain with the want of Josh Rivers.

Dawn broke with a pink and red sky, but with a hint of rain. They ate breakfast, and Josh joined them, he and Marybeth reading each other's thoughts, both wishing they had awakened in the arms of the other. There was a sweet, wonderful feeling between them now that ran much deeper than friendship. He had touched her breast, had crushed her against him, explored her mouth savagely and pressed himself against her in manly desire. For the first time she wanted to give herself to a man. He had asked her to marry him when they got to Oregon, and she knew he would marry her before that if she but said the word.

Clouds soon gathered on the western horizon, and after two hours on the trail clouds also gathered on the eastern horizon—not in the sky, but at ground level. The MacKinder wagons were approaching…

# Thirteen

Never had Marybeth's heart felt heavier than when she spotted the MacKinder wagon coming. "Remember your promise to yourself and to Danny," Delores reminded her. "You can do it, Marybeth."

"I'm going to wait until we get to Fort Laramie to tell them. After that I'll have a wagon to use." The women walked together beside the Svensson wagon, and Marybeth carried Danny on her hip. Part of her wished Josh was close by, and another part of her hoped he wouldn't come near. Right now he was hunting; he didn't know the MacKinders had caught up and were closing in at the rear of the wagon train.

Marybeth breathed deeply, trying to find the will to walk back and greet her in-laws, finding it absurd that she could hardly bear the thought of seeing them again. The train would stop soon for the noon meal, and she would have to leave Delores.

Only minutes later, Cap called a halt, and Marybeth's heart sank a little more. The wagons slowed, and she swallowed back a lump in her throat. "I had better get my things together. There is no sense putting this off any longer."

Cap rode up to her then on his big mule. "You goin' back there with the family?"

Marybeth shifted Danny in her arms. "For now."

The old man looked her over. "I don't want trouble, Mrs. MacKinder, but I don't blame you for how you feel either. I know about you and Josh, and I'll do my best to keep Josh in line, but he's young and a little bull-headed. I reckon John MacKinder and his pa are even *more* bull headed, and that spells big trouble."

"I don't want trouble any more than you do, Cap," she

sighed. "If I could change any of it, I would."

"Don't you fret. I'm on your side. Right now I'm goin' back to see if the MacKinders are in good shape, and I'm goin' to give them a little warnin' of my own."

She smiled wistfully. "Thank you."

She watched him ride to the back of the wagon train, but turned away when she heard John raising his voice about something. She climbed into the wagon and packed her things, depressed over the thought of not being able to be with Josh for a while. She climbed down and took Danny from Delores. "At least you can be alone again with your husband," she told the woman. "I'm sorry to have put you out this way."

"It was no problem," Aaron told her. He walked up to her, pulling a child's wagon behind him.

"You know you could have stayed with us for the rest of the trip," Delores told her.

"Here," Aaron told her, handing her the handle of the wagon. "A gift from us."

Marybeth frowned. "I don't understand."

"I bought it—from Stu Ellerbee. He didn't want anything at all for it, but I wanted to give him something. It belonged to his youngest son, who died of the cholera. He said he would be glad to see someone get some use out of it—another little boy. It is for Danny. Until he is big enough to play with it himself, you can use it to pull him instead of carrying him. I know John and Mac seldom let you ride in the wagon with the boy, and you don't like to leave him in there alone. But you can't be always carrying him, Marybeth. He's getting too heavy. You'll have a broken back climbing these hills."

Her eyes teared. "Oh, Aaron! What a wonderful idea! Oh, thank you so much!"

"It is my pleasure."

She looked up at him, seeing the same gentleness in his eyes she often saw in Josh's. Yes, Delores was a happy and a very lucky woman. "I will pray for both of you," she told them. "I hope you make it safely to Oregon."

"Well, we will see plenty of you the rest of the way," Delores answered with a reassuring smile. "You will still come and walk with me, won't you?"

"I'll try; but we've lost our place in line now and we're so far behind you."

"It won't matter during the day. Besides, soon you will be in your own wagon and you can do whatever you want."

Marybeth saw John MacKinder approaching and her heart sank. "I hope you're right, Delores." She put Danny into the wooden wagon, which had high sides on it that would keep him from falling out. She stuffed blankets around him to help him stay in a sitting position, then put in the rest of her belongings. She cringed when she heard John's voice.

"What kind of an ungrateful in-law are you," he growled, ignoring Aaron. "We have been away all this time, and when we return you do not even come back to see if we are all right."

Marybeth rose and faced him, looking him over. "You look just fine to me. I couldn't imagine that a MacKinder would be anything *but* all right. I had to wait until the wagons stopped so I could pack our things." She faced him squarely. "I don't suppose it occurred to you to come and see if Danny and *I* are all right. Didn't Cap tell you about the cholera? A lot of people died—women and children mostly. Poor Florence Gentry lost two children. Abel and Henrietta Lake lost all four of theirs and headed back east. Stu Ellerbee lost a son. Aaron bought this wagon from him so I could use it for Danny and not have to carry him all the time."

John frowned, looking darkly at Aaron. "What am I owing you?"

"Nothing," Aaron answered, his own blue eyes hard and angry. "It is a gift to Marybeth."

"We do not accept gifts."

"For heaven's sake, John, thank the man," Marybeth said disgustedly.

John noticed others watching them. "Thank you," he growled.

"I need no thanks, and it was not up to you whether or not to accept it. It is for Marybeth and the boy, not for you.

Marybeth has already thanked me, and sincerely, not as though it sets bitter in her stomach."

John gave Aaron one last look, then turned and stormed away. "Hurry it up, Marybeth," he ordered over his shoulder.

Marybeth looked apologetically at Delores and Aaron. "It is all right," Delores told her. "We understand. Be strong, Marybeth. We are behind you."

Marybeth turned away, pulling the wagon behind her. It was heavy with her belongings, but she got no offer of help from John or Mac, both of whom watched her approach. When she reached the camp site, she saw the look of anger that still lingered in Mac's eyes. "Did you enjoy your little vacation?" he sneered by way of greeting.

Marybeth met his eyes boldly. "Yes," she answered. "It was quite peaceful."

"I suppose you're going to be even harder to put up with now that the rest of them have spoiled you and put ideas in your head."

"I have no ideas in my head I didn't already have before you so stupidly drove the wagon into the river."

"You watch your mouth," John told her. She saw how his eyes moved over her. "In spite of your sass and the fact that you are not happy to see us, I will say that you are a fine sight to me." He grinned. "I think when we get to Fort Laramie, maybe we can find a priest. They say there are priests out here who administer to the Indians."

Marybeth pulled the little wagon to the MacKinder wagon and unloaded her things. "We won't be needing a priest. I am not even sure I will be staying with you the whole trip."

Mac rose. "What the hell are you talking about?"

Marybeth wondered where her courage came from. Inside, her heart pounded so furiously she thought she would faint. "I am talking about possibly using a spare wagon left when the Sleiters died." Ella looked up from the fire in surprise at Marybeth's bold remark. "I don't suppose any of you is interested in what happened to the Sleiters, or who was affected by the cholera," Marybeth continued.

"And just how would you get by—a woman with a baby and no money," Mac asked her, obviously as unconcerned about the tragedies others had suffered as Marybeth thought he would be.

"I would find a way. Anything would be better than what I have to put up with from you and John."

Mac grabbed her arm painfully, jerking her around. Her head snapped back at the sudden movement, and she felt the sting on her face before she realized Mac even had his hand up. Those closest to the MacKinder wagon gasped and walked away, and whispered word quickly spread that Mac had struck his daughter-in-law.

"I knew it would be this way when we caught up with you," Mac hissed at Marybeth. "This is why I did not want you to go on with the others!" She could smell whiskey on his breath. "I told you that you would not leave this family with Danny. If you want to go marching off on your own, woman, you will do it alone! It will be no other way, even if we have to break off from this wagon train. Do you understand? We've done it for the last two weeks, and we can do it again if we have to. I don't like Cap coming back here warning us he wants no trouble, you hear? I don't know what went on while we were gone, but I don't like the fact that you didn't even bother to come and see us when we returned."

"Why should I have," Marybeth seethed. "For *this*?" She jerked away from him. "You can't treat me this way, Mac."

"You're family. You're a MacKinder, and I'll treat you any way I like when you threaten to take away my grandson! You remember the boy still sucks at his mother's breast. That means wherever *he* goes, *you* go—and Danny MacKinder stays with *us*!"

The man stormed off, grabbing a bottle of whiskey. Bill Stone sat at the campfire waiting for Ella to give him something to eat. He glanced at Marybeth, a sly grin on his face.

John stepped in front of her. "You remember what Father said. You are back with us now, and this is where you stay. I have told Father how I feel about you, Marybeth. In spite of your sassiness, I still want to marry you. Dan never should have been allowed. I was the one who wanted you all along, and that is how it will be." He held a big, powerful fist in front of her face. "You remember that. Anyone who objects will feel this, even if it means having to leave this train. It might be the last thing he feels. You tell that to Cap and Aaron Svensson and anyone else who thinks he is going to help you!"

He left to water, the oxen, and Marybeth stood there a moment, stunned. Mac had just slapped more determination into her soul, but the sight of John's fist, as big as her whole face, dampened her spirits. The thought of the possibility of Josh being on the receiving end of that fist was enough to make her question her decision. She looked over at Ella, who gave her an "I told you so" expression.

"Don't you care about how many died from cholera while you were gone?" Marybeth asked the woman. "Don't you care that in her despair Wilma Sleiter shot her husband and then killed herself?"

Ella hesitated a moment, glancing up at Marybeth before returning to quietly stirring a pot of stew. She sighed deeply. "Everyone chooses his own way, Marybeth. We can bear up under our burdens, or take the easy way out, like Mrs. Sleiter did. It is too bad about the cholera, though."

Marybeth stepped closer. "You say Mrs. Sleiter took the easy way out from under her burden. Well, so do you, Ella. You just cow down and take whatever Mac hands you. That isn't being strong. Being strong is doing what you know is *right*. Can you look me in the eyes and tell me you've never thought about shooting *your* husband, or about putting a gun to your *own* head?"

Ella stopped stirring again. She looked up at Marybeth, and in that one look Marybeth knew the answer. "I do not intend to burn in hell forever in the afterlife, Marybeth."

"What is the difference between that and *living* in hell right here on Earth?" Marybeth turned away, wanting to cry at the realization that she had been back with the MacKinders only minutes, and already she felt full of hatred and anger.

She didn't like feeling like this. It wasn't good for Danny. Suddenly being on her own again seemed almost impossible. How was she going to do it without half the men on the wagon train having to hold guns on the MacKinders, or without Josh getting hurt? She didn't want to be the cause of such turmoil, and her mind whirled with indecision. She had no choice but to stay with them for now.

She leaned down and took Danny from the little wagon, thinking how kind it was of Aaron to get the wagon for her. She could only pray John or Mac wouldn't kick it to pieces out of anger. She looked off into the distance, wondering when Josh would come back, terrified of what would happen when he did.

Josh. The thought of him brought a sudden peace to her soul. She would miss his campfire stories, miss watching him play with Danny, miss his touch, his kiss, the feel of his strong arms around her.

"Get over here and help Ella dish up the stew," Mac barked, startling her from her thoughts.

Danny's lips puckered when he felt his mother jump, felt her tension. Marybeth kissed his cheek. "Zosh," he whimpered.

"Hush, Danny," she said softly.

"What's that he said," John asked. Both men had sat down to their noon meal.

"I don't know," Marybeth answered. "It's some new word he picked up and it means nothing." She set Danny on a blanket and began helping Ella.

The sun had almost set when Josh returned. Marybeth caught sight of him out of the corner of her eye to her left. She glanced in that direction as she walked, pulling the wagon and Danny behind her. She saw him slow his horse as he realized the MacKinders were back and Marybeth was with them. She couldn't help staring for a moment, drinking in the sight of him. He looked wonderful on a horse, so natural. He fit this land so perfectly. She noticed another deer on his pack horse, and her heart swelled with pride at what a good hunter he was.

He rode his horse at a slow walk for a little ways, watching the MacKinder men herd the oxen. To Marybeth's relief he finally rode on ahead with the deer. An hour later they made camp for the night, and Marybeth said nothing to Mac or John. She decided she was better off saying nothing at all to them until she found a way to sever ties completely. She could only hope not to feel the sting of John's or Mac's hands again by keeping quiet; and she reminded herself not to get caught alone with John. He had watched her all day like a hawk, and he had the look of a stud horse anxious to get over the fence to a waiting mare. She was not going to be John MacKinder's mare. She had suffered enough sexual humiliation under Dan MacKinder.

Night settled over camp, and somewhere in the distance someone played a harmonica. Marybeth thought wistfully about what a nice night it would be to share with Josh. She stayed near the fire, not daring to walk out into the darkness, something she knew John was waiting for her to do. She worked on a pile of mending, while Ella scrubbed at a stubborn fry pan and soaked some dried peas in another pot.

"You're damn lucky you and the boy didn't come down with the cholera, letting those little brats of Florence Gentry's take care of him," Mac grumbled to Marybeth.

"Don't call them little brats. Toby and Melinda both died. Florence Gentry has suffered dearly." She looked at him. "And they were a great help to me. How could any of us have known it would happen? We can only thank God for being spared."

The man grunted. "It only goes to show you you're better off sticking with your own kin and not mixing too much. It could have meant Danny's life."

*He's in more danger growing up with the likes of you*, she felt like saying, but she kept the words to herself. She heard the slow trot of a horse then, and her heart raced faster as Josh came into the light of their campfire. She looked up at him, longing to run to him. She could tell by his eyes that someone had told him Mac had slapped her earlier in the day. His dark eyes literally glittered with repressed anger as he turned his gaze to John, who sat against a wagon wheel drinking whiskey.

"What the hell do you want?" John asked him.

"I expect after being out there so long you folks wouldn't mind some fresh meat," Josh replied. He took a small burlap bag from his horse and threw it down in front of Mac.

"I see the cholera didn't get to you," John said by way of thanks.

"Sorry to disappoint you," Josh told him. He glanced at Marybeth again, his eyes telling her he wanted to be with her. She looked down at her sewing, and he could see her hands shaking. Josh looked at Mac, the leather of his saddle creaking as he rode the horse around behind the man, then between Mac and John. "Heard you gave your daughter-in-law a fine greeting when you got back. Must have made her real glad to see you."

Mac looked up at him, then slowly rose, as did John. Marybeth felt as though her heart was moving right up into her throat.

"What's it to you?" Mac asked, glaring at Josh.

"Of all the MacKinders, Marybeth is the best—stronger and braver than any of the rest of you for all your MacKinder blood. Maybe it's because she doesn't *have* the MacKinder blood in her. Cap already warned you two to ease up on the woman and not make trouble. I'm adding to that warning. Marybeth has a lot of friends along on this wagon train, MacKinder. You remember that. You can't get away with your abuse any longer."

"We'll treat our own kin as we see fit!" John said, moving closer.

"You'll by God follow the rules of this train and act like decent men," Josh told him. "If you don't, you'll be off this train, and right now I don't think you want that to happen. We picked up signs of Indians today. Devon rode back to say he'd seen two wagons burned out, and it was Indians, not cholera. He knows the signs. As long as we're as big as we are, we shouldn't be in any danger. But if you choose to drop back alone, it's your scalp! And you sure as hell won't take Marybeth and that baby with you!"

"You might be right about the Indians, Rivers," John told him, his fists clenched at his sides, "but I don't like the way you say Marybeth's name."

Josh's horse pranced in a little circle. "I'll say her name any way I want. And I'll be pitching my tent not far from this camp tonight. Cap wants this side of the circle watched. We're keeping extra guard on the wagons and the livestock because of possible Indian trouble. But I won't be watching just for Indians, MacKinder. You remember that."

"Get down off that horse, Rivers, and I'll fix it so you're not in any *shape* to watch for Indians!"

Josh just grinned and rode closer to John. "Our time is coming, MacKinder, but not tonight. For the next few days *and* nights we keep our eyes open for Indians. Cap needs everyone's cooperation, so make sure you give it to him. You might be a fighter, but you're no match for a warrior with a tomahawk, I'll guarantee it." He looked at Mac. "You're welcome for the meat." He turned his horse and rode out.

Marybeth kept her eyes averted, but she wanted to jump up and hug Josh, thank him for camping close by. She knew it had nothing to do with Indians, and it was difficult for her not to smile. Her heart felt lighter. She didn't have to worry about John MacKinder bothering her tonight.

For five days everyone traveled with the fear that they were going to feel an arrow in their backs at any moment. They passed a landmark called Chimney Rock and Marybeth stared at the odd formation that jutted up from nothing and seemed to have no reason for being there. The land was changing even more, hillier, more rocky. On the first night Josh warned about Indians, a few cattle were stolen, but nothing more happened, and as they neared Fort Laramie, people began to relax a little. Within another week they would be there, if everything went well.

To John and Mac's irritation and Marybeth's relief, Josh often rode, and camped, near their wagon. Even if they couldn't be together, she felt his watchful protection, yet dreaded the thought of an actual conflict and prayed such a thing would never take place. The Indian threat had seemed to subdue the MacKinder men somewhat, but tension was high among everyone. Those who had lost loved ones to cholera were surly and quiet. Everyone was tired and cranky, and hungry. Because

Indians could be lurking anywhere, Josh was unable to ride far from the wagon train to hunt. For the time being it was simply too dangerous, and every time he even went over a rise and out of sight Marybeth feared for him.

The weather turned hotter than ever, building tempers. John and Mac grumped constantly about the weather, and Danny cried often, picking up the tension of the people around him. It was at noon break, six days from Fort Laramie, when horror visited Marybeth. At nine months old Danny liked to try to stand on his strong little legs. It was so hot, Marybeth took off his shirt and let him walk. She walked behind him, holding his hands as he toddled on fat, bare feet, laughing at being able to stretch his muscles and vent some energy.

Finally she let go of him and let him toddle a couple of steps before he plunked onto his fat bottom and began crawling over soft, green grass. Whenever he came to a big enough rock, he would pull himself up and stand for a minute, then crawl again. Marybeth stayed behind him, and when she called to him, he would come toward her, grinning happily.

Suddenly Marybeth heard the dreaded hiss. Before she could get to Danny, he screamed in what was obviously terrible pain. Her heart pounding at the chilling cry, Marybeth ran to him, then saw the diamond-backed snake slinking away. She shouted Danny's name, picking the boy up in her arms. Her legs would not move as she stared down at her still-screeching son. "A snake!" she screamed. "Josh!" He was the first person who came to mind in her moment of desperation. "Josh! Somebody! Help us!"

People came running, the MacKinders, Josh, Cap, Delores and Aaron. "What happened!" John shouted to her.

"A snake! A snake bit him!"

"Look! There it is," someone shouted.

Josh drew his pistol and blew its head off, and Cap ran over to it, reaching with the barrel of his rifle to pick it up. "It's a rattler, Josh," he said, with just about the same gravity he would have used to announce cholera.

"Jesus! Give me the boy," Josh told Marybeth,

holstering his gun.

She handed Danny to him while John watched jealously. Josh ran with Danny to the wagon and grabbed out a blanket, throwing it on the ground and laying Danny on it. He began inspecting the child for snakebite, finding the ominous fang marks on his ankle.

"Hang on to him," he told Marybeth. "I've got to try to get some of the venom out." He quickly reached over and untied Marybeth's slat bonnet, ripping a ribbon from it and tying it tightly around the baby's leg, just under the knee. Then he pulled a hunting knife from its sheath on the side of his boot and to Marybeth's horror he quickly cut an x-mark across the bite while Danny screamed furiously. "Try to keep him as still as you can, Marybeth. Don't let him thrash around. Somebody hold down his other leg."

"What the hell is he doing?" John demanded to know.

Ella kneeled down to hold Danny's other leg.

"The boy's only chance is for someone to try to suck out most of the venom," Cap explained. Josh was already bent over Danny, sucking at the cut and spitting out blood and venom. "I expect Josh has seen his share of snakebite down in Texas."

Josh said nothing. He kept sucking at the bite for several seconds as people stood around watching and Marybeth kept a tight hold of Danny's arms, bending over the howling boy and talking to him soothingly. She struggled to stay calm for the baby's sake. Josh finally quit sucking at the bite and threw his head back. Marybeth knew by the agony on his face her baby could die. "That's all I can do," he almost groaned, looking at Marybeth.

"It was a young snake, Josh," Cap told him "The venom's not so powerful in the young ones, and you got to the boy quick. There's a chance he'll make it."

Josh looked down at Danny, bending over him and brushing his curly, damp hair away from his face. "He's already going under, Cap. He looks real sleepy."

"Josh, how bad is it," Marybeth cried. "What's going to happen to my baby?"

He met her eyes. "I don't know, Marybeth. It's like Cap says. It was a young snake, and Danny is a strong little boy. Get him inside the wagon out of the sun and keep cool cloths on him to keep his fever down. He'll get real sleepy. If he makes it, the area of the bite is going to be pretty sore for a while."

"Josh," she whispered, her eyes pleading.

He reached out and touched her face. "I can't do anything else, Marybeth. Do like I said and get him inside the wagon. Keep him cool and keep him quiet." He reached around and gently squeezed her neck. "Hey, it's just like the cholera," he told her, trying to smile for her. "Remember what I told you about that?"

"Told her when?" John stood in front of them, sneering down at them both. "Get your hand off her, Rivers."

"For God's sake, John, this is no time for your stupid jealous temper," Marybeth cried. "Danny might die!"

Josh let go of her and gently lifted Danny, walking to the wagon and climbing inside to lay Danny down. Ella climbed in after him.

"This is all *your* fault," he heard John yelling.

"It was an accident," Marybeth screamed back through tears. "And I'm not the one who chose to come on this journey in the first place. Now get out of my way so I can go to my son."

Josh heard a gasping sound. He heard John shout, "You're no good, Marybeth. I can see there is something between you and Josh Rivers. You've shamed this family, and now you've proven what a bad mother you are! You can run off with Rivers, but you'll not take Danny with you."

Josh hurriedly climbed out of the wagon to see John's big hands around Marybeth's throat. She pulled wildly at his big wrist to no avail.

"Let her go, MacKinder," Cap warned.

Aaron stepped forward, fists clenched. But before he could speak Josh walked up and grasped John's arm. "Let go of her or I'll kill you," he said quietly.

John just looked at him for a moment, still clutching her neck. Suddenly he tossed Marybeth aside with deliberate force, as though she were no more than a sack of potatoes. She fell against a wagon wheel with a jolt, while John turned to Josh.

"Go ahead, Rivers. What will you do, shoot me? I am not armed, Rivers," John sneered. "If you want to kill me, you will have to do it with your fists."

"Don't do it, Josh," Cap warned. Marybeth tried to do the same, but she could not even find her voice as she lay on the ground, gasping for breath. Delores and Aaron helped her up.

Josh heard no warnings. His eyes were on John MacKinder, as he unbuckled his gunbelt.

"Fists will be much more enjoyable," he growled. He threw the gunbelt aside and charged into MacKinder, both men crashing to the ground.

Marybeth gasped for breath as she whispered Josh's name and watched in horror, torn between the two worst tragedies she could have experienced. Danny could be dying, and so could Joshua Rivers. It was too late to stop it now. This fight had been coming on ever since the two men arm wrestled on the riverboat. But she knew John MacKinder. This was no arm wrestling contest. This was a duel to the death.

# Fourteen

Women onlookers screamed and turned away from the brutal fight, pulling their children along with them. Marybeth could hear the powerful punches as she struggled to get back her breath and walked toward the back of the wagon. She needed to go to her baby and for one frantic moment she wondered if she would lose Josh and Danny both. Her back and head hurt from hitting the wagon wheel, and already bruises were forming at her throat. She watched the vicious fight with wide-eyed terror, feeling sick at the bloody punches.

Others backed away. "Let them go," Cap warned one man who thought the fight should be stopped. "They've both been wanting this."

To everyone's horror they saw Mac pick up a shovel and raise it as John punched savagely at Josh and backed him toward his father. Aaron moved in quickly, grabbing the shovel away. "Oh, no you don't," he warned. "If they are going to fight, it is going to be fair." Mac glowered at the man, but knew that Aaron's youth and bigger size were more than a man his age could handle.

With shaking hands Marybeth climbed inside the wagon, kneeling down beside Danny, who lay still as death.

"He's still alive," Ella told her, "but his pulse is very slow."

Marybeth shivered with pain and fear. Her baby lay near death, and outside the brutal fight continued. She sat down, gently pulling Danny into her lap. The sides of the wagon canvas were rolled up because of the heat, and she could see the fight going on outside. How any man could withstand the punches both John and Josh were dealing and receiving, she could not imagine. For the moment they seemed almost evenly

175

matched, except for John's bigger size. That size seemed at times to be a disadvantage. Josh seemed to be quicker at ducking and punching, and his rage gave him an edge.

Marybeth gently stroked Danny's curly hair, feeling sick at the sight of the ugly, swollen bite mark. Outside, Josh grunted from John's blows, but he dealt just as much damage as his own big fist landed over and over into John's middle and his face. They tumbled together in the dust, growling like animals, and she felt responsible for all of it. What would the others think of two men fighting over her? She put a hand to her throat, which ached fiercely, realizing John could have killed her.

Men had gathered around the scene, all but Bill and Mac cheering for Josh. The women had left, except for Delores, and farther back Marybeth noticed Florence was watching anxiously. Ella wet a rag and handed it to Marybeth. She gently washed Danny's face, and Ella ran another wet cloth over the boy's chest and arms, more emotion on her face than Marybeth had seen since she had known the woman. She wondered what was going through Ella's mind at the sight of her son fighting, but then she had seen this sort of thing before. Perhaps she had given up getting upset by it.

Marybeth knew with shivering certainty that John would not give up until Josh Rivers was dead or close to dead. Still, Josh held his own. Both men were wearying, stopping to circle each other while they panted for breath, their faces and hands covered with blood, their clothes torn and filthy.

"No MacKinder ... finishes a ... fight ... on his back!" John spit out.

Josh wiped at a bloody nose. "There's a first time ... for everything," he hissed. He charged at John again, but John's booted foot came up into Josh's gut. Marybeth gasped, and someone swore in the crowd of men.

"Goddamn dirty fighter, is he? Get him back, Josh! You can get dirty, too!"

"Josh," Marybeth whispered, watching him roll to his knees, holding his ribs. "Stay down, Josh, just stay down." She closed her eyes and bent over Danny, imagining the horror of losing her little son, and the only man who had ever meant anything to her. She wished there were two of her at the moment, one to be with Josh when this was over, and one to be with Danny. Ella wet the rag again and squeezed it into Danny's curly hair to keep his head cool. The baby made no movement or sound.

Marybeth dared to look out again. Josh had got back to his feet, and John began taunting him. "Come on, Rivers. Come at me again. I've got ... plenty left." He was near the shovel, and he reached down and picked it up. Men gasped and swore and backed farther away, and Marybeth wondered where her next breath would come from.

"You're ... pretty brave ... when you've got your pa ... to help ... or you've got a woman ... to beat on or a weapon in your hand..." Josh growled. "Big, brave ... John MacKinder. You're ... a *coward*, MacKinder! You're all talk ... but bullshit doesn't ... win a fight. You're a braggart ... and a woman beater ... and this whole camp ... is sick of all you MacKinders!"

Marybeth gasped as John swung the shovel. It grazed across Josh's back as he ducked low, the corner of it cutting through shirt and skin. By then Josh was ramming into John again. Swinging the shovel left John off balance, and Josh kept shoving until John fell backward, landing in the hot coals of the MacKinder campfire. He screamed in horrible pain, and Marybeth looked away, but Ella was still watching.

Marybeth turned her eyes back to the fight to see John roll out of the fire, dragging Josh with him and jerking him up, kicking viciously at Josh while his back and shirt smouldered. Even some of the men had to turn away from the awful sight. In rage from pain, John used only his foot, kicking and kicking until Josh went down. John kicked at him again while he was bent over, and Marybeth cried out Josh's name. The crowd quieted, sure Josh was finished off.

John stood over him then, legs spread, still on his feet in spite of his smoking back. "I told you ... Rivers..." He grimaced with pain before finishing. "No MacKinder man ... finishes a fight ... on his back. Give it up, Rivers! You're ... no match ... for John MacKinder."

Marybeth and the others watched with sickening horror, everyone praying Josh would stay down; but he got to his knees in front of John. He was still bent over.

"Go ahead, Rivers," John panted. "Beg me ... to quit! Beg me, Rivers!"

Josh folded his hands together as though in prayer, and for a moment most thought he really would kneel there and give up the fight. Suddenly his hands came up between John's legs, ramming hard into the man's groin. John bent over in agony. Josh kept his hands locked as he brought them up hard into John's nose, sending the man reeling backward.

The crowd of onlookers cheered wildly. John rolled to his side, holding his groin and groaning, his nose bleeding profusely now and looking flatter.

"Come on, MacKinder," Josh taunted this time. "You said ... a MacKinder never ends a fight ... on his back."

John rolled to his knees, everything looking black.

"Give it to him again, Josh," Aaron yelled.

Mac stood by with agony on his face. "Get up, John! Get the hell up!"

John managed to get to his feet, hardly able to see Josh. Josh began punching again, sending John staggering backward while the men shouted and whooped in Josh's support. John went down again. When he rolled to his side, he spotted Josh's pistol that had been tossed aside. He grabbed for it, but Josh's booted foot came down hard on his arm. John cried out with the pain, screaming that his arm was broken. Josh reached down and yanked the gun from his hand.

"Serves you right ... for thinking about ... shooting an unarmed man." He tossed the gun aside, and although it was obvious he was in agonizing pain himself, he yanked John up again. One final blow to John's mid-section and another to his face again sent the man sprawling onto his back, out cold. Josh grasped at his ribs, standing over his opponent and managing a grin in spite of his battered face. "There's your first ... a MacKinder ... flat out cold ... on his *back*!" He wiped at his bloody face again and staggered over to Mac. "You bring ... any harm to Marybeth … and you'll end up the … same way. Soon as … Danny recovers … I'm coming to take Marybeth … away from your camp. And don't you … try to stop me!"

Aaron and Delores hurried over to him as he staggered away, and Aaron grabbed hold of him as his legs began to crumble from under him.

"Marybeth," Josh muttered. "Take me there." Aaron and Delores helped him walk to the MacKinder wagon, and Marybeth's eyes teared at the sight of him. "Danny—take care … of Danny."

"Oh, Josh," she wept. "Please let someone help you."

"I'm … coming back for you." His face was so battered Marybeth was sure she wouldn't have recognized him if she didn't already know who he was. "Danny—he'll be all right. You just pray over those … beads." He grimaced with pain, and started to slump. "Don't … let me pass out … in front of MacKinder," he told Aaron. "Get me to a wagon."

The Svenssons helped him walk away, and Marybeth heard Florence telling them to take him to the Sleiter wagon. "I'll take care of him," Florence was saying. Marybeth was glad. Florence needed the distraction. She knew Josh was in good hands.

"Get him into my wagon," she heard Bill Stone telling the men who were lifting John. He was still unconscious. She looked at Ella, who was watching her son being carried off. Ella met her eyes then.

"It has been a long time coming, but I knew that it would," she told Marybeth. "I should feel sorry for him, but for some reason I don't. I only feel sorry for little Danny." She ran another cool rag over the boy. "He brings a sweetness and joy to this family that has not been with us for years—since Dan and John got older and Mac taught them the MacKinder way."

Her words surprised Marybeth. They were spoken in bitter resignation. She looked at Marybeth again. "Sometimes I hate you, Marybeth for having the courage to do and say things I have held inside my entire married life. I do not always like you, but I respect you, and I love this child. You are in love with Josh Rivers, aren't you?"

Marybeth watched her eyes, trying to read them. "Yes," she answered firmly.

"Would he make a good father for Danny?"

"He would be a wonderful father."

Ella looked down at Danny. "Then go to him when he comes for you. I don't want Danny to grow up to be like Mac and John." She sighed deeply. "Our religion does not allow us to leave our husbands. I have never once considered divorce, and neither would you have. But God saw fit to give you a second chance by taking Dan to Him and leaving you a free woman. I only hope there will be a way I can see Danny once in a while. Once you leave this camp, Marybeth, I don't think there is any way you can ever be a part of this family again."

She looked at Marybeth. "You were right. Mrs. Sleiter took the easy way, and in a sense, so have I. I think you are strong enough to take the hard way. And Josh Rivers has proven he is the man who can help you. John fought out of pride and meanness. Josh Rivers fought for *you*. You are a lucky woman."

Marybeth felt a lump rising in her throat. Never did she dream she would hear such words from Ella MacKinder. She knew the woman well enough, though, not to thank her. A thank you would embarrass her and make her withdraw again. "Stay with Danny all you want," she told Ella. "At least … if you aren't able to see more of him after he's recovered, you can be with him now."

They heard a terrible scream then from Bill's wagon, as Cap yanked John's broken arm into place. "Get me somethin' to use for a splint," Marybeth heard Cap ordering. "Soon as I'm done here, these wagons get moving, wounds, snakebites and all. You MacKinders have cost us enough problems. This is the last of it, unless you want to go out there and see how you do alone against the Indians. With John all broken up, I don't think you want to be in that kind of a fix."

John groaned again. Bill came to the back of the MacKinder wagon to ask where Ella kept the salve for bums. The woman took a jar from one of the pockets in the wagon and handed it out to him. "Tell Mac to tend to him himself. I am staying with my grandson until he wakes up."

"Goddamn bastard!" They could all hear John's half sobbed words. "I'll kill him! This isn't the last of it! I'll kill Joshua Rivers! He stole her! He stole Marybeth from me, and he'll *die* for it!"

Marybeth looked at Ella, who just closed her eyes and turned away. Marybeth felt a cold shiver at the words. She leaned over Danny, kissing his cheek. "Please wake up, Danny. Please wake up."

For the rest of the day and through the night Danny lay in a sleep that seemed more like a coma, while Marybeth and Ella kept him constantly bathed. Mac checked on him occasionally, refusing to even look at Marybeth. He spoke only to Ella and asked about the boy as though Marybeth was not even there. John lay groaning in Bill Stone's wagon, the pain of his broken arm and his burns agonizing.

By mid-morning the next day, while the wagon bounced and jolted over rough terrain, Danny opened his eyes and looked around, as if in a daze. Marybeth leaned over him and spoke to him, her heart taking a leap of joy when he smiled at her. But when he began to move slightly, his face contorted into a frown of pain and he started crying. Ella examined his ankle and saw it looked puffy and sore. She sprinkled some whiskey on it, bringing even louder screeches from Danny's strong lungs. Marybeth tried to soothe him, and soon the wagon began to slow as Mac halted the oxen. Moments later Cap appeared at the back of the MacKinder wagon.

"By golly, I thought that was Danny I heard squawkin'," he told Marybeth with a grin. "I could hear him clear up ahead. Josh will be glad to know he's awake."

Marybeth smiled through tear-filled eyes. "I was never so happy to hear him cry," she replied.

"Just don't be givin' him any laudanum or whiskey or anything that might put him back to sleep. He's better off stayin' awake and cryin' his lungs out and workin' up a good sweat now—work more of that venom out of his system."

Marybeth nodded. "We'll keep him awake." Their eyes held, and Cap saw the question in her own.

"He's gonna be all right, Marybeth. A few cracked ribs and hands so swole up he can't even make a fist. His face ain't so pretty either, but it will get back to normal."

Marybeth longed to go to Josh and comfort him. "Thanks, Cap. Tell him—tell him I love him."

Cap glanced at Ella, who had begun sponging the baby again. The woman said nothing. "I reckon he already knows that," he told Marybeth, "but I'll remind him."

Cap left, and Mac climbed up onto the wagon seat to look again at Danny. "He looks and sounds back to normal."

"I think he'll be all right, Mac," Ella told him.

The man glowered down at Marybeth. "What you've done to this family is worse than a sin, Marybeth MacKinder! You might think you can get away with this, but by God you won't! We'll not make trouble for now, and if you want to go whore around with Josh Rivers, you're welcome to him! But Danny will end up back with us where he belongs, I promise you that!"

He climbed down, and Marybeth closed her eyes against tears at his cruel words. Her throat still ached fiercely, and it showed dark bruises from John's big hand. Her back was bruised where it had hit the wagon wheel the day before.

Ella said nothing as the wagons started rolling again. Danny cried until noon break, then fell asleep on Marybeth's lap, his fist in his mouth. Nothing Ella or Marybeth could do would keep the boy awake. Cap rode up to check on him again, and Marybeth looked at the man anxiously. "Cap, he went back to sleep!"

Cap just grinned. "With all the hollerin' I heard, I expect he's out of danger. He's just wore out now. Let him sleep. When he wakes up again, I expect it would be all right to feed him." The man turned his horse, and Marybeth could hear him exclaiming, "What the hell are you doin' on your feet?"

"I want ... to see the boy," she heard Josh's voice answer. Her heart quickened as Josh came to the back of the wagon, Aaron holding his arm for support. Her heart ached at the sight of her beautiful Josh, his face bruised and swollen and covered with scabbed cuts. "I reckon I'd scare Danny half to death if he was awake," he told her, trying to grin.

"Oh, Josh, you shouldn't be up at all," she told him.

He shook his head. "Damned if I was going to let John MacKinder get to his feet before me. He went down first—and he'll get up last."

Her eyes misted as she studied him lovingly.

"What the hell are you doing at my wagon," Mac yelled then. He approached from where he had walked off to relieve himself.

"You touch him and there will be another fight here," Aaron warned the man. "He has come to see the child and you will let him do it."

Cap and Devon both rode closer to Mac. "That's right, MacKinder. You stay out of it," Cap told him. Devon looked down at Mac with the eyes of an Indian looking for revenge. Mac looked away, and then shouted to Ella, "Come out here and fix me something to eat."

Ella looked at Marybeth. "Things are back to normal. You stay here and talk to Josh." The woman climbed out of the wagon, looking up at Josh. "It was a good fight," she told him, astonishing him with the remark. She smiled a little and walked off.

Josh looked at Marybeth, who smiled sadly. "It *was* a good fight."

He managed another crooked smile through swollen lips. "Wish I could have watched instead of participated," he told her. He turned to Aaron. "Help me up, will you?"

"Oh, Josh, be careful," Marybeth said as he hooked his arms over the wagon gate. He couldn't grab the gate because of his crippled hands, so he used his arms, and Aaron gave him a boost. Josh grimaced with the pain of cracked ribs but he managed to climb into the wagon. His shirt was open because of the heat, and Marybeth could see his ribs were wrapped tightly with bandages. He sat down gingerly near her. Marybeth kept Danny in her lap as she turned and touched Josh's shoulder gently. "I was so afraid for you," she told him.

He put a hand to her hair, his fingers stiff and curled, but he managed to stroke it gently. "You have bruises on your neck. And what about when you fell? Are you—all right?"

"Yes. I'm just very sore."

"Danny. I heard him crying earlier. I prayed all night for him, at least when I was alert enough to remember what happened before the fight." His words came out slightly slurred because of his swollen lips.

"Cap says he'll be all right now. He cried himself back to sleep, but it's just an exhausted sleep—not the coma the venom caused."

"I've never been so scared in my life, as when I saw those— bite marks."

She touched his face gently. "You saved his life." A tear slipped down her cheek. "Here you are, all beat up and in pain, and you're asking about me and Danny. You shouldn't even be up. There could be internal damage."

He grinned again. "Not me. My pa was tough, and so are his boys." He laughed lightly, then grimaced and grabbed at his ribs. "My God, I sound like a MacKinder—talking like that. I guess it rubbed off on me."

Marybeth studied him lovingly. "You could never be like a MacKinder. That's why I love you."

Their eyes held. "Marry me—Marybeth." Her eyes widened at the surprising request. "I don't want to just let you use my wagon," Josh added. "I want *us* to use it—together. I know it seems … crazy and … too soon and totally illogical; but I do want to marry you. I want you to be my wife, and I want to be able to lie in your arms at night—and wake up to you in the morning. God only knows what could happen … before this journey is over. I don't want to miss the chance of knowing the joy of lying with you. I don't want to wait … until we get to Oregon."

Her eyes teared with love and joy. Of course it was too soon, totally illogical, just as he had said. But didn't Delores say love was that way sometimes? "Oh, Josh," she whispered. "Yes. Yes, I'll marry you!"

He tried to smile and laughed softly. "I'm not in much of

a condition to be a husband to you—but by God I'll make an effort to heal fast."

She felt her face redden as her blood rushed hot at the meaning of his words. "I love you, Josh," she said in a near whisper. "Yesterday, I was afraid I was going to lose you and Danny both. Oh, Josh, I was so scared for you ... for Danny ... I felt so torn." A tear slipped down her cheek. "I just ... want to get away from this wagon now—this camp. I just want to be with you."

"Don't cry, Marybeth. Everything is going to be all right now." He managed to touch her face. "You just have to hang on until we get to Fort Laramie. It's only a few more days. I'll be healed by then—at least enough to walk like a normal man. John isn't in any condition to give you any trouble, and people are watching Mac. You'll be all right. After Fort Laramie, we'll have a wagon to use. If we're lucky we can find a way to be married—at the fort—and we'll share that wagon together. When we get to Oregon, I'll buy up some ... horses and round up some mustangs; and we'll have a big ranch, Marybeth. I'll be married to the most beautiful woman in the Willamette Valley, and there will be all kinds of Rivers descendents running around. And Danny ... will be as much my son ... as the children we'll have together."

It seemed as though fire moved through her blood at the thought of being his wife; never had she known such joy as realizing she wanted a man with utter wanton passion. She leaned close and gently kissed his sore lips. "I'm scared, but I'm happy, too," she told him.

Josh looked down at Danny, gently touching the boy's sunburned cheek. "What a miracle. He's a strong boy, Marybeth. You've got to hand that much to the MacKinder blood." He met her eyes. "I love you, Marybeth."

She gently kissed his cheek. "And I love you, Joshua Rivers, but you'd better go back. We'll have to break camp soon and I have a feeling you can't walk very fast."

He grinned as much as his swollen lips would allow. "I think you're right." He turned away then, grunting with pain as he moved to the back of the wagon and Aaron helped him climb down. He looked at Marybeth once more before limping away.

John MacKinder managed to rise up on one elbow when Bill Stone told him Josh was walking toward the wagon. "He's been inside Mac's wagon with Marybeth and the kid," Bill told him.

John grimaced with almost unbearable pain. "Give me another drink of whiskey," he groaned, breaking out in a sweat. He watched Josh walk by, the sides of the canvas top still rolled up against the heat. "You're a dead man!" John managed to call out to Josh.

Josh just looked at him. He said nothing, as he kept walking.

"A dead man!" John yelled the words as loudly as he could, and Marybeth felt the sick feeling return to her stomach. "You hear me, Rivers? You're a dead man!"

# Fifteen

Marybeth returned to the MacKinder campsite with an armload of wood to see Aaron and Delores, Sam and Florence, the lay minister Raymond Cornwall and his wife Lillith, as well as Cap and Josh, standing at the campfire. She walked closer and laid down the wood.

"Get your things, Marybeth," Aaron told her. "We all agree you should not stay here another day. We will all take turns taking in you and Danny until we get to Fort Laramie."

Marybeth looked at Josh, then at Ella, who watched with sorrow in her eyes. Mac and Bill were inside Bill's wagon changing the dressing on John's burned back. Marybeth walked up close to Josh and took his arm, leading him away from the others.

"It's all right, Josh. We'll share a campfire with others at night and be together; but during the day, I'll stay with the MacKinder wagon."

Josh frowned. "You don't have to, Marybeth."

"It's only a few more days. I—" She leaned up closer to him. "It's for Ella," she said quietly. "She's afraid she won't get to see much of Danny once I leave the wagon."

Josh sighed, grasping her shoulders. "I don't know why you would want to do anything for *any* MacKinder, but if you think it's right—"

"It is. I'll be all right. I'll be with you evenings, and Mac is too busy driving the oxen during the day to give me any trouble. John won't be raising a ruckus very soon." She sighed. "She's Danny's grandmother, Josh. After the fight ... she said some things that made me realize how much she's suffering."

"But she can see Danny whenever she wants. I would never stop that."

187

Marybeth shook her head. "Once I take my things and go Mac will never let her come and visit with me and Danny, and he'll never allow me back into their own camp. I don't trust them to come and take Danny to *their* camp. Mac is determined Danny will stay with the family, so I can't trust what they might do if Ella comes to get Danny to keep him with her for a while."

"You sure?"

She leaned up and kissed at a cut on his cheek, her heart aching at his battered condition. "Yes. And tonight I want you to get your rest. You need to heal, Josh. We need you to hunt for us, remember?"

"You're more important."

"Than food?"

He touched her hair. "I get my nourishment just looking at you."

She smiled and reddened. "Well there are others in this camp who need to eat."

His eyes moved over her in a way that made her feel undressed, and she was surprised that she looked forward to allowing him to see and touch her naked body. Could a woman ask for more ecstasy than to lie in Josh Rivers' arms?

"Look at them out there," Mac was grumbling inside Bill's wagon. He took another slug of whiskey. "He comes around here like he owns our Marybeth and our Danny. He's got no right filling her head with ideas of going off on her own. None of them have the right to stick their noses into MacKinder business."

"You might as well let it go, Mac," Bill told him. "I don't aim to leave the safety of this wagon train."

Mac glowered at the man and looked down at John's burned back. "There will be a way some day. We'll find it."

"You bet we will," John groaned.

Josh and Marybeth walked back to the others. "She's staying until we reach Fort Laramie," he told the others. "It's all right. I'll explain later."

Marybeth looked at all of them, her heart swelling with love for these loyal and supportive new friends she had made. She knew some of the others along still gossipped and frowned on her religion, but these few friends were all she needed. "Thank you—all of you. But I don't want to put anyone out any more than I already have. And please take Josh back and make him rest. I'll come see him in a few minutes. I'll visit with all of you every night, unless there is too much work for Ella. You are all being too good to me. I will not forget." She put a hand on Josh's arm. "Florence, take this man back and don't let him up any more tonight. I'll come and see him in a little while."

Florence smiled, the terrible grief still showing in her eyes. "He has kept me busy, and I need to be busy right now."

Marybeth walked up and hugged her. "I know. I'm just glad to see you rejoining us in the evenings. Oh, I'm so sorry, Florence. When I thought Danny—" She hugged the woman tighter. "God help you, Florence. We all love you."

"Thank you, Marybeth." The woman pulled away and wiped at tears. "Are you sure you don't want to come stay with us?"

"No. I'm all right here, really." She grasped Josh's arm. "Please go back and lie down, Josh."

He looked around the camp warily, then leaned down to kiss her cheek. "Anything goes wrong, anything at all, you scream just as loud as you can, understand?"

"I will. Thank you for coming for me."

He looked around the camp again, his eyes resting on Bill Stone's wagon. "I have a feeling I should have finished him off," he muttered. He looked down at her. "I was sorely tempted when he went for my gun. But the fact remains they're still family, to Danny at least. I wasn't sure how you'd feel about me if I had killed the man."

A chill moved through her at the thought of either of them killing the other. "It would have been a terrible thing." She searched his eyes. "But if it came to his life or yours ... God forgive me that I would choose a man I have known such a short while over my own brother-in-law."

He smiled in sympathy. "I figured even somebody like John MacKinder is allowed one more chance." He sobered then. "If it ever comes to him and me again, Marybeth, I can't guarantee the outcome."

"I know that. And I understand."

"I still don't like leaving you here." He started to leave with the others, but they hesitated when Mac climbed out of Bill Stone's wagon and headed toward them, his eyes on fire. "Marybeth MacKinder, what makes you think you can pick and choose when to stay with us and when to leave?"

Josh started to push her away, but Marybeth moved in front of him, facing Mac. "Ella wants to have a little more time with Danny."

"To hell with Ella!" Mac shouted The woman looked up sadly from the campfire, then rose, watching her husband. "If you're so damn bent on leaving this family, then go!" Mac nearly screamed the words. "I'll not have you prancing around in front of us with Josh Rives panting at your feet. You've shamed us enough!"

"She hasn't done one thing to shame you," Josh spoke up. The anger in his words frightened Marybeth. If Mac decided to land into the man, Josh wouldn't have a chance in his condition. She noticed Aaron and Sam step closer and thanked God they were nearby, but Mac's remark was humiliating, even in front of her friends, let alone the fact that most of the others could hear.

"You stay out of this," Mac shouted at Josh. "I'm saying right now that if she's itching to go live in sin with you, then she goes *now*. But by God I'll find a way to keep the two of you from raising my Danny!"

"He's *my* Danny, and you'll never take my son from me!" Marybeth was surprised at her own words.

Josh grasped her shoulders. "Let him keep showing everyone what a stubborn fool he is," he said angrily, his eyes on Mac. "If he wants you to leave now, then let's get the hell out of here!" He gave her a light shove, walking past Mac, not too sure himself whether or not the man would land a blow.

"Go on with you! I'll not have the two of you flaunting around in front of poor John. He loves you, Marybeth! You're doing a foolish, sinful thing!"

"Don't argue with him," Josh told her calmly. "Just get

your things."

She looked up at him, and Josh could see the devastation and humiliation in her eyes. "You're right and he's wrong," Josh went on. "You know it in your heart, Marybeth. God means for us to be together, and there's nothing sinful about it. Now get your things."

She hurried away, while Mac ranted on. Aaron moved to stand beside Josh, and Mac walked to the back of the MacKinder wagon, full of enough whiskey to batter Marybeth verbally. "My God, I wish I could use these hands," Josh muttered.

"He's just drunk," Aaron reminded him. "We'll have her out of here soon."

Marybeth handed Danny to Florence. "Take him to Ella to hold while I get everything together," she told the woman.

Florence obeyed, giving the boy to his grandmother, who took him with tears in her eyes. Marybeth packed her belongings into a blanket and a carpetbag, then climbed out and piled everything into the little wagon Aaron had given her. Delores pulled the wagon while Marybeth went to get Danny. Her heart ached at the look in Ella's eyes.

"I'm sorry, Ella. I wanted to keep him here a little longer."

"I know."

"I have to do this. I love Josh and we're going to be married. I wish I could feel differently about John, but you already know how I feel."

Ella nodded, kissing Danny and handing him over. "He will try to get the boy. But there is really nothing he can do. Don't fret about it. Be happy, Marybeth."

Marybeth felt a lump growing in her throat. She leaned forward and kissed Ella's cheek. "Good-bye, Ella."

The woman just turned away. Marybeth walked over to Josh. "You can stay with us again," Delores told her.

Josh put an arm around Marybeth. "It will just be for a few days," he said. "We're getting married as soon as possible, and then Marybeth MacKinder will be Marybeth Rivers, and she'll stay with me."

Marybeth's eyes teared with a mixture of love for Josh, and

humiliation at Mac's ranting. She walked off with Josh—away from the MacKinder camp, away from the MacKinder family, this time for good. She felt as though she was walking out of a dungeon into the light of day. She was free, truly free! Free to be with Josh Rivers, free to be a full woman. Josh had told her there were often traveling preachers at the forts for the army men, sometimes priests. She would pray fervently that there would be someone at Fort Laramie who could marry them, for she wanted nothing more now than to lie in Josh Rivers' arms and know the ecstasy of belonging only to him.

"Zosh," Danny said, reaching toward the man with a big smile.

The next five days were the most delightful Marybeth could remember, in spite of everyone being bone weary, and edgy from one night's theft of some horses by Indians. By day she walked with Delores, and Florence often joined them again. Evenings were spent either at Delores' campfire, or with the Gentrys, or with Cap and Devon. Danny was so popular with all of them that Marybeth had a great deal of help with the child, especially from Florence, who needed the diversion, and the joy of a baby's laughter.

Josh's injuries and an Indian threat kept him close, and in spite of a hunger for fresh meat, Marybeth was grateful. It felt good to be open about their feelings, to be able to share the news that they intended to marry. No one seemed to think there was anything wrong with her marrying again so soon.

"Out here things happen fast," Cap told her one night over a plate of beans. "Folks have to be practical—a man loses his wife and is left with kids to raise, he's got to have a woman. A woman loses her husband—same thing. It's hard out here for a woman alone. When she's lucky enough to actually love the man like I can see you feel about Josh here, well, that's all the better. Sometimes out here, a person has to marry first and *then* learn how to love their partner. You and Josh are startin' off the right way."

There were no questions about her first husband, no accusatory looks. Marybeth felt nothing but friendly support, and just before reaching the fort, several more families from the wagon train came together with surprise gifts for both Marybeth and Florence Gentry.

"You'll need things to start your own home when you get to Oregon," Lillith Cornwall told Marybeth, handing her a homemade quilt.

"And you need to replace so many things," Bess Peters told Florence, presenting her with a blanket and a coffee pot.

Others came forward. How they came up with so many things from such meager supplies, Marybeth could not imagine.

"Cap says we have to lighten our wagon even more," another woman told her. She set a crate down in front of Marybeth. "This china belonged to my mother. Jed says I have to get rid of something. I know you will take very good care of it for me. Mother would have been happy to give it to you if I couldn't have it."

Marybeth was overwhelmed by their generosity. When they were through, she and Florence both had a good start of supplies to set up housekeeping. Florence wept. Her emotions over the gifts and the memory of having lost everything in the tornado, then losing everything again, along with two children because of the cholera, brought forth a wash of tears that soon had all the other women quietly crying.

"No more of this!" Cap whipped out a harmonica, and Raymond Cornwall retrieved a fiddle from his wagon. After a round of ear-curling notes in an effort to get their tunes in harmony, the two men managed to keep in time with each other well enough to play a few rousing songs that soon had husbands and wives whirling in circles, tattered skirts flying, booted feet stomping. Those who stood aside clapped rhythmically for those who danced, and the two men who had lost wives to cholera danced with the two women who had lost their husbands. It had taken considerable cajoling from the others, but everyone understood all of them were grieving. No one saw anything wrong with taking one evening to forget, just for a little while—to laugh and dance and try not to think about cholera and Indians, mountains and hunger. For Marybeth and Josh, it was a night to forget about the MacKinders, who chose to stay to themselves.

Although still badly bruised, the swelling in Josh's face had gone down, and his hands were more limber. "I think I can at least shoot a rifle if I have to," he told Marybeth. They danced to a slow tune drawn out on Raymond's fiddle. Others twirled around the large campfire all had built together out of wood gathered from dead cottonwoods along the river, using buffalo chips as hot coals at the center to keep the wood burning.

Marybeth and Josh had eyes only for each other, both of them feeling the fire move through them at the thought of other reasons for needing the use of his hands. Josh drew her own hand up to his mouth and kissed it, the glitter in his eyes making her feel weak.

"How about your ribs," she asked, reddening as she attempted to change the subject.

"They're healing."

"Oh, Josh, I hope we never have to go through that again."

"We? I'm the one with all the bruises," he said with a grin.

"And I had to watch. I'm not sure that was any easier."

He loved the feel of her long hair brushing across his hand at her back. How many nights had he lain awake picturing that hair draped over bare shoulders and full breasts? "I suppose not." Someone laughed, and he turned his head. "It's good to hear laughter, isn't it?"

"Yes. More than that, it feels good to be the one laughing. There was a time when I wondered if I would ever want to laugh again. You make me so happy, Josh."

"Well, then we're a good match. You do the same for me.

"All I've done is get you hurt."

He frowned. "We both know whose fault that is. I want no guilt feelings on your part. Let's not talk about that tonight. Let's talk about Oregon. We're half way there, you know. How big of a house do you want?"

She laughed lightly. "I don't care if we live in a cave."

"Fine. That will save me a little work and money." They both laughed then, and the thought of sharing a home brought a surge of desire that made him draw her closer. "And how many children do you want," he asked.

Their eyes held. "As many as I can give you, many sons to help you with our vast ranch; daughters to bring gentleness and etiquette to the Rivers' home. It will be a grand home, won't it?"

"Maybe not at first, but some day, Marybeth, some day." He whirled her away from the others, out of the light of the fire and around behind a wagon, where he pulled her tight against him.

"You'll hurt your ribs," she told him.

"It's not my ribs that ache right now." He leaned closer, brushing her lips so lightly it was more of a tease than a kiss. She moved her arms around his neck and he kissed her again, gently, being careful of his own still-sore mouth. Burning desire helped him forget his healing injuries, and the kiss deepened. The thought of being his wife made Marybeth whimper with the want of him. She wondered how a man so strong and able and sometimes fierce could also be so gentle, so sweet. His mouth was warm and delicious and seemed to mold against her own lips in a perfect fit. She wondered if she was crazy to so quickly agree to marry this man; yet she knew if she didn't, she risked falling into sin. There was a time when she could not have imagined wanting a man so badly that she would risk going against her own religious beliefs to have him.

He left her mouth and kissed her eyes. "It's done now, Marybeth," he said, his voice husky with desire. "You're going to be mine. I fought for you and I won. What's more important, you would have left on your own strength, even if I had never come along. I know you would have because you're so strong, and you love Danny enough to know what is best for him and you have the courage to act on that love. To find a woman strong and brave and beautiful all in one package is something I never expected." She rested her head against his chest, being careful not to hug him too tightly. "I wish my sister and brother could meet you. I've thought about going back, but I need to start all over someplace new, Marybeth. We've come this far now, and I've heard so much about Oregon I feel compelled to keep going."

"I want to go wherever you go. This land is all new to me. I will be happy as long as I'm with you." She leaned back. "Oh, Josh, I am getting excited now about seeing the mountains, after hearing Cap tell us about them. They sound so beautiful— dangerous and difficult, but beautiful. Already the land is changing, getting higher, hills and low mountains all around us. I thought at first that what I was seeing were the mountains people talked about. But Cap says they are much higher, so high the snow at the top never melts! Did they have mountains that high in Texas?"

He grinned, enjoying her girlish excitement. In a way she had never had the chance to be a young girl, free and happy; had never been allowed to truly love and enjoy life, love and enjoy a man. He ached to show her how good and sweet it could be. "Not the part I came from," he told her. "Oh, there were lots of canyons and buttes and rocky mesas. But not the really high mountains. Even I haven't seen them."

"Buttes and mesas? What are those?"

He kept an arm around her and ran a hand through her hair. "Oh, low-range, flat-topped hills. I guess you could maybe call some of them low mountains. Most of the part of Texas where I lived was pretty flat—hard and dry and flat, but it had its pretty, green places, too." He sobered. "God, how I wish my Pa could meet you. My Ma, too. They were such good people, Marybeth. They struggled to keep their love together, just like you and I have had to do. Ma, she was a big Bible reader— named all of us after Bible characters, taught us we should live by the Good Book. She treasured her Bible." He kept caressing her hair. "I meant to always keep it, but it got burned up when the comancheros set fire to the house." She felt him tense at the words. "A traveling artist came by once, made a pencilled drawing of my parents. It was the only picture we had of them. That got burned up, too. I wish I had it to show to you. She was such a pretty woman. If you could see Rachael, you'd know. Rachael looks a lot like her."

"I can tell by looking at you. And your father must have been a handsome man."

He grinned. "You should have heard the way my Ma's voice would go all soft when she talked about him. River Joe. Her River Joe. You would have thought no stronger, braver, more handsome man ever walked on two feet."

She reached up and touched his bruised face. "I can understand how she felt. I feel the same way about his son."

He sobered. "I miss them so much sometimes, Marybeth, like it was only yesterday I was a kid running in and out of that house, Ma inside cooking, Pa outside yelling at us to get out chores done, my brother Matt still alive..." His voice trailed off and she ran her hand over his back.

"We all have things we miss that we can never get back again, Josh. I miss my own mother and father, and I miss Ireland terribly. I suppose we are more alike than we realize. All we can do now is start a life of our own, and try to be the kind of people our own parents were. Surely they are with us in spirit. I think they know about us. Josh, and they are smiling."

He smiled through tears she could not see in the darkness. "I expect they are." He breathed deeply and cleared his throat. "I didn't intend for the conversation to get so deep. I brought you out here for more pleasurable things." He moved his hands up her ribs, pressing them to the sides of her breasts. She grasped his wrists.

"I think perhaps we should go back and join the others." She could feel him trembling, and her own resistence was weakening. "Please, Josh. I want to keep it honorable and right."

He sighed deeply. "My respect for honor is getting weaker every day. I sent Devon on ahead to see if there are any missionaries or preachers or whatever at the fort: If there are, he'll make sure they stay there and wait for us." He drew her close again. "In two or three days, if we are lucky, Marybeth MacKinder, your name will become Marybeth Rivers, and I won't have to worry about honor and sin and all those things that keep coming between us. And if dreams count, I've already sinned with you and thrown honor out the window."

She closed her eyes, desire pulling painfully at her insides. "You have a way with words, Joshua Rivers, that makes it very difficult for me to stick to my convictions. I demand that you take me back this very minute."

He laughed lightly. "One more kiss first."

"No!"

His mouth met hers almost savagely, and she gave no more argument.

At the MacKinder campfire, John slowly climbed out of Bill Stone's wagon. For the past several days he had got up only to relieve himself, unable to do anything more. Tonight he felt a little stronger. He limped over to the family campfire, his swollen and purple arm in a sling. He wore a light shirt, leaving it unbuttoned so that it hung loose and did not rub against his badly scabbed back, which would forever carry ugly scars. Wincing with pain, he sat down on a barrel, and his mother handed him a plate of beans.

"Beans again," he muttered. He glanced over at the bonfire, where most of the other travelers danced and sang and laughed. "I suppose she's over there with him?"

"What do you think," Mac grumbled. "Bill says he heard folks saying they plan to marry soon as they can find a preacher to do it. He's over there right now seeing what he can find out."

"If they are not married by a priest, it won't count."

"Depends how bad they want to be married. I have a feeling Marybeth will compromise, as long as Rivers isn't Catholic himself. They aren't going to want to wait."

John swallowed a spoonful of beans. "He's got no right! No right!"

"Let it go, John," Ella spoke up, surprising them both. "You had your fight and you lost. She has chosen and it's over."

He rose, tossing his plate into the fire. "It's *not* over," he hissed. "Are you turning against your own son?"

She met his eyes. "I am tired of the fighting, that's all!"

"Well, you will have to put up with it!" John turned and glared at the gathering in the distance. "Let them dance all night! The day is coming when Joshua Rivers will never dance again!

And the woman in his arms will be in *my* arms!" He walked off into the darkness, and Ella met her husband's eyes. She saw the dark anger there.

"Don't you ever talk in that woman's favor again. Sometimes I think she made you start thinking *you're* not a MacKinder either!"

*I'm not*, she wanted to shout at him. *I am Ella McGuire. Have you ever thought of me as a person, Murray MacKinder?* "I just want some peace, Mac," she said aloud.

"Then keep your mouth shut and tend to your chores." He handed out his plate. "Give me a little more."

She dipped some beans onto the plate.

# Sixteen

Devon rode up to the cook wagon, where Marybeth watched Ben Stramm take buffalo tongue meat from a pot of boiling water. Devon had shot the buffalo three days earlier, and as he scraped the hide for drying, he had explained to Marybeth the many uses the Indians had for the buffalo. After divying up the meat, Ben had cut some into small strips to dry, and he spent his nights smoking more of it. Marybeth wanted to learn to cook foods uniquely American, and was curious about buffalo meat, which Hank insisted tasted much better than beef or pork, especially the tongue.

"The secret is to kill a young buffalo, like this one Devon got. The meat of an old buffalo is tough and stringy," he was telling her as Devon dismounted. "Plenty of salt and onion—bay leaves if you can find them. I always stock up on spices before I set out on one of these trips." He carried the meat to a board set on the tailgate of the cook wagon and began slicing it thinly.

Devon walked up to the campfire and sat down across from Josh. "Many soldiers and Indians at Laramie," he said.

Marybeth turned to listen. She had learned not to be afraid of the wild looking half-breed, who seldom spoke unless it was to give information. After all, he was a friend of Josh and his brother-in-law.

"Trouble," Josh asked.

Devon shook his head. "Your president plans a great treaty. Only Indians there now are Sioux, but more will come—hundreds, maybe thousands, the soldiers say. Not for two moons yet, but already missionaries gather to try to bring their religion to the Indians." He looked up at Marybeth. "I saw two black-robed men like the ones you describe. Are they the kind you say must marry you?"

Marybeth brightened. Surely God *did* mean for her to be with Josh. "Yes." She looked at Josh, who bounced Danny on his leg. He smiled and winked at her.

"I don't know why it's so important to you to be married by one of them," he said, "but if it makes you happy, it's all right with me. Far as I'm concerned, any old minister will do."

She folded her arms. "Not for an Irish Catholic."

His eyebrows arched as his eyes moved over her. "I'd like to see how long that Irish Catholic stubbornness would hold up if we couldn't find a priest at Laramie. I reckon I'd have to spend a lot of time hunting."

All the men laughed, even Devon. Marybeth only reddened, turning to watch Ben slice the buffalo tongue. In the next moment Josh had handed Danny to Cap and was standing behind Marybeth. He put a hand to her waist. "I didn't mean to embarrass you. I just like to tease."

She looked up at him and broke into a smile, shaking her head. "I know. That is part of what I love about you." Their eyes held. "Josh, a priest! I prayed so hard we would find one. I hope Devon told him not to leave."

Josh looked over at the Indian, who was checking his rifle. "You told the black-robes to hang around, didn't you," he said louder.

Marybeth was unable to look at the rest of them as they chuckled again.

"I told them. I said a lady who prays with strange beads wishes to be married by a priest when she comes. And I talked to the soldier who leads the men at the fort. He tells me one officer's cabin is empty right now. He said the man and woman who wish to be married can use it. He even sent men to clean it up. I think the soldiers look forward to celebrating the wedding. They are bored."

Marybeth felt Josh's arm come around her. "Now are you satisfied we're supposed to do this?" he asked her. "Not only do we have a priest, but we have a place to spend our wedding night."

She felt suddenly warm and breathless at the thought of it. She looked up at him and they embraced lightly. "Josh, do you think you're well enough?"

She heard Ben chuckle and suddenly realized how the question sounded. Josh kept his arm around her, realizing she had to be even more embarrassed, and he grinned. "I have a feeling I'll be able to overcome the pain," he teased, making Ben laugh even harder.

"Oh, Josh," she said quietly, pulling away and folding her arms.

"It's all in good fun," Ben told her. "Here, Marybeth, taste this here tongue meat. I know you think it's going to be awful, but believe me, this here is a delicacy. You remember how I cooked it."

Marybeth took the thin slice of meat and tasted it, her face still flushed. Her eyes widened at the wonderful, sweet flavor. "It's delicious," she said.

Ben grinned. "I told you." He studied her pretty face. "I'm glad about the priest, Marybeth. Josh here is getting the prettiest woman west of the Mississippi. We're all happy for both of you."

"Thank you, Ben; and thank you for helping me learn the way you cook. The last buffalo meat I made with Ella tasted awful."

"Well, there is a knack to it. You can help me dish up some of this for the others."

Marybeth helped him while Josh went back to the campfire. "How soon will we make Laramie," he asked Devon.

"I would say tomorrow—maybe early afternoon. Depends how long it takes to get across the river in the morning. River's down. Shouldn't be too difficult."

Marybeth's heart pounded harder at the words. By tomorrow night she could be lying in Josh Rivers' arms, sharing his bed.

"Unless some idiot like MacKinder decides to take a different route again," Cap joked. They all laughed, but the mention of the name gave Marybeth the shivers. She could not forget John's bitter hatred, his talk of killing Josh.

"I hope he does," Josh spoke up. "I'd like to see him off

this train completely."

"Wouldn't take much to do it," Cap answered. "One more wrong move and they're gone."

"Hell, Josh, you can handle that big ape," Ben put in. "I'll tell you one thing—ain't none of us sittin' here that's gonna let any MacKinder spoil you and Marybeth's big day. That's a promise." He put a hand on Marybeth's shoulder. "If we have to tie and gag that loud-mouthed bully, we'll do it. It might take six of us to get him down, but we'll handle it."

"I don't think he's in any shape yet to cause much trouble," Cap said. They all chuckled, and Marybeth had never felt so much love. Years with the MacKinders had almost made her forget how it felt to love and laugh and share. Her only link to such feelings had been Danny. She carried a plate to Devon.

"Thank you," she told him. She turned to Cap. "Thank all of you. When we get to Oregon, I hope you all know that if you should stay, you would always be welcome in our home." She looked at Josh. Home. What a nice sound it had.

The wagon train passed by a circle of tipis outside the grounds of the fort, and Marybeth stared at dark-skinned women, some in doeskin tunics, others wearing cloth skirts and shirts, an array of beads draped around their necks. The Indian women stared back, and it struck Marybeth how many different kind of people there were in the world and within this country called America. It was full of immigrants like herself; rugged whites born to it, like Josh; black slaves from Africa; and these natives who watched her now. She could see Devon in the half-naked men who walked among the camps or sat smoking beside tipis. A few rode by on painted horses that carried no conventional saddle.

"Cap says these Indians are friendly. I have heard some frightening stories about what they can do when they are unfriendly," Delores said as she walked beside Marybeth.

Devon rode by and dismounted, greeting two of the Indian men in their own strange tongue, and Marybeth tried to imagine what Josh's brother-in-law might be like. Josh had told her he was familiar with some Pawnee and Cheyenne. Devon had said these were Cheyenne—his people. He was half white, yet he seemed to recognize only his Indian side.

"Devon says some day there will be big trouble between whites and Indians," she told Delores.

"I just hope it waits until we get to more civilized places in Oregon."

"So do I."

They followed the wagons across the parade grounds of the sprawling fort, which covered several acres and was not surrounded by the conventional log walls Marybeth had seen pictures of in books. It was much more open than she had anticipated. Soldiers milled about in every direction, some being drilled, others relaxing. The sight of their blue coats made her feel more secure, and she was glad the train was here now and not a month from now, which was when Devon said thousands of Indians would gather here for a great treaty signing. She prayed the treaty would alleviate any problems with the Indians, and she also prayed that the Indian trouble they had experienced earlier was not a sign that there was more trouble ahead. What other reason could there be for planning a treaty than the Indians must be restless and angry? She wished she knew how to explain to them that she and the others who came through their land meant them no harm. Maybe that was what Devon was telling them now.

This was Josh's first day back on a horse. Although his ribs were still bound and badly bruised, he was able to function as long as no pressure was put on them. His hands worked well enough to handle the reins, and Marybeth knew he had been anxious to get back in a saddle. He seemed to be most comfortable and look most natural on a horse, and she watched him ride up to someone who looked like an officer. She went on with the others, making camp with Delores on the north side of the grounds, where Cap ordered the wagons to circle. Soldiers and buildings stretched between the wagon camp and the Indian tipis, a deliberate move by Cap to help ease any tension and keep them well separated from the unpredictable Indians.

Several minutes later Josh rode up to the Svensson wagon, smiling as he dismounted. Marybeth wondered if he was really more handsome than she had seen him yet, or if he just seemed that way because tomorrow he would become her husband.

"I've seen the cabin," he told her, walking up to her and kissing her cheek. "They went all out cleaning it up. And one of the soldiers went to get one of the priests. They're camped among the Indians. One of them will be by soon to meet us. Get cleaned up and I'll walk you to the commissary and supply store. I want to stock up on ammunition. We'll buy some supplies to set up our own wagon, and you can look for a new dress. I want you to buy the prettiest dress there. There are wives living here at the fort, so there should be some women's clothes at the supply store. What time do you think we should announce we'll be married tomorrow?"

"Oh, Josh, you are going so fast! I cannot think."

"Too late for thinking. Time for doing. I say two o'clock. What do you say? That way we can celebrate all afternoon and share our happiness with everyone else."

She smiled nervously, loving him for telling her earlier that they would wait one day after arriving at the fort before being married. He knew she was nervous, sensed her sudden apprehension. He grasped her small face between his hands. "Tomorrow night we'll do only what you *want* to do. We'll even just go to sleep if you want—enjoy lying in each other's arms and waking up that way."

She held his eyes. "I would not do that to you on your wedding night."

"What? Lie in my arms? You won't do that?"

She smiled. "Josh Rivers, you know what I mean."

He smiled warmly. "I just want you to understand that I'm not the animal I suspect Dan MacKinder was," he said softly. He kissed her forehead. "Come on. Let's get cleaned up and get ready to meet the priest." He put a reassuring arm around her, and Marybeth said a secret prayer of thanks that she had found a man she could love totally, a man of whom she would never have to be afraid.

• • •

"It is a fine young lad you have here," Father O'Grady told Marybeth. He handed Danny to Josh, and Marybeth smiled proudly, overjoyed at not only finding a priest, but to discover that he was Irish. "And it's a father he'll certainly be needing."

They sat on barrels near an Indian camp on the outskirts of the fort.

"You—don't think it's wrong then, that I marry again so soon," Marybeth asked the man.

Father O'Grady frowned, rubbing at his chin. "You have already explained the kind of husband Dan MacKinder was. Only God can be the judge of your feelings for the man, but if I, a human, can understand, surely God can be even more understanding. When I look at you and Joshua, see the look in your eyes, I know that you truly love each other. And in this land, a woman with a child should not be alone. I will tell you the truth. I have seen women marry out here with their husbands barely cold in their graves, Marybeth. It is common. People cannot live by what is necessarily proper, in this land. They must think about survival. If, at the same time, their hearts are true, as are yours and Josh's, they are all the more blessed."

Marybeth took Josh's hand. "I married once out of necessity, Father. I vowed I would never do so again. I love Joshua, and he loves me."

The priest eyed Josh. He liked what he saw, liked the honesty in his eyes. They had told him why Josh was still bruised, and he felt sorry for Josh and Marybeth both. "Marybeth is Irish and Catholic," he told Josh. "I know from experience how some people feel about that. I think perhaps to a man like yourself, being Irish means nothing. You are a man who judges a person for what is on the inside. But what about the religion, Joshua? How will young Danny be raised?"

Joshua shrugged. "If Marybeth wants him to be raised a Catholic, that's fine with me."

The priest arched his eyebrows. "Ah, but it is best if both parents practice and understand the religion. Would you be willing to convert?"

Josh smiled, feeling a little unsure. "I don't know what I'd convert *from*. I believe in God, if that's what you mean. I have a brother-in-law who is part Indian and who, I expect feels a lot like these Indians around here about his God. God is a lot of things to a lot of different men."

"And what is He to you, Joshua?"

Josh took off his hat and ran a hand through his hair, balancing Danny on his knee. "Well, God is God. I mean, my ma, she raised us up on the Bible. We never had any formal churching, but I've done my share of praying a time or two, usually when a snake was looking hungrily at my ankle or an Indian had me in the sight of his arrow."

The priest laughed. "And did you feel God's presence?"

"I reckon so. I'm sitting here talking to you, aren't I? There hasn't been a rattler or an Indian got me yet. Not even John MacKinder could best me, so I suppose *somebody* heard my prayers."

Father O'Grady chuckled again, shaking his head. He folded his hands, looking at Marybeth and Danny before meeting Josh's eyes once more. "Would you be willing to take the Catholic religion, son? It takes a few weeks of lessons. There is no time to do it now, but might I have your promise you will do so when you reach Oregon?"

Josh looked at Marybeth, squeezing her hand. "Why not?" He looked at the priest. "A little religion sure can't hurt a body, now, can it?"

The priest reached out and touched his arm. "It's good for the soul, my son. And it will be good for Danny. As long as you agree to convert, I will gladly marry you and Marybeth."

"Oh, thank you, Father O'Grady," Marybeth spoke up.

The man leaned back, folding his arms. "It always warms my heart to see two young people in love. You are both strong and determined. You will need that where you are going. I can see that little Danny is already getting attached to his new father. That is a good sign."

It seemed strange to Marybeth to be talking with a Catholic

priest in what seemed the middle of nowhere, in this land called America, with soldiers and half-naked Indians milling around them. She could not quite get over the variety of people and places and nationalities of this land—from the civilization of New York City, to the empty plains. Joshua was purely American, from a strange place called Texas, which sounded different from anything she had seen yet, but still it was a part of America.

The priest rose and put his hands on Josh and Marybeth's shoulders. "God bless and be with you both," he told them. "When I perform the ceremony, I will annoint you both with Holy Water. Marybeth, if you would like Confession, I have a tent set up for such things."

"Yes, I—I would like that." She looked at Joshua. "Do you mind?"

"Of course not." He looked at Father O'Grady. "I understand more about your religion than you think, Father. I'm from Texas, you know. Lots of people of Spanish descent there—lots of missions. There was one not far from where I lived. I remember going there sometimes just because it was cool inside, and because it was so peaceful. I felt closer to God there, even though I didn't understand the religion."

Father O'Grady nodded. "Then you will have no trouble taking Marybeth's religion for your own," he answered.

Marybeth and Joshua both rose, and Joshua put out his hand, shaking the priest's hand firmly, holding Danny in his left arm. "I'll wait here for Marybeth," he said then.

Father O'Grady smiled at Marybeth. "Never be ashamed of loving this man, Marybeth, in spite of what anyone else thinks, especially the MacKinders. If you follow your heart, God will bless you for it. Come, I will take your confession and give you Communion."

Marybeth took her Rosary beads from her pocket, turning to look at Joshua. "Thank you, Josh. I'll be back in a little while."

"I'll be right here."

Her eyes teared. "I know. That's what I love about you." She turned and followed the priest, her heart warmed by the thought of Communion, by the Father's Irish accent; most of all by Josh's willingness to convert for her and Danny's sake. Yes, he would be there when she returned. Surely he would always be there for her.

The day passed quickly. After visiting with the priest, Josh and Marybeth went inside the fort and bought supplies. Marybeth found a soft pink dress with a bodice that was cut in a scalloped design and revealed just enough of her full breasts to bring out all her womanly beauty. The fitted waist accented her own small waist, and when she looked at it in the mirror in a back room of the supply store, she was surprised at the happy face that looked back at her. Yes, she felt beautiful, more beautiful than Dan had ever made her feel. She bought pink combs to match the dress, which she would use to pull back her auburn hair at the sides. Her shoes were badly worn, and Josh insisted she buy new ones—a good pair for her wedding, and a sturdier pair for walking. He bought clothes for Danny and food and other supplies, and Marybeth bought a nightgown that she would not let him see.

"Josh, you'll run out of money before we get to Oregon," she fussed.

"Don't worry about that. I've never had much to spend my money on up to now, and I saved a long time for this trip; figured I might get married after I got there and would need money. I sure never figured I'd get married *before* I got there."

Her eyes saddened. "I am so sorry I cannot present you with a dowry. In Ireland it is the custom. I am embarrassed."

Josh lit a thin cigar and grinned. "Well, you're not in Ireland, so don't worry about it. Besides, you do have a dowry. You've got Danny, and he's worth more than a few coins and property. And your own beauty is your dowry. Just getting you is treasure enough."

She smiled softly, and they left the store, so loaded up they needed Delores and Aaron to help carry their supplies. "Now, don't you think I had a good idea saying we'd wait a day?" Josh asked her. "We could never have done all this and got married, too, and we still have the wagons to rearrange."

They slowed as they noticed the MacKinders coming toward them. Marybeth's heart pounded wildly at the sight of John MacKinder back on his feet. He walked using a thick branch for a cane, grasping it with his left hand. His right arm still hung in a sling. His face was mottled green and purple, and at the moment he glared at Josh with more hatred than Marybeth had ever seen in any man's eyes.

"Afternoon, folks," Josh spoke up jovially. "Good to see you up and around, John. I guess a MacKinder man can still get up and hold his head proudly, even after landing flat on his back for the first time."

Josh and Aaron both grinned at the remark, but it was obvious John saw no humor in it. He turned dark eyes to Marybeth, and Josh felt a silent rage at the thought of how the man's brother must have once treated her. "Is it true you are marrying this man, Marybeth?" John asked in a low growl.

Marybeth stiffened. "Yes. We will marry tomorrow."

"Two o'clock," Josh spoke up, obvious sarcasm in his voice. "You folks planning on coming?"

Marybeth didn't know whether to laugh, or faint from fear for him at his brashness.

"This is not over, Rivers," John told him.

"It is for me. If you want to go on stewing about it, go ahead. Hell, you're a handsome man, MacKinder. You ought to be able to find yourself some other woman. Of course, considering your temper and bad attitude toward them, maybe it *won't* be so easy. Women out here are tougher and smarter than you think, MacKinder." He looked down at Marybeth. "Let's go. I'm not too fond of the company." He walked past John, and Marybeth followed, pulling the wagon. Ella stared longingly at Danny, who grinned at her. John watched Josh with smouldering eyes.

Once several yards were between them, everyone breathed a sigh of relief, and Aaron laughed. "You were pushing it back there, Josh. You remember you're in no condition to get into another fight."

Josh shrugged. "Neither is John MacKinder."

"Oh, Josh, you had me so nervous," Marybeth told him.

"He isn't going to try anything. And after tomorrow, it will be too late." The words sounded wonderful. After tomorrow ... After tomorrow her name would no longer be MacKinder.

# Seventeen

It was as fine a wedding as Marybeth could have imagined, even in a more civilized place. Everyone from the wagon train gathered, and so did most of the soldiers from the fort. A few women were among them, and one military wife baked a cake. Another offered the bedroom of the quarters she shared with her husband for Marybeth to use to bathe and get dressed, and the women from the wagon train gathered wildflowers for a bouquet.

Marybeth walked between two columns of soldiers, Aaron on her arm, leading her to the priest where Josh stood beside him waiting. Raymond Cornwall played a lovely tune on the fiddle, and most of the men from the wagon train stayed at the back of the crowd, keeping an eye out for any movement from the MacKinder wagon, ready to put a stop to anything John or Mac might do to disrupt the wedding.

In spite of his lingering bruises, Marybeth had never seen Josh look more handsome. He wore a dark suit and a white shirt with a ruffled front, and a black string tie. His dark eyes watched her with near worship, his thick, sandy hair blowing in loose wisps about his face. She kept her eyes on his, trusting his promises, thanking God for bringing her such a wonderful man.

Josh had never known such beauty as what he saw coming toward him in soft pink. He had had his share of women, but never had one excited him like Marybeth MacKinder. Never had one kept him awake nights, disturbing his thoughts painfully; never had he felt he could not go on without one of them.

They stood together through a long ceremony, much of which Josh did not understand. The priest spoke in a strange language at times. Finally he was placing the plain gold wedding band on her hand. Josh had bought it just the day before, wishing there was more of a choice. He promised himself he would some day get her a really beautiful ring, but to Marybeth there could be nothing more beautiful than the little gold ring that said she now belonged to Joshua Rivers, and he to her. He kissed her lightly, gently, then embraced her while everyone else cheered and threw rice that the fort commander had provided.

Marybeth clung to Josh, crying, and he gave her a light squeeze. "Come on, Mrs. Rivers, we have a cake to cut and some celebrating to do."

Danny was passed around from one person to the next, enjoying all the attention, while the musicians in the group struck up some lively music and the dancing began. The air was full of the smell of a side of beef roasting over an open pit, and Indians began to mingle with the crowd, enjoying the white man's celebration. Men broke open the whiskey, and someone handed a bottle to Josh, who laughed and took a swallow.

"Josh, no!" Marybeth spoke up, grabbing his arm as he started to raise it again.

He frowned and bent close to her, kissing her ear. "This is the happiest day of my life, Marybeth. Now I'm not a drinker, but an occasion like this calls for a slug or two."

"Please don't," she begged him, looking up at him with a mixture of fear and pleading in her eyes. He understood when he remembered how much the MacKinders drank, how drunk and abusive Dan MacKinder probably was on his wedding night. He smiled softly and set the bottle down.

"Marybeth, I've only been truly drunk a couple of times in my life, and even then I just get happier, not mean." He kissed her cheek. "But I won't drink any more."

He turned and handed the bottle to someone else, and Marybeth was astonished he had quit just because she asked him to. A MacKinder man would have slapped her silly for daring to object to anything, especially if it involved his right to drink.

Josh pulled her out into the middle of the parade ground, where emigrants, soldiers and Indians formed a circle to watch the newlyweds dance. Soon others joined in, but Marybeth was aware only of Josh. "Thank you," she told him, holding his eyes.

"Actually, I just didn't want my senses dulled by the whiskey," he said, grinning.

Marybeth felt a powerful surge of desire rush through her at the remark. "*I* don't want your senses dulled either." Their eyes were riveted by desire. "I love you, Josh, and I do trust you." How wonderful it felt having his strong arms around her, knowing she was his now to do with as he pleased, yet knowing he would not abuse that privilege. He leaned down and kissed her, and people clapped and whistled, bringing them out of their own spell to realize everyone was watching. Others made teasing remarks, and Josh kept a constant arm around her as though to tell her not to pay any attention.

They danced for hours, with each other, with others. The beef was sliced and served, and the wedding cake was cut. The men of the fort presented them with money they had collected. "You'll need it to set up house when you reach Oregon," the commander told them. Marybeth was touched, again overwhelmed at how good and kind people could be.

Danny started crying from hunger, and pieces of soft cake would not do. Josh took him in his arms and walked with him and Marybeth to the little cabin they would use, located on the east side of the parade grounds. People remarked and whistled about the two going to their "honeymoon cottage."

"She's just going to feed the baby," Josh called out with laughter.

"Sure she is," someone yelled back.

Marybeth was too embarrassed to look at them. "Won't they be surprised when we come back," Josh told her, following her inside.

Marybeth laughed and took Danny as they went in. Her eyes widened as she looked around the little one-room cabin. It was clean and tidy, and there were curtains at the windows. There was a bed in one corner, made up with clean sheets and blankets. A checkered tablecloth covered a small table, and an oil lamp sat on it. The sun was setting, and Josh lit the lamp for a little more light.

"Oh, Josh, it's wonderful."

"I thought so, too. There is a little room off the back where there's a wash bowl and a couple of buckets of water. And there's an out-house just outside the back door there, so you don't have to go far."

"It will be nice not to have to hold up blankets or go searching for someplace private—at least for a day or two."

He laughed lightly. "I'll go get our things while you feed Danny. I know we're going back out, but we might as well get everything over here for later." He kissed her cheek and left, and she could hear others teasing him when he went back outside.

Marybeth unbuttoned her dress and put Danny to her breast, then took hold of a bed blanket at the end of the bed and drew it over herself. After several minutes, Josh came back inside with her carpetbag, and an armful of clothes for himself.

"They didn't make it very easy for me," he told her. "The ribbing got worse. I even got offered more whiskey, but I turned it down like a good boy."

She smiled, and their eyes held. He set the things aside and came to the bed, sitting down beside her. Marybeth felt the fire beginning to move through her at his very closeness. Josh Rivers was her husband now. He put an arm around her and reached over to gently pull the blanket away. She made no protest, her heart pounding wildly as his eyes rested on her breast as Danny took his nourishment. She trembled as he leaned down, gently kissing the white of her breast. His lips moved over her breast then and to her throat.

"I love you so much, Marybeth. I'm so proud you're my wife." He met her lips with sweet desire on his own, grasping the back of her head and drawing out the kiss seductively. Already she wondered why she thought earlier she might be afraid of him. Josh Rivers didn't know how to be anything but gentle with a woman.

He left her mouth, and she studied his eyes, seeing the need and love in his own. "Let's not go back out," she said, surprising herself at the words. "When Danny is through, take him to Delores and … come back. I'll go and change."

He searched her sea-green eyes, on fire for her. "You sure?"

She nodded. "Yes."

He smiled. "It's hard to believe any of this, isn't it?"

Her eyes misted. "I am so afraid I am only dreaming—that I will wake up and find myself still traveling with the MacKinders. If it *is* just a dream, I want to experience the best part of it before I do wake up."

Danny's eyes were drooping. It had got to the point where he fed very little in the evening. She could tell she was going to be able to wean him early. It had been a long day for the boy, and Marybeth knew he would sleep soundly all night. She gently pulled him away from her breast, and Josh took him from her. Suddenly it was so easy to let him see her breast; she handed the boy over with the feeling she was giving him to his father. Josh went to the door, and alarm suddenly came into her eyes. "Josh!"

He turned, frowning. "What's wrong?"

She pulled her dress over herself. "Don't leave him with Delores. Lay him here on the bed and go and get some bedding and his little wagon. We'll let him sleep in that. He'll sleep through the night. He won't be any bother to us. I ... I don't want him out of my sight tonight."

"What are you afraid of?"

"I don't trust John or Mac. I know them. If they could steal him, they would. With all the dancing and noise, Mac could ride away with him."

"You don't really think he'd do a thing like that, do you?"

"Yes, he would. They are still very angry. Please, Josh. I thought we should leave him with Delores for the night, but I want him here near us."

He walked back over and laid the boy on the bed. "All right. Just don't get all upset." He kissed her lightly. "Nothing is going to happen to him—or you. You've got me now, remember? And lots of friends. You just stay relaxed and go and change. I'll go get the wagon."

She reached around his neck and he rose, still embracing her. "Thank you," she told him. "And be careful, Josh. You must be careful, especially tonight."

"I'll be back here in five minutes. Then we'll bolt that door, and nobody can bother us the rest of the night." He kissed her lightly and set her on her feet, then left. She bolted the door behind him, then took the soft, white cotton nightgown from her bag and hurriedly took off her clothes. She went to the washroom and washed and dried off her breast, then pulled the sleeveless nightgown over her naked body. She walked back into the main room and took out her brush, brushing her hair nervously. She studied herself in an old, stained mirror, pinching her cheeks for color, then took a bottle of lilac water from her bag, sprinkling some on herself. By then she already heard Josh at the door. She walked over and unbolted it, letting him inside.

Josh stood there for a moment, his eyes moving over her, studying the hard points of her breast that were easily discernible beneath the thin material. She felt herself reddening as she stepped back a little and folded her arms in front of her.

"You look beautiful," he told her softly. He brought in the wagon and bedding, then closed and bolted the door. He set the wagon near the bed and filled it with a couple of feather pillows and blankets, then took Danny from the bed and laid him carefully into the wagon. He covered the boy, smiling at Danny's puckered lips. "He sure is a good kid," he remarked.

Marybeth watched him lovingly as he made sure all the curtains were closed tightly, then turned down the oil lamp. He looked back at her, and she smiled nervously, moving to the other side of the bed.

"I'll turn down the blankets," she told him. She drew them back and sat down on the other side of the bed, rubbing her arms. "I know it is hot out, but suddenly I am very cold."

He grinned and shook his head, removing his suit coat and vest, untying his tie and throwing everything over the brass rail at the end of the bed. "Marybeth, you don't have to sit there and shiver like a lamb waiting for slaughter." He unbuttoned and removed his shirt.

She swallowed, consumed with both apprehension and anticipation. "Is that how I look?"

He sat down in a chair near the bed and put out a foot.

"Yes. Relax and grab hold of this boot, will you? I'm too sore in the middle to bend over and pull it off."

She grasped the boot and pulled, and he winced with lingering pain at the strain. He sat there a minute breathing deeply. "If it's going to hurt that much, we might as well do the other one and get it over with." She grasped the other boot and pulled again, and he let out a disgusted gasp. "I hope to hell things go nice and easy for us for a while. I'm still not in any shape to go one on one with some Indian brave or with one of your relatives."

He leaned back for a moment, and she studied his handsome form, the powerful arms and shoulders. Although he still wore linen strips wrapped around his ribs, it was obvious his stomach was flat and muscled, and above and below the bandage she could see soft, dark hairs. The memory of another big, hairy chest flashed into her mind, hovering over her virgin body, its owner laughing and panting as he too quickly introduced her to man.

She quickly pushed the thought away. "I'll pull off your socks," she told Josh. She removed them, and he stood up, unbuttoning his trousers. Marybeth looked away as he threw them aside and stood there in his longjohns.

He sat down beside her, touching her face, feeling her tension. It amazed him that she had had a husband and had even delivered a child, for she seemed almost as hesitant as a virgin. "You said you trusted me, remember?"

"I remember," she answered quietly.

He leaned behind her and pulled back the covers. "Why don't you just crawl under these sheets, and I'll lie down beside you and just hold you. If that's all we do all night, then that's all we do. At least we'll wake up together. We've both been wanting that for a long time."

Again came the memories—Dan MacKinder yanking off her wedding gown before she had time to change or think. There had been no tender words beforehand, no gentle caresses— just an eagerness to get at her and satisfy his own needs. She looked at Josh.

"Do you mean that?"

She saw no teasing grin, no little sparkle that was usually in his eyes when he was teasing her. "I mean it."

She dropped her eyes and moved under the covers. He turned the lamp down to an even dimmer light and moved into bed beside her. She lay rigid, feeling awkward, haunted by fears Dan MacKinder had instilled in her, yet wanting this man with more passion than she thought she had in her. He moved an arm under her neck. "Come here."

She nestled into his shoulder and felt the fire begin to move through her when he rested a hand on her belly. "That was one fine wedding, wasn't it?"

"Yes, it was," she answered. "Everyone was so nice to us. I would rather have that wedding than the grandest church wedding. I'll always remember it, and the friends we've made. I'll miss them when we all go our separate ways in Oregon."

"Well, maybe we'll find a way to settle near some of them—at least Delores and Aaron. You'd like that, wouldn't you?"

"Oh, yes! And I want to be with Delores when she has her baby. I hope it all goes well for her. She deserves to be happy." His hand massaged her belly in gentle, circular movements as they talked, and she began to relax more, a fire building deep inside her. She realized she wanted him more with every word, every movement. Was he deliberately doing this? Dan had never moved his hand over her this way.

"Yes, she deserves it. And so do you," he answered. "You deserve happiness more than anyone I can think of. I'll try to make you happy, Marybeth."

"You already have. You made me your wife."

He kissed her hair, and she knew what he was thinking. She was his wife only on paper. She still did not belong to him completely. She had to know if it was really true—if she could really enjoy a man. She knew he meant it when he said he wouldn't do anything if she didn't want to. But she also knew he wasn't about to let the night go without at least trying. Yet she didn't mind. He wasn't raking over her, forcing himself into her. He was being so sweet about it, so gentle. She smiled.

"You're trying to trick me, Joshua Rivers."

"Trick you? I'm just trying to relax you."

She turned her face to his. Their eyes held, and in the next moment their lips met. That was all either of them needed. Her passion for him far outweighed her apprehension, and she found herself returning the kiss with as much need and desire as he felt for her. She wanted him! She was enjoying his touch! It seemed so incredible.

She whimpered as his hand moved around to her bottom and down her leg, then up under her gown, massaging her bare hips, moving to the inside of her thigh. His fingers moved into secret places, drawing out her moistness as he made lovely, circular movements that brought out an aching desire she had never felt before. What was this magical thing he was doing to her? He made her want to move her tongue wantonly over his lips, made her want to open up to him; he brought forth a wonderful, agonizing throbbing from somewhere deep inside that made her cry out his name over and over when his lips left her own.

He pushed up her gown and moved on top of her, and she knew what he wanted. To her amazement she wanted it just as much, could hardly wait for him to unbutton his longjohns. It had all happened in what seemed seconds. Never had she wanted a man this way, with such utter agony and passion, with such sudden wantonness.

She cried out when he entered her, and he covered her mouth with his own, running his tongue deep, just as he ran himself deep inside her belly, filling her with his manliness, making her arch up to him in sweet abandon in the most joyful act she had ever experienced. There seemed no limit to her ecstasy as he filled her hard and deep. She could not get over the fact that she wanted him, that she was enjoying this act, that she wanted to take him and take him like some kind of harlot.

The ecstasy of finally being inside Marybeth MacKinder Rivers was more than Josh could handle, especially after going so long without a woman. His life spilled into her sooner than he would have liked. He shuddered with the ecstasy of the deep relief. He rested on his elbows then, still on top of her, breathing deeply, kissing her eyes.

"I'm sorry. I wanted it to last longer for you. I know you were enjoying it, and I wanted that for you more than anything." He kissed her gently.

"Oh, Josh," she whispered, reaching around his neck and drawing him to her. "What was it you did to me? The way you touched me, it was so beautiful. It was just like you said it would be—that I would take pleasure in it, too."

He frowned, wondering if she meant Dan MacKinder had never touched her first, never brought out her own needs and desires. But he didn't want to mention the name tonight. He didn't want her to think about the bad times.

"Was I all right?" she was asking. "Did I please you?"

He couldn't help a light laugh. "Marybeth, did I seem like I wasn't enjoying it?" He could see her blush, even in the dim lamplight. "For someone who didn't think she even wanted to do this tonight, it happened awful fast," he teased.

Her eyes widened. "Oh, dear God, what must you think?"

He grinned. "I think you're wonderful, beautiful, more woman than I thought you would be. And I think I want to do this all over again." He kissed her. "I want you to enjoy and enjoy, all night, Mrs. Rivers." He kissed her again, running his tongue over her lips seductively. "I want you to know all the best things about being a woman, and I'll be enjoying the best things about being a man."

He raised up and pulled off his longjohns, and for the first time in her life she wanted to look at that part of him that had always frightened her with Dan. He was beautiful. She never thought she would enjoy looking at a naked man, or that she would delight in letting a man remove her last remnant of clothing as Josh did now. She sat up as he pulled the gown over her head.

"God, you're beautiful, Marybeth." She lay back down and closed her eyes, moving her fingers into his thick hair as he bent down to caress her breasts with his lips. His tongue moved over a nipple, and his mouth came around it, making her gasp in ecstasy. She had wanted this, yet never dreamed it was going to be this wonderful. Before she had only hoped it could be beautiful, imagined it. Now it was real. She whispered his name as his lips kissed and caressed, moving to the other breast, moving over her belly, lightly kissing at private places Dan MacKinder had only ravaged and abused. It was just like he had promised, beautiful, gentle, enjoyable.

In moments he was moving inside of her again, this time more slowly, with deliberate circular motions that made her wild with desire. He raised up, massaging her breasts, drinking in her beauty as he took her. She didn't mind his looking at her; Dan had always made her feel dirty. Josh Rivers made her feel beautiful, made her understand it was all right to want and enjoy a man, made her want to please him. Her joy knew no bounds.

She grasped his muscular forearms, remembering the day of the fight, remembering John MacKinder out cold on his back. Josh Rivers had done that. He had done it because John had hurt her. She was safe with Josh. He didn't buckle under men like John MacKinder. He knew what he wanted, and he took it, yet she gave it so willingly. He *had* tricked her into this bed, but she didn't mind. She was Mrs. Joshua Rivers now, in every way, and for the first time she was glad she had come to America.

Dawn broke with the sound of birds chirping, and Danny pulling himself to his knees and looking out over the side of the wagon at his sleeping mother. "Mama," he said, grinning and showing two front teeth half grown in. He laughed a baby's soft laugh and put a fist to his mouth for a moment, then reached out again, starting to pout. "Mama."

Josh opened one eye and looked over at the boy, then gave him a little wave. Danny grinned and giggled. He plunked back down into the wagon and began sucking on the corner of a blanket. Josh studied Marybeth for a moment, wondering how a woman could look even more beautiful when her hair was tangled and her face puffy from sleep. He grinned at the thought of how surprised she had seemed that she had enjoyed their first intercourse. How many more times had they made love after that? He wasn't sure. He only knew he couldn't get enough of her, and he took great pleasure and manly pride in the fact that she had enjoyed it as much as he. He kissed her cheek. "Marybeth."

"Mmmm," she murmured, turning to him.

"Danny's awake. I think he's hungry."

She stretched and opened her eyes, studying him for a moment as though not realizing at first where she was. Then she smiled.

"Good morning, Mrs. Rivers."

"Good morning, Mr. Rivers."

"How about feeding me before you feed your son?"

She reddened and looked over at Danny, who seemed content for the moment. She looked back at Josh, reaching up and touching his tangled hair. "Whoever is the hungriest," she answered softly.

He bent down, lightly kissing her breast, drawing forth her desires all over again. Their bodies were warm and soft from sleep. He moved down, kissing her belly, her thigh, her knee. He hooked his arms under her legs and drew them apart. She was warm and relaxed and didn't mind that this time there had been no foreplay. She didn't need it to want this. She could hardly believe she was giving herself so openly, so brazenly, letting him touch and taste and explore and invade her in ways she once thought were ugly and painful.

He pushed hard and deep, and again, as she had experienced for the first time the night before, she felt the wonderful explosion while he was inside of her that she had first felt when he made magic with his fingers. It made her gasp his name and push harder. As he grasped at her hips and drew her to him, their bodies moved in perfect rhythm, and she felt on fire as his eyes drank in her naked beauty in the morning light. Danny gurgled "Mama" again, but Mama was occupied with his new Papa, praying that soon there would be another baby, one of Josh Rivers' seed. She felt his life spilling into her, and he came down close, drawing her to him and kissing her several times over.

"You satisfied now that I was telling you the truth?"

She laughed lightly and kissed him back. "Yes." She sobered. "Oh, Josh, I love you so. What would I do now if anything happened to you?"

"Nothing is going to happen to me. I told you this was all meant to be. Now you go wash and I'll change Danny and entertain him until you're ready to feed him." He sat up. "And be ready for some teasing from our friends today. We'll both get plenty of that."

"I don't mind, as long as the MacKinders don't come around and make trouble."

"They know better." He got up, reluctantly, and she watched his firm thighs and bottom as he picked up his longjohns and walked to the wash room. She heard him pour some water into a wash pan. "I'll be out in a minute. And quit worrying about the MacKinders. Our bigger worry is Indians. There has been some trouble, which is why the government is anxious to get a treaty signed. With the dangers there are out there for a man or a wagon alone, even the MacKinders aren't stupid enough to risk losing the safety of traveling in numbers."

"I suppose you're right." Marybeth could not forget the hate in John's eyes, or his threats to kill Josh. What would she do now without Josh Rivers in her life? "Is the wagon train in a lot of danger, Josh?"

"Oh, I don't think so—not with as many wagons as we have. Besides, Devon's pretty good at parleying with them; and Cap and Trapper and I have had some experience dealing with them. As long as everybody obeys orders and no one does anything stupid, we should be all right. You have to be real careful dealing with Indians."

He came back into the main room, wearing his longjohns. He leaned over and took Danny from the wagon, and Marybeth wondered if anyone could love someone as much as she loved Joshua Rivers. She sat up and picked up her gown, holding it over herself as she walked to the other room to wash. She brushed out her hair and scrubbed her teeth with baking soda and walked back into the main room wearing the nightgown. She sat down on the bed. Josh handed Danny to her and she pulled down one shoulder of the gown to expose her breast. Danny latched onto his food hungrily, and Josh grinned, sitting down beside her.

"I think I'm jealous," he told her.

She laughed lightly, meeting his eyes. "I must look terrible."

"You look prettier than I've seen you yet."

She studied the kind, brown eyes. "Are you happy, Josh? Truly? Are you really pleased?"

He kissed her mouth gently. "Don't ever ask me that again. Not ever. Right now I feel like the luckiest man in the world. We're going to make it to Oregon, Marybeth, and life is going to be good to us from now on. We both have things from the past that we have to forget now. We're starting a whole new life."

"We are, aren't we? And it's going to be a good life, a wonderful life, with a big ranch and lots of babies."

"Now you're talking." He kissed her once more and left her side, going to a window and parting the curtains to look outside. It was a bright, sunny morning. He prayed inwardly he was right about not too much danger ahead, that he was right everything would be good for them from here on. He didn't want her to worry so much about things. In the distance he noticed the MacKinders walking toward the supply store. John still used a cane. The man stopped for a moment, glancing over at the cabin.

Contrary to what Marybeth thought, Josh had not underestimated John MacKinder's threats. He had no fear of the man now, but he did not trust him, not for a minute. The man would take some watching. He turned to Marybeth, putting on a smile. "Our first full day as Mr. and Mrs. Joshua Rivers is going to be sunny and beautiful. When you're through with Danny we'll get dressed and go join Delores and Aaron for breakfast, if it isn't too late. I don't even know what time it is."

She smiled. "Right now time seems to mean nothing. I wish we could stay right here forever."

"Well, I'd like that, too, but it wouldn't be too practical. In a couple of months there will be more Indians swarming around here than either one of us could hope to see in a lifetime. If any place is going to be dangerous to live, it's right here in the thick of things. We're better off getting ourselves to Oregon." He leaned over and kissed her. "Home."

She met his eyes. "Home. It has a nice sound to it."

He gave her a smile and began pulling on his clothes. *Let's just hope we get there with no trouble*, he thought, keeping the smile on his face for Marybeth. Joshua Rivers had seen a lot of death and loss in his own life. He was as ready for security and happiness as Marybeth was, and he would fight to his dying breath to get it for her.

# Eighteen

Cap held the wagon train at Laramie for an extra day, giving animals and humans a much-needed rest, and giving Josh and Marybeth another night alone in the cabin.

Marybeth still wondered when she would wake up from the lovely dream she was living. Josh had kept every promise, and she relished the love and attention he gave her, lapping it up like a starving animal. She was a loving, generous person herself, who had been too long deprived of support and affection. Her happiness knew no bounds as she helped set up the little "home on wheels" she would be sharing with Josh until they reached Oregon.

The commander of the fort gave the Gentrys a wagon that had been abandoned there, and once again Sam and Florence set up their own wagon, with the supplies others had donated, and more supplies purchased at the fort. Marybeth admired their courage and fortitude in continuing on, determined to make it to Oregon in spite of their horrendous losses, traveling now with their only remaining child.

When Marybeth thought about Sam and Florence, her own earlier predicament seemed less painful, and now she felt almost guilty for being so happy, but there was no need for the guilt. Others were happy for them both, and all knew that disaster could strike any one of them, at any time, in the form of disease or Indians, hunger or accidents. The journey had taught them all to be grateful for the good times and happy moments, never knowing who would be the victim of random misfortune that might lie ahead.

On their second morning in the cabin, Marybeth turned tear-filled eyes to Josh, nestling into his shoulder. "I hate to leave here," she told him. "It's been like our own special heaven. I'll never forget these past two days." She kissed his neck. "And nights."

He turned on his side and drew her into his arms. "I won't either. But this is just the beginning, Marybeth. We're going to make it." He kissed her eyes, her lips. "And right now we'd better take advantage of this last little bit of privacy."

He moved on top of her. "Will we be able to do this after we leave?" she asked.

"You know how it is on that trail," he told her. He nibbled at her lips. "We'll find a way. We'll just have to be more quiet about it."

She smiled, returning his kiss and opening herself to him in sweet abandon. He took her slowly, quietly, each of them deliberately drinking in every movement and touch, giving and sharing and taking with a building intensity brought on by the anxieties of what might lie ahead. This was their special moment, and they must remember it; they must burn this magic moment into their minds and hearts and souls, and treasure it.

By the time they were through, Danny was awake and the eastern sky was red with a rising sun. Josh kissed her gently. "We'd better get going."

A tear ran out of one eye and down her face, then another and another, as she studied her handsome new husband. She reached up and hugged him tightly. "I love you, Josh. I love you so much sometimes it scares me."

"Everything will be all right," he assured her. He kissed at her tears. "Come on. Cap will be wanting to head out pretty quick. At least we have our own wagon now."

"Yes." She wiped at her tears. "I am sorry. I just ... I get so frightened something will happen to spoil it all. I never thought I could feel this way, and I don't ever want it to end."

He gave her one last kiss and stood up. "It won't. No more tears now, Marybeth. Let's get ourselves to Oregon so we can have a nice solid home under our feet. I promise you one thing. It will be bigger than this little room."

She rose to wash. "I don't care how small it is, as long as

we're safely in Oregon and still together."

They dressed and gathered their things. It was decided she would feed Danny when they got to the wagon, in case Cap was ready to leave. They walked out of their little honeymoon cabin. Marybeth looked at the closed door with tear-filled eyes and Josh put an arm around her, giving her a light hug. "Let's go, Mrs. Rivers."

The land turned into a rolling, yellow-green sea of buffalo grass, broken by rock-studded plateaus, the distant hills looking like a velvet patchwork quilt. The wagon train again crossed the North Platte, which meandered into the Sweetwater, heading almost directly west. Here the land was higher, the arid atmosphere making the nights cooler; but Josh and Marybeth had no trouble keeping warm inside the wagon. Weariness and danger and aching muscles did not deter them from quiet lovemaking deep in the night. They lay together on a feather mattress, and Josh would take her with slow thrusts, both of them kissing wildly to keep from crying out. Their love was too new and exciting to let the physical aspects of it be detered by hardship or lack of privacy. They simply closed up the canvas and forced themselves to be as quiet as possible. But sometimes Josh would whisper teasing remarks afterward that would make it impossible for Marybeth not to break into soft laughter that she could not control, and Aaron enjoyed embarrassing her the next morning by asking what she was laughing about in the middle of the night. Josh would make things worse by frowning and shrugging, saying he slept hard and didn't hear a thing.

"My Delores, she sometimes laughs in the night, too. I do not understand these women." The first time he made the remark, Delores chided her husband; both men laughed until Josh had tears in his eyes by the time he rode out of camp to hunt.

Cap positioned Josh and Marybeth's wagon directly ahead of Delores and Aaron, and behind Sam and Florence so that when Josh rode out to hunt, Marybeth would always be near people who could keep an eye on her. Josh paid Ben Harper, an eighteen-year-old young man who was strong and able, to guide the oxen while he hunted. Ben had lost his mother and two of four siblings to cholera, and he enjoyed the diversion of helping the newlyweds on what had for him so far been a boring and tragic journey.

Marybeth dreaded every morning that Josh rode out, fearing that something would prevent him from ever coming back. Whenever she heard a gunshot, she shivered with the dread it could be an Indian shooting at Josh, or perhaps some kind of outlaw. Cap had told them that from here on the wild land was peppered with men who for one reason or another had never made it to California during the gold rush, some of them men who had made it but never found their dream. They survived by robbing emigrants of horses and supplies.

Every evening when Josh rode back to the wagons, Marybeth thanked God. Evenings were often shared with the Gentrys and the Svenssons, and the three women helped each other with the endless chores of cooking, washing, unpacking at night and repacking in the mornings. Florence was a tremendous help with Danny, since the lonely woman had grown more attached to the baby, and at night Marybeth prayed over her rosary beads that one day Florence would conceive again and have a baby to help replace the terrible losses of Melinda and Toby. There were still nights when they could hear her sobbing quietly, mourning the fact that she would never even be able to visit her children's graves.

Marybeth could not help wondering how many of the women along, especially those with children, had secretly hated and dreaded the idea of the trip, but had said nothing because their men had a dream. She realized now that she would have done the same for Josh, and her love for him helped her realize why a woman would be so willing to submit herself to the deprivations of trail life, leaving behind fine homes and relatives. It had been different when she traveled with the MacKinders. She had resented and hated them, coming along only because she had no choice. Perhaps most of these women also had no choice, but at least they had the one supporting incentive that kept them going—a love for the men they followed west.

Still, for some it was a nightmare, and it was obvious more than a few harbored a deep resentment, some from the beginning, most after several weeks or months of agonizing hardships. But it was not like that for her and Josh because she had met him on the way, not followed him. And she loved him so much she could not imagine anything he could do ever affecting that love. She could never hold a gun to his head the way Wilma Sleiter had done to poor Cedrick.

She thought of them now, as she lay inside the wagon unable to sleep. She turned to Josh, needing his nearness at the memory of the horror of the Sleiter murder and suicide.

"What's wrong," he asked quietly, petting her hair.

"You awake, too?"

He sighed deeply. "I came across the camp of some shifty looking characters today. They didn't see me, but I saw them. Cap's got Devon and Trapper taking turns keeping guard, but I can't help worrying a little. I'm also upset that there isn't more game around here. The damn Forty-niners did a good job of killing everything for miles over the last couple of years. No wonder the Indians are so hostile. They need food to survive too." He stretched. "We should be able to stock up at Fort Bridger, but that's about three weeks away."

"We'll manage somehow. I'm being careful with the food."

He rubbed at her arm. "You didn't tell me what's keeping *you* awake."

She listened to a wolf's howl, a new sound she was learning not to fear. The foothills of this place Cap called Wyoming seemed to be full of new sights and sounds, plant life she had never seen before, like layered rocks lined with something Cap called lichen, and scraggly bushes with feathery growths on the ends that Cap called buck brush. "The deer love it," he had said.

"I was just thinking about the Sieiters," she said aloud to Josh, "wondering how two people can first love each other and end up hating so much that one of them kills the other. I never even loved Dan, and sometimes I regretfully wished bad things for him. I still feel guilty over being unable to truly mourn his death. Yet even though I never loved him in the beginning, and cruel as he was to me, I never could have killed him. How does it happen to someone who must have started out loving?"

"You don't know that they did. Besides, you're a much stronger person than Mrs. Sleiter was. Some people break easily, but not you."

"Or you. You watched those horrible Comancheros murder your brother, and they almost killed you." She put an arm across his chest. "Oh, how glad I am that they didn't. And I can't imagine anything that could ever change how much I love you."

He turned and pulled her closer, meeting her lips in a long, sweet kiss. Suddenly he stiffened, pulling away and putting fingers to her lips. "Don't move," he whispered.

She watched with alarm as he sat up and quietly took his pistol from its holster. It was then she thought she heard something just outside the wagon. They both waited a moment, suddenly noticing a light outside. It came close to the wagon, then got brighter as if someone was holding a burning brand against the canvas. In that instant the canvas caught fire. Marybeth screamed and began beating at it, and Joshua jumped out of the wagon.

"Hold it," she heard him order. A shot rang out and someone cried out. "Don't let him get away, Devon," Josh yelled. "Marybeth, get Danny and get out of there." Someone threw water against the side of the wagon, some of it coming through the hole and splashing onto Marybeth as she turned to grab up Danny. In the next instant Josh was at the back of the wagon. "Marybeth!" Danny wiggled awake and began to whimper as she handed the baby out to him and climbed down, too shaken to worry that she wore only her flannel gown and Josh wore only his longjohns.

Already people were shouting and asking what was going on as they climbed out of wagons. Devon was herding someone toward the central campfire that was almost burned out. Cap came hurrying over, holding up a lamp. Cowering next to Devon was John MacKinder. He held the shoulder of his broken arm, and blood seeped from a deep flesh wound.

"You sonofabitch!" Josh reached for the man, but Aaron and Cap held him back, while Devon kept a pistol steadied on John.

"Can't a man take a night stroll without being shot at?" John whined.

"You tried to set fire to our wagon! If we had been sleeping hard you could have caused your own nephew a horrible death!"

"And you are a liar, Rivers!"

"You've been caught red-handed! I heard you outside the wagon, saw someone hold a light up against it. When I looked out, you were running."

"He was running," Devon confirmed to Cap. "It was no nighttime stroll that I saw. It is Josh's bullet that cut his shoulder."

"Here's the lantern," Sam spoke up, coming from beside the wagon. "The wick's turned all the way up."

All eyes turned to John MacKinder in disgust and anger, even those who had previously determined to stay out of MacKinder affairs. Mac and Bill came hurrying to the scene, Ella following behind, wrapped in a shawl. Danny started to whimper and Marybeth put him against her shoulder, patting his bottom. "I know you hate me and Josh," she hissed at John. "But how could you stoop so low as to risk Danny being burned alive!"

"He would not have been! I only meant to leave you without a wagon!"

Josh jerked desperately to get at the man, and Sam joined in restraining him, and Sam and Cap holding his arms while Aaron crooked an arm around Josh's neck.

"Your ribs are still too battered to try to fight," Aaron growled at him. "And the man has a broken arm."

"He'll have more than a broken arm when I get to him!" Josh's eyes were burning with rage. "You bastard," he snarled at John. "You risked Danny's life, just because you couldn't stand me and Marybeth being together!" He jerked again. "I knew you'd try something, but I figured it would be against *me*, not Marybeth and Danny! I want him off this train, Cap! If he doesn't leave I'll *kill* him, I *swear* it! I don't give a damn if you *hang* me for it!"

"You can't turn him out of here," Mac growled. "We're getting into the worst of the wilderness, headed toward the mountains."

"He should have thought of that before he pulled a trick like this," Josh yelled at the man.

"I say he goes," Aaron spoke up.

"Me, too," another put in. "We can't have this constant upheaval between these two men the whole rest of the way. One of them has to go, and it isn't fair to make it Josh and Marybeth. They haven't done anything wrong."

"The man could have killed them all," Al Peters spoke up.

"I agree," Cap said. He slowly let go of Josh, while Devon continued to hold a pistol on John. "Josh, I'm trustin' you to keep your head. Neither one of you is in any condition to fight, and a fight wouldn't solve this anyway. It's obvious the first one didn't, and I'm not going to have the women and children submitted to that kind of violence again, much as I understand your feelings."

Josh glared at John, breathing deeply for self control. "I'll keep back," he snarled, "but only if he leaves—tonight! And when guards are posted, one of them stays near our wagon at all times."

"No! You can't turn him out," Mac protested again.

"You can go with him if you choose," Cap told him. "I've a mind to force you out anyway, considerin' you can be as much of a troublemaker as your son. But you are not the one who got in a fight or set fire to the Rivers wagon, so I'm givin' you your choice. I'll remind you you've got a woman along, and there are outlaws and Indians in those hills. If you've got a shred of decency in you, you'll stay with the train and with your woman. Your son brags about his strength and size. I reckon' he'll find a way to take care of himself and face up to anybody he comes across."

Aaron and Sam cautiously let go of Josh, and Mac looked around, realizing what people would think of him if he took Ella and left the wagon train. He turned to his son. "That was a damn stupid stunt!"

John gritted his teeth, the veins of his temples standing out in his anger. "Without a wagon he could not be with Marybeth," he hissed.

"For God's sake, it's done now," Mac told him. "I told you to wait until we get to Oregon."

Marybeth felt her heart pounding with fear and dread. "Wait for what!"

They both looked at her. "Danny belongs with us," he told her, the old threatening look in his eyes.

"And so do you," John added.

"She's my wife now, and Danny is my son," Josh said sharply, his fists clenching.

"You're living in sin! It wasn't a legal marriage. You aren't Catholic," John roared.

Marybeth felt her face turning crimson, felt everyone staring at them. "We were married by a priest," she answered, her voice shaking. "He wouldn't have married us if he didn't deem it legal. He knew how much we love each other, and Josh is going to convert when we get to Oregon. There wasn't time for all of that, and the priest knew it."

"Don't listen to him, Marybeth," Josh said, his voice calmer now. "He's just looking for excuses, trying to hurt you. He knows damn well the marriage was legal." He stepped a little closer to John, and John, surprisingly, stepped back from him, holding his broken arm. For the first time in her life Marybeth saw fear in John MacKinder's eyes. "You're done, MacKinder. You get some supplies together and you go find somebody else to get you to Oregon. But I'll tell you this, if I see your face again, either before we get there or after, I'll kill you. That's a promise."

John's eyes shifted to Cap. "And what if I refuse to go?"

"Then I'll keep you tied in the cook wagon the rest of the way. By day you'll walk with your wrists tied to the wagon with a length of rope and you'll walk behind it like the common criminal you are. I'll not let you loose for anything but seein' to personal needs. They've got laws in Oregon now. When we get there I'll have you tried for attempted murder, and we've got plenty of witnesses. Only trouble with the law out here is it's not quite as civilized as it is back east. Hard tellin' what the punishment would be. Leavin' this wagon train is a lot better than your other options."

John's dark eyes turned to Marybeth, and she shivered at the look she saw there. He moved his eyes over her hungrily, making her feel like a harlot, before he turned his gaze to his father. "We never should have left Ireland," he hissed. "And you never should have let Dan marry her instead of me!" He stormed away, and Mac looked at Ella, whose eyes were tearing. She walked away without a word and Mac followed.

"Devon, you go along and make sure he does what I told him," Cap told the scout. Devon nodded and walked off into the darkness.

Josh stared after them, then turned angry eyes to Cap. "I don't trust him. I want our wagon watched!"

"It will be. If there's no sign of him after we get past Fort Bridger and Fort Hall, I expect you can rest easier. If he's smart, he'll head back toward Laramie and hope to hook up with another wagon train. I just pity the ones who take him on." The man grasped Josh's arm and squeezed. "You two all right?"

Josh looked down at a shaken Marybeth and put an arm around her shoulders. She could still feel his rage in the grip. "By God's grace," Josh answered. "We were both having trouble sleeping. I was wide awake and I heard something. God only knows what would have happened if we were sleeping soundly. The way that canvas went up, he must have poured some of the coal oil onto it before he set the wick to it."

"Devon and I will see that he goes. You stay out of it, understand?"

"It won't be easy."

"I know that. But you have a wife and child who depend on you now. There's no sense riskin' your neck if you don't have to. I was afraid if you lit into him in front of his pa, John bein' still wounded and all, his pa would have lit into you. A couple of good blows to your middle could have done you in good."

"Some things are worth the pain."

"And you can't go flyin' off any more. You've got

responsibilities. As long as you've got help and we've got laws, there's no sense usin' up your energies on trash like John MacKinder. We might need you for more important things. We've got a long way to go yet, Josh. We need you to hunt, and we might need your shootin' skills. Most of all, we need you completely healthy, and so does Marybeth."

The man left them, and Marybeth patted Danny's back, resting the baby on her shoulder. "Cap's right. Let him go, Josh. He's lost now, and he knows it. Did you see how he backed away from you?"

He turned and walked to the wagon, taking his pants from a nail and pulling them on. "We'll see about patching the canvas when it's light. You get back inside and tend to Danny."

"What are you going to do?"

"I'm going to go have a smoke with Ben and Trapper. I'm too wound up now to sleep."

"You've got to try to get some rest before morning."

"I'll manage." He sighed deeply, putting a hand to her hair. "A man like that ought to be dead," he said then. "I won't rest easy until we go a hell of a long time without seeing a sign of him. In the meantime, I'll not let him ever get near you, Marybeth. So you just climb in that wagon and get some rest. I just wish to hell I could have seen better. I didn't mean for that bullet to just graze his shoulder. I wish it would have gone right through his black heart!"

He reached inside the wagon again and picked up a shirt.

"Josh, will you come back later? Please don't let me lie here alone worrying about you."

He leaned down and kissed her lightly. "There is nothing to worry about. I just need some time to cool down." He took the baby from her and held him until she climbed back into the wagon. He handed Danny up to her. "I'll be back soon," he promised. He walked off into the darkness, and Marybeth sank down into the feather mattress, keeping Danny beside her. She lay staring into darkness, listening to loud voices in the distance. She knew it would be John and Mac.

She closed her eyes against tears, feeling sorry for Ella,

thinking back to Ireland and how much had happened since the terrible potato famine. Apart from little Danny, Josh Rivers was the first good thing that had come into her life since that awful time of losing her mother and being married to Dan MacKinder. Josh had been her husband only one week, and already it was difficult to imagine life without him.

The loud voices continued, as well as the sound of someone banging things together—*Probably John trying to pack*, she thought.

At the MacKinder wagon Mac brought a horse and saddle to John. "I bought her off Beckman. He was the only one who would consider selling me a horse," he spoke up. "She's not much for speed, but she's strong."

"Looks like a worthless nag to me," John grumbled. He began tying a sack full of supplies to the pommel of the saddle, hardly noticing the hurt look in his father's eyes.

"It was the best I could do. If you hadn't pulled such a stupid trick, it would not be necessary," Mac answered. "I told you to wait until we get to Oregon." He turned and walked to his wagon, coming back with a brand new rifle he had purchased at Fort Laramie. "Here. You'll be needing this worse than I will."

John turned, looking down at the rifle. He took hold of it with his strong hand. "Worth a lot more than the horse, that's sure."

Mac handed him a leather bag full of ammunition. "We'll be praying for you, son. Just because you're kicked off this train doesn't mean you have to be far away. A man could get lost easy in these hills. You hang back, stay close if you can, meet up with us in Oregon. We'll take care of unfinished business then."

"I'll try to stay close. I ought to shoot down Josh Rivers first chance I get, is what I ought to do."

"No. They'd know it was you. I don't want you being a hunted criminal. We'll find a way when we get to Oregon. You've just got to be patient, son."

John shoved the rifle into a boot on the old, worn saddle that had come with the horse. "Patience is something I have little of when it comes to Marybeth MacKinder." He met his father's eyes. "Good-bye, Father."

Mac squeezed his arm. "Good-bye, son. Stay alert. And stay close."

"I will try to do both." John looked over at his mother. Their eyes held for a moment. John could not remember the last time he had thought of her as anything but his father's wife, the woman who cooked his meals and washed his clothes. He felt the trace of an urge to hug her, but almost all feelings of affection had vanished when she favored Dan marrying Marybeth instead of himself. Dan had always come first in her eyes, and John could not quite forgive her for it. Ella in turn wanted to embrace her son, but Mac had taught them both at an early age that hugging was a "sissy" thing to do.

"Good-bye, Mother," John spoke up. She nodded to him, holding her chin high, hiding the urge to cry. Mac didn't like weeping women.

John mounted up. "I will see you in Oregon." He nodded to Bill Stone and turned his horse, heading east, away from the wagon train.

Back at her wagon Marybeth heard the sound of a horse riding off. Several minutes later, after her eyes had begun to close in a fitful sleep, someone moved inside the wagon. She jumped awake at first, remembering the fire, and John MacKinder's threats.

"It's just me," she heard Josh saying. A moment later he crawled under the blankets with her, and she gently moved Danny to her other side and snuggled up against Josh.

"Hold me, Josh," she whispered.

He drew her close, kissing her hair. "He's gone," he told her. "I just hope to hell it's for good."

# Nineteen

The wagon train lumbered on over an undulating sea of yellow grass that sported clusters of cottonwood trees along the Sweetwater. An array of small to medium-sized rocks dotted the landscape and made walking difficult for both humans and animals, causing unending problems with well-worn wagons. Cap had strayed slightly from the main trail because of lack of grass for grazing. Both grass and game along the now well-used trail was becoming more and more scarce, gobbled up by the thousands who had gone to California over the last two years. The trail continued to be littered with the bones of oxen and other animals that had died along the way, as well as with rotting, discarded furniture and lonely graves.

Food became so scarce that women began looking for edible berries, and one man accidentally shot another in the leg when he fired his rifle wildly after spotting a rabbit. While Devon dug the bullet from the screaming victim, Cap gave orders that no one was to touch his gun unless ordered to do so under an emergency. "Leave the huntin' to Josh and the scouts."

The food scarcity compelled Josh to ride farther from the wagon train to find game than Marybeth liked. She worried not only about outlaws, but about being followed by John MacKinder. For the next two weeks, as they neared Fort Bridger, there was no sign of him. She wished she could feel sorry for him, a greenhorn alone in this new wilderness, but she could not. She could only imagine the wagon on fire and little Danny dying a horrible death.

By day her worries were soothed by the changing land, the almost constant sunshine and the cool nights, the sight of the snow-covered mountains on the northern horizon, which Cap told her were called the Bighorns because of Bighorn sheep that roamed there in abundance; and the Rocky Mountains to the west, to which they came closer every day. And every evening she breathed a sigh of relief when Josh returned to camp again, especially the night he showed up with two antelope and two rabbits draped over his pack horse. Several women with hungry children quickly converged to help clean the animals and divide the meat as evenly as possible.

"It's damn good to have somebody who can ride out and hunt for us," Cap told them over the night's campfire. He licked grease from his fingers. "I've been on wagon trains where folks got so hungry they was about ready to kill their own animals and eat them. Only thing that kept them from that was the thought of bein' stranded in the middle of Indian country."

Josh fed a piece of bread to Danny, who sat on his lap. "I'll keep trying, but there isn't much out there."

"Should get better in another month to six weeks. The animals will come down out of the mountains because of winter comin' on."

"In August?" Marybeth was surprised. "Since I have been in this country, it seems August is the hottest time of the year."

Cap chuckled. "Maybe in the East it is. Out on the plains, too. But in this country, from August on, you learn not to count on how the weather is *supposed* to be. You take a day at a time and hope for the best, especially when we get farther into the mountains. I've known it to blizzard up there the first of September. 'Course them early snows generally don't last, but when they come, they come hard and bury you deep for a few days.

"Don't you be worryin', though. I'm just givin' you the worst picture. If things go like normal, we should make it to Oregon sometime in October, and once we get through the Rockies in Idaho country, we get into lower, flatter land again where the weather shouldn't be too bad. There's mountains in Oregon, but once you get to the Willamette Valley, the weather is pretty decent. 'Course they can get some pretty wild storms there in winter, what with the Pacific Ocean bein' so close, but you'll be in a nice, cozy cabin by then."

He winked at her and she smiled, feeling the reality of a home in Oregon with Josh coming even closer.

"We taking Sublette's Cutoff?" Trapper asked Cap.

Cap threw a bone aside. "I've been thinkin' on it. It's a hard decision. If we head down to Fort Bridger, we can stock up a little. But if we just go directly west on the cutoff, we'll save ourselves five, maybe six days of travel. In another week or so we'd be at Fort Hall." He looked at Josh, who was handing Danny to Marybeth. "Which do you think is best—takin' the south loop and pickin' up supplies at Bridger, or takin' the cutoff and savin' a week's travel?"

Josh finished lighting a thin cigar. "I'm not the one to ask. I'm as new to this trail as the rest of them."

"Maybe so, but you've got a feel for the land, and you have a good idea of how low the rations are. Can we afford to pass over Fort Bridger?"

Josh puffed the cigar for a moment. "If it will save a week's travel and there will be plenty of supplies at Fort Hall, we can."

"Well, I don't know about plenty, but there will be supplies. And if we can save a week's travel, we can afford to rest an extra day or so after we get there. I expect folks would like that."

"I'm going to put Danny to sleep," Marybeth told Josh, rising. "You men can make your plans."

They all bid her good-night, and she carried Danny to the wagon, laying him inside. She started to climb up when she heard her name spoken softly by a woman. She turned, looking into the darkness beyond the wagon, and Ella stepped from the shadows. "Hello, Ella," she said quietly.

Somewhere in the distance a wolf howled as the woman came closer, swallowing nervously before she spoke. "Mac is sleeping hard from too much whiskey," she told Marybeth. "Ever since ... since John was sent away ... he's been drinking more."

Marybeth sighed. "I'm sorry. I know what he's like when he drinks. And I'm sorry about John—not for him, but for you. But he brought it on himself, Ella."

"I know that. I am not here to accuse you of anything

or make excuses for him. I just thought—as long as Mac is sleeping—maybe you would let me see Danny for a little while."

Marybeth studied the woman's eyes, always afraid of a MacKinder trick. But after her last conversation with Ella, she was sure the woman was sincere. "I guess so, but I do not want him taken from the wagon. You can climb inside and see him for a while."

Ella nodded, struggling, as always, to show no emotion. "Thank you." She climbed into the wagon, and Marybeth heard her coo Danny's name like any doting grandmother. She felt sorry that the woman couldn't see more of the boy, but Marybeth refused to allow Danny to go near Mac, and Mac would not allow Ella to come and see him.

She waited outside, deciding to let the woman have time alone with the boy. After several minutes, Josh approached the wagon, smiling when he saw Marybeth standing outside. "I figured you'd be inside waiting for me," he told her, putting his arms around her and drawing her close.

She kissed his cheek and pulled away from him. "Ella is in the wagon with Danny."

"Ella?" His alarm was immediate, and he looked around into the darkness.

"It's all right. Mac is in a drunken sleep. She wanted to see Danny, and this was her chance. I said it was all right as long as Danny didn't leave the wagon."

He sighed impatiently. "I suppose it is. I just don't want Mac storming over here causing problems."

"He won't." The words came from Ella herself, as she came out of the wagon. Josh reached up to help her down, and she looked at him as though shocked that he would offer. She waved him off. "No man has helped me do anything in thirty years. No sense starting now." She climbed down by herself and looked at Marybeth. "Thank you again. If I can find a way, I will come again."

"It's all right with us, as long as there is no trouble with Mac."

The woman nodded and hurried off into the darkness. Marybeth looked up at Josh, blinking back tears. "I might have ended up like her." Josh pulled her into his arms and she rested her head against his chest. "Oh, Josh, thank God I found you."

He kissed her hair. "Let's get inside and get Danny to sleep."

He helped her inside and pulled down the end canvas flaps while she lit a lamp and fixed Danny's bed in a corner of the cramped wagon. There was just enough room in the center of the wagon to roll out the feather mattress at night, but neither Josh nor Marybeth minded having to sleep close.

"I must look a mess," she said as she unlaced her shoes. She was grateful for the flat-soled, leather shoes Josh had bought for her at Fort Laramie. They looked more like a man's boot, but Marybeth didn't care. All that mattered was that they were much more comfortable than the shoes she had been wearing.

"You look fine. Help me get these boots off."

She held the boots while he pulled his feet out of them. "I need a bath," she answered. "And I long to wash my hair."

"Your hat keeps the dust out of it, and you brush it out every morning and night. Nobody can be their best on a trip like this, so just remember you aren't alone."

She unbuttoned her blouse and scooted out of her tattered skirt. "I just wish I could look prettier for you."

He laughed lightly, pulling off his shirt and pants. "You'd be beautiful if you were covered with mud. And how do you think *I* feel? I'd like to be all scrubbed up and wear my best clothes for you. We're stuck with things as they are for now. We're getting into much dryer country now, Marybeth. We have to conserve our fresh water more than ever. But Cap says up in the mountains, the streams flow as clear as glass. If we come across water like that, he says it's safe to drink. Maybe up there you and I can find a place to take a bath together. Sounds like fun to me."

She smiled and blushed at the thought of it, and Josh moved closer as she reached for her nightgown. He grasped her hand and kissed her cheek lightly. "Leave it off." Before she could answer, he met her mouth in a soft, sweet kiss, moving his fingers under the lacy strap of her cotton camisole and drawing it down over her shoulder. He moved his lips to her neck, pulling

244

off the other strap and tugging the camisole down to her waist.

"Josh, we've agreed we can't do this too often," she whispered. "There isn't enough water for washing."

"We'll just have to go thirsty then. It's better than this craving hunger I have for you," he said softly, kissing lightly at her breasts and moving his lips to taste their sweet fruits.

She wanted to object more strongly, feeling self-conscious about being dusty and ragged. But then she realized he was the same way, and she didn't even care. And how could she say no to him when he gently tasted her breasts this way, almost like a hungry child. He had a need, and she never minded fulfilling that need, for he always took her with such gentleness and respect. "Cap would be angry that we'll have to use water for washing," she said as he laid her back into the feather mattress, his lips lingering at her breasts.

"Cap doesn't have to know," he answered softly, moving his lips back to her throat as with one hand he untied the camisole and pushed it open. "And if he had a woman pretty as you in his own wagon, he'd forget about the water supply, too."

He kissed her lightly, then raised up a little, meeting her eyes in the dim lamplight. "You think we're the only ones going against the rules?" He grinned. "This journey might have its pain and hardship, Marybeth, but the needs of a man and woman don't change. Maybe we can't do this as often as we'd like and can't fancy and perfume ourselves up for it, but by God I love you, and I need my new wife. Things are going to get worse instead of better for a while, so let's take what we can get for the moment."

She watched his eyes. "I hate having to be so quiet about it," she whispered. She raised her hips, letting him pull off her bloomers. "It will be so nice when we're in a real house, with a real bedroom and a real bed."

"That it will, my darling," he answered, mimicking her Irish accent.

She leaned up and met his lips in an effort not to giggle, but they laughed a smothered laugh with their mouths together as he moved on top of her. She opened herself willingly, and in the next moment the laughter turned to sweet moans of ecstasy when he entered her in one quick, hard thrust. After that they moved slowly, quietly, loving each other too much to care about comfort and bathing and perfumed hair. What mattered was that one never knew what the next day would bring. What mattered was that they were here, together, alive, well and in love. They made up for lack of privacy as best they could, keeping as quiet as possible while outside night birds called and wolves howled … and John MacKinder struggled as best he could through wild country he knew nothing about, determined to stay within riding distance of the wagon train.

They chose Sublette's Cutoff, taking the more direct route to Fort Hall to save time. Oxen strained up steep, rocky embankments and down again, and already people were discarding more of their personal items to make the wagons lighter. Some women wept, others only watched with cold eyes as precious belongings were tossed aside. Men's items, such as heavy tools, were usually not considered dispensable. Hammers and hatchets stayed, while china, beds and rockers went, putting new strains on relationships already tested nearly to the limit. Still, there were no more Sleiter incidents.

It was toward the end of the cutoff that tragedy struck again, always too sudden. A rattler caused the head oxen of the Peters wagon to balk and veer off the beaten path. Al Peters shouted and cursed as he snapped his whip in an effort to get the animals headed in the right direction again, while old Tillie James, Bess Peters' mother, clung to the wagon seat. The woman seldom walked, finding it too difficult for her aging legs.

The lead oxen swerved, while others held up their wagons and waited for Peters to get back into line. The lead oxen bolted one way, while those behind them went another, and Al kept whipping at all six of them. The animals made a sudden, sharp half turn bringing the wagon around in an arc, and before Al could bring the powerful animals under control, the right front wheel of his wagon rolled up onto a high, round rock, causing the right side to suddenly tip up so high everyone thought the entire wagon would fall over. Tillie lost her balance and went rolling off the wagon seat, while Bess screamed in horror.

The oxen kept going, pulling the wagon in such a sharp circle that it slid off the rock, and before Al could stop the team, the left back wheel ran over Tillie James. By then several other men had run to Al's aid, finally getting the oxen under control. Marybeth ran with Josh to where Bess was bent over her mother. She pulled the old woman into her arms, and it was obvious by the way her head dropped back that her neck was broken. Marybeth turned away from the sight, burying her head against Josh's chest.

"Somebody get Cap," someone called out.

For the next few minutes, as everyone stared in shock and sorrow, the only sound that could be heard was Bess' pitiful sobbing, and her husband's soft-spoken words as he attempted to comfort her.

"Somebody dig a grave," she heard Cap saying then. "Aaron, you and Josh check out the Peters' wagon. See if there's any damage."

Josh patted Marybeth's shoulder and left her, and she wiped at her eyes and turned to Delores. The two women put their arms around each other, while Florence, the memory of the graves of her children still too fresh in her mind, turned away, hurrying back to her wagon and climbing inside. She was not going to watch another burial.

With expediency that would seem cruel and ludicrous in any other situation, a hole was dug, Tillie's body was wrapped in blankets, and men lowered it into the lonely grave. They were nearing the mountains, and time was of the utmost importance. The wagons had to keep going. Again Raymond Cornwall read from the Good Book, and Marybeth prayed over her beads. Men shoveled dirt into the grave and piled rocks on top of it to keep away the wolves.

Bess knelt beside the grave and lay over the rocks, weeping. Al, his face stained from his own tears, bent over her and gently but forcefully pulled her away. "We've got to go, Bess."

"Not this soon," she wept. "I didn't even … get to tell her … good-bye." The Peters children, Andy, thirteen, and Lilly, ten, both stood on the other side of the grave, crying and holding hands.

Marybeth turned and wept against Josh's chest, again imagining the horror of being without him.

"It … can't be," Bess sobbed. "It can't be! Just this morning she was saying how good she felt … talking about finishing a quilt … laughing with the children."

"Give her another fifteen minutes," Cap told Al Peters. "I'm sorry, Al." Cap motioned to the man to come and talk to Josh and Aaron. Josh kept an arm around Marybeth as the men talked. "Al, you've got a cracked axle, and one of the oxen broke a leg," Cap told the man.

Al turned away and rubbed at his eyes.

"With five oxen, you'll only be able hitch four. You can alternate each day so one of them gets a rest. But we're headed into even higher country and you've got a bigger wagon than most of the others. It's gonna put a strain on only four oxen. If there's anything you can get rid of, do it. I'm sorry to have to put this extra burden on you."

Al rubbed at his neck. "I know."

Cap put a hand to the man's back, then walked away.

"Al, I think the wagon itself will make it if you lighten it up," Josh told him. "The crack has weakened the axle, but if you're careful, it will hang together. It might help to lash it, if we can find some rawhide. If we wet the rawhide first and pull it around good and tight, it will draw the crack together even tighter as it dries and shrinks."

Al nodded. "Okay. I'll see what I've got." He turned bloodshot eyes to Josh. "The only really heavy item we've got left is a chest-size music box that her mother brought over from Germany. She treasured it and we promised to let her bring it." His tears spilled over. "I can't ask Bess to just dump it off, especially not now. It would kill her."

Josh removed his hat and ran a hand through his hair. "Look, for the time being, don't tell Cap. We aren't that far from

Fort Hall. When we get there, I'll buy a couple more oxen and you can load the music box into our wagon. We'll make room for it somehow. Our wagon is a lot smaller. With two more oxen we should be able to handle the extra weight."

Al wiped at his tears. "I could get a couple more oxen myself. You don't have to do that."

"Even with more oxen, you can't take a chance with that cracked axle, and if you stop to put on a whole new one, you'll fall behind and never catch up, not in this country. And right now I think it's important for your wife to stay with friends for the rest of the journey."

Al nodded, watching his wife and children. "Yeah, you're right." He met Josh's eyes. "I appreciate it, Josh." He put out his hand and Josh shook it.

"I can't guarantee I won't have my own problems and we won't have to dump the music box ourselves, but we'll give it a try. At least it gives Bess some time to get over this first shock."

"Yeah," Al answered quietly. He sighed and walked back to his wife, and everyone left the graveside to give the family a few minutes alone. Josh and Marybeth headed back toward their wagon, pulling Danny behind them. One of Josh's horses stood saddled and ready for Josh to go hunting. "I'm glad you offered to take the music box, Josh," Marybeth told him.

"All we have to do is find a place to put it. I reckon I'll end up sleeping outside on the ground after all." She looked up at him and he kissed her tears, then pulled her into his arms, both of them frustrated over the difficulty of not being able to share their love the way they would like. "It sure will be nice to get to Oregon, won't it?"

"Yes," she whispered. She kissed his cheek. "We'll find ways to be together, Josh." He met her lips and kissed her tenderly, running a hand through her hair.

"Sure we will," he said softly.

For a moment she cried softly on his shoulder. "Oh, Josh, poor Bess. It's so sudden and cruel."

"I know, honey, I know. Do you want to keep walking, or do you want to ride in the wagon for a while?"

She pulled away and took a handkerchief from a pocket on her skirt. "I'll walk with Delores," she said, wiping at her eyes. She looked up at him. "Please stay with the wagon train today. Don't go hunting. I want you near."

"I have to go, Marybeth. It's too important."

She met his eyes, loving him all the more for offering to take the music box, proud of his generosity in doing most of the hunting. How utterly different he was from a MacKinder man. "I know. I'm sorry. It's just—seeing that grave dug and all…"

He grasped her arms. "Marybeth, the only graves with our names on them are going to be in Oregon, and they won't be dug for a lot of years yet. Nothing is going to happen. How many times have I told you we're supposed to be together? We haven't gone through all this hell to let anything keep us from reaching our dream. Tillie James is dead, but I'm standing right here alive and well, and so are you. Now where's that strong, fiesty woman I married?"

She smiled through tears. "She isn't feeling so strong today."

He kissed her cheek. "It will pass, Marybeth. My heart hurts for them as much as yours does. Besides, I'm to stay behind until the wagons are out of sight, then shoot the ox with the broken leg. We didn't want to do it while Bess was around."

Marybeth nodded. "I understand."

From the front of the wagon train Cap whistled. "Everybody gather up! We can make a few miles yet."

People quietly prepared to go on. Al half dragged his sobbing wife to their wagon, where Josh and Aaron had already hitched the spare ox. They had loaded the extra yoke onto the side of Aaron's wagon. Bess and the children climbed inside, and the wagon train was underway. Marybeth watched Josh mount up. He rode his horse back a ways, and she walked on with Delores, pulling Danny behind her in the wagon.

Her heart ached fiercely for Bess and the fresh grave they left behind. It was frightening to think how a person could be so alive one moment, and dead the next. She wept as she walked. It was perhaps fifteen minutes later that she heard the gunshot in the distance. The ox was dead. Marybeth felt sorry for it. None of them could realize their dreams about starting over in a new land without the strong, dependable brutes that got them there. The oxen seemed as much a part of the triumphs and tragedies of this journey as the people.

# Twenty

John led his horse by the reins, walking gingerly because of blisters on his rear end. "Damn American saddles," he grumbled. He looked at the aging mare that walked behind him. "No wonder Beckman sold you," he growled at the animal. "You're worthless. Pa should not have given a nickel for you."

He trudged through a rocky, heavily forested area, trying to keep panic from setting in. He had managed to stay within a day's ride of the wagon train, always hanging behind it so the scouts, who usually stayed ahead of the wagons, would not spot him. But yesterday he had spotted a deer. His hefty appetite longed for the meat, and he had shot at the animal, hitting it but not killing it. The deer had bounded away, and John had gone after it. By the time he realized the old, slow mare his father had purchased for him would never keep up with the animal, he was totally lost.

"That damn deer is probably lying dead somewhere, food for wolves, while I go hungry," he grumbled at the horse. "It's all your fault."

The horse just snorted and shook its head. John halted, looking around the unfamiliar terrain. "I will probably die in this godforsaken place," he said aloud. He turned to the horse. "And I was wrong. It wouldn't be your fault, you useless old woman. It would be Josh Rivers' fault!"

The horse's eyes widened at the loudly growled words, and she reared back as though afraid of the man. John just grinned. "So, you are afraid of me, too," he said. He laughed. "Some day there will be fear in Josh Rivers' eyes when he sees me ... and I will see the fear in dear Marybeth's eyes also."

He looked around again, his stomach growling, his own fear

building at realizing he had no idea which way to go. Evening was coming on, and there was a chill in the air, reminding him that he was in country where Cap said the weather could be very unpredictable. He did not relish the thought of wandering these woods until a mountain blizzard came along. He had not experienced such a thing, but some of the winters in New York had been unbelievably cold and snowy; the way Cap described it, those winters were nothing compared to a mountain winter.

"I've got to figure out something or I am going to die here," he told the horse. Somehow it was comforting to talk out loud, even if it was to an animal. "If hunger does not kill me, the winter will. This is all their fault, Josh Rivers, Marybeth, Cap—*all* of them! They might as well have shot me! Sending me out here—me, a man who does not know about this land. It is the same as a death sentence, and they knew it! If I ever get out of this, they will all pay!"

He headed up a steep embankment, looking for a good place to make camp for the night. It was then he heard the laughter, sounding like several men. His first thought was Indians, a danger he dreaded most. He had not the slightest idea how to converse with them. On previous encounters, Devon had always done the talking. The only thing John knew was that sometimes they could be appeased with a bottle of whiskey. Mac had given him four bottles. He closed his eyes at the memory, missing his father. *We will be together again, Father, you will see. And together we will get Danny.*

He didn't want to talk aloud now. First he had to find out where the voices were coming from. He tied the old mare and took the rifle from it that Mac had given him for protection. It was a good rifle, one of the newest in repeaters. He moved to the top of the embankment to see four men sitting around a campfire on a flatter piece of ground just on the other side of the ridge. Four tents were erected around them, and the four sat leaning against saddles, drinking whiskey.

"Hurry it up, Pat," one of them called, turning his gaze to one of the tents. "We're waitin' our turn." John could hear an odd squealing sound coming from inside the tent. He stayed low, studying the camp setting, noticing about eight horses tied nearby. Apparently there was one more man in the tent, making at least five all together. It was then he spotted the naked body of a man, lashed to a fir tree. He looked bloody, and his head hung oddly. John realized he must be dead. He also realized by the dead man's long, straight hair that he was an Indian.

"You want somethin', mister?"

John whirled at the voice behind him, and a bearded, grizzly-looking man wearing a deerskin jacket chuckled, as he held a pistol on John. John instantly told himself not to look afraid. No MacKinder man showed fear. He took a deep breath, realizing these men were probably some of the wild mountain men who had stayed in the hills after failing to make it to California, some who had headed back home and simply never made it. Cap had told them about such men, but these were the first John had seen.

He stood straighter, making sure the man with the gun realized how big he was, but he warned himself that this was an unfamiliar setting, the men just over the ridge and the one with the pistol unlike any men he had known before. For once he would not brag. After all, although he had taken his arm from the sling, it was still not healed. He was in no shape to get himself into a fight. Besides, he was used to fists, not guns.

"I am lost," he admitted. "I was part of a wagon train and I rode out to hunt for them. But I am not familiar with this country, and I am afraid I lost my way." He looked down at the pistol and put out his hand. "You do not need that gun. I am called John MacKinder, and I am from a land called Ireland. I am glad to find someone who might be able to help me."

The man with the pistol watched him warily. "I ain't one to shake hands with strangers." He looked around. "You alone then?"

"I am. And I would consider it a great favor if you or one of your friends could help me find the wagon trail."

The man looked him over. "You're a big one. Don't seem like a big man like you should have much trouble makin' his way out here."

"I told you, I do not know this land."

"Why'd they send you out to hunt then?"

"We all take our turns. I shot at a deer and chased it. By the time I realized I was not going to find it, I had lost my way."

The man glanced at his horse and chuckled. "With a nag like that, it's no wonder you didn't catch it."

John grinned nervously. "I agree. My family brought no horses along. I borrowed this one." He could not tell the man the truth about how he had come to be here. He had no idea how men like this would feel about someone cast out of a wagon train. "I … I have some whiskey. I will gladly share some with you and your friends, if I might have some food in return, and if you would consider helping me find the trail in the morning. Do you know which way it is?"

The man eyed him cautiously. "You put that rifle away, and I might consider your offer."

John nodded, turning and shoving the rifle into its boot. "What you limpin' for?" the man asked as he watched John walk.

John rubbed self-consciously at his back end. "I am not used to a lot of riding. Back in Ireland my family used mostly buggies—we used horses on our farm for plowing. We did ride, but not so much every day. And I do not like American saddles."

The man burst out laughing. "You really *are* a greenhorn, aren't you?"

John felt his anger rising but told himself he could not afford to lose it here. He put on a grin. "I told you I was." He kept hold of his horse's reins, realizing that if he did have to flee these men, the old mare would never outrun them. His only choice was to be friendly and unchallenging for the moment. "How about my offer—whiskey for food and directions?"

The man finally holstered his pistol. "You see the Indian down there?"

John nodded. "I know nothing about these American Indians. How you treat them is your own business, not mine."

The man grinned a little. "That's a good way to look at it, MacKinder. You have a woman with the wagon train?"

John's blood rushed with the thought of Marybeth, but he

only said "No."

"Well, we've got one down there in that camp. We came across an Indian couple alone. They're young—maybe they were on some kind of Indian honeymoon; I don't know." He laughed. "All I know is we caught them havin' a hi-ho time in the grass, and the sight of it—well, she's awful pretty, too pretty to just sit and look at. Out here, men like us don't get much chance to be with a woman. Kind of gets to you after a while."

John nodded. "I agree."

The man looked toward the sound of his comrades' laughter, and John heard another scream from the tent. The man with him met his eyes. "Usually we trade somethin' for an Indian woman. But this one came along free, know what I mean?" John nodded. "They're Crow. We ain't got much use for Crow. We figure to be long gone by the time their friends find them. You, uh, you got a need for a woman?"

John took a deep breath, again thinking of Marybeth. "It has been a long time."

"Well, then, come on down to our camp and take a turn at the little Indian gal we found. They're wild little things. You'll enjoy it."

John frowned, confused by the right and wrong of it.

"Come on, come on!" the man urged. "These things go on all the time out in these parts. It's survival of the fittest. Ain't you ever heard that? Besides, to most of us, killin' an Indian is like killin' a rabbit. And Indian women are only good for haulin' wood, cookin' meals and pleasin' a man."

John grinned. "I thought that was what *all* women were for, Indian or white."

The man laughed loudly. "How right you are, Irishman." He finally put out his hand. "I like your attitude. Name's John Hanna. Come on down to camp and meet my friends. Which would you rather do first, take care of manly needs, or eat?"

John shook his hand. "Eating would always come second for me." The man chuckled and headed up the bank. "But you men found her first," John added. "I will eat and wait my turn. Will you help me find the trail in the morning then?"

"Sure, why not?"

John followed the man over the ridge. Hanna yelled out to his friends that he was bringing in a stranger. John glanced at the dead Indian as they came closer to the camp. This was indeed an unusual land, where there was apparently no law and order. These men seemed to think nothing of killing the Indian, and raping his woman. Apparently, that was the accepted way in this wilderness. He felt an ache at his own need of a woman, and he decided it couldn't be wrong to take his turn with the Indian woman. After all, these Indians were uneducated, animal-like creatures that probably didn't have the same feelings as civilized whites.

His aching need of a woman had been magnified by the thought of Josh mating with beautiful Marybeth, taking what was rightfully John MacKinder's. He would gladly relieve his needs with the Crow woman, and some day Marybeth MacKinder would share his bed and find out what it was like to be with a *real* man.

He accepted a plate of stew from one of the other men, while yet another went inside the tent where the Indian woman lay tied. John handed the others a bottle of whiskey and bit into a juicy piece of venison. He decided a man could get used to this kind of life. What he liked most about it was its lawlessness. Apparently if a man wanted to kill another man, he just did it.

"Don't let 'em drink!" Cap ordered. "Keep to the right! Keep to the right!" Everyone struggled with oxen, mules, horses and cattle that smelled the poison water. "We'll be in the foothills of them mountains ahead by nightfall. There's fresh water there."

Marybeth pressed a handkerchief to her neck, intrigued by this strange land that could change from rolling green hills to flat, dusty, hot nothingness. She longed for the cooler mountains toward which they were headed, as they neared the area where Cap said Sublette's Cutoff met up with the regular trail again. This land seemed a myriad of desert and mountain, poison and fresh water, green grass and boulders. Her feet ached from constantly stepping on small stones. Josh preferred she ride in the wagon, but the last two days had been hot, and the water supply was very low. She didn't want to strain the oxen.

She prayed the strain on herself would not bring harm to the baby she suspected was growing in her belly. She had not told anyone yet, not even Josh. She wanted to be very sure. More than that, Josh had so much on his mind that she didn't want to place an extra worry on him. Hunting had not been good, and besides being thirsty, everyone was also hungry. Fort Hall would be a welcome sight.

She put a hand to her belly, hoping she was right about the pregnancy. Josh would be so happy. She was certain it must have happened during those two glorious days and nights she spent with Josh after their wedding. She had flowed two weeks before that, but had not had her time since then. Still, she and Josh had only been married a month, and since Danny's birth, because of nursing, she had only had two periods before the last one. But they had at least been regular, which meant that missing one now could very likely mean she really was pregnant again. She could only pray she was right. She longed to give Josh a baby; but she worried the strain of the journey might cause something to go wrong. There was a time when she was pregnant with Danny that she thought she might lose him; that was after an argument with Dan, followed by a slap that had sent her sprawling. There would be no more such heartache and misery in her life.

She shivered at the sight of the bleached bones of animals that lay scattered about the poison water hole. Never in her years in Ireland, nor even after first coming to America, did she imagine a land like that she had seen since coming west. Her nostrils stung slightly from the permeating scent of sage. It was not an unpleasant smell, and often welcome as opposed to the odor of dead animals they often passed, left behind by other wagon trains. It just seemed that sage grew everywhere and overwhelmed all other smells until one got tired of its sweet, strong scent.

She looked back at the foothills they had left two days ago, always afraid she would see John MacKinder riding farther back, but she saw nothing. She wondered if he was still alive; and if he was, where was he? Much as she wanted to forget he existed, she could not.

"All of a sudden this walking is hurting my back so," Delores said, drawing Marybeth's thoughts away from John.

Marybeth looked at Delores's swelling stomach. "It is because of the baby," she told her. "Maybe you should ride, Delores. This is your first child. You don't want anything to go wrong."

"Oh, I don't want to be a burden. All the other women are walking."

"They aren't six months pregnant." She was tempted to tell Delores her own suspicions, but decided against it. Josh should be the first to know, and it was much too soon to be sure.

Delores put a hand to her belly. She wore her cotton shirt outside of her skirt now, since she could no longer button her skirt at the waist. "Do you think we will make it to Oregon before my baby is born, Marybeth?"

"Of course we will. Cap promised, didn't he?"

"Did you have any problems with Danny?"

Marybeth thought again about Dan's beating. "No. And you won't have any problems either. But if your back is hurting you, you should ride in the wagon for a while. Don't worry about being a bother. Aaron would want you to be careful. If you don't say something to him, I will," she threatened.

Delores reddened at the thought of her pregnancy being discussed openly in front of Josh and Aaron. "No, no. I will talk to Aaron."

"Promise?"

"Yes, I promise." She smiled. "You are a good friend, Marybeth." She wiped sweat from her brow. "It will be good to get higher into the mountains again, won't it? At least we will be cooler."

"Yes, but after some of the frightening roads we have already taken, I am not so sure which is worse, the mountains or this hot, lonely flatland. It frightens me to be so high, depending on the animals to keep us from falling over a ledge. And Cap says the road gets higher and more dangerous in some places ahead."

Delores looked around. "Some of this land looks as though it doesn't even belong to the Earth that we know. I sometimes wonder, Marybeth, if there is really an Oregon out there. It seems as though we are walking into an eternal wilderness from which we will never return." She had to raise her voice above the shouting and cursing of the men who continued to steer their oxen away from the tainted water.

Marybeth looked around, studying the mountains that hovered all around them. Everywhere she looked, there were rocks and sage and alkaline soil that would grow only scrubby, prickly brush. She thought about the rich soil of Ireland, the green hills. Would anyone ever be able to plant anything in this strange land? How she prayed Cap was right about how beautiful and green Oregon was. "Yes, it does," she answered. "But surely it is true there is a beautiful land beyond the mountains, or there would not have been so many go before us."

She looked behind her then to see a rider coming. Heat waves made him look eerie and ominous, and again she thought about John; but soon she realized it was Josh who was coming. She breathed a sigh of relief. Soon they would be in the cooler foothills and in another week they would reach Fort Hall, where they hoped to find enough supplies to get them through the last part of their journey over mountain passes and into Oregon. She noticed with disappointment that again there was no meat on Josh's pack horse.

He rode closer to her and dismounted, taking the wagon handle from her and pulling Danny with one hand while he walked his horse with the other. "I don't like you walking in this heat, pulling Danny besides. He's getting too heavy."

"I am all right."

Their eyes met. They missed each other. The journey had been extra strenuous the last week, leaving them both too tired at night to spend needed energy on lovemaking. He sighed, bending down and giving her a peck on the cheek. "We'll be out of this in a day or so. After that you'll *have* to ride in the wagon most of the time. The roads will be too steep for you to be climbing them dragging this wagon behind you." He looked over at Delores. "How are you doing, Delores?"

The woman reddened and tugged at her loose shirt, making sure her belly was covered.

"She is having problems with her back," Marybeth answered for her. "I think she should ride in the wagon, Josh."

Josh nodded. "I agree. You be sure to tell Aaron, Delores. If you don't, I will."

"Marybeth has already told me the same."

Josh's horse reared slightly, smelling the water. Josh noticed everyone herded their animals past it. "Another poison water hole?"

"Yes. Cap says by tomorrow we'll be in the foothills. He knows where we can find some fresh water."

"Good. Now if I could also find some game, we'd be in a lot batter shape. I hate seeing the looks on these peoples' faces every time I come back empty-handed."

"It isn't your fault. You do the best you can, riding out there every day. It worries me so, Josh."

"I haven't seen any sign of Indians."

"It isn't just Indians I worry about." She looked ahead again. "I don't trust him, Josh."

"Well, I haven't seen any sign of him either. And you know I can take care of myself. If we're lucky, he won't survive."

"I do not like to wish bad things on anyone. But in his case, God forgive me, I cannot help it."

"Doesn't bother me one bit wishing the worst. Trouble is, bastards like MacKinder never die. That big, loud-mouthed braggart will probably find a way to hang on. He'd just better never let me see his face again." A chilly wind picked up, and dark clouds came spinning from over the top of the mountains to the west.

"Storm coming—and fast," Josh said. He handed Marybeth the wagon handle and grabbed Delores's arm. "You get on my horse. We're going to run." He helped her up, then grabbed up Danny into one arm. "Bring the wagon, Marybeth. Let's get all of you under cover."

Cap was already slowing the wagons and telling women to get inside, as rain began to pepper their faces. Marybeth was beginning to grow accustomed to the wild, unpredictable weather in this land, and learning not to be afraid of it. The wind was almost constant, a hot, dry wind that made her wonder if she would shrivel into an old-looking woman at an early age. Now the temperature dropped in a matter of seconds, the endless wind changing to cool and wet. The mountains seemed to do strange things to the weather, and often hid approaching storms until suddenly clouds broke over the mountain tops and came swirling down on whatever was on the other side.

Josh helped Delores and Marybeth into his own wagon, handing Danny up to Marybeth and hanging the little wagon on a hook outside the bigger one. He tied his horse to the back of the wagon and ran to help young Ben Harper calm the oxen. Suddenly they all heard a loud pop, with a horrendous clap of thunder coming at almost the same instant. Women screamed and children began crying at the sudden noise. Marybeth held Danny to her and rocked him, trying to calm his own wailing.

"Oh, dear God," Delores exclaimed then. "Someone's wagon is on fire!"

Stalking Bear, leader of the band of Crow warriors, knelt over the dead body of his blood brother, Black Wolf. "They put a knife through his heart," he said, rising. He turned angry, black eyes to the others. "White men did this!"

"White Feather has a bullet in the head," one of the others told him in their native tongue. "She wears no clothes. She has been used by men many times."

Stalking Bear, walked away from them to hide the pain in his eyes. Black Wolf and White Feather had come to this place in the forest to consummate their marriage. For many months Black Wolf had courted the young, pretty maiden, whom he had loved since she was but a child. Stalking Bear's rage was great. He pulled a knife from its sheath and stabbed it into the trunk of a pine tree over and over while the others watched. When he finally stopped, he was shaking.

"White men must *die* for this!"

"Two sunrises past, I see white man's wagons going by not so far from here. Perhaps they were the ones," one of the others told him.

Stalking Bear turned to face him, his bare chest shining with sweat, his jaw flexing in anger. "Red Foot and Jumping Crow, you take Black Wolf and White Feather back to the village for proper burial. Tell White Feather's mother we have gone on to seek revenge for this!" He ran his eyes over the rest of them. "We go through the flatland and find the white man's wagons. Men riding free on horses can catch them quickly. We will wait until they are in the hills, where we can use the trees and rocks for shelter." He slammed the knife back into its sheath. "Come! Let us paint our faces and pray for proper vengeance! White men must die!"

# Twenty-One

Again, those who had survived the calamities that had beset the wagon train since leaving Independence, stood over two more graves. Lightning had struck the wagon of a childless couple, setting it and its occupants aflame in an instant. Josh and two other men who had tried to get inside the wagon to rescue the man and woman were haunted by the sight of blackened, smoking bodies.

"Ashes to ashes," Raymond read. Josh shuddered at how fitting were the words.

Rain fell lightly now. Marybeth wore her hooded cape, and Josh wore a rubber raincoat, keeping it over Danny as he held the boy. Marybeth was grateful for the way Josh could keep Danny calm. The boy was growing fast, energetic and strong, and often a little too rambunctious for occasions such as funerals. Josh had a stern but gentle way of making the boy behave, and Marybeth's heart swelled with love at the way he had so easily and thoughtfully stepped in as father.

They all sang a hymn, again acutely aware of how near they all were to death's doorstep. Those left had survived windstorms, cholera, accidents, snakebite, and an array of sickness and infection. Since leaving Independence they had lost five men to death, plus five women and nine children, as well as an assortment of oxen, cattle and horses that died from over-exertion, from disease, or were stolen away in the night by Plains Indians. They had lost an additional two men and a woman, when Abel and Henrietta Lake turned back after losing all four of their children to the cholera; and when John MacKinder had been banished from the wagon train.

The oxen that belonged to the burned wagon had survived,

but two oxen belonging to another wagon had been struck down by lightning. The surviving oxen were given to the man who had lost his own.

The bodies of Harold and Eileen Rogers were lowered into their graves, and people quietly left the site while men shoveled dirt into the gaping holes.

"We'll camp right here for the night," Cap told Josh. "This thing has held us up till it's too late to go on. We'll be in those foothills to the west of us by noon tomorrow. I don't like all these delays, but there's nothing any of us can do about it. Either one of you know them people?"

Josh shook his head. "They were always pretty quiet."

Cap sighed. "Well, I've got their names wrote down on a list I always make before we start off—where they're from and all. When I head back next spring I'll get word to next of kin as best I can." He shook his head. "Every spring there's always folks at Independence or St. Louis inquirin' about family members they ain't seen in a year or more. Must be hell watchin' a daughter go off in a wagon, never knowin' for months, maybe years, whether or not she made it. The looks on their faces when I have to tell them they didn't is right pitiful."

"I can imagine," Josh answered. "Which reminds me, I've got to send a letter to my sister and younger brother back in Kansas—let them know about my new wife and that I'm all right. Any possibility of finding a letter carrier at Fort Hall?"

"Sometimes. You never know. Might be you'll have to wait till we reach Oregon. Either way, it will be months before they know." A wary look entered his eyes then as he turned to see Murray MacKinder coming toward them. "Be alert," Cap told Josh.

Josh handed Danny to Marybeth, who put her cape around him to protect him from the rain.

"You see those graves?" Mac asked, storming closer. His breath reeked of whiskey. "My son is probably dead out there somewhere, and he won't even get a decent burial! Do you realize what this is doing to me and my wife?"

"John should have thought of that before setting fire to

Josh's wagon," Cap answered.

"I want him back here," Mac snarled. "Send one of your scouts back to find him. They could do it easily enough. He's going to die out there."

"Somehow I can't imagine John MacKinder not being able to handle himself out there," Josh put in. "But if he doesn't survive, it sure won't be the fault of any of us."

"You stay out of this, Rivers! This is all your doing in the first place." The man ran his eyes over Marybeth as though she was a naked harlot. "You! You as much as killed my son!"

"That's enough, MacKinder," Josh told him, stepping closer.

"Get on back to your wagon, MacKinder," Cap told the man. "If you're worried about your son, go look for him yourself."

"You know I can't do that!"

"Then get back with your wagon and leave these people alone."

The man glowered at Marybeth, then stormed off. Marybeth watched him, trembling.

"I ought to give him what's coming to him, just like John," Josh growled.

Cap touched his arm. "You just let it be." He walked away, and Josh looked down at Marybeth.

"Don't you let anything that man says upset you."

"I don't anymore. The only thing that upsets me is the fact that they're near us at all, the memory of what life was like with them." She looked up at Josh. "I love you. Every time we bury someone I realize how much I need you. You've made me so happy, Josh."

He took Danny from her again. "God has been with us so far. He's not going to stop now. As far as MacKinder goes, I think he realizes he's lost all the way around. If he wants to be civil and admit he's been wrong, he's welcome to see his grandson." He held Danny in one arm and put the other around Marybeth. "You've beat them, Marybeth. You did what you knew was right and you've beat them. There won't be any more problems with the MacKinders."

Mac turned and watched them, then returned to camp

and kicked a bucket several feet into the air. "Damn them," he grumbled. "I feel so helpless," he said, turning to Bill Stone.

"You'll figure something out," Bill told him. "And I have a feeling John is just fine." He drank down some whiskey and offered some to Mac. "We're here for the night. Might as well take advantage of it."

Mac grabbed the bottle and guzzled. Ella watched, hoping he would drink enough to put him into another deep sleep. She longed to go and see Danny again.

John threw off his blanket, cursing at its dampness. He had managed to find a drop in the flat land, where a shelflike rock overhung a slight indention in the narrow dropoff, just enough room for a man to curl up under it and be at least a little protected from the torrential rain that had fallen the day before and had turned to a drizzle the rest of the night. He moved out from under the cramped shelter and stretched to sunshine that he hoped would dry out his clothes and gear. It was a little cooler, a good day to ride.

He scanned the horizon. Somewhere up ahead was the wagon train. He wondered if the storm had given them any problems. He walked to where his horse was tied, grateful the old mare had not managed to break free and run off on him during the terrible storm.

He took a can of beans from his gear, wishing he could taste more of the succulent deer meat John Hanna and the others had given him three nights ago. That night had been one of the most pleasant he could remember in a long time: male companionship, good food, whiskey and a woman. The young Indian girl's resistance had only made his adventure with her more exciting, especially when he imagined doing the same to Marybeth, watching her squirm and fight him, imagining her resistance turning to passionate desire once she discovered how he could make her feel.

"I've got a lot more to offer her than Josh Rivers," he grumbled, shoving a knife into the can and twisting it open.

He held the can to his lips and let beans fall into his mouth, his eyes scanning the horizon again. He wondered where Hanna and the others had gone after Hanna showed him the trail and went back to their camp. He had been surprised to find out just how close he was to the wagon route, after thinking himself lost. He wondered if the Indian woman was still with the men and decided he wouldn't mind having a squaw along himself. He could understand now why he'd heard mountain men often took Indian wives. It sounded handy, having a woman along who could be discarded whenever necessary.

But there was one woman he would not discard, if he could ever get his hands on her. He had always wanted her; and he had thought after Dan's death, it would be easy to claim her—her and the boy who rightfully should have been his own, not Dan's. It angered him that all the trouble he had taken to make Dan's death look like an accident had gone for naught. Sometimes he woke up with nightmares, remembering the look on Dan's face when in that instant before he fell into the molten steel, he realized his own brother had pushed him. But it had been necessary. John was convinced of that. The problem was, it had not been so easy stepping in and taking Dan's place.

His frustration was painful and maddening. He was determined to dog the wagon train, determined one way or another to make Marybeth his own. His feelings for her were mixed now. He still desired her, but he also hated her. Now he wanted her not because he thought he loved her, but because she made him feel defeated, and John MacKinder did not like that feeling. It was bad enough losing a contest to a man, but totally unacceptable to lose one to a woman. Marybeth had to pay. Somehow he had to win, to see the look of defeat in her eyes—defeat and desire.

He heard horses then, heard odd shouting and hooting. To the east he saw several riders coming hard. Instinct told him that in this land everything new could mean danger. He quickly pulled the old mare behind a growth of yucca bushes just barely wide enough to hide him and the horse. He watched through the shedding bushes as the riders passed by perhaps a hundred yards away.

"Indians!" He whispered the word, his heart pounding with fear. They were painted and shouting, and they looked angry. Had they found the Indian man Hanna and the others had killed? Maybe all of them were dead. Whatever had happened, these Indians were mad, and they were headed in the direction of the wagon train. His first thought was of his father and mother. Were these Indians aiming to attack the wagon train? He realized there was nothing he could do alone to help. He knew nothing about fighting Indians, and there was no way on God's Earth his old mare would catch up with and out-run the painted warriors so that he could warn the wagon train.

"All we can do is follow, you useless old nag," he grumbled. He quickly gulped down more beans, then threw the can aside. He draped his damp blanket over the horse and mounted up, waiting until the Indians were nearly out of sight. He looked around, hoping there weren't more of them, then rode off behind them, heading in the direction of the wagon train.

Marybeth stirred a pot of peas and onions, relieved when she looked up to see Josh riding in with an antelope draped over his pack horse. She loved the way he looked on a horse, was fascinated by how well he handled things like horses and guns.

"In Texas, instead of a cradle and a rubber toy, your folks stick you on a horse and put a gun in your hand when you're born," he had teased once. She was beginning to think his exaggeration was not far wrong. He dismounted and patted his horse's neck. "Sorry, boy, but you've got to stay saddled for a while yet." He turned to Marybeth, a teasing glitter in his eyes. "You care if we just eat what you're cooking there and wait till tomorrow for some of this meat?"

"I suppose not. Why?"

He grinned. "I don't want to wait for the meat to cook. Ben and Cap are going to take care of skinning the antelope and divying it up. They'll salt down our share for us. I want you to get Danny to sleep. I have something to show you."

"Show me? It's getting dark, Josh."

"Doesn't matter. Just don't ask questions. I'm taking this meat back over to Cap." He tied his lead horse and led the pack horse away. They were camped in rolling green foothills, with a steep, winding road heading upward ahead of them. Everyone gathered water from a fresh stream they had just crossed, where the animals had stopped to drink, delaying the crossing and making supper very late. The sun had set behind the mountains, and Danny was already sleepy. Marybeth climbed inside the wagon and fed him; within minutes he was sound asleep. She put him to bed and returned to the pot of peas. Josh came back and climbed into the wagon, and Marybeth watched curiously when he came back out carrying two blankets with something rolled up inside them.

"Josh Rivers, what are you doing?"

"No questions. Let's eat some, then you and I are going for a ride."

"A ride? Josh, it's dark. And what about Danny?"

"I told you not to worry about the dark. Besides there's a big, bright moon up there. And Florence said she would keep an eye on Danny. You know how attached she is to him. She'll watch him like a hawk."

She sighed. "Well, I can see I have no choice." She dished some of the peas onto a plate.

He took the plate, grinning. "You'll like it, I guarantee."

She smiled in return, dishing up some food for herself. "I have a feeling what it is, and it is more than a little embarrassing to realize others know, too."

He laughed lightly. "I never said living with me wouldn't have its embarrassing moments, did I?"

"No, but you also did not warn me that it would happen nearly every day. You are a terrible tease, Josh Rivers."

He hurriedly gobbled the peas, a man with a big appetite she knew would keep her busy in the kitchen whenever they got a house of their own. "Better to laugh and be a little embarrassed every day than to cry and be afraid, right?"

Her smile faded as she thought of the MacKinders, and her

heart swelled with love for the man who had changed it all for her. "Yes," she answered quietly.

He gave her a wink. "Hurry up and eat."

They finished their food, and Josh plunked her on his horse, then tied the blankets onto his gear. He mounted up behind her and guided the horse off into the darkness, moving an arm around her waist and pressing her close as he kissed her neck.

"Josh, how can you see where you are going?"

"Woman, you are a profound worrier, aren't you? When are you going to have confidence in my riding? Besides, horses see very well in the dark—a lot better than humans. Ole' Sunset here won't go stepping into any holes."

"I didn't know horses could see in the dark."

"There are a lot of things you don't know. I've got a lot to teach you when we get that ranch started, don't I?"

She leaned her head against his chest and enjoyed the soft, night air. "All right, I won't look and I won't worry."

"That's the spirit." He leaned around and kissed her cheek, his hand moving to her breasts. "I love you, Marybeth. There is some real rough country ahead, Cap says, the most dangerous we've come on yet. The men will be doing a lot of hauling with ropes, cutting trees to drag under the wagons on downslopes, things like that. We're going to be awful damn tired at night, and so will you be when you get done climbing some of those passes." He looked ahead, guiding his horse around boulders that looked eerie in the moonlight. "We won't be having much chance to make love, or the energy to do it." She could hear the sound of water falling then. The horse splashed across a stream. "I believe you were complaining farther back about wanting a real bath. We're going to take one."

She laughed. "Josh, are you serious? That sounds wonderful!"

"Yes, ma'am. And there's a nice private place over here where we can do some catching up on other things."

A shiver of sweet desire moved through her. It had been so long since they could make love in complete freedom, outside the confines of the cramped wagon, or been able to give vent to their burning desires. "But the water must be so cold," she protested.

"Not this water." He rode a little way past the waterfall and dismounted, helping her down. "Stay right here. And don't be afraid. You can't see the wagon train, but Devon knows where we are, and a gunshot will bring him fast. I checked it out real good—no bear dens or anything like that around." He removed the blankets, spreading them out on a dark spot that looked like grass. "I've got a change of clothes here for me, and your nightgown and robe here—some soap and some of that lotion I bought you back at Laramie. You don't use it often enough, Marybeth. You have such pretty skin."

"I hate to waste it when I can't bathe first."

"Well, you can bathe now." He came over to her and began unbuttoning her blouse.

"Josh, are you sure—" Her words were cut off by a kiss, a sweet, delicious, tender kiss that gently parted her mouth while he moved his hand inside her shirt and caressed a breast with the back of his hand.

"I told you to quit worrying," he said then. "Just enjoy, Marybeth. This is probably the last chance we'll get to do something like this before we make Oregon." He pulled off her blouse and pulled down the sleeves of her camisole, bending down and kissing her breasts. He went to his knees, tasting lightly at her firm nipples as he unbuttoned her skirt and pulled it down, bringing everything else with it. He kissed her belly, kissed at the warm love nest that he needed to invade.

"Josh," she whispered, grasping his hair. In moments she stood there naked, and he rose to strip off his own clothes. She studied him in the moonlight, so much man. She stepped forward and kissed his bare chest, reaching down and touching that part of him that brought her pleasure instead of the humiliation and pain it had once brought her from another man. So soft it was, and already swollen with need for her.

Josh picked her up and carried her to the blankets, setting her down on one of them. "I'm not waiting for the bath," he told her. He laid her back, and she gladly opened herself to him, gasping when he quickly entered her, filling her with such power and manliness that she sometimes wondered how he even fit in her. Dan had once told her she would be useless to a man after the baby, that no man could enjoy her. "A man would have to be built like a damn stud horse to get any pleasure out of you then," he had told her during one night of his verbal abuse. He had not lived long enough to find out. Now here was Josh Rivers, taking great pleasure in her.

If Dan MacKinder's statement was true, then her man was built just as Dan had described, for he filled her to the point of light-headed ecstasy. She felt the wonderful explosion building deep inside as he moved rhythmically, in that special way he had that brought out wild, wanton desires. Then it came, the wonderful, pulsating climax that made her cry out his name. She could hear his own groans of pleasure as he raised up, grasping her hips and pushing deep, his eyes drinking in her naked beauty in the moonlight. He moved in circular motions then, destroying any modesty she might have left, making her pant his name and arch up to him in glorious abandon.

Moments later his life spilled into her. He stayed on his knees, throwing back his head and breathing deeply. After a moment he pulled away from her, grabbed at a bar of soap, and picked her up in his arms. "Now for that bath," he told her. She screamed lightly as he carried her over to a pool of water behind the bigger waterfall.

"Josh, we'll freeze!" She screamed again as he plunked her in the water and waded in after her. Marybeth's eyes widened in pleasant surprise. "It's warm!"

He laughed, pushing her deeper into it. "I told you I'd surprise you. It's some kind of hot spring. I very selfishly didn't tell anyone else about it because I wanted to be here alone with you."

"Oh, Josh, we should at least tell Delores and Florence. They would so much like a bath."

"Well, don't feel too selfish. There isn't time for everyone to come over here and take turns. I think Cap would rather they *didn't* know." He lathered up the soap and laid it on a rock, then reached out to rub his soapy hands over her neck and down over her breasts. "I'll wash you. This is the first time we've used this fancy soap I bought in St. Louis. Don't ask me why I bought it. I think clear back then I knew I'd find a need for it. Feels a lot better than plain old lye, doesn't it?"

"Oh, yes!" He moved behind her and soaped her up, and for the next several minutes she enjoyed a glorious massage over an aching back and legs and feet. "Josh, you're too good to me."

"No, ma'am. You deserve every good thing I can do for you. Just relax."

She leaned against him, and his soapy hands moved over her breasts again, gently massaging, down over her belly. His fingers moved into secret places as he whispered to her to again relax. Moments later she felt the wonderful desire building again, and the exotic pulsation again came to her just from his magical touch. She groaned his name, and he turned her. She wrapped her legs around his waist and he pushed himself inside of her, setting her down on the bottom of the shallow pond. She rested on her elbows, and he moved big hands under her bottom to support her while he made love to her again.

It became a night of magic for her. When he finished with her they bathed each other again and got out to roll up in a blanket together. They slept a while under the full moon, spoke little, made love again, bathed again. Finally they dressed and stretched out on a dry blanket, pulling another one over them.

"We should get back to the wagon train while it's still dark," she told him.

"We can go back in the morning."

"Please, Josh. I can only take so much embarrassment. Please don't make me ride back in front of everyone in the morning in my robe. Everyone will know."

He laughed lightly and nuzzled her neck. "All right, we'll go back in a while." He kissed her eyes. "I love you."

"And I love you." She touched his face, tempted to tell him about the baby; but he had talked about rough country ahead and hard work for the men. She didn't want him burdened with the worry of her pregnancy. "This was so sweet of you, Josh. This has been the second most memorable experience of my life."

"The second?"

"The first was our wedding night."

He grinned, pulling her close and kissing her lightly. "I hope you've stopped worrying about pleasing me."

She smiled and kissed him back. "I never thought it could be like this. Oh, Josh, I can't wait for Oregon. We'll settle in that pretty green valley everyone talks about. It will be so wonderful." Her eyes teared. "God has been so good to me."

He sobered, pulling her close. "And to me." They lay there quietly for a few minutes. "We'd better get back before we get too sleepy."

"We'll have to be very quiet. The whole camp is probably asleep by now."

"Except Trapper. He's keeping watch." He rose and rolled everything into a blanket. He pulled on his boots and loaded up the gear, then helped her onto his horse and climbed up behind her. They rode quietly back to camp, unaware that they rode past Trapper's dead body, lying behind some brush, an Indian knife in his back. All around them, more Crow warriors settled into positions, waiting for dawn.

# Twenty-Two

Josh lay awake, listening to the howling of wolves and the nearby calls of night birds. He felt uneasy, but was not sure why. Some of the night birds sounded different, and there seemed to be more of them than normal. He sat up and searched through the pockets of his deerskin vest that hung inside the wagon, finding one of the thin cigars he enjoyed smoking. He put it to his lips and prepared to light it when he heard a rustling sound outside the wagon. Immediately he reached for his pistol and cocked it, the still-unlit cigar in his mouth.

"Josh." The name was softly spoken from the back of his wagon. "It is I, Devon."

Josh pulled up the canvas flap. "What is it?"

"Wake your woman quietly—tell her to dress and be ready. Something is wrong."

Josh lowered his pistol and took the cigar from his mouth. He looked past him into the darkness. "I feel it, too. I haven't been able to sleep. Seems like an awful lot of night birds out there."

"Not night birds. Indians. They are giving signals."

Josh felt his chest tighten at the threat. "Have you checked with Trapper?" he asked, his voice a near whisper.

"He does not answer my signal," Devon whispered back. "Something has happened to him, and I dare not go out into the darkness to find out what it is. But I suspect he has been killed."

"Killed! What the hell for? We haven't done anything to any Indians. We haven't even run into any since leaving Laramie."

Devon looked around with eyes that reminded Josh of a wild animal sensing danger. "I do not know what the reason could be. But they are out there, watching the wagons. I suspect they are waiting for dawn."

"They?"

"Crow, most likely. The Crow and Shoshoni have been pretty peaceful the last couple of years. If they plan to attack us, something has happened to provoke it. We will probably never know what it was. I must go now—warn the others to be dressed and alert. Raise the canvas slightly on the outer side of your wagon and keep watch. Watch for any movement the moment the sun rises. If we are not caught off guard, it will be better for us. From listening to the exchange of signals, I suspect perhaps twenty of them. That is almost the same number of men we have, plus a couple of young boys who know how to shoot. These farmers are not going to be very good shots, and many of them have old muskets, but it will be the same for the Indians—mostly bow and arrow and old muskets. Still, you and I and Ben and Cap will have to make our shots count. Stay alert."

The man left, and Josh lowered the canvas, turning to Marybeth with a heavy heart. How he hated having to tell her the news. He could not imagine what could have spurred the Indians to move against them, but he did not doubt Devon's suspicion that they were indeed out there. He quietly pulled on a shirt and his vest, then slung a holster and his revolver over his shoulder. He leaned over Marybeth, kissing her awake.

"Josh, I'm too sleepy," she muttered.

He grinned, but his heart ached at the thought of her coming to any harm, and he prayed that would not happen. "Honey, you have to get dressed."

She blinked and looked around the still-dark wagon. "What?"

He put a finger to her lips. "Be very quiet. We have to do this without others knowing it."

"What others," she whispered. She sat up, rubbing her eyes. "Josh, what is going on?"

He sighed, pulling her close for a moment. She felt the gunbelt. "Josh! Why are you wearing this in the middle of the night?"

He held her arms reassuringly. "Devon just came by," he whispered. "Something is wrong outside. I felt it, too—couldn't sleep for all the bird calling. Devon says it's Indians."

Her eyes widened, and he felt her stiffen. "You mean … Indians that mean us harm?"

"Possibly. Devon says they're giving signals—he suspects they intend to attack the wagon train come morning."

"Oh, Josh!"

He quickly kissed her. "Just stay calm. I want you and Danny dressed in case you have to get out of the wagon quick. And we're supposed to roll up the canvas a little on the side of the wagon facing out—not too much so it's not too conspicuous; just enough to peek through at dawn to see if anyone is coming."

Her throat tightened with fear, not for herself but for Danny and Josh. "Oh, Josh, if it happens, please be careful." She put a hand to her chest. "There are hardly any men on this wagon train who know anything about fighting Indians."

"Maybe not; but most of them have at least hunted. That's better than nothing. Devon, Cap, Ben and I have fought Indians before."

"Trapper, too. I wonder how many Indians there are, Josh?"

He decided not to tell her Devon suspected Trapper was already dead. He shivered at the realization he had been out there alone with her earlier in the night. He kissed her forehead. "Hard to say. Just get dressed. I'm going to roll up the canvas just a little and keep my eyes open the rest of the night."

He turned and quietly moved things aside so that he could turn up the canvas without climbing outside the wagon, afraid if he were spotted, the Indians would be alerted and attack sooner. Marybeth pulled off her gown and quickly pulled on a shirt, not bothering with her camisole. She pulled on some bloomers and a clean skirt, then felt around in the darkness for her brush. She began vigorously brushing her hair, realizing it was a silly thing to do. Her hair might end up on some Indian's trophy belt. Yet she nervously kept brushing, desperately needing something to do to curb her terror.

Indians! Why? They had come so far without Indian trouble. Why did this have to happen? The happiness she had known just a few hours earlier in Josh's arms beside the hot springs seemed an odd contrast to the tension of the moment. She could lose him, and Danny, too.

"Oh, dear God!" A woman from some other wagon wailed the words, probably upon hearing she must be prepared. She exclaimed something else, but the words were muffled, no doubt by her husband clamping a hand over her mouth.

"If nobody panics we'll be all right," Josh told her, hoping he was right. Although fairly evenly matched, he knew the kind of fighters Indians were, even without good weapons—vicious, intent, having no fear of death. Their attitude and skill in battle far surpassed most of the men with the wagon train, who were mostly peaceful farmers who had used their guns for little more than rabbit hunting.

"They're afraid, Josh. *I'm* afraid." She put down the brush as he finished tying off the canvas.

"Don't think I'm not. I know how Indians fight. But in situations like this you can't let fear get the better of you. That's one thing Indians count on when it comes to whites." He turned and embraced her. "You sit tight. I'm going to find Devon."

She grasped his arms, whispering his name. "Earlier tonight—it was so wonderful," she told him. "I love you, Josh."

He met her lips in a tender kiss. "And I love you. We'll be all right. You remember what I told you about things working out for you and me." He kissed her again, and she could sense his own apprehension in spite of his air of confidence. He climbed out of the wagon and disappeared into the darkness.

John waited in terror in the darkness, the sound of Indian calls all around him. Although he was not accustomed to this land and its night sounds, he knew the Indians were ahead of him; he had watched them gather near the foothills, then split up. Instinct told him the sounds he heard now were those same Indians. They had surrounded the wagon train, and John knew he could not go in without being spotted and killed. For the moment he could only hope the savages would not spot him right where he was.

*Not that I give a damn about one person on that wagon train except Danny and my parents … and Marybeth*, he thought. *I'd like to see them all die, especially Cap and Josh Rivers.*

His emotions were mixed. After the way he had been treated, he could enjoy watching the wagon train burn, its people murdered and scalped. It would serve them right. They had left him to what could have been the same fate if not for nerve and luck. If only his own parents and nephew weren't along. He wondered if all this could have anything to do with Hanna and the others killing the Indian man. Had they also killed the woman? Hanna had mentioned he couldn't let her live to run and tell her kin what had happened. Had the Crow blamed the incident on the travelers in the wagon train?

He settled down against an embankment, shivering with the thought of being caught himself. If he lived through the night and the next day, he would be a lucky man.

Josh watched from inside the wagon, as dawn awoke to pink and gray, and a crane squawked somewhere in the distance. He saw the movement then, a man darting from one tree to another. He cocked his rifle, while Marybeth lay flat in the wagon bed, holding Danny against her and watching Josh with desperate fear for him. She saw him take aim.

Someone from another wagon fired at something.

"He's got a flaming arrow," she heard Josh say as he fired his own gun. The Indian with the bow and arrow cried out and fell backward, but he had already got off the arrow.

It seemed then that everyone was firing at once. Danny started crying at the loud noise as Josh shot several times from inside the wagon. Guns seemed to be roaring everywhere. A woman screamed, and Marybeth looked out the end of the wagon to see the canvas of one wagon on fire. A woman was scrambling out of it, and at almost the same time another flaming arrow landed into another canvas top. The woman who climbed out of the first wagon suddenly jerked, and fell with an arrow in her back.

"Get out of here *now*!" Josh ordered. "If we wait till they put a flame to us, they'll be watching for us to climb out and shoot us like sitting ducks!"

Marybeth did not question his instructions. Filled with horror at the sight of the arrow in the woman's back, she grabbed Danny and quickly scrambled out of the wagon. Josh was right behind her. "Get down underneath," he told her, pushing her down. "And stay there!"

She crawled under the wagon, and now she could hear the yips and calls of the Indians as they moved in closer. A man cried out, and Marybeth saw him fall, an arrow in his chest. She could also see Josh's boots and buckskin leggings, watched him moving back and forth, heard his gun explode several times. She tried to see the MacKinder wagon, worried about poor Ella.

A few of the Indians suddenly rode hard toward the wagon train. Marybeth could see their painted horses coming from where she lay. She kept her body over Danny to protect him, and as one horse came very close to their wagon she heard Josh's gun go off again. The man cried out and flew from his horse, sprawling onto his back, his chest bloody. Marybeth looked away, only to see another Indian break through and swing a hatchet at the man whose wife had been shot with the arrow. A horrible bloody gash opened up across the side of the man's neck, and Marybeth felt ill at the sight. The Indian dismounted and daringly slung the dead woman's body over his horse. Marybeth recognized her as Anna Mae Billings, who lost a child to cholera. Her other three children scrambled out from under the now-burning wagon screaming for their mother, but to Marybeth's surprise, the Indian brought them no harm. He rode off with the body, and someone fired, knocking him from his horse. Another Indian rode in, grabbing the dead Indian's horse and riding into the trees with Anna Mae.

More Indians tried to come in close, but the almost constant volley of gunfire sent them retreating. Everything became suddenly silent, almost too silent. The only sound was the dreaded crackling and popping of two wagons that were on fire, the Billings wagon, and the other one Bill Stone's. A frightened woman began sobbing. One of the Billings children whimpered for his father, as the child bent over the man's body, which had been nearly beheaded.

Josh bent down to look under the wagon. "You and Danny all right?"

"Yes," Marybeth answered, her eyes moving over him. "What about you?"

"I'm okay."

"Can you see Ella? Is the MacKinder wagon still all right?"

It took him a moment to look around. He knelt back down. "Looks okay so far. I can see Ella under it, loading Mac's rifle." He rose again. "Stay put, no matter what happens, understand? If I go down, don't try to crawl out to me."

"Everybody stay where you are," Cap called out. "They'll be back." Marybeth felt sick at the words. "Somebody tend to the Billings children."

"Oh, God, why did they take Anna Mae's body," a woman wailed.

"Marybeth, are you all right," Delores called from under her own wagon.

"Yes. What about you and Aaron?"

"We aren't hurt so far."

Florence Gentry hurried over to the Billings wagon with Sam, and the two of them scooped up the three Billings children, Ruth, twelve, Fred, Jr., six, and little Nina, only two years old, who was toddling around crying for her Mama.

"Dear God, Josh, why are they doing this?" Marybeth asked with a groan.

"We'll probably never know."

"Here they come again," Cap shouted.

Again the guns roared and children screamed and cried. An Indian moved in boldly, Anna Mae's body on his horse. She was naked, and from where Marybeth lay she could see the body was covered with deep gashes as though deliberately desecrated. Most of her long, blond hair was gone, with only an ugly, bloody spot remaining where her scalp had been lifted.

A woman screamed in horror at the sight as the Indian

flung the body toward the wagon train, then whirled and rode off. Marybeth turned away from the sight, feeling nauseous.

John tied the old mare and took his rifle from the horse, moving in closer at the sound of gunfire. He had to know if his parents were all right. He stayed well above the line where the Indians crouched for their attack. The air roared with booming guns, screams and the yips of Indian war whoops. From his side it appeared as though the Indians were very close to the wagon train and moving toward the other side. He saw no horses, and guessed the Indians on his side had left their horses across the way, since the terrain on this side was very wooded and brushy.

He darted behind a huge boulder, noticing that right beside it was a rock formation that left a hole big enough for a man to duck inside it. He quickly moved into the hole, crouching down and removing his hat, then daringly peeking up. His heart quickened when he realized he had found an excellent vantage point to watch the wagon train. He could see his father's wagon, which was at the edge of the circle farthest from him; he could see his father standing on the inside of the circle, firing at Indians. He saw his mother handing him a loaded musket, while he threw her an empty one. He breathed a sigh of relief that they were all right.

He scanned the rest of the train, seeing the two wagons that were burning. Then he saw him—Josh Rivers. There was no mistaking the wagon, or the buckskin pants and the blue checkered shirt he recognized. He realized his hated enemy was within shooting range.

Even John was surprised at how quickly the thought came to him. *He could kill the man, and everyone would think the Indians had done it.* Because of the Indian attack, he could literally get away with murder. He struggled with the idea, realizing that to shoot Josh would mean one less man to help fight the Indians and thus defend his own parents and Danny. Still, there were plenty of other men on that wagon train, and John knew there were not enough Indians to keep up the battle forever. The wagon train was better equipped for both protection and weapons.

He cautiously raised his rifle. He had had plenty of chances to practice with it, and his arm was healed enough to at least be able to hold up a rifle and pull the trigger. He took careful aim, unable to resist this most wonderful temptation. He fired, then realized he had missed when Josh moved to the other end of the wagon and kept firing at Indians. John noticed the Indians on his side were moving downhill. One came daringly close to his hiding place, and John ducked down as he heard the screeched warcry. He heard someone run past him. He stayed low for several seconds, then cautiously looked out again to see Indians running through trees and down the bank toward the other side, where he was sure the horses of those on foot were kept.

The firing slowed somewhat, and again John took aim at Josh. He realized the Indians were preparing to ride off. He had to do this quickly, or he would miss his chance. He took one more look to be sure his parents were still all right, then cocked the rifle.

"They're retreating again," Marybeth heard Cap yelling to the others. "Keep firing!"

She watched Josh's feet, her only link to him, her only way of knowing he was all right. She heard him fire twice more, as the shots began to dwindle. Suddenly his feet jerked strangely. She saw his rifle clatter to the ground, and her heart seemed to freeze as his body tumbled after it. "*Stay under the wagon no matter what happens*," he had told her. She stared at him in horror, clinging to Danny as the man she loved more than her own life lay sprawled on his belly, a bloody hole in his back. He looked lifeless.

Shots continued, and for the moment she could only stare in disbelief, sure some Indian was going to come crashing through to grab her and Danny if she came out from under the wagon. In the next few seconds the shots dwindled, and again came the odd silence, made more eerie and horrible by the sight of her beloved Josh lying motionless only a couple of feet away.

"Josh," she whimpered.

She heard someone running. "Josh!" It was Aaron's voice. "Dear God!"

"Oh, no! No!" The words came from Delores, who watched from under her own wagon.

Marybeth crawled out from under the wagon, and Aaron took Danny from her as she bent over Josh's body while Devon and Cap came running. She told herself what she was seeing was only a nightmare, that this could not possibly be real. Hadn't Josh promised nothing would happen to their love? Hadn't he promised they were meant to be together, that they would reach Oregon and live happily ever after?

"Josh," she moaned, bending over the body and moving an arm under his head and turning it to kiss his face and hair. His eyes were closed, and he made no sound or movement. "Josh! Josh," she wept. "Oh, God, no. Please no!"

"Let me look at him, Marybeth," Cap told her, gently pushing her away.

"I will look around," Devon was saying. "I think they are pulling out. This must have been for vengeance. They have killed enough of us to be satisfied."

A woman screamed at the sight of Anna Mae's body, and a man quickly ran toward it with a blanket to cover it up. Children wailed and women cried at the horror of the attack, while several of the men attempted to douse the flames of the two burning wagons to try to save at least some of the belongings and the wagon beds.

Marybeth folded her arms over her belly and rocked in an effort to keep from losing her mind, as she watched Cap rip Josh's shirt away to examine the wound.

"How bad is it, Cap?" Aaron asked the question cautiously, afraid of the answer.

The man sighed. "Bad enough, but he's still alive. From the looks of this wound, it was a higher caliber repeating rifle, not a musket." He looked at Ben, who had also come to Josh's side. "I didn't know any Indians had got their hands on those new-fangled rifles yet."

Ben shook his head. "Must have. No white man could have been up in those hills with so many Indians around."

Cap ran his hands around the wound, and Ben helped him gently turn the body over while Marybeth watched in agony. Delores knelt behind her and put a hand to her waist.

"No exit wound," Cap grumbled. "The damn bullet is still inside him. Look at this bruise near his ribs. I expect he's bleedin' on the inside." He turned troubled eyes to Marybeth. "This is about as bad a wound as a man can have and expect to live, honey," he told her. "You better do some prayin' over them beads of yours. I've seen plenty such things in my time, and I don't hold out much hope for him."

She met his eyes, trembling more and shaking her head. "No! You've got to help him, Cap!"

"I'm going to try. But I ain't no great surgeon, Marybeth. And a bullet inside like that—all them vital organs in there. Ain't nothin' worse than a bullet in the back, let alone lodgin' in his belly."

She looked down at Josh's face. It looked an ungodly white, his eyes closed. "Josh," she whispered. "Wake up. Please wake up." The tears came then as she bent closer to kiss his hair. "Please, please wake up."

"The pain he'd be in, he's better off stayin' unconscious, Marybeth," she heard Cap saying. "Some of you men help me get him inside the wagon. Put plenty of gauze and towels under the back wound and lay him on his back. I'll have to cut in from the front. The bullet's most likely closer to that side, somewhere in the middle of that purple spot."

"Move back, Marybeth," Delores told her, "so they can lift the body."

*The body.* The words sounded so deathly, as though Josh were already a corpse. This couldn't be happening! Delores tried to pull her away, but Marybeth would not budge. Sam came over then and grasped her about the waist, pulling her away. She screamed then. Oh, how she *needed* to scream. She fought Sam, screaming Josh's name over and over, screaming at him to wake up, cursing God. "Not Josh! Not Josh," she wailed. She crumpled then, grasping her belly, realizing Josh Rivers might never even see the baby she wanted to give him. Only moments before she had seen him moving around, had heard him ask if she was all right, heard his gunshots. It was just like Bess's mother, alive and happy and talking one moment, dead the next.

Dead! He looked so dead! Would there be another grave dug, one for her Josh? Only hours ago she had lain beneath him, taking him inside herself, enjoying his virile, strong, eager body, feeling his tender kisses, splashing in the warm spring water with him, letting him gently massage her with his gentle, soapy hands. How could the man she watched carried inside the wagon be that same man, now so lifeless and white and limp ... looking so dead.

Sam started to let go of her, but her legs didn't seem to want to work. Josh! Josh! Sam grabbed hold of her again. "We'd better take her to your wagon while Cap tries to get the bullet out," he told Delores.

Suddenly new life came into Marybeth's legs. "No! No, I want to be with him."

"Marybeth—"

She turned and hit at his chest with hard fists, hardly realizing what she was doing. "No! You let me sit with him! I have to be with him!"

Sam grasped her arms and shook her. "All right! But you've got to calm down, Marybeth, or you'll be no use!"

Her chest heaved in gasped sobs as she stared up at the man. "Oh, I'm so sorry, Sam. You ... and Florence ... have suffered so much ... loss. You're both so—strong..."

"And so are you. I'll bet Josh himself told you that many a time."

Tears streamed down her face as Florence came up to her. The two women embraced.

"Help me, Florence," Marybeth sobbed. "How did you do it? How do you go on?"

"We go on because we know our children are happy and romping in a better place, removed from danger and pain. And if something happens to Josh, you will go on, too, Marybeth.

You still have Danny to think about."

Marybeth pulled away, taking a handkerchief from the waist of her skirt. "I didn't even tell him yet—that I'm carrying his baby."

Florence looked at Delores in surprise. "Marybeth," Delores exclaimed. "Are you sure?"

She wiped at her eyes. "Pretty sure." She looked at both of them pleadingly. "Can you watch over Danny for a while?"

"Of course we can." Florence grasped her hands. "You're one of the bravest, strongest women on this journey, Marybeth. And right now Josh needs that strength. You've drawn on his strength, depended on him up to now. Now he needs you for the same thing. He isn't dead, Marybeth. And with all our prayers, he *won't* die." She embraced her again. "Be strong, child."

Sam took her arm and helped her climb into the wagon. From his perch on the hill, John watched Marybeth, his heart elated at the distant sound of her sobbing. He grinned with victory, moving from his hiding place and hurrying away to find his horse. The Indians were riding off in another direction. All he had to do now was lay low for the winter. No one would ever suspect. Come spring, he would find his parents, then pay the lonely, twice-widowed Marybeth a friendly visit.

At last he had visited the final defeat over Joshua Rivers!

# Twenty-Three

Those first few hours after Josh was shot were the most excruciating of Marybeth's life. Josh came around slightly while Cap was cutting into him, and his horrible moans of pain while Devon held his arms and Aaron held his feet tore at Marybeth's heart like a double-edged sword. She refused to leave his side in spite of the bloody, painful operation. Cap tried to get laudanum and whiskey down Josh's throat, but he kept choking on it and spitting most of it back up.

"I ain't never gonna be able to do this right if we can't make him lay still," Cap told them all. The man was obviously shaken himself. Cap was very fond of Josh Rivers. "I sure don't like bein' the one to have to do this, but I ain't got no choice, Marybeth."

She looked at Cap with a tear-stained face, the horrible grief and terror evident in her eyes. "Just do what you can," she said, her voice gruff from her screams of agony earlier.

"You're a brave woman, and he loves you. That's gonna help."

Finally, between what laudanum did stay down, and the horrible pain, Josh passed out. Devon and Aaron quickly tied his hands and feet in case he came to again.

Marybeth handed Cap whatever he needed, and Delores brought hot water. More low moans came from Josh when Cap dug for the bullet, and it was evident that somewhere in his semiconscious mind Josh Rivers was in horrifying pain. Marybeth wished she could take some of it upon herself, anything to relieve his suffering. Blood seemed to be everywhere, and Cap kept packing the wound and sewing organs with the supply of cat gut he always carried for emergencies, dumping whiskey onto the cut in hopes of preventing infection.

"Our first worry is that he don't bleed to death," the man grumbled as he kept searching for sources of the bleeding after finally finding the bullet.

Marybeth held Josh's head in her lap. Outside she could hear hymn-singing. She wasn't sure how much time had gone by, but apparently it had been enough for the others to dig more graves. She shuddered at the horror of putting Josh's young, handsome body into one of those graves. Such a short time ago he had been so vital, smiling, teasing her, making love to her. How could one small bullet bring down such a big, strong man?

Devon washed off the bullet and studied it. "You were right, Cap. This is from a repeating rifle. I do not understand it. Those Crow must have already attacked some other whites, perhaps mountain men, stole their weapons."

Suddenly Marybeth thought of John. Was he dead? Josh had mentioned something about Mac giving John a new repeating rifle to take with him. Perhaps that was where the Indians got the weapon. If there were angry Indians out there, it was unlikely John in his inexperience had managed to avoid them. Her emotions were a mixture of sorrow and relief at the thought of it. Yet if John were alive, perhaps this never would have happened. Perhaps no Indian would have got hold of a repeating rifle. Even in death, John MacKinder had come back to haunt her, had inadvertently got his vengeance on Josh.

"You are thinking John MacKinder is dead," Devon said aloud, seeing the far-away look in Marybeth's eyes.

"What?" She met his dark eyes, for a moment wanting to hate him because he looked so Indian. But it was just like she and Josh had talked about. She had asked him not to judge all Irishmen by the MacKinders. And she could not judge all Indians by those who had attacked them today, especially when she did not know the reason. "How did you know?"

"I thought of it myself. I helped see him off. His father gave him a new repeating rifle. It is possible the Indians got hold of it. If so, John MacKinder is dead."

She closed her eyes and bent her head down, kissing Josh's forehead. "I would rather he lived if his death has been the cause of this."

"I think I got most of the bleeding stopped," Cap said then, his whole body drenched in sweat. "I ain't never seen anything like this." He sighed. "That bullet ripped through a lot of vital organs." He looked at Marybeth. "I don't like to take away your hope, honey, but…" He swallowed.

"He won't die. He can't! He promised me we'd make it to Oregon."

Her throat ached fiercely, and she wondered how long she could keep going without losing her mind. Danny. She had to stay sane for Danny's sake.

"Marybeth, a wound like this, a man would have trouble makin' it even with the best of care; but … hell, I patched him up like a woman tryin' to make an old ripped-up quilt useful again. It can't hardly be done. Only God knows if I sewed up the right spots. And it's almost a sure bet there's gonna be infection."

"He'll live," she said firmly. "I know he'll live."

Cap glanced at Devon, seeing the doubt in the scout's eyes. Devon too had realized how bad the wound was. Cap sighed again. "Let's get him sewed up." He removed some of the gauze he had packed inside the wound. "Looks like I got most of the bleedin' stopped."

"I think there could be another problem even if he lives," Aaron said then. He met Marybeth's eyes. "When he was in so much pain and thrashing about with his arms, I held his legs because I thought he would kick them around. But he was not really moving them at all. A man in that much pain, does it not seem likely he would have moved his legs also?"

Marybeth felt the horror sinking even deeper.

"You think they're paralyzed?" Cap asked.

"The bullet went into his back, not far from the spine."

Marybeth lowered her head again, pressing her cheek against Josh's. Cap just shook his head and began sewing Josh up. "I've done all I can do inside," he announced finally. "I'd better see what's goin' on outside." He reached over and touched Marybeth's shoulder. "You know we have to keep goin', don't you?"

"Yes," she answered quietly.

"Best thing we can do is get the hell out of here and higher into the mountains. The Crow won't bother with us up there. If we can make decent time, we'll be at Fort Hall in about four days. If Josh is still alive when we get there, we'll decide then what to do."

She raised her eyes to meet his. "What do you mean?"

"I mean he'll be lucky to make it that far. If he does, he'd be best to be left there to rest. A man in this condition can't hope to make it through what's ahead after that. There's cliffs that we have to lower wagons over with ropes. He couldn't even stay inside for somethin' like that, and he sure couldn't be moved around. There just ain't no way he can hope to survive unless he can stay in on place and not be moved. There are men at the fort who would look after him."

"I'll do it myself," she said, sitting straighter. "He'll need me."

Cap looked at Devon, and the Indian turned his eyes to Marybeth. "It is no place for a woman and a baby to spend the winter."

"I don't care! I'll not leave him!"

Cap put a hand on Devon's arm, warning him not to say anything more for the moment. "We'll talk about it when we get there. You just stay calm for now, Marybeth, while I get him sewed up and bandaged."

She stroked Josh's forehead and temples while Cap pulled the skin back together over Josh's right side as best he could. "Untie his wrists and roll him up real gentle," the man told Devon. The Indian obeyed, and Josh let out a heart-wrenching moan when he moved. "This here entrance wound is small. I'll give it a couple of stitches and we'll wrap him up."

For the next few minutes there was no talking. Marybeth argued with herself about staying with Josh at Fort Hall. She didn't care what Devon or anyone else said, she was not going to leave her husband. If he lived, he would need her, especially if he really was paralyzed. And if he died, she would not let him die all alone.

Cap finished, and Devon retied Josh's wrists. "You stay here with Josh, and let me know if he comes around and starts rarin' up again," Cap told Marybeth.

She nodded, and the men climbed out of the wagon, leaving her alone with Josh. She looked down at him, running her fingers through his thick, sandy hair; over his now-closed eyes that only hours earlier had sparkled with love for her, over the strong lines of his handsome face, the finely etched lips; and over the strong shoulders and arms. So much man he was to be lying so near death. It didn't seem possible, yet here he was, lying unconscious in her lap.

The tears came then, tears that had had to be withheld because she was needed. Now it seemed there was nothing else to do but vent her terrible grief and somehow find the faith to pray and believe God would answer those prayers. At the moment, it seemed God was surely against her. She would rather have never met Joshua Rivers and still be living in hell with the MacKinders, than to find such happiness and lose it so quickly. Her sobs welled up in great waves of sorrow. She could not fathom never again being held by Josh, not seeing his warm smile, or hearing his teasing laughter; even if he lived, she could not picture her virile husband unable to walk.

"Marybeth?" Delores climbed into the wagon, moving carefully around Josh to touch Marybeth's shoulder.

"What am I going to do, Delores? Cap ... doesn't think he'll live at all, and if he does, he might be crippled."

Delores's eyes filled. "I don't know what to tell you, Marybeth. But you always seemed to have so much faith. You *are* very strong, like Josh always said. Now you have to be strong for him, like he has been for you. Why don't you find those beads you pray over, and we'll pray together."

Marybeth raised up and wiped at her eyes. "I don't know ... if I can pray any more."

"You can. Praying will help you, too."

Marybeth looked at her, dark circles showing under her eyes. "If I have to bury him, I won't want to live myself," she told Delores.

Delores grasped her hand. "You have Danny to think

about—and you said you were carrying Josh's child. Marybeth, if Josh dies, you still have his life, inside of you. You'll have a part of him to treasure forever. How do you think he would feel if you ended your life and ended his only hope of leaving a part of himself behind? If you take your life, you leave Danny an orphan, taken in and raised by MacKinders; and you'd also be taking the life of Josh Rivers' baby. I don't think you really want either one of those things to happen. You're just talking out of grief."

Marybeth closed her eyes. "It isn't fair," she wept.

"There are a lot of things in life that are unfair—like Bess losing her mother that way; Florence losing two children. Somehow people manage to go on. You have lots of friends now, people who will help you." She squeezed her hand. "Let's pray, Marybeth."

With shaking hands Marybeth reached for her rosary, which hung inside the wagon. She took it down and stared at it, grasping it tightly, hanging her head. Delores began praying, and slowly Marybeth moved the beads through her fingers, praying over them in a faint whisper. She leaned down and kissed Josh's cheek.

"Mary ... beth," Josh groaned.

Her tears came again at the misery she sensed in the way he spoke her name, but she thanked God that somewhere in his subconscious he was with her.

Enough of Bill Stone's wagon was saved that he could keep going, although there was no canvas left. Florence and Sam took in the orphaned Billings children, and the wagon train headed into the mountains, leaving behind the graves of Fred and Anna Mae Billings, a single man named Walt Madden, and Trapper. Out of the original twenty-six men, seventeen were left, although one of them, Josh Rivers, would be no help to the others. Thirteen of nineteen women were left, and only nineteen of twenty-eight children. The Billings wagon, burned too badly to be used, was abandoned.

The wagon train snaked slowly up the side of a mountain, stopping frequently so that the animals could rest. The combination of constant climbing and less oxygen made the animals weary easily, and some collapsed. Some of those were either left behind or shot.

This stage of the journey was one of terror for most of the farmers along, who were accustomed to wide, flat land. Now they were on a narrow road that followed the side of a mountain, around and around, twisting and winding upward, with places barely wide enough for animals and wagons to pass over. Every time a wagon hit a rut, hearts tightened. Children were told to be very quiet. There could be no loud noises around the animals, since to have a team panic would mean certain disaster. No one relished the thought of watching their wagon tumble hundreds or thousands of feet over the cliff that loomed beside them as they climbed.

Most walked, afraid to stay in the wagons in case of just such a disaster, and one single man, the last of a party of three men, suddenly clutched his chest and collapsed from a heart attack. Since there was no way to bury him along the narrow road, valuables were taken from his wagon and divided up among the rest of the travelers, the man's oxen unhitched; the body was placed inside the wagon, and men turned the front wheels and pushed it over the edge. The chilling crashing sounds that went on for several minutes left everyone filled with silent terror.

There were now fifteen wagons left, sixteen men. Cap himself herded the dead man's team of oxen along in the same spot his wagon had occupied, since at that point the road was too narrow to move the animals out around the other wagons or to break them up and divide them among those who needed extra oxen.

Marybeth remained inside her wagon in spite of the danger. Josh could not be moved, and she would not leave him. Danny was brought to her for feedings, then taken away again because he was crawling and too lively to be around Josh. His crying every time he was taken away from his mother and his "Zosh" tore at Marybeth's heart. She wanted to be with her baby. But she knew that Florence and Delores would take good care of him, and the Billings children, who desperately needed the diversion, did a good job of entertaining Danny and making the baby forget he wanted his mother.

Marybeth's terror of the dangerous road was overshadowed by her terror of Josh's dying. She could only watch in horror as he went through spells of violent shaking and sweating, and frequent vomiting, mostly blood. Never had she felt so helpless and desperate. She comforted him as best she could, bathing his face and neck with a cool cloth, talking to him soothingly in the rare moments when he seemed to be conscious enough to realize she was there.

After two full days of climbing they reached a summit, where they camped and rested for another full day. Cap came to check on Josh, and together with Marybeth and Devon, they changed the bloody, pussy bandages, none of them expressing their most dreaded suspicion, that already infection was setting in—infection in an area where nothing could help but prayer. If it were an arm or a leg, a limb could be amputated. Horrible as the thought was, it at least could save Josh's life. But the only hope for infection deep inside his middle was Josh's own strength and determination. His pants and longjohns had been removed, and towels were wrapped around him diaper fashion for elimination.

Every time they moved him even slightly, it brought an agonizing groan that made Marybeth ache with pity for him.

"His fever is rising, Cap," she told the man.

"Keep his head cool. That's the most important thing. If he's worse by the time we get to the bottom of this mountain in a couple of days, I'll have to cut him and drain out the infection I suspect is buildin' around the wound. Trouble is, it's gonna spread all through him even if I manage to get some of it out, and there ain't a damn thing I can do about it. I'm sorry, Marybeth." He frowned when she met his eyes. "You been gettin' any sleep?"

"Just a few minutes at a time."

"Well, you look it. You get some rest, young lady, or you'll be no use to him at all—or to your baby. And what about the one you're carryin'? You're gonna lose it if you keep this up. Is that what you want? That baby could be all you have of Josh if he doesn't live."

She closed her eyes and hung her head, stroking Josh's hair. "I can't leave him, Cap."

"Yes, you can. There are others who would be willing to help out. Here." He held out a bottle of whiskey. "Drink some of this."

"Oh, I couldn't."

"Drink it! That's an order. You swallow some of this and you get out of this wagon for a while. I'll have some of the other women take these soiled bedclothes and get some fresh ones under Josh. You wash up and change your own clothes and get some sleep in the Svensson or the Gentry wagon."

"Cap, I don't want to leave him."

"You've got no choice. Devon, you take her out of here. I'll stay with him till somebody else comes."

Devon nodded. "Get some clothes."

"Drink that whiskey first. Come on, a couple swallows," Cap told her.

Marybeth took the bottle and curled her nose at the smell. She tipped the bottle and swallowed, then felt her insides catch fire. She gasped and coughed. "How do you ... men ... drink this!"

Cap grinned. "You get used to it. Now you go get something in your stomach. I won't let you back in this wagon come mornin' if you don't go eat and get some rest. I mean it."

Marybeth knew he was serious. She leaned down and kissed Josh's forehead, telling him she would be back soon, wondering if he even heard. She looked at Cap, her eyes tearing. "If he's ... going to die, I hope it will be quickly, Cap. I can't stand watching him suffer so."

"He's a strong man, and he's got you to live for. Go on now. Do like I said."

She reluctantly climbed out of the wagon, feeling lightheaded from lack of food and her first taste of whiskey. The rest of the evening seemed to pass in a kind of fog. She ate a little, washed and changed, remembered lying down on someone's feather mattress. When she awoke, dawn was breaking and women were preparing breakfasts. Panic immediately filled Marybeth's heart. She climbed out of the Gentry wagon and hurried over to her own, paying no attention to Delores, who called out to her to come and eat some breakfast. What if Josh had died during the night, and she was not with him!

She climbed up onto the seat of the wagon and looked inside. Bess Peters looked up at her, the woman's eyes still dark and lifeless from her own lingering sorrow over her mother. "I told Cap I thought it would help my own grief if I could help nurse your husband for a while," the woman told her. "Delores, she's pregnant and not feeling so good lately. And Florence is busy with the Billings children and taking care of Danny."

Marybeth moved inside. "Thank you, Bess. How is he?"

"About the same. Very feverish." She touched Marybeth's arm. "I'm so sorry for you, Marybeth. You had such a short time together, and he made you so happy. Everyone could see how much in love you both were." She looked down at Josh, bathing his face with a cool cloth. "He spoke your name a couple of times. I answered for you. I figured he probably wouldn't know the difference, and if he thought you were with him, it would help." She shook her head. "It's such a shame. Such a vital, handsome man he was."

Marybeth sat down beside the woman, noticing Josh seemed to be looking thinner. His face was so pale he already looked dead, and dark circles had formed under his eyes. "I don't know what I'll do if he dies, Bess."

"You'll go on. We all go on." She put the cloth back in a bucket of water and met Marybeth's eyes. "My husband told me about Josh's offer to take the music box. The trouble is, we couldn't wait until we reached Fort Hall. That climb was much too taxing. And with Josh lying in your wagon, we couldn't give you the added weight, let alone make room for the box. We left it behind." The woman's eyes began to tear. "I ... had Al set it high against the cliff, where it wouldn't be noticed or stolen."

Marybeth grasped her hands. "I'm so sorry, Bess. We would have gladly taken it."

"I know," the woman choked out. "I just keep telling myself Mother would have understood, and all I really need is her memory. And I have some of her other ... personal belongings left."

Their eyes held, both feeling the pain of realizing how near death always hovered. They embraced and wept, and Bess finally pulled away and left. Marybeth leaned down and kissed Josh's cheek.

"Please don't die, Josh," she cried. "Please, please hang on for me!" She grasped one of his hands, and to her surprise, she felt him lightly squeeze it. The tiny movement brought unspeakable joy to her heart.

Another day was spent chopping down trees and rigging them to the underside of the wagons, creating a drag that would help the animals hold back the weight of the wagons as they headed down the steep winding road that would take them into flatter land and on to Fort Hall. Josh had not shown any more recognition of Marybeth's presence, other than to groan her name over and over while he lay in a pitched fever. When she answered him, he continued to groan her name, seemingly unaware she had spoken to him.

Delores brought Danny to her for another feeding, and Marybeth clung lovingly to her son, realizing it was possible they would again be alone against the world. She thanked God for the life in her womb, knowing that if something happened to Josh, she would indeed want to stay alive not only for Danny, but to bear Josh's son or daughter. But to think of either child growing up without Josh's love and influence, of never realizing their dream of a ranch in Oregon and lots of children, brought agony to her heart. She longed and needed to be held by Josh, but those arms might never hold her again.

She was nearly through feeding Danny when to her surprise, Ella MacKinder climbed up onto the wagon seat. Their eyes held for a moment, and Marybeth clung to Danny warily.

"How is Josh," the woman asked.

"Do you really care?"

Ella nodded. "I care. Just don't tell Mac I asked." Marybeth looked past the woman almost fearfully. "Don't worry. He is busy helping cut trees. I told him I wanted to see about helping take care of Danny today. The women who have been helping you have had extra work. I'd like to see my grandson, and so would Mac."

Marybeth frowned. "I suppose Mac only agreed because he thinks Josh is going to die. Does he really think that if Josh dies I would come running back to the MacKinders? Does he think this little gesture is going to make me think he's changed?"

Ella shook her head. "What difference does it make what he thinks? I just want to be with my grandson. Way up here, what harm is there, Marybeth? We certainly can't go anywhere with him, and Mac won't be through helping tie the logs under the wagons until nightfall."

Marybeth sighed, tired of the hate and distrust. "All right. I know *you* at least are sincere, Ella." She readied Danny. "If you really want to know about Josh, it's hard to say if he'll live or die. The wound is very bad. Cap did what he could, but now he's full of infection. He has convulsions and vomits. He's in a lot of pain," Her eyes teared. "And I wish there was more I could do for him."

"I'm sorry, Marybeth. Whether it was right or wrong for you to leave this family, I know you loved him."

The words surprised Marybeth. She handed Danny up to his grandmother. "Ella, did Cap or Devon tell you—the bullet came from one of those new repeating rifles? That it could have been John's?"

The woman's eyes misted over. "Cap told us." She held Danny close, patting his bottom. "You can imagine what Mac had to say about that. I won't sting your ears with it. He won't grieve because he's positive John is alive. You know how stubborn a MacKinder can be. But I..." Her voice choked. "I have no doubt my only remaining son is dead. My biggest regret is that I let them both become what their father was, and so, God forgive me, perhaps the world is better off without them."

The remark astonished Marybeth, and she saw the woman's determined effort to show no feelings. "We don't have much more reason now to keep going, except that we cannot turn back. And then there is Danny." She sighed. "I will bring him back when he is hungry. Thank you, Marybeth."

The woman climbed down, and Marybeth felt sorry for the years of unhappiness Ella MacKinder had suffered. Surely she had once longed for the kind of love Marybeth had found with Josh. She would not begrudge the woman whatever little bit of joy she had left in life by denying her the right to see Danny. But she worried how she would manage alone in Oregon if something happened to Josh. Would Mac find some way to get Danny away from her, like he had promised? She still had not got over the fear she felt at the memory of the look in Mac's angry eyes, and it sickened her to think the man was probably rejoicing over Josh's fate.

She looked down at Josh, and for the first time he opened his eyes and looked at her with a hint of recognition in his eyes.

"Josh?" She leaned closer, touching his face. "Josh, it's me, Marybeth. Do you see me? Can you talk?"

He searched her eyes, unspeakable pain evident in his own. He licked his lips and opened his mouth, managing to whisper the word water.

Marybeth smiled through tears as she dipped a ladle into a bucket of water Cap had set inside the wagon for her. She moved an arm under his head and held the ladle to his lips, letting him sip the water. She put the ladle back when he began shaking, and she leaned down, putting her arms around his shoulders.

"I'm right here, Josh. Please hang on for me. Please. I'll help you through this. I need you so."

"Marybeth," he whispered. "Hurts ... everything ... everything..."

"I know." She kissed his eyes. "It will get better, Josh. Thank God you're talking to me." She swallowed back tears, not wanting to break down in front of him.

"What ... happened?"

"You were shot, Josh, in the Indian raid. Do you remember the raid?"

He closed his eyes again, his breathing shallow. "How ... bad? Can't ... move."

"That's just because the wound is so fresh and you're still in so much pain," she lied, hoping she was at least partly right. "You'll get better, Josh. You have to—for me—me and Danny and your own child. I'm going to have your baby, Josh. *Our* baby. You have to get well before it's born. We have to get to Oregon and start that ranch, remember?"

"My God ... the ... pain," was his only answer. She suspected he didn't even understand what she had just told him. His head flopped sideways, his eyes closed, and for one panicky moment Marybeth thought perhaps he had died. She put her fingers to his neck and felt a faint pulse, then broke down into tears.

"Dear God, take away his suffering," she wept.

# Twenty-Four

The journey down the other side of the mountain seemed more taxing than the climb up. Now animals had to hold back the weight of the wagons rather than pull it, a more dangerous task. Marybeth stayed inside the wagon with Josh, praying not only for his life, but for the safety of the wagon that carried them, and the skill of young Ben Harper, whose dexterity with oxen was tested to its limit.

Marybeth ventured to look out only once, and regretted it. What she saw would have been something exciting to share with Josh, for in spite of the terrifying height and narrowness of the mountain trail, the view was so vast Marybeth stared spellbound for a moment. She tried to guess how many miles she must see, wondering if she was literally looking at Oregon in the distance. The land below was spread out like some mystical, heavenly place, with a vast valley below and more mountains in the distance. It was all purple and green and yellow, and hazy from the afternoon sun.

But there was no Josh with whom to share this amazing, once-in-a-lifetime sight, and without Josh to help her through this danger, the sight caused Marybeth's heart to tighten and made her whole body tense up with every bump and jolt of the wagon.

It took sixteen hours to make the descent, and when the last wagon made it to flatter land, a round of cheers went up from those weary emigrants who waited at the bottom, already making camp for the night. Young Ben guided Marybeth's wagon into position and stepped up to the wagon seat. "He make it through all right, ma'am?"

"I think so, Ben. Thank you so much. What would we do

without your help?"

"You know I don't mind, ma'am." He removed his floppy hat and wiped his brow. "I just hope I never go through somethin' like that again. Trouble is, Cap says there's more up ahead. I'll try not to think about it till the time comes I have to." He grinned. "I'm goin' to my pa's wagon now. I hope Josh is gettin' better."

"Thank you, Ben."

Josh heard the voices. They sounded so far away. "... *hope I never have to go through somethin' like that again.*" Whose voice was that? Ben? What had they been through? Was Marybeth all right? Why did voices seem to echo in his mind, like a dream? Why did everything hurt so horribly that he wanted to scream; everything but his legs? Why couldn't he move them? Why couldn't he sit up? He should be on his horse, out hunting for meat. He wanted to wake up from this nightmare and be with Marybeth at the warm pond, make love to her, pick up Danny in his arms, go hunting. He had never before had such a continuing nightmare.

He felt something cool on his face, heard a woman's voice. Someone dribbled something wet and cool into his mouth, and he swallowed. Thirsty! He was so thirsty and hot, so hot! Were they in the desert? Was that what Ben was talking about? His mind scrambled to remember where they might be, what had happened. Indians. He remembered Indians—and Anna Mae Billings's bloody, naked body. Marybeth. She was under the wagon with Danny. And he remembered a ripping pain, a horrible burning in his back and guts, and even more horrible pain when it felt as though someone was gutting him alive. The memory brought a gasp of pain from his lips, and he felt gentle hands press against his face.

"Josh? Josh, can you hear me?"

Marybeth. That was her voice. Why was it such an effort to wake up, to speak? Something deep inside welled up, a deep need to know what was real, to wake up from this nightmare. He struggled to shout Marybeth's name, little realizing it was coming out in a groan. Finally his eyes opened, and he looked through a haze at a woman's face, saw by the light of a lamp that the face was surrounded by a cascade of auburn hair.

"Mary … beth," he managed to mumble.

"You spoke to me once before, but I don't think you remember," she told him. "Josh, are you with me this time? Do you hear me?"

"So … hot."

"I know. I'm trying to keep you cool. It's the infection. If you can just hang on through the next couple of days, Josh, Cap says you have a good chance of making it. But you can't be moved too much. That's why you're having trouble getting better, riding in this bumpy wagon. We'll be at Fort Hall soon. You'll rest better there."

He struggled to see her better. "Where … are we?"

"We're over the mountains, well past Sublette's Cutoff— on our way to Fort Hall. Cap says in another three weeks we'll be in Oregon Territory." He felt her kiss his cheek. "Oh, Josh, I love you and need you so. Please, please get well, Josh. Remember your promise? We're supposed to be together, Josh."

He could tell she was crying. How he wanted to hold her, but even the minimal effort of raising his arms brought excruciating pain. Why? This was something different from anything he had ever suffered—different from the arrow wound he had taken down in Texas, different from the bruises he had after the fight with John MacKinder. MacKinder! He had to protect Marybeth from them. He couldn't just lie here like this. He tried to rise, heard his own scream, felt Marybeth pressing on his shoulders and heard her yelling for someone to get Cap. Now he felt the sickness coming, heard Marybeth crying, tasted blood and bitterness in his mouth.

"Cap, he tried to get up," Marybeth was saying.

"You crazy fool," Cap was telling him. "Take that towel out from under his head, Marybeth. We'll put a clean one there. Throw that one out and Florence will take care of it. Let's look at the bandages."

The next several minutes were filled with pain, as familiar voices, Cap, Aaron, Marybeth, talked about a wound being infected and discussed cutting him open again. Him who? Himself? No one was going to do any such thing! He wanted to reach up and grab Cap and tell him so, but his body was useless. All he could do was scream at them to stop touching him, stop moving him around, but his protests came out only as horrible moans and mumbled abuse, as pain caused him to cuss out Cap and whoever else was probing at him. He searched for the worst words he could think of, that, unknown to him, were shocking to Marybeth.

"It's just the pain talkin'," he heard Cap tell someone. The man chuckled. "Ain't the first time I've been called them names. Look at it this way, Marybeth. At least he ain't dead."

"Oh, Cap." Josh could hear her tears. How he wanted to comfort her.

"I'm hopin' he can hold out till we reach Fort Hall," Cap was saying. "That way, once I cut into him again, he won't have to be moved." Someone wrapped his middle tightly with something. "Marybeth, I ain't brought it up since that first night, but I'm tellin' you again, you can't stay at Fort Hall. There are men there who will watch after him. It ain't safe for you to stay there alone through the winter, especially with a baby comin' on."

A baby? Whose baby? Did he mean Danny? Surely not. Comin' on could only mean a new baby. *Was Marybeth pregnant?*

"No! I won't leave him, Cap. I won't!"

"You ain't got a whole lot of choice. What if he dies after all? You'd be left there alone all winter, have a baby out here in this wilderness with nothin' but a bunch of no-good men to help you. You'd have to wait for a new wagon train to come along to take you on to Oregon—travel with complete strangers. If you go on with us, you'll be safe, among friends, people who care about you and Danny, womenfolk who will be able to help you when you have the baby."

*Have the baby.* It was true then! Marybeth was going to have a baby, *his* baby! And here he was unable to raise even a finger. What in God's name had happened to him? Marybeth needed him, and he was useless!

"Cap, you can't ask me to leave him. You can't."

"Honey, if he lives, you know damn well he'll come chargin' out to Oregon as fast as he can ride. We can send messengers back here in the spring to find out what's happened to him. He'll understand, Marybeth. If he was in his right sense now, he'd be tellin' you exactly what *I'm* tellin' you. He'd want you to go on, Marybeth, stay with people who love you and care about you, people who will watch out for you. Hell, you don't even know for sure if John MacKinder is dead or alive. You can't be caught out here alone. You think real hard on it, Marybeth. You'll see I'm right. You've got little Danny to think about."

Someone fussed more with him, and he heard more tears. Then he sensed the men were leaving. Someone sponged his face again. "Oh, Josh, they want me to leave you at Fort Hall. I won't leave you; I won't. You'll need me so very much the next few weeks, maybe months. I love you so much, Josh. Please, please get better."

He thought about what he had heard, realizing even as he struggled with full consciousness just how badly injured he must be. Now he remembered Marybeth saying something earlier about his being shot. Was he that bad, that they had to leave him at Fort Hall? He couldn't be moved? If that was true, Cap was right. Marybeth couldn't stay buried in the mountains for the winter, not with Danny, and not if she was going to have a baby. What if he died? Cap had said he might. If he did, the baby Marybeth was carrying was all that would be left of him.

He longed to talk to her, to tell her he agreed with Cap. But for the moment the words were too difficult. He had drained his meager strength trying to fight Cap, screaming out in pain. Forcing out enough air to speak now was impossible.

"Marybeth," he managed to mutter. "Love … you."

"And I love you, Josh. I love you so. Please hang on." Oh, if only he could hold her.

John stayed hidden in the trees for a while as he watched the cabin. Smoke curled slowly from its stone chimney. He watched one man come outside and get some wood. He wore a heavy bearskin coat and a floppy hat. His hair was long and mingled into a shaggy beard.

John dismounted, shivering against the cold air, realizing he had to find shelter soon. Each night seemed colder than the last, and he remembered stories he had heard about winters in the mountains. He would rather have followed the wagon train into Oregon, but now he was afraid. Although he celebrated watching Josh Rivers go down under his gun, he was afraid that if he made an appearance too soon, someone might put two and two together, especially someone clever like Cap or Devon. They were all friends of Josh's. They would be eager to find his killer, and the Indians who had attacked the wagon train didn't carry repeating rifles. Those John had watched had only one or two old muskets. Someone like Devon probably knew that. Was there a way to tell a bullet hole from a musket ball hole? Had Josh lived long enough for them to remove the bullet and see what kind it was?

One thing he was sure of. No man lived through being shot in the back. Either way, he decided not to show his face until spring. By then his parents and Marybeth would be settled somewhere in Oregon. The wagon train would be broken up, everyone would have gone their separate ways, and Marybeth would not be surrounded by so many do-gooders. She would be alone and vulnerable, and lonely.

He walked cautiously toward the cabin, leading his horse by the reins. He told himself that if the man inside gave him trouble, he could just shoot him. After his brother and Josh, killing was becoming easier for him. It still amazed him how easily one man could get away with such things out here. He was beginning to like this country. It by God fit him—big, wild, strong. He could learn a lot living out the winter here. His arm would heal completely, and when he showed up in Oregon, Marybeth would see he could be just as skilled at survival in this land as Joshua Rivers. She would be surprised to see him, and he would tell her stories of killing bears and surviving a horrible winter, whether the stories were true or not.

He was not so sure how he felt about Marybeth or Danny any more. Part of him said to hell with the whole thing. He had got his vengeance on Josh Rivers, which was what he had wanted more than anything. But there was a principle involved that had still not been settled. Marybeth MacKinder had given herself to another man. She had taken Danny away from the family. She had not turned to him after Dan's death the way he was sure she would have. She was a bitch of a woman who still had not learned a woman's place, and her hateful spurning of his love and his desire for her had left a burning need deep in his gut to prove to her he was the only man for her.

He kept his rifle in his hand as he tied his horse and went to the door, knocking on it.

"Who's there," came a gruff voice.

"I'm a man who's lost his way—need a place to winter. Can I come in and get warm?"

"Door's open."

John slowly opened the door to see the man sitting in a chair with a rifle pointed at him. "Set the gun aside till I hear your story, mister. Out here it don't always pay to be too neighborly."

John carefully laid his rifle on the table. He guessed the man to be perhaps close to fifty. But he was so hairy it was hard to tell, and it seemed that men who lived out in these parts aged faster. "My name is John MacKinder. I had a little problem with a wagon train I was traveling with to Oregon. They left me on my own."

"What was the problem?"

"That is my business; but I have become lost and am afraid to try going on until spring. I need a place to stay for the winter. I saw your cabin."

"Close the door."

John obeyed, staying near the door. "I am strong. I can help you hunt, cut wood, whatever. I have an arm that was broken but is healing now, so for a while I cannot do hard work. But I will do my share, and I have whiskey ... and a little money to pay you."

"What's that funny accent?"

"I am Irish."

"Mmm-hmm. You kill a man or somethin'?"

"No. I just ... got in a fight."

"Over a woman, I'll bet."

John grinned. "Is that not the reason most men fight?"

The man chuckled. "Women or gold, and you don't look like a rich man." He nodded toward a chair. "Sit down. I'll get you some coffee." He rose as John took a chair. The man picked up his rifle and looked it over. "One of them new repeating rifles, I see."

"Yes. You can have it if I can stay the winter here."

The man eyed him closely. "You mean it?"

John nodded.

The man looked the gun over again. "Well, I just might take you up on that. But for the first few days, you don't touch a gun, and at night you sleep on some bearskins there on the floor near that big support post." The man indicated a thick pine trunk that seemed to be the primary support in the center of the cabin. "I've got me a chain with a lock I used to use to chain up a wild wolf I captured once. I'll fasten one ankle to the post every night till I'm sure I can trust you. I ain't gonna give quarters and share my food with no man who's aimin' to shoot me in my sleep and keep himself warm all winter on wood I cut, keep his belly full on food I hunted."

"I mean you no harm. You can teach me things I need to know. This land is new to me."

The man looked over the rifle again, then at John. "I'll teach you. You treat me right, I'll treat you right. And I'll be keepin' this gun as payment. You got more bullets for it?"

John nodded. "I will not be chained to a post like a dog, though. If you do not trust me, I will sleep outside the next few nights in your horse shed. You can bolt your door."

The man nodded. "All right." He moved to the fireplace and hung the new rifle over it. "Name's Nick Eastman. Came out here from Michigan in '49. Didn't have no luck findin' gold in California, but I like this country—like bein' alone. But sometimes even I like some company. I'm up here pannin' for gold. Nobody else around here is doin' it, so I figured maybe I'll be lucky and hit it big. Gold could be anyplace out in this country. A man just has to keep tryin'."

"I would like to learn how to do that—pan for gold. I will help you however you need it."

The man nodded and grinned. "All right. But if things don't work out the next few days, you gotta leave. You'll get your rifle back and I'll lead you to the nearest shelter. Agreed?"

John nodded. "Agreed."

Marybeth decided that during the whole journey, Fort Hall was the most welcome sight so far. Finally Josh could lie in a real bed that would not jostle him around and make his misery worse. His infection seemed to be worse, and his fever was raging; and he had not been able to carry on an intelligent conversation with her yet, although there had been a few lucid moments.

They all made camp, most grumbling about the fact that the army had abandoned this fort and left it to a few mountain men. "It's no wonder we had that Indian trouble," one man grumped to another. "I thought the government was doing a better job of protecting the emigrants."

The fort was hardly more than a passable trading post now, once belonging to the Hudson's Bay Company, taken over by mountain men first, and then the military, now turned back to the mountain men, who made an effort to keep a few supplies around for the wagon trains.

Cap, Devon, Aaron and Sam came to get Josh from the wagon, while Raymond Cornwall and Al Peters stood at the back of the wagon with a makeshift stretcher. Cap lowered the tailgate of the wagon.

"I've talked to the man who runs this place," he told Marybeth. "Name's Frank Powers. I know him. He can be trusted. We fixed up a bed in that big log building over there. Used to be officers' quarters when the army was here. We're gonna' try slidin' Josh onto that stretcher and carry him there."

"Be careful, Cap."

The moment the men began sliding Josh toward the back of the wagon, his screams could be heard by the whole camp. People shuddered and prayed, everyone pitying Josh and

Marybeth both.

The men managed to get Josh onto the stretcher, and Marybeth quickly followed them across an open area to a two-story log building. They carried Josh inside and laid him on a homemade, rope-spring bed covered with a feather mattress and clean blankets. Marybeth looked around the small, crude room; the inner walls were also made of logs, and there was one window. It did not let in enough light, however, and Aaron lit a lantern that hung near the bed. Josh's face betrayed his hideous pain, and Marybeth felt sick herself at how ill he looked.

"Marybeth, this is Frank Powers," Cap was telling her, indicating a huge, bearded, buckskin-clad man standing on the other side of the bed. The man removed his hat and nodded to her.

"Mrs. Rivers," he acknowledged. "Cap here, he told me what all happened. I take great store in Cap's opinions, and he tells me your husband here is a good man and will need a lot of carin'. Me and some of the others, we'll be here all winter. We'll do all we can for him."

"I appreciate your offer, but you won't need to go out of your way, Mr. Powers," Marybeth told him. "I'll be staying here with him."

Josh could hear the conversation, but was in too much pain to speak out.

Powers looked at Cap in surprise. He looked back at Marybeth. "Ma'am, it just wouldn't be a smart thing for you to do. Winters around here are awful rough, and there's always the danger of Indians. Cap says you've got a young boy, and…" He looked her over. "And another one on the way. It's most likely your baby would be born before the weather was good enough for you to leave this place, and believe me, this ain't no place for a woman to be havin' a baby."

"I won't leave him," Marybeth said firmly.

Powers shook his head. "You got to think about your boy, ma'am, and your baby and what your husband would be wantin' you to do. Fact is, you ain't got a whole lot of choice. I just plain out won't *let* you stay. This ain't no place for no woman except the kind that's made for this land—Indian women. You got my word, your husband will be took good care of."

Marybeth's heart began to pound with panic. They were all against her! They were going to make her leave Josh! "You *have* to let me stay," she said, angry with herself for the quiver in her voice. "He'll need me—need to know I'm near."

"He'll need to know you're *safe*," Cap put in. "Use your head, Marybeth. Josh ain't gonna rest easy knowin' you're buried in these mountains with him, knowin' at any time Indians could come along and murder Danny and run off with you. Damn it, Marybeth, do you know how they'd treat you? You'd be wishin' you was dead, and once they was through with you they'd *grant* your wish." Marybeth reddened. "I'm sorry to be so blunt, Marybeth, but you've got to think about what is *really* best for Josh, and worryin' about you bein' here alone ain't gonna help him heal."

Their eyes held, and he saw the desperation in her own. "Cap, I belong with him," she pleaded.

"You belong with people who can see to your safety, and the safety of Danny and Josh Rivers' unborn child. You know I'm right, Marybeth."

She turned away, torn with indecision, with love for Danny and her unborn baby, and her love for Josh. Cap gave orders to bring hot water and to cut off Josh's bandages. "Get some laudanum down him if you can. I've got to try to drain that infection and get the fever down. He ain't gonna last long the way he is." The old man touched her arm. "You stayin' for this? It ain't gonna' be pretty, Marybeth."

She breathed deeply. "I'll stay." She turned and faced him, and his heart went out to her at the look in her eyes. "Cap, please at least don't leave until he's conscious enough for me to explain to him what's happening, why I ... can't stay."

"We can't be waitin' too long, Marybeth. It's gettin' to be the time when anything could happen up in them mountains, and we've got more to get through before we're home free."

"I know. Maybe—maybe once we get rid of some of the infection and the fever goes away, he'll be more aware of his surroundings."

"Maybe."

Men came back with hot water and towels, and they tied Josh's arms and legs.

"Cap," Marybeth spoke up before he got started.

"What is it?"

"It's not just the thought of him being in pain and alone. I'm worried how he'll react if he discovers he's paralyzed. Out here ... all alone. How long can we depend on these men helping him once he's healed but can't walk? How will he get out to me? I'm the only one who loves him enough to take care of him the rest of his life."

"Marybeth, I'll give you my personal promise. If he don't show up next spring in Oregon, I'll come back here myself to see what happened. If he can't walk, I'll get a wagon and I'll bring him back over them mountains to you myself."

A tear slipped down her cheek. "Thank you, Cap."

"We are ready, Cap," Devon spoke up.

Marybeth took a deep breath for courage and leaned down to put a cool cloth to Josh's forehead. "Mary ... beth," he mumbled.

"God help me," she whispered. "Please take away his pain."

# Twenty-Five

Marybeth sat through the night by Josh's side, putting Danny to sleep on her feather mattress, which Aaron brought to her from the wagon and laid out on the hardwood floor. It felt good to be in a solid building, and it made her think of how wonderful it would have been to arrive in Oregon with a healthy Josh, to build their cabin and have a real home, but the pain and suffering she had witnessed when Cap relieved Josh's infection made her hope dwindle.

In the morning she fed Danny and carried him outside for Florence to watch over him so that his natural squealing and childish noises would not disturb Josh. She was carrying him toward the Gentry wagon when she noticed Ella approaching, Mac walking with her. Ella called out to her, and Marybeth's heart quickened. She could hardly stand to look at Mac any more, and had managed not to for several weeks now, in spite of their proximity. When Ella came for Danny, she had always been alone.

She stopped and waited for them, clinging to Danny. "Marybeth, I'd like to have Danny again today if I could. While we're resting here, I'll have more time to spend with him."

Marybeth looked at Mac, feeling the old dread and hate all over again when his cold, dark eyes drilled into hers. "Well, now, we are not about to go running off with him in a wilderness like this, are we?" he said sarcastically.

"I suppose not," Marybeth answered cooly. She handed the baby to Ella. "He's been changed and fed. Try giving him a little bread or something. He's eating more solid foods every day. I'd like to get him weaned in another two or three weeks and give myself a rest before I start feeding another one."

"Another one? Are you with child?" Ella asked.

"Yes," she answered proudly. She looked at Mac and saw the anger and chagrin in his eyes. He looked her over scathingly.

Ella turned and hurried away, but Mac stepped closer to Marybeth. "You're going to be alone soon, Marybeth. You'll need us again." He grinned a little. "You do have a way of going through men, don't you? I wonder who your next victim will be?" He laughed a hard, cruel laugh. He saw Cap approaching then and left her.

"Marybeth, that man givin' you trouble again?" Cap asked her.

She watched after Mac. "He doesn't upset me so much any more, Cap." She swallowed back tears and turned to face him. "Josh's fever has gone down some. Do you want to come and look at him?"

"That's what brought me over here." They walked back to the log building and went inside, and Cap checked Josh's bandages. "He looks a little better, don't you think? His color is better."

Josh opened his eyes. "Don't ... tell me this ... buffalo skinner ... has been putting ... the knife to me."

"Josh!" Marybeth leaned closer. It was the most lucid statement he had made since he was shot, and the digging remark sounded more like the old, teasing Josh. She leaned down and kissed his cheek. "Josh, are you really with us this time?" Her eyes filled and she sat down carefully on the bed and touched his hair. "Oh, Josh, how do you feel?"

He closed his eyes. "Like ... somebody took a ... pitchfork ... and raked it all the way ... through my body. I need ... some water."

Marybeth hurriedly got him some, and Cap leaned closer. "I take it you ain't real happy about bein' my patient," he said with a grin.

Josh smiled weakly, but Cap caught the tears in his eyes. "I can't ... move my legs, Cap."

Cap's grin faded, and Marybeth felt a lump rising in her throat. She leaned over and Cap held his head while she helped him drink the water. "It's just temporary," Marybeth told him.

"Cap thinks after you've rested a good, long time and healed more, you'll get the feeling back in your legs."

Josh looked at Cap, fighting an urge to drift off to sleep again. He couldn't let that happen. There were too many things he wanted to tell Marybeth. He knew she was lying about his paralysis being temporary. How could anyone know that for certain? He felt the horrible panic rising. Useless! He would be useless to Marybeth now—never stand up like a man and hold her again—never make love to her again. He felt the helpless tears wanting to brim over, but he breathed deeply and forced them away. "What—was it," he asked Cap. "Musket? Arrow?"

Cap looked at Marybeth, then back to Josh. Marybeth put back the ladle of water. "It was a bullet from a repeating rifle, Josh. We think it's possible Indians got hold of John MacKinder and stole it from him. Devon says there ain't no Indians got their hands on rifles like that yet."

"That would mean ... MacKinder is dead."

"Most likely."

Josh moved his eyes to Marybeth, seeing the mixture of relief and sorrow there. "I can't ... say I'm ... sorry," he told her.

"You don't need to."

Josh looked back at Cap. "Leave me ... alone ... with Marybeth for ... a while," he said.

Cap nodded. "You just make sure you don't overdo things. You're far from bein' out of the woods yet, Josh. You're a very sick man, and you're best off not doin' any kind of movin' around on your own for quite a while yet." Cap looked at Marybeth. "I'll have one of the women fix up some broth for him and you see if you can get something into his stomach. The man's fadin' away to bones."

Marybeth nodded and Cap went out, leaving them alone. She pulled up a chair and sat down near the bed, taking Josh's hand. "Oh, Josh, it's so good to be able to talk to you and know you hear me and understand me."

He studied her for a moment, so young and beautiful and vibrant. He felt sick at heart at not being able to take proper care of her. "Where's ... Danny?"

She decided not to mention the MacKinder name. "He's being watched after."

He squeezed her hand with as much strength as he could muster. "I remember … hearing things … hearing people talking. You're … going to have a baby, aren't you? Our baby?"

She smiled. "Yes. I was waiting to tell you when I was positive, but I'm more sure of it all the time."

He closed his eyes, and a tear slipped out of his eye. "Damn," he whispered.

Her own eyes teared and she quickly dabbed at his with a handkerchief. "Oh, Josh, don't do this. You'll be all right. I know it in my heart."

He took several deep breaths, gritting his teeth, disgusted with his weakness. "I'm … a sorry … mess, aren't I?"

"Josh, you've been through some horrible things. Your resistance is just very low right now. Good heavens, Josh, there is nothing wrong with tears."

He took another deep breath, biting his lower lip. "I don't … need this right … now. We need … to talk."

"We can talk another time."

"No!" He spoke the word through gritted teeth, and with a sudden firmness that made him wince with pain from the effort. He swallowed before continuing. "Marybeth, I heard … all of you talking … yesterday. At least I think it was yesterday. Cap, the others … they're right about you—going on with the wagon train."

Her heart tightened at the words. "Josh, how can I leave you alone in this condition? You'll need me. I'm your *wife*. I can't bear the thought of leaving you behind all alone and in such pain. Just the thought of it tears at my soul."

"You've got … no choice. I'm … ordering you … to go." He met her eyes, his own bloodshot and hollow looking. "You're going to have a baby." He looked past her, studying the room for a moment. "This place—it's no good for a woman. I heard Cap talking about it. Like he said … there are men here who will … take care of me. I want you to be with … friends. I might … die, Marybeth."

"Don't talk that way, Josh," she said, the tears starting to come. "You've lived through the worst."

"Can't be sure. I've seen people live ... a couple of weeks with ... bullet wounds and still—not make it." He squeezed her hand. "You know I'll try—for you, Marybeth ... for my baby. If you stay here and something happens to me ... you'll be left alone, to find a way to ... Oregon. Please, Marybeth. I ... don't want that ... on my mind. And—it's dangerous here." He studied her eyes. "If I never walk again ... if you want to be free of me—I'll understand."

Her eyes widened with anger. "How dare you suggest such a thing! I love you. Nothing will separate us, Josh. And you aren't going to die. You're going to *live*, for me, and Danny, and your unborn child. If it's so important to you, I'll go on to Oregon, but I'll do it unwillingly. And come spring, you're going to come out to me. Cap is going to come and get you, and I don't care if you come in the back of a wagon. You're coming to Oregon, and I'll figure out a way for us to survive. We can do it, Josh, because we love each other, no matter what has happened." She barely paused for breath. "I don't intend to be twice widowed, and no matter what condition you're in, I'm better off with you than without you."

She stopped and gasped, putting her head down on the edge of the bed, her lips against his hand. "Darling Josh, you've got to live—for me. Don't make me watch another grave being dug—for someone I love more than my own life."

He managed to open his hand, and he moved it to touch her hair as she lay weeping at the side of the bed.

"My poor ... Marybeth." He again fought his own tears. "You know I'll try, Marybeth."

"I know you will!" She looked at him, wiping at tears. "You said it yourself, Josh. You said we were meant to be together. Surely God will make you well and bring you out to me." She put his hand to her cheek. "I don't want to leave you, Josh. It will be the hardest thing I've ever done, and I don't feel right about it."

He took her hand. "It *is* the ... right thing, Marybeth. You have to take ... care of yourself—and our baby—for me."

"I will. And I'll pray for you constantly, Josh." She raised up, leaning over him. "I can't bear the thought of you lying here all alone and in pain."

He managed to muster a grin. "I'm—a big boy."

"Oh, Josh, you know what I mean."

He held her eyes, longing to stand up and embrace her fully, comfort her. "I'll rest a lot … easier … knowing you're with people who … care about you. You do like Cap tells you."

She leaned closer and kissed his lips lightly. "I love you so much, Josh. I need you. And I know you need me."

"That's why … I want you to go. If you stay here … something could happen to you—and then I'd have … no reason to go on living."

The door opened, and Delores came in with a tray, a bowl of broth sitting on it. "Is it all right to come in?"

"Yes." Marybeth straightened and blew her nose and wiped at her eyes. "He's talking, Delores. I think—maybe he can try eating."

"That's what Cap said. Are you all right, Marybeth?"

She met Delores's eyes. "Everyone tells me—I have to go on to Oregon with the rest of you. How can I leave him behind, Delores?"

"Because it's best for you and Danny and the baby. Everyone knows that, including Josh." She came closer to the bed and looked down at him. "You agree, don't you Josh?"

"That's just what I've been … telling her."

"There, you see?" Delores set the tray down on a table. "I'll let you feed him, Marybeth. Do you need me to stay?"

"No. I'll be all right. Thank you so much, Delores. You've all done so much for me. I feel so guilty."

"Don't be silly. You're our friend. If the tables were turned, you would do the same for us." She looked at Josh, trying to hide her horror at his gaunt, deathly palor. "Now you get some food in you. Nothing solid, mind you. Just broth. Try to finish it even if you don't feel like it. You'll never get better without something in your stomach." She touched his arm. "We all love you, Josh. And we'll all be waiting for you in Oregon. I know you're going to make it."

"I'll ... do my best."

Delores left, holding back her tears until she was well away from the building.

Marybeth and Danny slept together on the feather mattress on the floor the second night. Marybeth was so exhausted from so many nights with hardly any sleep, that even her worry over Josh could not keep her awake.

Josh watched them both, wanting to weep at the possibility of never being a proper husband to Marybeth again. They had had such a short time together. He tried to understand why this had happened, how God could have let it happen. It was torture not being able to lie with Marybeth, to love her, provide for her, protect her. And he had already established such a close relationship with Danny, who needed a father. Would he ever be a proper father to the boy, be able to take him fishing and hunting, to teach him how to ride a horse? Right now just trying to move his arms was torture. He had wanted Marybeth to sleep beside him, but the moment she sat down on the bed, the shifting movement brought him too much pain.

All he could do was lie there and watch her sleep, so beautiful, her arm around her baby boy. He loved her all the more now for carrying his seed, and he could only pray he would live to see the fruit of that seed, and to be a father to his son or daughter. He clenched his fists, promising himself he would live and he would walk again.

The day and night had gone by too quickly. There had been too little time to get a good look at her, to instill in his mind every feature, to remember her voice, the feel of her hair, remember her smile. He had moved fitfully in and out of sleep brought on by the laudanum he had taken for pain, and they had not been able to talk as much as he would have liked.

All too soon the sun peeked through the one window of the room. He hated waking her, but the dreaded time had come, and he wanted to be sure she got in that wagon and kept going.

"Marybeth," he called. How he hated doing this! He would have to be as brave about her going as she. It would be torture for her to leave him, and torture for him to let her go. At the moment he felt like a frightened young boy, unable to admit his fear to anyone else. How he would love it if she could stay with him, be the one to change his bandages and bathe him and talk to him in his low moments.

He needed that love and care so much right now, but his love for her was much too deep to allow his own selfish needs to come before what he knew was best for Marybeth and Danny. He practiced smiling. He would have to be as cheerful as possible this morning, to assure her he would be perfectly all right without her. He had met Frank Powers, liked the man; but being cared for by a grizzly mountain man who was also a total stranger was not going to give him the love and support he needed so badly right now.

He breathed deeply, feeling a little ill again. He told himself to quit giving in to the pain, and to his childish need of Marybeth. He called her name again, and this time she stirred. "It's dawn," he told her, his voice weak.

She sat up, her green eyes filled with terrible grief. "Already?" She got up, agonizing over the fact that the wagon train was leaving today. Oh, for just one more day, just one more! She said nothing, afraid if she tried to carry on a conversation she would start screaming. She washed her face and brushed her hair, changed Danny and fed him. She set him in the middle of the mattress then, handing him a tin cup and a spoon while she tended to Josh. The boy stuck the cup over his nose and mouth and made noises into it, laughing at the sound.

"I'll shave you," Marybeth told Josh, taking a razor from the gear Cap had brought in from Josh's horse and pack horse. "The water is barely warm, but with enough soapy lather, I can probably do a reasonable job."

"Just don't cut me," he answered. "I've ... lost enough blood."

She smiled and got everything ready. She gently but firmly shaved off a six-day-old stubble.

"Where did you learn this," he asked.

"Dan. He said it was a woman's duty."

"Well, not in my book. When I'm able I won't make you shave me. I can take care of myself."

"Oh, how well I know that." She gently turned his head and trimmed his sideburns. "I'm glad you said 'when I'm able.' At least you're planning on living."

"You think I'd let ... anything keep me from you and Danny? I'll live all right. Question is ... will I be able to walk?"

"Of course you will." She tried to keep her voice positive. "Father O'Grady said we were blessed. God will make you well, Josh."

"Do me a favor—write my sister. She should ... know, but not not till spring. Wait and see, Marybeth. If you write her now, she'll just worry. Might as well wait to see whether you should ... tell her I'm dead—or alive."

Marybeth gently washed his face. "Just a moment ago you had no doubt you would live. You had better make up your mind, Josh Rivers." She pulled back the covers and began gently washing him as best she could without disturbing him too much, and to his embarrassment, she changed the towels on which he lay. She did it all so willingly, so lovingly.

Soon Cap was there to check his bandages again. He and Marybeth got Josh's head and shoulders elevated against a mound of animal skins Cap brought with him. "I seen a man die once just from layin' flat on his back too long," Cap told them. "Somethin' about the lungs gettin' full of water. I heard that from a doctor on another wagon train once. I sure wish there had been one on this one. I got no idea if I did anything right. But I know you're best off sittin' up more, Josh."

Delores brought more broth, which was the only form of food Josh could manage to keep down for now. Cap assured him Frank had promised he would be well cared for, and that there were plenty of supplies at the fort to get them through winter.

"I'm damn sorry, Josh," the man said. "We've got to keep goin', but there will be times when nobody can be inside the wagons, and you've got to be someplace where you won't be moved around, or bounced around in no wagon. You've got to be as still as you can be the next few weeks. You understand, don't you?"

Josh swallowed some broth Marybeth fed him. "I understand, Cap. You just see that … Marybeth gets there safely. That's … all I care about."

"You know I'll do that. And next spring I'm comin' back here for you. Whether you're walkin' or not, I'm takin' you to Marybeth. I promised her."

Josh looked at her and kept a look of confidence. "I'll be walking."

"That's the spirit, boy," Cap told him. He reached out and put a hand on Josh's shoulder. "All your personal supplies are here in the room, and your horses will be kept here. You can trust Frank, Josh. He won't do you wrong."

"If you … recommend him … I'm not worried."

Cap looked at Marybeth. "We've got to get goin'," he told her. "Fifteen more minutes, Marybeth. That's all I can allow. I'm sorry."

To Marybeth it was like a death sentence. She felt as though either she or Josh were going to the gallows. "All right, Cap."

Cap squeezed Josh's shoulder. "Good-bye, Josh. Thanks for all the help you've been. I'll see you come spring."

He caught the tears in Josh's own eyes, realized how frightened the man had to be deep inside. "Bye, Cap. Take … good care of … my wife."

Cap nodded, unable to say any more. He turned and left, and Josh met Marybeth's beautiful green eyes, studying them intently, wanting to never forget them.

Marybeth's throat ached so badly it was difficult to speak. She realized with horrible reality that this could be the last time she set eyes on her husband, and even at that, she was not looking at the vibrant, handsome man she had married. He was ravaged with pain and infection, and he looked it. His skin was sallow, his eyes dark and sunken, and already he looked thinner. *"I've seen men hang on for up to two weeks and still die,"* Josh had said.

She set aside the broth and grasped his hand. "Josh, no

matter what happens, you've made me the happiest woman alive," she told him. "I wouldn't trade the last six weeks for all the riches in the world. You're the only man I've ever truly loved or ever will." A tear slipped out of her eye. "And if it weren't for Danny, and the baby I'm carrying, I would never consider leaving you here like this. I don't care what horrible things might happen to me. It wouldn't matter."

He squeezed her hand. "I know. I realize you're only going because of the baby ... and Danny. Believe me, Marybeth, I *want* you to go. I'll ... rest a lot easier. You've got Delores and Aaron ... the Gentrys ... Cap. They'll all take good care ... of you. And that makes me feel ... a lot better." He ran a thumb over the back of her hand. "I'm going to make it, Marybeth. And ... I'm going to come to Oregon on my own ... riding my own horse ... walking on my own two legs. You'll see."

She wanted to weep openly, but she knew that this was not a time to show her absolute despair. He needed her to be strong, and from the trace of tears in his own eyes, she realized he was being strong for her in return.

There was a knock on the door then, and Delores came inside, followed by Aaron, the Gentrys, the Peterses, Ray and Lillith Cornwall, Ben Harper and Devon. Some of them had to struggle not to show their shock and sorrow over the way Josh looked.

"We came to tell you we'll be praying for you every day, Josh," Ray told him. "Don't think you're alone after we leave. We'll all be with you in spirit." He looked at Marybeth. "Marybeth, we'd like to pray together here, right now, for Josh's recovery. With all this prayer power, how can he *not* recover?"

Marybeth kept hold of Josh's hand. "Thank you, Ray." The man took hold of Josh's other hand, then reached out and took his wife's hand. They formed a circle of hands, Florence completing the circle and taking Marybeth's other hand. Devon stood off alone, not one to join in white men's worship. Ray prayed fervently for their "brother in spirit" who had been a "good servant of God." By the time he finished Marybeth's heart was lifted, especially by the fact that all these Protestants had prayed for a Catholic woman and her husband.

"Thank you all—for coming," Josh told them. "I'll be with you—when you cross those mountains and rivers. Good luck to all of you, and … take care of … Marybeth."

"You know we will, Josh," Aaron told him. "I look forward to seeing you again next spring, friend. I am going to look for some good land for you right next to where I settle so we can all be together again once you get to Oregon."

Josh managed a smile. "Thanks, Aaron. I … look forward to it too."

They all said their good-byes and filed out. Delores held Danny, leaning close to Josh so the boy could give him a sloppy kiss. "Ba-ba, Zosh," he said, waving a fat, dimpled hand.

"Good-bye—son," Josh answered. "You … be a good boy … for your mama." Aaron picked up the feather mattress and Marybeth's blankets, and left. Marybeth leaned over Josh.

"Wherever I am, Josh, no matter how many miles are between us, I am with you. Always remember that. Please don't let yourself feel lonely, because you will never be alone."

A tear finally slipped down his cheek. "Neither … will you, Marybeth."

"We will always be together in spirit—always." *Even if you never make it to Oregon*, she thought, but did not say aloud. She chastised herself for thinking it. Surely the prayers of so many people would make him well. "I love you, Josh."

He searched her eyes. "And I love you—more than anything—anyone. More than my own life."

She leaned down and kissed him lightly. He wanted to kiss her back in his old, teasing way, to grab her and roll her over, feel her pressed against him, make love to her. But that might never be. At least his seed had taken hold in her womb and at least one child would come of their union.

"See you … in the spring—Mrs. Rivers," he told her, giving her his best smile and a wink.

"I'll be waiting."

Her heart sank when the door opened and Frank stepped inside. "Cap says you've got to go now, ma'am," he told

Marybeth. "I'm sorry."

She did not look at him. She leaned down and kissed Josh once more, more tears coming now, her voice shaking. "I love you, Josh. I love you."

"Go ahead … get going," he told her, hoping he could hold back his own tears until she was gone. "I … love you too. I'll see you … in the spring. I promise. I … haven't broken a promise to you … yet … have I?"

She kissed his cheek and rose. "No. And I'll be waiting, Josh. I'll be waiting." The lump in her throat was so huge she wondered where her next breath would come from. She turned and gathered her things, looking at him once more but saying nothing, then hurried out, bursting into tears as she did so. Frank walked closer to Josh.

"Sorry, friend. You need anything right now?"

Josh closed his eyes. "Yeah. I need to be left alone—before I make a … fool of myself in front of … another man."

Frank smiled sadly. "Sure. I'll check on you later." He reached down and pressed Josh's shoulder. "She's a fine woman, a good reason for you to get yourself well and get on to Oregon."

The man turned and left, and Josh heard Cap shouting for the wagon train to get under way. Men shouted and cursed and cracked their whips at the oxen, and minutes later the voices and the sounds of wagons and animals faded. Josh could not stop the tears then, glad there was no one to see them.

# Twenty-Six

Marybeth's grief was overwhelming. To her, leaving Josh behind felt as if she had buried him and had to leave his grave behind. She had watched the log building where he lay until it was no longer visible, and then had come the wracking sobs so devastating that Florence had had to hold her up as they walked. Nothing anyone could say would comfort her.

The only thing that kept her going in the days that followed was Josh's own promise that he would come to her in the spring, and the fact that he was still alive at all. But sleep did not come easily. Every night she lay listening to the wolves and other night sounds, shivering against the cold night air, remembering how unafraid and how warm she had been lying in Josh Rivers' arms.

"*If you follow your heart, God will bless you for it*," Father O'Grady had told them. Her faith and the priest's blessing were all she had now. Every night she went to bed with her rosary, praying to the Virgin Mary over the beads, clinging to her religion, the only source of hope and sanity for her. She hoped she would find a Catholic church in Portland, and a priest who could offer up prayers in Josh's behalf.

The wagons rolled ever farther away from Josh, along dangerous roads that wound back up into high mountains. Marybeth thought how much more beautiful this country would be for her if Josh were along to enjoy it with her. Never had she seen such grand views, such color. Never had she been in a place that seemed so close to heaven. She prayed that come spring, Josh would see all of this, would ride through here on his own horse, vital and healthy again.

Everywhere she looked she saw snow-capped peaks, gray and purple mountains, their sides deep green with fir trees. They moved along mountain roads that nearly stopped her heart with their height. The view from their path was spectacular, and she realized that none of the descriptions she had heard about this land had been completely accurate. How could any man fully explain its grandeur? It had to be seen to be believed. She prayed Josh would see it also.

After several days the wagon train reached a point where the wagons would have to be lowered over a cliff by rope, while the animals would be herded down a road too steep and narrow to take the wagons. The dangerous project took all day, straining men's muscles to the limit. That night women rubbed linament into their husbands' backs and arms, and Marybeth wished Josh was here and she was doing the same for him. Under normal conditions his virile strength would have been a big help on a day like today; but she told herself she must be prepared for the possibility he would never be that strong and vital again.

On and on they journeyed, ever farther from Josh, putting three weeks between themselves and Fort Hall. The nights got colder and colder, and ice formed a thin crust on top of the water supplies so that the women had to break through it every morning to get water for cooking and washing. Finally they moved down out of the mountains and into wide, open land, welcomed by all. Marybeth could see more mountains far, far to the west. That night when they made camp, Cap made the announcement that brought joy to everyone's hearts, but a strange sadness to Marybeth's, for this was a moment she had planned to share with Josh.

"Folks, we're in Oregon Territory," he told them. "We've got about a month to go now before you're where you want to be, but at least you can say you made it to Oregon."

Cheers went up, and a few men broke out some whiskey. That night harmonica and fiddle were brought out again, and the weary, tattered travelers, many of them still grief-stricken by graves left behind, sang and danced and celebrated. Marybeth watched the dancing, imagined Josh sweeping her around in his arms.

"We're here, Josh," she said softly as she watched the

others. "We made it to Oregon." *In another month we'll be home*, she thought. *Home, like we talked about so often. Oh, how I wish we could share this moment together. Please be alive, Josh. Please hang on for me.*

She felt a sudden wave of warmth move through her, as though his arms were around her. "He's alive," she whispered aloud. She put her face in her hands. "I just know it. He's still alive."

They camped near a river that roared so loudly it was difficult to sleep. The emigrants had traveled for two weeks through mostly flat land. Now they were into rolling foothills and headed closer to mountains again. Tomorrow they would cross a wild river on rafts fashioned by Cayuse Indians who charged exhorbitant prices for their services. Marybeth decided that whoever said Indians were ignorant didn't know what they were talking about. These Indians were as clever as the best white businessman, although their wild appearance frightened her, after the encounter with the Crow that had nearly destroyed Josh.

Indians were a mystery to her. Some could be wild and murderous, others, like Devon, nearly like white men. Now there were these Cayuse, looking wild and untamed, but harmless, except for robbing the emigrants blind with fees for getting them across the river.

Ella again came and asked for Danny, but Marybeth hesitated. "We're in Oregon now, Ella. Mac could ride off with him and steal him away from me if he wanted."

Ella stiffened with what was left of a pride that was once strong in her soul. "I will not let it happen, even if he would beat me to death. I promise, Marybeth. I just want to be with my grandson for a while. Please."

Marybeth sighed, feeling sorry for the grief in the woman's eyes, finding it impossible to deny her a few hours of pleasure with Danny. "Just an hour or two then. Bring him back here to sleep."

The woman nodded, smiling a rare smile when she took Danny, who went to her readily and called her "Na-na."

Marybeth watched the woman walk off with him, thanking God that she was out from under the ugly, frightening shadow of Murray and John MacKinder. But it was all thanks to Joshua Rivers. She hoped she could continue to be strong against Mac, even without Josh to back her.

Morning brought bright sunshine, and people readied themselves for the trip across the river. Animals were unhitched, and women took from the wagons a few clothes and precious belongings to carry in case everything else should end up in the river.

Marybeth hung on to Danny, and Delores clung to Marybeth as the two women were oared across the river in a canoe by a dark Indian whose skin was greased not only against the cold but to protect him from icy waters should they end up in the river. The Indian's skill in handling the canoe against the mighty waters was nothing less than amazing, and Marybeth decided that these natives of the land at least earned their fees. She clung to Danny with one arm and to the edge of the canoe with the other, as water splashed against the side of the boat and sprayed them with its chilly beads.

She ducked and prayed, feeling Delores's fingers digging into her arm, while the canoe lurched and tipped and threatened to roll them all into the water. When they finally reached the other side, Marybeth was never more relieved to step on dry ground again. Of all the rivers they had crossed, this one seemed the most dangerous. Once ashore, she and Delores joined several other women and children who had already crossed. Others came over, some of the children crying from fear of the churning white water.

Marybeth watched for Ella, but the woman was not among the rest of the women who came across. Men were herding animals and wagons onto rafts, preparing to bring across two teams and two wagons at a time on four separate rafts. It was then Marybeth heard Mac's shouting, and she strained to hear him over the roaring waters. She could see Ella standing beside him, and saw him facing Cap.

"... no goddamn Indian—get near my wife," Marybeth

made out. "… savages killed my John! … ride over—wagon—raft's good and sturdy … stays with me and the wagon!"

"Mac won't let poor Ella come over in a canoe," Marybeth said to Delores.

"I think he enjoys being obstinate and having his own way, even if it puts a family member in danger."

Cap was shouting back, then waved the man off. "… your own damn way then," Marybeth heard him say then. "I'll be glad—rid of you—another couple of weeks … biggest pain in the ass…" The man rode off to help some others.

Several rafts came across safely. Then came the MacKinder team and wagon. Marybeth watched Ella climb into the wagon, which was then rolled onto one of the rafts. Mac helped herd his oxen onto another raft, and both rafts were pushed into the waters. Strong, experienced Indians worked with poles and an excellent knowledge of the river's currents to steer the rafts safely.

Midway across one of Mac's oxen panicked. Against orders to stay calm, Mac began cursing at the animal, snapping at it with his whip when it kicked at him. The ruckus stirred up the rest of the oxen, and the Indians guiding the raft were shouting something to Mac in their own tongue. One of the oxen stumbled and knocked one of the Indians into the water, the ox falling in after him.

The entire incident happened before Marybeth's eyes like a living nightmare. Without the second Indian, the first one could not hold the raft. It began swirling away from him, and then Mac fell into the water. The raft and the struggling, swimming ox both slammed into the raft carrying the MacKinder wagon, and the rest of the oxen slid off. Two of them scrambled desperately to climb onto the raft that carried the wagon, tipping it slightly. Marybeth heard a scream from inside as the wagon rolled forward into the water.

Everyone stared helplessly as both rafts, the wagon, the oxen, Indians and the MacKinders bounced and bobbed down river, the humans trying to grasp onto rocks, the wagons and rafts smashing into the same rocks and splintering. To everyone's shock it took only seconds before everything, humans, animals, wagon and all, disappeared under water. Marybeth remembered Cap saying that not far ahead the water was even more turbulent, and churned into a steep waterfall.

"Dear God," she muttered. She felt no great remorse for Mac, but still, it was a terrible way to die, and her heart ached for Ella. For several minutes there was no movement, no talking. People just stared. Marybeth put a hand to her stomach, watching the churning waters in disbelief. Two of the Indians, adept at mastering the river, managed to swim to safety. Some of the men helped pull them to shore, and Bill Stone quickly borrowed a horse and rode with Devon downriver to see if they could find the MacKinders. Two Cayuse Indians followed.

Delores put an arm around Marybeth. "Are you all right?"

Marybeth's heart pounded with a mixture of emotions. Gone! So quickly gone! Poor Ella, her whole life wasted, not one moment of it happy, except for the few precious moments she got to share with Danny. "I don't know," she answered Delores.

Delores led her to a campfire, and people watched with their hearts in their throats as the undaunted Indians brought over the rest of the wagons and animals, a day-long project. People came up to Marybeth and told her they were sorry, everyone secretly feeling the loss of Murray MacKinder was no great tragedy, yet understanding that they were after all kin to Marybeth, and that Ella MacKinder's life had ended as tragically as it had been lived.

In spite of feelings for the MacKinders, people were overwhelmed with shock at what they had witnessed, and nerves were close to breaking. Cap walked around camp that evening, assuring everyone that they had mastered the last great danger of the journey. "There was a time when The Dalles was the biggest danger of all," he told them, referring to a stretch of the Columbia River all travelers once had to traverse to reach the Willamette Valley. "A man named Barlow lost family there—made it his personal project to see that a road got built to by-pass The Dalles. We'll be takin' that road."

People breathed easier, but the experience still left them

shaken, and the shadow of death again hung over the group of travelers. Marybeth went to bed full of fear again for Josh, feeling the hand of death had come much to close. Would it also grasp Josh?

"Holy Mary, Mother of God, Pray for us sinners now and at the hour of death," she whispered over her rosary. "If there is any way to forgive Murray MacKinder of his cruelty, please do so and accept him into your Kingdom, Lord. Perhaps there was a reason for his actions that only You understand. And bless and be with Ella. Give her the peace and happiness she has so long been deprived of."

She fell asleep in tears, thinking about Josh, holding her last prayers for her most beloved. Was he calling for her? Was he being properly fed and looked after? How she hated this helpless, helpless feeling.

In the morning Bill Stone and Devon returned dragging travois behind their horses, two bodies wrapped and tied to the travois. No one needed to ask who they were.

"They were bashed up pretty bad," Devon told Cap. "The Cayuse took their own back to their village. They said we were lucky to find the bodies at all. Many who fall into the river are never found."

Again graves were dug. Marybeth found it difficult to believe they were for Mac and Ella. In spite of her feelings for them, it seemed so tragic to have come so far, to be so close to the end of their journey, never to reach their destination.

Gone! All the MacKinders were gone. A chill moved through her at the realization of how much had happened since she first left Ireland the unwilling bride of Dan MacKinder, leaving those first sad graves behind her—her mother's and father's. There had been so much death and heartache since then, and her only bright light, her only happiness besides Danny had been Josh Rivers.

She stared at the dark holes as the bodies were lowered. Was someone lowering Josh's body into a grave? The thought seemed absurd. Not a big, strong, vital man like Josh Rivers. Not her Josh! Others prayed over the MacKinders, but Marybeth prayed for Josh, realizing with sudden shock that she truly was alone now. Much as she would not have wanted to depend on the MacKinders again, the fact remained there was no one left but her and Danny. Somehow, if Josh never came to her, she had to find a way to survive in this new land. She couldn't depend on Aaron and Delores or Sam and Florence forever.

She felt a flutter in her stomach, remembered the life that was growing there. In a few months not only Danny would depend on her, but a new baby—Josh's baby. He or she could be all she had left of the man she had loved with such exquisite passion.

The sound of a shovel brought her back to the present, as Aaron threw dirt into Ella's grave. Two more people and another wagon were gone. Bill Stone wept from the shock of losing two people with whom he had traveled closely over some three thousand miles. Marybeth felt her own tears coming then, not for Murray MacKinder, but for Ella, who had never known the kind of love Marybeth had known in Josh Rivers' arms.

Josh lay in a sweat, finding it incredible that bending his arms to lift the rocks in them could be such a strenuous task. Frank had brought him the rocks, and Josh was determined to start rebuilding his strength. Because of constant sickness since the wagon train left, he had not eaten anything but broth for a month. Today was the first time a piece of bread had stayed in his stomach, but pain was still a constant companion. There had been moments when he literally begged God to take him, moments when he truly wanted to die. But in those moments, Marybeth's face would come to mind, her green eyes crying, her ruby lips forming the words to beg him to get well. Her auburn hair cascaded over creamy skin, and her hands were always reaching out to him for help.

Outside the wind howled, and an early mountain storm was dumping wet snow on everything. Josh hoped the wagon train had made it through and everyone was safely in Oregon and out of the mountains. A month had passed already. It seemed impossible, and he found it hard to realize how far away

Marybeth was now. Sometimes she seemed like some distant dream, something that was not real at all.

He laid the rocks aside, panting for breath, wondering if the day would ever come when he would be normal again. Frank came inside, carrying a cup of hot coffee. "How did you do," he asked, always jovially trying to encourage Josh.

Josh closed his eyes. "Not so good. I bet you don't believe I used to be a strong man."

Frank came closer and handed him the coffee. "Here. Drink this."

Josh looked at it and breathed deeply. "Set it beside me there. I can't even lift a damn cup of coffee till I rest my arm. How in hell am I going to ever get back to normal, Frank?"

The man grinned. "I've seen that woman of yours. You'll get back to normal, all right. And I *do* believe you were a strong man. Cap told me all about that fight you had with some big Irishman who'd never been beat. I'd sure like to have seen that one."

Josh smiled ruefully. "Yeah. Well, I couldn't fight a kitten right now."

Frank pulled back the covers and checked the bandages. "We'll have you fightin' mountain lions come spring." He pressed around the wound. "I don't hear any screams."

"It doesn't hurt so bad any more when you press on it."

"That's good. Means most of the infection is gone."

"How come everything inside still hurts when I move around then?"

"Well, I expect there's still some infection deeper inside—and you're just plain sore, Josh, muscle sore from that bullet rippin' through you—maybe some damage to your nerves. Hell, I'm no doc. I'm just guessin'. But as long as that fever says down, you're sure as hell gettin' better."

Josh rubbed at his legs, feeling nothing. "Maybe so, but I've got a long way to go, Frank. First I've got to get the strength back in my arms so I can use some crutches. Then I get busy on these legs." He looked at the man. "You think the life will ever come back into them?"

Frank sobered. "Who knows, Josh? Like I say, I ain't no doc. I expect your own determination will have a lot to do with it. But I'll help all I can."

Josh nodded. "I'm obliged to you. You're a hell of a friend, to Cap and to me. You didn't need to volunteer to put up with this—me being so sick all the time."

"Well, I figured what the hell? Out here things get pretty boring come winter. Fact is, I brung along a deck of cards, thought you might be interested. Got some good cigars and a little whiskey, too. None of them things can do you much harm. The whiskey will help kill the pain, the cigar will relax you, and a little card game will keep you primed up for when you get to Portland and play against some of them fancy gamblers there."

Josh managed a grin. "All I want to do when I get to Portland is find Marybeth. I'll have a lot more on my mind than cards."

Frank chuckled. "I reckon so. Well, how about it? You want to try some cards? I've got me a bag of dried beans here we can use in place of money—till you're better. Then, my friend, we play for the real thing."

Josh grinned. "Why the hell not?" He reached over and picked up the coffee, sipping some of the strong, hot brew. The howling wind outside only enhanced his feelings of terrible loneliness, and he wondered how Marybeth was holding up. It tore at his heart to think of her arriving in Oregon without him, spending a lonely winter not even knowing if he was dead or alive. "I could use the company," he said aloud. "It gets awful lonely in here."

Frank laid the cards beside him and walked over to stoke up the fire in the potbelly stove that sat in the corner of the room. "Well, the storms up here can get pretty bad. I think I'll move my bed and gear in here for a couple of months so's I'm right nearby if you need me or if the fire goes out. I would have sooner, but sometimes when a man's as sick as you was, extra commotion only makes him feel worse." He pulled a table over next to the bed. "Now, deal up them cards. It will give you some practice usin' them arms and hands. Before you know it, we'll have you dealin' them cards with your toes."

Josh smiled wryly. "Right now I'd be happy just to wiggle them." He picked up the cards and dealt them, and Frank poured two small glasses of whiskey. "Between the laudanum and the whiskey I've drunk the last few weeks, I'm going to be an alcoholic by the time I'm healed," Josh joked.

"Better a walkin' alcoholic than a dead man, don't you think?"

Josh looked at his cards and thought about that first night, when Marybeth looked so frightened because he drank some whiskey. "Maybe, but I want to stop taking the laudanum, and don't bring me any whiskey for a while after this. Maybe I *need* to feel the pain. Maybe it will help me get to feeling my legs again if I'm not all tanked up with pain killers."

"Whatever you say, friend." He threw down two cards and asked for two more. "Whatever you say."

Josh twisted slightly to deal the two cards. To his surprise he felt an odd tingle in his right thigh. He sat back with his cards, still feeling the tingle but afraid to get his hopes up. Marybeth! How happy she would be if he came back to her standing on his own two feet.

"I'll bet two beans," Frank said. He waited, then frowned. "Josh? You with me?"

"What?" The tingling had stopped, and Josh threw down his cards. He picked up the glass of whiskey and drank some. "I'm sorry, Frank, I really am; but I'm just too tired from lifting those rocks. Maybe tomorrow."

"No problem. I'll just leave everything right here. I'll go get my bed and gear. Want me to bring you anything?"

"No."

The man left, and Josh felt the leg that had tingled. Again he could not feel his own touch. He cursed and hit the leg with his fist.

# Twenty-Seven

The emigrants arrived in Portland in late October. Some, including Bill Stone, paid their dues to Cap and kept going, having little to say to the others, wanting only to be on their way and try to forget the tragedies that had plagued their journey. Young Ben Harper could not help a few tears when he said good-bye to Marybeth. He had lost his mother and two brothers to cholera. Another brother and a sister had lived, and Ben's father wanted to head for the Willamette Valley. There were other towns farther south, and Harper hoped to settle in one of them for the winter.

Marybeth wondered if her life would be only full of goodbyes and never anything permanent. She paid Ben what Josh had promised the boy for driving their oxen for them, and she embraced him, wondering if she would ever see him again. It seemed odd the way perfect strangers could become so close on such a venture, and then suddenly turn back into strangers when they reached their destination, each family moving on to start their own lives. The Cornwalls headed for Oregon City, and Al and Bess Peters went with them. Devon headed for California, a man who never stayed in one place for too long.

"I believe Josh will make it," he told her before leaving. "He is a strong, determined man. He will come, and you will be happy again. I am sorry for what happened to him. Tell him Devon will come by sometime and see him walking strong again."

"Thank you, Devon. I'll tell him."

Cap took a room in a boarding house in Portland for the winter, but the rest of the travelers scattered until the only ones left were the Svenssons and the Gentrys.

Portland was a town of contrasts. Only recently

incorporated, it had a population of about eight hundred, with newly built stores standing next to sagging cabins that had been around since the days of the original fur trappers who had settled the area. Some called the place Stump Town, because the main street had been cut from a virgin forest, and many of the stumps were left for horses and wagons to make their way around. They were painted white so they could be seen more easily at night, but many men had cursed them as a nuisance, having lost more than one horse and broken the wheels and axles of more than one wagon on them.

By day men could be heard chopping away at the stumps, sawing lumber for even more new buildings, pounding nails. It was obvious Portland was growing fast, and Aaron had heard another town farther south, Oregon City, was growing even faster.

The whole area was simply a tiny bit of civilization in the middle of a wilderness. Wild roses grew everywhere, as though God insisted on beautifying the gray buildings and muddy streets. In spite of the cold weather setting in, dainty flowers clung to life. Seeing them gave Marybeth hope, as though God was showing her there was beauty and life in everything, and that even a fragile rose could exist in a harsh wilderness. If the rose could survive, so could Josh...

Sam and Aaron hired a couple of extra men to help build two cabins, one for Delores and Aaron, which would have an extra room for Marybeth and Danny; and one for Sam and Florence, who had a new family in the form of the Billings children, Ruth, twelve; Fred, six; and little Nina. Their own eleven-year-old son, Billy, got along well with the Billings children, the entire Gentry family needing the extra noise and work to help them forget the two graves they had left so far behind, graves they could probably never find again even if they tried. Florence had not mentioned the graves in a long time, and both Delores and Marybeth prayed the woman was slowly healing on the inside, although both knew a woman surely never fully recovered from such a loss.

For awhile they all continued to live out of the wagons while the cabins were being built, the children running and playing together; little Nina played endlessly with Danny, who was crawling everywhere now, sometimes getting to his feet and walking. Marybeth was amazed at how fast the men from these parts knew how to raise a cabin. Within ten days they were inside the crude but warm structures. Neither family intended to build anything fancy. The cabins were simply shelter for the winter. Come spring, Aaron and Sam would build homes in the Valley; during the winter they planned to head into the Valley to look for good land, confident their families would be safe living in Portland, which was well settled.

It felt good to be in the arms of civilization again. None of them had seen anything resembling a city since leaving Independence. Marybeth remembered the day the wagon train had headed west, remembered being disappointed that Josh Rivers had not shown up; and she remembered how she felt the first time he rode into camp offering his services as a hunter. Every time she pictured him then, her heartbeat quickened. She was sure she had loved him almost from the day she had bumped into him in St. Louis.

It all seemed so long ago now, and so unreal. But the fluttering in her belly reminded her it *was* real. She had married Josh Rivers, and he had made her his woman. Now his life was growing inside of her. Every time she felt that life move, she was reminded that Josh was still with her.

The cabins had dirt floors covered thickly with clean straw, and the men had worked hard at chinking all cracks well to keep out drafts. Large, stone fireplaces served for both heating and cooking. It was a new form of cooking for Marybeth, who had used a gas stove in New York, and then had learned to cook over campfires. The fireplace was not much different from a campfire, but it was more convenient, and at least when she used it she was out of the elements.

When they moved into the crude but sturdy structures, the women baked, and everyone celebrated being in a home that didn't rock and sway and bounce. Cap was invited to a fine dinner at the Svensson cabin, with dessert and singing afterward. All the Gentrys were there, and there was a lot of laughter. Marybeth forced herself to join in the celebrating, even though inside she wanted to weep as she had never wept before. Here was everything she and Josh had planned to do. How many times had they talked about reaching Oregon, about building a cabin, about having a real roof over their heads and a real bed to sleep in? The ache in her heart made her feel almost physically ill. If only Josh could be here with her, with all of them. She could almost see him standing with the men, joking, laughing, giving her that teasing smile that meant he wanted her.

They celebrated well into the night in the Svensson cabin. Florence had put all "her children" to bed in their own cabin, which was only a few feet away from the Svensson structure, and had rejoined the eating and singing for a while before finally going "home" Marybeth had long since put Danny to bed. Everyone slept on home-made beds with rope springs and feather mattresses. No one had much in the way of furniture, using mostly crates and barrels for the time being.

"When we get settled in the Valley and have the home I have planned for you, then we will have nice furniture again, Delores," Aaron told her.

"I am just glad to be here," she told her husband. They embraced, and Marybeth had to look away to hide her pain.

Sam and Cap finally left, and Delores, growing big with the child she expected to deliver in only a couple of months, went into the bedroom to get ready for bed. Aaron knelt in front of Marybeth, who sat by the fireplace.

"He will come," he told her, taking her hand. "When Sam and I go to look for that land, I am claiming some for Josh, just like I promised. And you will come and live with us until he arrives to build you a home of your own."

She looked at the big, sometimes clumsy man with tears in her eyes, loving him for his goodness. "Aaron, I do not intend to be a burden to you and Delores forever. You have your own lives to lead. If Josh doesn't come in the spring—"

He grasped her hands more tightly. "I told you he will come, and I do not want to hear you talk that way. There will be no more mention of being a burden. You are going to have Josh's baby. You are Delores's best friend. She would be heartbroken without you nearby. She is afraid inside, being in this new land, having her first baby. You are good for her. I consider you a welcome friend, not a burden. Now I think you should go and get some sleep."

A tear slipped down her cheek. "Thank you, Aaron."

He gave her a wink and rose, going into his own bedroom. Marybeth went into her room, closing the pine door and removing her dress. She put on her nightgown and crawled into bed beside Danny. Minutes later she heard sounds coming from the other bedroom, and she knew Delores and Aaron were making love, happy to be at least somewhat settled. The thought of Josh holding her, making love to her, tore at her heart and passions like a sword. She ached to feel his strong arms around her, to taste his kisses, to be a woman to him. But there was no Josh in Marybeth Rivers' bed. There was only a little boy, and soon he would have his own bed to sleep in. Hers would be empty, and she knew it might always be empty. She drew Danny close and cried herself to sleep.

Christmas approached, and a gentle snow fell on the land. Marybeth and Delores worked hard at knitting and baking and sewing, making gifts and cookies and pies for Christmas. Aaron brought a fir tree inside and set it in a can of water, steadying it by tying it to the upper beams. The Gentry children helped decorate the tree with popcorn, and Marybeth watched, thinking what a glorious Christmas this would have been if she could have shared it with Josh. She watched Danny with great joy, wishing Josh could see how the boy walked now, toddling everywhere on his fat little legs, laughing at the antics of the Gentry children, who all did such a good job of entertaining the boy and little Nina.

Danny was weaned now, and Marybeth's stomach had

swollen to obvious proportions. She was forced to wear her skirts unbuttoned and her shirts hanging over them, as Delores had been doing the last few months. Often she wore her black calico wrap dress, which was gathered across the bosom and had no waistline. The baby inside her belly was active and often kept her awake nights, and she had to smile at the thought of what a healthy child she surely carried because of the handsome, healthy man who had given it life.

It was two days before Christmas when Delores went into labor. There was still no doctor in Portland, and it was up to Florence and Marybeth to help the frightened Delores deliver her baby.

"Don't leave me, Marybeth," Delores kept whimpering between screams of labor. Marybeth was reminded of her own first birth, the fear, the pain.

"It will all be over soon, Delores," she assured the woman. "And you'll have a beautiful little son or daughter to present to Aaron." She sponged Delores' face, hoping there would be no complications and no heartbreak for Delores. They had all seen too much of trial and tribulation. The birth of a healthy baby would be a welcome joy.

For hours Delores lay moaning or crying on the crude bed, while Marybeth and Florence gently coached her, and Aaron paced outside, smoking one cigar after another. Finally the little head appeared, and above Delores's screams the other woman told her to push. A baby boy was soon expelled, red and wrinkled and bloody and squalling at the top of its lungs. Delores's screams turned to smiles and tears at the sight of her new son, and Marybeth wrapped him and took him to the outer room to show him to Aaron and clean him up.

"Merry Christmas," she told Aaron. "You have a beautiful, healthy son."

The man looked down at his new son, dwarfing the boy's tiny face with his huge hand when he touched his cheek. His eyes teared. "At least his *lungs* are healthy," he commented with a smile.

Marybeth grinned. "I'll clean him up for you." She looked

up at Aaron. "Just think. Some day you can tell him that he walked almost all the way across America before he was born."

He nodded. "What a long, sad journey that was." He met Marybeth's eyes. It had been nearly four months since they left Josh behind at Fort Hall. He knew what she was thinking. "If I could find a way to get to him, I would do it," he told her. "But it is winter in the mountains—"

"Don't keep thinking you should be doing something, Aaron. There is nothing any of us can do right now but pray. Cap will go in the spring. You just claim that land for us like you promised. Make sure it's good grazing land. Josh wants to raise horses." Her throat tightened and she could say no more. She walked to the table. "Fill a pan with warm water, will you? I'll wash the baby." She smiled through tears. "What a beautiful Christmas present he makes."

Several grizzly mountain men came into Josh's room carrying whiskey and cards and crutches. Frank handed the crutches to Josh. "Merry Christmas," he said jovially. "No more draggin' around hangin' on to our shoulders. You start usin' these things, and before you know it, them legs will be movin' on their own."

Josh tried to smile, taking the crutches and wondering what Marybeth was doing for Christmas. Was her pregnancy going all right? Had Delores Svensson had her baby yet? How wonderful it would be if they could have shared their first Christmas together. He studied the hand-carved crutches. "Thanks, but what makes you think I can use these?" he asked Frank.

"Because you've got your arms and shoulders back in good shape. Now we've been pickin' you up and helpin' you around—I say it's time you tried it by yourself. Come on now. Give it a try, and then we're gonna play some cards and drink a little whiskey to celebrate Christmas. Ole Barnes has a nice piece of venison roastin' back at the other cabin. He'll be bringin' it over in a while."

Josh winced as he sat up. He had regained a little feeling in his thighs though not his lower legs, but at least he had got back all feeling through his hips. The awful pain in his belly and back every time he moved had finally begun to subside, and for the last month he had been able to eat solid foods. He grasped the crutches.

"Okay, now, everybody leave me alone," he told them. "And don't be laughing at me."

"Nobody's gonna laugh, you crazy Texan," one of them spoke up. "Hell, we're all rootin' for you. Give us a reason to drink, boy."

Josh laughed lightly and shook his head. "After all I've been through, I'll probably fall and bust a bone." He hung on to the crutches and started pulling himself up. He had worked hard with the stones, making Frank bring him bigger ones every few days. The muscles in his arms and shoulders flexed firmly as he strained to pull himself up. He was still alarmingly thin, although lately he felt that he had finally begun to put on a few pounds.

"Come on, Josh, you can do it," Frank told him.

Josh felt his whole body shaking, and he felt light-headed, but he managed to get to a standing position and hook the crutches under his arms. The men cheered as he stood balancing himself. Using the feeling in his thighs, he managed to get one leg ahead of the other and take one step before starting to fall. Frank caught him.

"Hell, that was damn good for your first try," he told Josh, helping him back onto the bed.

Josh was drenched in perspiration from the meager effort. "It felt damn good to get up by myself. I'll be walking around this room by nightfall," he told the man.

"Hell, in another month we'll have you ridin' a horse," one of the others volunteered. "I gotta say, Rivers, you sure have broke up the boredom around here this winter. Want us to find you an eager little Indian gal to come visit you so's you can see if other things are still workin' right?"

They all laughed, and Josh felt a rush of desire for Marybeth. Little did anyone know how much Josh worried about being able to be a man for her again. "No, thanks," he told them. "I'll experiment with my own wife."

They made hooting sounds, some of them saying paralyzed or not, no man would have trouble with his sexual needs around a woman like Marybeth. The remark made Josh realize that there must be a lot of single men around Portland, a lot of ex-gold miners who had wandered up from California; surely many men who had headed west had lost wives along the way. Marybeth would catch their eyes, he had no doubt of that. He hoped she was safe, but more than that, he wondered how good those men would look to Marybeth if he never walked again or could never be a husband to her again.

"Give me a drink of that whiskey," he said.

They gladly obliged, and Josh set the crutches against the wall near his bed, determined to start using them every day, no matter how much pain it brought him.

Helping care for a new baby and watching after Danny kept Marybeth busy through the drizzly, dark winter. It seemed to rain more than snow in Portland, warm ocean winds rising over the mountains and dropping rain on the valley. People who had lived in Oregon longer told them that after the winds rose again and moved over the Cascades, they picked up colder air and usually dumped a lot of snow on eastern Oregon. But the weather in the Valley area was not so severe.

Little Stanley Svensson was a delight to everyone, spoiled by all the women in the settlement as winter wore on. Delores had trouble with heavy bleeding after the baby was born, and it took her nearly a month to get back on her feet. By then it was Marybeth who was feeling tired, and when she looked in the mirror, she was glad Josh could not see her now. She had swelled all over, not just in her stomach, and she would be glad when this second child was born.

She smiled at the thought of how Josh would tease her about how fat she was getting; she knew that he would love her just as dearly in this condition as he did when she was slim. After all, it was his baby she was having.

She managed to waddle to church every Sunday, settling for

a Protestant church where people sometimes stared at her when she made the sign of the cross and prayed over her rosary. But going to church was important to her. The prayers and hymns gave her courage, and every week the whole congregation offered up prayers for Joshua Rivers, a man most of them had never even met. But they knew his faithful wife, Marybeth, and prayed the baby she was going to have would have a father to care for it.

Not a few of the single men of Portland were watching and waiting to see if the mysterious Josh Rivers would show up, all of them realizing the beautiful Marybeth would need a husband if he didn't. In spite of her present bloated condition, they all recognized it was just her pregnancy; the beauty of her face and hair, and her exotic green eyes, were obvious in spite of her condition.

The long, lonely months of winter moved into spring, and Oregon was as beautiful as others had promised it would be. Little Stanley was feeding well and getting fatter, a big baby who would obviously take after his father. Marybeth was so big and uncomfortable, she could do no more than walk just outside the cabin door. She longed to go shopping with Florence and Delores, but when she was on her feet for too long, they became too swollen. She would sit outside, smelling the spring air, pretending Josh was sitting beside her. Sam and Aaron would be leaving for the valley soon to see about some land. They were only waiting for Marybeth's baby to be born.

If only Josh could be here for the birth. If only Josh was here to go with Sam and Aaron and start building their cabin in the valley. She dared not dwell on the thought and worry too long at a time. Was he alive? Could he walk? Sometimes she felt she would go insane with not knowing, and with the frustration of needing him, missing him. She could not help being plagued with feelings of guilt for leaving him, still unsure she had done the right thing. What if Indians had come and Josh had died some horrible death after all he had already suffered?

The first of April one concern was answered. Marybeth went into labor. She wondered how a woman could so easily forget this kind of pain. Perhaps it was because of the beautiful baby it produced. Now here was the pain again, the terrible clawing at her insides, the contractions over which she had no control. The baby was ready to come, whether she was ready or not. This time the pain seemed worse than with Danny, and she was sure her screams could probably be heard all over Portland. She had planned on just gritting her teeth and not making a sound, but there was no holding back.

"Josh," she moaned. "If ... Josh were here ... it would be easier."

"It's never easy, Marybeth," Florence told her. "You just remember that Josh is coming soon, and you want to show him a nice, healthy baby when he gets here."

The pain brought out all her fears and sorrow. "What if he doesn't come," she wept between spasms. "What if he's dead? I want Josh. I want him to be here."

Delores and Florence both kept reassuring her he would come, neither of them quite so confident now. It had been seven months since they left Josh behind. They concentrated for the moment on just getting the baby born.

Through the black pain Marybeth could see Josh, his warm, beautiful smile; his teasing brown eyes. She could feel his kiss, remember the feel of his strong arms around her, so reassuring and loving. Oh, how happy she had been in those arms! He had brought her such joy, made her laugh, made her feel so beautiful. Josh, her beloved, the father of the baby now eager to be born. She cried out his name with every gasping breath, as voices told her to push.

Finally she heard the wonderful words—"It's coming!" She pushed harder, and someone said the baby was out. "Oh, look, it's a little girl," she heard Delores exclaim.

Marybeth felt more pain, and couldn't understand why, until she heard Florence gasp. "Delores, there's another one! No wonder she got so big!"

"Twins!" Delores exclaimed. Marybeth heard a smack and a little squawl. "I'll wrap the little girl and clean them both up after the next one."

"Marybeth, you'll have *two* babies to show Josh when he gets here," Florence told her. "You've got to push some more, Marybeth. Another baby is coming."

It was all like a strange dream. The pain finally faded, and people were laughing and talking. Marybeth could hear Aaron in the outer room. "By God, that Josh went and had twins! He was always joking about Texans doing things in a big way."

She heard Cap's laugh, heard babies crying. She opened her eyes and saw Florence, who was gently massaging her belly to work out the afterbirth. "Florence?"

The woman looked at her and smiled. "Marybeth, you've had twins—a boy and a girl, and they both seem healthy. Hear them crying?"

Her eyes teared. "I want ... to see Cap."

Florence straightened, seeing determination in Marybeth's eyes. "All right." She covered her. "I'll go get him. Delores is cleaning up the babies for you." The woman left the room, and a moment later Cap came inside, holding his hat in his hand.

"That's a couple of fine babies you delivered there, Marybeth. Josh will be one proud man!"

"Cap," she spoke up, her voice weak. "Go ... and get him ... please." A tear slipped down her cheek. "Are you able ... to go now?"

"Well, I reckon I could start out. It's a dangerous time in the mountains, what with spring runoff and spring snowstorms, but it won't be so cold now. I've done it before."

She reached out for him and he took her hand. "Bring him to me, Cap. I don't care ... if he's crippled. Just ... bring him. I need him so much. And I want ... him to see ... his babies."

Cap nodded.

"Tell him ... I'm naming the babies after his mother and father—Joseph and Emma. He'll ... like that."

Cap squeezed her hand. "That he will. You take good care of yourself so's when I come back with Josh, you'll be all well for him."

"I will, Cap. God ... be with you."

He gave her a reassuring smile and left the room. Marybeth

lay listening to her new babies crying, realizing the hard reality of her situation. She had three children now, and no man to provide for them. She couldn't stay with Aaron and Delores forever, and the money Josh had given her was slowly being used up. She had insisted on paying her own way, helping buy food and share other expenses. She had no idea what she was going to do if Josh did not get well and come to her. She wanted to be happy about the babies, but her situation was a worry to her, as well as wondering what had happened to Josh. Soon she would know.

Delores brought in the babies, holding them where Marybeth could see them well while Florence finished cleaning her up.

"They're beautiful," Marybeth said, the tears coming again. "Oh, if only Josh were here to see them!"

Little Joe and little Emma. God had truly blessed her with such healthy babies, but would He bless her with the return of their father?

Outside Cap made preparations to go back to Fort Hall. That very same day, John MacKinder rode through eastern Oregon with his head bent against a sleet storm, determined to get to Portland and find his parents—and Marybeth Rivers.

# Twenty-Eight

Without any help from his crutches, Josh walked gingerly toward Frank. The man greeted him with outstretched hand. "How far today, friend?"

"At least two miles, the way I judge it. I think I'm ready to leave, Frank. I don't want to wait any longer."

Frank laughed lightly. "With a woman like yours, I'd not be wantin' to wait, either. Think she's had that kid by now?"

"Most likely." Josh breathed deeply of the sweet-smelling spring air. "I just hope to hell she made it all right. I don't know if I'm really well, Frank, or if it's just the thought of finding Marybeth that makes me feel this good."

Frank looked him over. "Well, you're still awful thin, but you've kept solid food down now for a couple of months, and you ought to be gettin' stronger with all that walkin'. I gotta say, I've never seen a man try harder. I know them first few weeks after you got on them crutches you were in a hell of a lot of pain."

"Well, there's still some. But if Marybeth has had my baby, she's needing me more than ever, and I know she's worried. I'd like to leave tomorrow, Frank. Will you help me pack my horses?"

"Sure thing. We're gonna miss you around here, you know."

They both started walking toward the building where Josh had lain sick for months. "I'll miss all of you. But I won't miss this place, if you know what I mean. Too many bad memories."

"I can understand that." Frank shook his head. "I've never seen a man as bad off as you were live to tell about it. Just goes to show what love can do for a man, huh?"

Josh grinned. "You bet. What about you? You staying here?"

"Well, I've lived in these parts for a lot of years. Been

through a couple of Indian wives and one white wife—outlived all of them. I like it here—like to hunt and trade with the Indians. But by gosh, if I ever come to Oregon, I'll sure look you up."

"You'd better. I'd be glad as hell to see you." They stopped at the doorway, and their eyes met, two strangers who had become close. "You're an even better man than Cap said you were, Frank. I can never thank you enough for everything you've done for me. Without you I'd have died or gone crazy."

They shook hands again warmly. "Oh, I doubt that. It's your wife who pulled you through, even though she wasn't really here."

"I suppose you're right there. But I'm obligated to you for everything you had to put up with, sick as I was. I'll pay you something before I leave, and if you come to Oregon, you'll always have a place to stay."

"Well, I don't want no pay. Hell, you made the winter go by mighty fast. We all enjoyed your company."

Their hands were still clasped. "I want to pay you something, and I will." Josh squeezed the man's hand harder. "Thanks a lot, Frank."

Frank squeezed back. "By God, you're gettin' stronger than I thought," he told Josh. He laughed lightly. "I sure would have liked to have seen that fight between you and that MacKinder fella."

They released hands. "Well, if I'm lucky, the man is dead. I know one thing, if I got into the same fight right now, I'd be a sorry man. A few good blows to these insides would put me right back down again. I might be walking and stronger, but it's still going to be a while before I can exert myself much or take a punch. I'll feel lucky just to make it on horseback to Oregon."

Frank scratched at his beard, and Josh secretly wondered when was the last the man had bathed. Clean or dirty, he was one of the finest men he had known, outside of Cap and his own brother-in-law back in Kansas. "Orville Dunne, he's goin' to Oregon. Said last night he'd be glad to accompany you. I think you'd be wise to travel with one other man, Josh, just in case you find out you ain't as strong as you think."

Josh nodded. "Might be a good idea. Thanks again, Frank. I'm going inside to pack some of my things."

"Come over to the main cabin in an hour or so. Billy's makin' some fine stew."

"I'll do that." Josh went inside the room that had been his prison those first horrible weeks after Marybeth left. He put a hand to his side, where he still experienced odd aches and pains, and where he carried two ugly scars. He knew he would probably always have problems from the near-fatal wound, but he felt strong now, and he could eat just about anything without any trouble. Once he had got on his crutches, he had used them daily, walking and working with himself for hours at a time, the feeling and strength slowly coming back to his limbs. He could finally discard the crutches and now walked a mile or two every day.

His best medicine had been the thought of going to find Marybeth. Old desires swept through him at night, telling him he could be a man for her again. He had been determined from the beginning not to go to her until he could stand on two good legs and hold her in two good arms. He could do all that and more, he was sure, but for a while he would have to pay someone to help him chop wood and build a cabin for his new family. He warned himself he would have to be careful for a long time to come, but to have accomplished this much seemed like a miracle.

"The miracle of Marybeth's little beads," he muttered to himself. He had once thought the beads a little silly, although he had never told her. But he had soon realized how strong was her faith, and he had no doubt it was that faith that had kept him from death's door.

He breathed deeply and flexed his muscles, praying he was well enough to make the journey to Portland. He couldn't bring himself to wait another month or another week or even another day. The men said April was a dangerous time in the mountains, but others had made it through, and so would he. Besides, the worst of the mountains were behind him. He realized it was their personal mountains that confronted people, that gave them the most trouble—death, heartache, danger. He and Marybeth and so many others had got over those mountains. They had been through so much together. Now Marybeth had had their baby all alone. He should be with her, and the sooner the better. He grabbed a canvas bag and began stuffing clothes into it, wondering how long it would take to again fill out his shirts and pants, which all hung loosely on him now.

*Marybeth's good cooking will help,* he thought with a smile.

It was the third week of April when John MacKinder rode into Portland. He saw no familiar faces at first, and wondered what had happened to all the people on the wagon train. In such big country, he knew it would not be easy to find his parents or anyone else, but he felt confident now of his knowledge of survival in this land, and of the strength he had regained over the winter. His arm was healed, and he was itching for a woman, as well as anxious to locate Mac and find out what had happened with Marybeth.

The well-worn trail had been easy to follow, and he had come part way with a Mormon supply train that had come up from Salt Lake City. He had traded the old, slow mare to them for a better horse, a young roan gelding, and he had purchased himself another rifle from them. The old man with whom he had spent the winter had kept his other rifle as payment for putting him up. It was a winter John would just as soon forget—long and lonely, with nothing but a gnarly old man for company. He had ridden on ahead of the supply train, anxious for people who liked to drink and raise hell; anxious to find the traveling prostitutes. But there was only one woman he really wanted now—the one woman who would fight him, who had spurned him.

He rode up to a tavern, deciding the only way to find anyone was to start asking questions. He lumbered inside, figuring he must make quite a commanding figure now that he had grown a beard. He looked like a real man of the mountains. Several gaudily dressed women inside the tavern looked him over hungrily, and he had no trouble being waited on. He ordered whiskey and walked up to a table of men playing cards. "I'd be enjoying a game myself if you can use one more," he told them in his Irish brogue.

One of them looked up at him and nodded. "Have a chair."

John sat down, and a woman brought his whiskey. He looked her over and grinned. "Do you do more than serve drinks?" he asked, putting a hand to her waist.

The woman smiled. "I might. Stay around until closing time and I'll let you know."

John laughed his loud, hearty laugh, patting her bottom as she left.

"She gives you your money's worth," one of the men at the table told him.

"That's good enough for me." John slugged down some whiskey. "My name is John MacKinder, and I am looking for some people who came through here last fall with a wagon train from the east."

"Wagon trains come through here by the hundreds every year," one of the others answered. He dealt the cards. "Pretty hard to learn who they all are. Most go on south of here."

John picked up his cards and studied them. "The ones I am looking for are my parents—Murray and Ella MacKinder. My father is called Mac. They had a friend along; Bill Stone was his name. And my sister-in-law, Marybeth." He watched their faces. "I believe Marybeth married again—my brother died before we left New York. Marybeth might go by the last name of Rivers now, but I believe she might have been widowed again."

They all placed their bets. "Portland is getting pretty big now," one of the others spoke up. "Can't say as I've ever heard of any of those people."

The man to John's right looked at him suspiciously as he laid down three cards and asked for three more. "If you left with all of them, how come you're just now getting here? Why weren't you with the wagon train?"

John drank some more whiskey. "Got myself hurt—Indians. I had to stay behind while I mended; hurt so bad I couldn't be moved."

"You don't look too awful sick to me."

John folded. "I spent the winter mending." His short temper began to rise. "What's it to you? I was only asking if any of you know where my family might be. Your personal life is none of my business, and mine is none of yours."

The man looked him over, judging John MacKinder to be at least six and a half feet tall and built like a buffalo. He also looked like he enjoyed a good fight, and the man was not about to be on the receiving end of one of MacKinder's big fists. "Just curious, that's all. In these parts men are always suspicious of strangers. You have to learn to accept that, Irishman."

John stood up, scooting back his chair and towering over the man. "I don't have to do anything I don't want to do, mister. I came to this table being friendly enough."

"Don't get all lathered up, mister," one of the others told him. "You gonna play cards or not?"

John finished a glass of whiskey. "I would rather put my money on a good round of arm wrestling, if anybody here wants to challenge me." He said the words loudly, and the room quieted. A big, barrel-chested, bearded man in a checkered flannel shirt rose.

"I'll take you on, Irishman."

The room immediately broke into a frenzy of betting. Tables were moved away and one sturdy one set up for the contest. John was in his glory. It had been a long time since he had been the center of attention this way, and a long time since he had had the chance to prove he still had his old strength. The fight with Josh Rivers had taken a lot out of him, but Josh Rivers was dead now. No one needed to know that at one time a man had beat him at this, and had laid him out flat on his back another time. From now on it was John MacKinder, number one.

The smoke-filled room was a din of voices and shouting once the match started. The prostitute watched with building passion for the big Irishman, as he quickly defeated the first man and continued challenging others, raking in money on every match. John was overjoyed to discover how well his arm had healed. By the time it started to ache, he had defeated eight strong men and was being slapped on the back and praised. He explained he had to quit because of the once-broken arm, while around him men exclaimed at how he had managed to beat his opponents in spite of it. He accepted free drinks and basked in being the center of attention.

This was the life he had missed. It had been this way nearly every night in the pubs of Ireland and the taverns of New York. He wished Mac were here to see this. He pulled the prostitute close and kissed her savagely, imagining she was Marybeth. Men laughed and cheered, and John decided not to worry any more about his parents tonight. Tonight he would catch up on other things. Tomorrow he would try again to find Mac and Ella— and Marybeth.

John rolled away from the prostitute, whose name he could not remember at the moment. His head ached from too much whiskey, and he wondered why he had awakened at all, until he realized someone was knocking on the door.

"John? John MacKinder. You in there? It's me, Bill Stone."

John just lay still for a moment, letting the words sink in. Bill Stone. *Bill!* He sat up, holding his head. "Bill? Come on in." He turned to look at the woman with whom he had shared bed and body through the night. She lay face down, the blankets fallen to her waist so that her bare back showed. John made a face at the sight of her plump back. In the light of morning she was not so much to look at, but she had served her purpose. Making a man feel like a man was all women were good for anyway, even ones like Marybeth. But a man didn't need whiskey to want Marybeth.

The door opened, and John looked up to see Bill Stone come inside. The man glanced at the prostitute. "Don't mind her," John told him. "She hasn't got a brain in her head anyway."

"John!" Bill walked over to him, putting out his hand and John shook it, managing a grin despite his aching head. "I couldn't believe it last night when some men came into the tavern where

I was and said some big Irishman had arm wrestled several men. When they said they thought the name was MacKinder—" The man pulled up a chair and John remained seated on the edge of the bed, keeping a sheet over his nakedness. "They said you'd gone upstairs with some whore, so I figured I would find you here. My God, John, we all thought you were dead!"

John rubbed at his eyes. "It's damn good to see somebody I know again, Bill. How about Mac and Ella? Where have they settled? Are they in good health?"

Bill sobered, removing his hat. "I'm damn sorry, John. Your folks ... they drowned at a river crossing."

John raised his head, looking at the man in wide-eyed disbelief.

"The rafts carrying their wagon and oxen broke loose and—well, it was only seconds before they were gone."

John just stared at him a moment, then put his head in his hands again. "My God," he muttered. "Both of them?" He threw back his head, breathing deeply, and the woman behind him turned and groaned, touching his back.

"Get out of here," he told her.

"What?"

"Go on," John repeated, fighting tears. "Get out of here." She sat up, rubbing her eyes. "Look, Irishman, this is *my* room."

"Get out!" He shouted the words, turning and giving her a shove with a powerful arm. The woman screeched as she went flying out of bed and to the floor.

"You big bastard," she whined, grabbing a robe. She stood up and pulled it over herself. "I'll get the boss up here. You can't throw me out of my own room!"

John, eyes blazing, rose to his full height, storming toward her. Her eyes widened and she ran out of the room. John slammed the door and turned to Bill, too angry to care about his nakedness. "I should have been *with* them!"

"John, your being there wouldn't have changed anything."

"I should have been with them," he repeated. "Maybe my being there *would* have made a difference! Maybe I could have helped in some way." He slammed a big fist against the wall.

"This is *her* fault," he growled through gritted teeth. "Every bad thing that has happened to us from the very beginning has been her fault!" He walked over and picked up his longjohns to pull them on.

"Who are you talking about," Bill asked.

John buttoned his underwear. "Marybeth MacKinder, that's who," he hissed. He looked at Bill. "I suppose *she* arrived nice and *healthy*!"

"I haven't seen her, John. I went on south after we got here. Without your folks, I just didn't have the heart to get into farming. But I came back here and got a job at the lumber mill. Oh, I've asked around a time or two—heard Marybeth had twin babies not long ago; Josh Rivers' offspring. I don't know what she'll do with three kids and no husband. Josh got shot in an Indian raid. They left him at Fort Hall to recuperate."

John looked at the man in surprise. "Rivers didn't *die*?"

Bill frowned, curious at the way John asked the question, as though he already knew about Josh. He kept his suspicion to himself for the moment, never sure of John MacKinder's temper. "Nobody knows. Cap was going to go back this spring and see what happened to him. There's a good chance that if he lived, he can't walk. It was a real bad wound. He suffered mighty bad."

John only grinned. "He did, did he?" He turned around. "Good. That makes up for my own suffering—being turned out into the wilderness like that, losing my parents." He faced Bill again, holding up a fist. "They all thought *I* would die. But nothing gets the best of a MacKinder!"

Bill shook his head. "I sure am surprised. The reason we thought you were for sure dead was because Rivers was shot with a repeating rifle. Devon said no Crow Indians would have such a new weapon; figured you'd been murdered by them and they stole the rifle from you."

A strange look passed through John's eyes. He looked Bill over as though the man was suddenly an enemy, then turned away. "They must have stolen one off someone else. No Indians bothered me. I found shelter with an old mountain man; gave him the rifle this spring in payment for putting me up." He turned back to face the man. "I bought another one off some Mormons—a better horse, too." He grinned. "Look at this beard. I did pretty good, huh? They all thought I would die, but I *survived*!"

Bill smiled nervously. There was something different about the man. He seemed wilder, even more boastful, if that was possible; no longer just a big, brash, bragging man. There was more than anger in his eyes. They held a murderous threat, an almost evil gleam.

"Now the person responsible for all that has happened to me and my parents is going to *pay*," John went on. "My father swore little Danny would grow up a MacKinder, and by God he will! I'll just bet Marybeth celebrated when Mac and Ella drowned in that river! And I'll bet she's praying *I* died, too! But it's Joshua Rivers who died, and John MacKinder who lived; and now that woman is going to learn once and for all where she belongs!"

Bill frowned. "John, she's got two more babies now. And nobody knows if Josh is dead for sure."

"*I* know! I know because in the end the one who is right wins out! And *I* am the one in the right! I don't give a damn about those two bastard Rivers babies. They aren't even legal, just like that excuse of a marriage was not legal! All I care about is Marybeth MacKinder and my nephew. They *belong* to me— *both* of them. If I didn't claim them and make us a family, I would be bringing shame to my poor father's memory! It is what he wanted, and by God that is what will be!"

"John, you're in a civilized town. You can't just go and take what you want, especially if she's unwilling."

"Can't I? I can do whatever I want. She owes me, Bill! She owes me! She has caused me nothing but pain. She doesn't know! She doesn't know what I did for her—what I did to be able to marry her!"

"What are you talking about?"

John blinked, as though suddenly realizing he was saying too much. He turned away. "The fact remains … if I had been with my mother and father, maybe they would still be alive. My having to leave the wagon train was her fault. She treated all of us badly—all of us, her only family, Danny's only kin. No woman should get away with that! I have practically sold my soul to the devil for that woman, and I'll not have her nursing some other man's brats and pining away for a lesser man than me! When we were with the wagon train, there was not much I could do. But now—now I am free to do what I want, and she is a woman alone, with no Josh Rivers or Cap or anyone else to get in the way! I came here for one reason, Bill—to find my parents and to take Marybeth to live with us. Now they're dead, and I owe it to their memory to do what is right and keep Danny in a MacKinder household." He began dressing. "Where is Marybeth now?"

Bill swallowed, not sure he should tell the man. He had liked the MacKinders as drinking companions, and he had taken considerable pleasure in the MacKinder antics back in New York, enjoying the nightly challenges of strength and drinking capacities. He had considered the situation with Marybeth none of his business, and had turned the other way many times when he knew she was being abused. After all, she was a MacKinder, too, and how she was treated by her own family was not his affair. Besides, Bill didn't like her independent ways any more than John and Mac had. But he had seen her suffering after Josh was hurt, and she had genuinely grieved over Mac and Ella, although John would probably never believe that. Recently she had given birth to twins, not even knowing if her husband was dead or alive. She surely was not even fully recovered from the birth. Bill was not eager to be a party to sending John MacKinder to threaten and harass the poor woman.

"I'm not sure," he answered aloud.

"Aren't you now?" John buttoned his shirt. "I will remind you how determined I am, Bill Stone. And when I am determined, I can get mean."

Bill frowned and rose. "Are you threatening *me*?"

John grinned. "I am. You know where she lives and you are not telling me."

Bill's eyes darkened. "I will remind you I was your father's best friend, and a good friend to you, too."

"All the more reason to tell me where Marybeth lives." John stepped closer, and Bill's concern for his own person far outweighed any concern he might have for Marybeth MacKinder. He sighed, putting his hat back on his head.

"I would have thought you would take some time to mourn your own parents' deaths—that the first thing you would want to do is let me take you to their graves. This thing with Marybeth has completely taken over your ability to reason, John MacKinder. You're a sick man!" He walked toward the door. "I think she lives in a cabin on the north end of town—shares it with the Svenssons. That's all I know."

He opened the door, anxious to get away from the man. "I came here because for your father's sake I was glad you were alive, and because I considered you a friend and felt I should be the one to break the news to you about Mac and Ella. But I can't consider a man a friend when he threatens me. You're wrong to do this, John, dead wrong!" He quickly left, just as afraid of John MacKinder as most other people were. He thought about going to warn Marybeth John was in town, but he decided he did not want the risk of having MacKinder angry with him. The man had become dangerous, and Bill wanted nothing more to do with him.

# Twenty-Nine

Josh lit a thin cigar and puffed on it quietly for a moment. He and Orville Dunne had just made it through the last ridge of mountains, held up for three days by a spring blizzard. They were well on their way into the eastern Oregon flatlands now, but had stopped to make camp early because Josh couldn't seem to quite make it to nightfall without wearying. It frustrated him that he couldn't put in a full day's ride, and Orville could see the anger in his eyes.

"It will all come back, Josh," the man told him. "I was hurt bad once by an explosion in a gold mine in '50. Some dimwit set the powder wrong—like to blowed out my insides. Takes a long time to really get over something like that. It's been two years and this past winter up there at Fort Hall is the first time I started feeling like I was up to my old strength."

Josh sighed. "I wouldn't mind so much if I wasn't in such a hurry to get to Marybeth. Every minute counts."

"Well, better to be rested and healthy when you get there than all wore out. You want to save your strength for when you find your woman, right? After all these months apart, you'll need it."

Josh smiled, his blood rushing warm at the thought of holding Marybeth's soft body against his own again. "Yeah, I reckon I will."

Orville stirred a pan of beans as Josh stood up and puffed on the cigar again, studying the spectacular scenery, wondering what Marybeth had thought of all this. Most likely she would have wished they could see it together.

From their campsight on a rise, they could see the trail for a good mile ahead, and Josh spotted someone coming. "Hey, Orv, look out there. Looks like a man leading a pack horse."

Orville stood up and studied the trail. He was a lean man who needed a shave and who wore a bearskin coat so worn that half the fur was gone, another of the men who had gone to find gold and never realized his dream. A drifter now, he probably loved the West and couldn't bring himself to go back home. Josh could understand how this land could capture a man's heart as strongly as could a woman. Now he felt captured by both.

"Yup. He's coming this way," Orville said. "I wouldn't mind some extra company myself. If he's from Portland, maybe he'd know something about your woman, or at least what's happening there. It's just one man—can't be much of a threat."

"Fine with me. Give him a signal."

Orville picked up his rifle and shot it off twice into the air. He waved it then and gave a call, cupping a hand to his mouth. "Hey, stranger! Come join us!" He watched as the man stopped, then headed in their direction. "He's pulling out his rifle," Orville told Josh. "Get yours ready. I reckon he's just being careful like any other man. There's all kinds of no-goods in these hills."

Josh went to his horse and took out his own rifle. Both men watched as the stranger came closer. Suddenly Josh lowered his gun. "By God, I think it's Cap!"

"Cap?"

"Harley Webster, the man who guided our wagon train and took the bullet out of me. You remember him, don't you? He's the one who left me off at the fort and got Frank to take care of me."

"Oh, Frank's friend ... yeah, I remember him."

"I'll be damned. He said he'd come back to get me in the spring." Josh laughed and set aside his rifle, walking out to greet the man. "Hey, Cap, it's me—Josh!"

Cap halted his horse, slowly lowering his own rifle. His eyes widened as he watched in total astonishment. Joshua Rivers was walking toward him, looking thinner but healthy. "Josh? Goddamn if you ain't the best sight!" Cap dismounted and walked up to him, and they embraced, laughing. "Hey boy, look at you," Cap said, stepping back and quickly wiping at his eyes. "Marybeth's gonna be the happiest woman ever walked the earth when she sees this. How'd you do it, Josh? How do you feel? How long did it take you to walk?"

"Hold up, there! First tell me about Marybeth." He wiped at his suspiciously damp eyes. "Is she all right?"

"Well, when I left, she had just give birth to twins—a boy and a girl."

Josh sobered, love and concern moving into his eyes. "Twins!" He ran a hand through his hair. *"Twins?"*

Cap laughed. "Yes, sir. Named them Joe and Emma—said you'd like that."

Josh smiled through his tears. "Those were my parents' names. Twins," he repeated. "I'll be damned."

"I reckon you are, son," Cap teased. "You got three kids under your belt already, and you ain't even set up house yet. You'd better go easy or you won't be able to build a house big enough to hold all the young 'uns."

Both men laughed lightly and embraced once more. "Come on up to our campfire, Cap," Josh said. "I'm traveling with a man who spent the winter at the fort—Orville Dunne. You probably don't remember him. You didn't have much time to meet the others when you were there. By the way, that Frank is a hell of a man. It's him that got me through a lot of this, encouraged me to walk."

"Well, maybe so, but everybody knows it was your desire to get to Marybeth in one piece that really did it. By God, you don't know how good it is to see you walkin' like this. Soon as Marybeth had them babies, she called me in and said for me to get goin' and come for you—bring you back no matter what shape you was in. It was awful hard on her, Josh, havin' to leave you behind. She's stayin' in a cabin in Portland now with Delores and Aaron. Delores had a baby boy last Christmas—name's Stanley."

"Good. I'm glad for her and Aaron." Both men reached the campsite and Josh introduced Cap and Orville, who remembered each other vaguely. Orville offered Cap some beans and coffee, and they all sat down around the campfire.

"You think Marybeth is all right?" Josh asked. "You say you left soon as the twins were born?" He turned to Orville. "Marybeth had twins, Orv—a boy and a girl."

"I heard Cap telling you. Congratulations, Josh!" The man put out his hand and Josh shook it, grinning. He turned back to Cap.

"What about it, Cap?" He picked up the cigar he had laid aside on a rock and relit it. "Was she okay?"

"Far as I know. I reckon she'd be a little weak for a while—had kind of a hard time of it. And keepin' up with twins ain't gonna be the easiest thing in the world, especially with Danny runnin' around gettin' into things. That boy is walkin'—I should say, runnin'. He's growin' fast, Josh. Gonna' be big, no doubt about it."

Josh's smile faded. *Big as any MacKinder*, he thought. "How about Mac," he asked. "Where'd they settle? They give Marybeth any problems?"

Cap sobered. "We wouldn't have let them. As it turns out, they're no longer a worry. They was both killed crossin' the river up in Cayuse country."

Josh frowned with surprise, his emotions mixed. "*Both* of them?"

"You know how Mac is ... or was. He wouldn't let Ella come across in a canoe with the Indians like the rest of the women—said Indians had likely killed his son and besides, he could look after his own woman. Damned, bull-headed bastards those MacKinders were. I said to hell with him and let him do what he wanted. He made Ella ride inside the wagon. The oxen was loaded onto one raft, and the wagon on another. The oxen started acting up, and Mac started yelling like always. Got them all excited and the next thing you know most of the oxen and two Cayuse was in the river. One raft rammed another—the wagon toppled over." He shook his head. "I don't know. It all happened so fast I can't hardly remember *how* it happened. Devon and that Bill Stone, they found the bodies and we buried them beside the river."

Josh sighed. "I'll be damned." He puffed on his cigar for a

moment. "The only thing that bothers me is the fact that there is one body that *hasn't* been found, and that still leaves me uneasy."

"John MacKinder?"

Josh met his eyes. "Anybody ever catch sight of him around Portland?"

Cap shook his head. "Not the whole winter."

Josh looked around at the distant mountains, breathing deeply of the spring air. "I'm worried he's still alive and he wintered it out somewhere like I did and he'll still try to find Marybeth. At the least he'll surely try to find his parents. If he finds out they're dead, he'll be on a real rampage. You know how he is. He'll say it was my fault, yours, Marybeth's—everybody and anybody but his own fault."

Cap ate a spoonful of beans. "I think he's dead, Josh. Everybody figures if the Crow had a repeating rifle, it was probably John's. Hell, most of the men up in those mountains don't have one of those yet."

"That's true," Orville told Josh. "All me and the others have at the Fort is muskets. Frank, he sent a man to Fort Laramie to see about getting some new repeaters."

"I figure with that Indian attack bein' so soon after we kicked MacKinder off the wagon train, that gun couldn't be anybody else's but his."

Josh puffed the cigar quietly for several minutes. He glanced at Cap. "I've had a lot of time to think these past few months, Cap. And I'm thinking, what if the Indians *didn't* take that gun off John MacKinder?"

Cap frowned, setting his plate on his knee. "What are you talkin' about?"

"Cap, I've gone over that day in my mind a thousand times. Those Indians had a few old muskets—most of them had only bows and arrows. Just before I was shot, they were riding off. The ones from my back side were running through the trees to their horses. During all the fighting, not one emigrant or animal was shot with the kind of bullet that hit me. Why was *I* the only one? If they had a rifle like that, why weren't they using it throughout the battle? If an Indian was a good enough shot to hit me, he could have hit a lot of others. They could have killed half the people on that wagon train, but I was the only one who got hit—and even then, it was while the Indians were running off."

Cap frowned, weighing Josh's words. He met the man's eyes. "You think it could have been John MacKinder that shot you?"

Josh's voice was sober and firm. "I think it's a strong possibility."

"Hell, them hills was alive with Indians! MacKinder didn't know nothin' about Indians. There ain't no way he'd have run into Indians and lived through it."

"Maybe he was just sneaking around up there following the wagon train. Maybe even the Indians didn't know he was there. And maybe he took advantage of an ideal situation—he could kill me, and everyone would think it was the Crow that did it. Then he just waits for Marybeth to get over her grief, and he moves in on her again. If I'm right, and John finds out about his parents, Marybeth won't be safe. Neither will my babies."

Cap shook his head. "I don't know, Josh. It sounds pretty far-fetched."

"Maybe so. But as far as I'm concerned, I can't get to Portland soon enough. I think I'm in a foot race with John MacKinder. I wasn't really strong enough to leave, but I knew I couldn't waste any time about it. It just pisses me off that I can't seem to get in a full day's ride."

Cap leaned forward and put a hand on his arm. "Look, Josh, you want to be as healthy as you can be when you reach Marybeth. Don't overdo things just because of a wild notion. Ain't many men who would live through a wound like you had. You could even have a setback yet. You just take it easy. Marybeth is surrounded by friends, and she's right in town. Ain't nothin' gonna happen to her, you hear? I'll ride back with you, and I ain't leavin' Portland till I know there ain't no more problems for you and Marybeth."

Josh breathed deeply, giving him a faint smile. "Thanks, Cap. I hope I'm wrong about all this. But I'll tell you one thing. If I'm right, there won't be any place John MacKinder can go to get away from me." His jaw flexed with repressed anger and hatred. "I'll not forget that pain for the rest of my life. I think MacKinder deliberately shot me in the back, and if I find out that's true, the man is going to pay!"

"A lot of us will want him to pay—and we'll see he does, Josh. Don't go tryin' somethin' alone, not the shape you're in. You remember you've got a wife and three babies who need you to be well."

Josh puffed on the cigar again, staring at the flames of the campfire. "I know." He pictured John MacKinder grinning, aiming a rifle at his back. "But he'll pay, Cap, and it's me who will *make* him pay. It's my right." He sighed and looked at Orville. "Dish me up some beans, and let's get some sleep. I'd like to pull out before sunup. How long will it take us to get to Portland, Cap?"

"Oh, about three weeks."

Josh took the beans from Orville. "I'll try to stay in the saddle longer from here on. I just hope to hell I'm wrong about John MacKinder."

Marybeth laid little Emma into the small bed Aaron had made for both babies to sleep in. They were five weeks old now, and Marybeth was feeling stronger, but tired from almost constant feedings. Her bleeding had stopped, and most of her old dresses fit her again, although still tight in the waist. She walked over to the mirror she had bought and hung on the wall of her room. She brushed at her hair, studying her face, trying to decide if it still looked too pudgy. She had lost most of the water and weight she had gained with the babies, but the strain of childbirth and keeping up with double feedings showed in her eyes. She tied her hair back at the sides and hoped Josh would still think she was pretty.

Josh. Perhaps he would be so crippled, her looks would mean little to him. She contemplated how she could provide for her children and her husband if Josh was unable to be the provider. Even if she could find some kind of work, who would look after the babies? How could she keep up with their feedings? The worry of it left her more tired than taking care of them.

Also she hated being such an intrusion in Delores' and Aaron's lives. They had not planned on adopting an entire helpless family when they headed for Oregon. Never once had they given any hint that they minded, but Marybeth minded. She did not like being a burden on anyone, and she again took down her rosary and knelt by her bed, praying fervently that Josh would return a healthy man.

She rose then, checking the sleeping babies, smiling at the wonderful gift Josh had given her. In spite of the tremendous responsibilities she would shoulder if Josh was dead or crippled, she would always treasure the beautiful little boy and girl that had come from her union with Josh Rivers.

She walked over and checked on Danny, who was napping, and she smiled at his puckered lips and dark, curly hair. Although his conception was far different from the twins', her firstborn had for a while been the only shining light in her life. He would remain a MacKinder, and for Ella's sake alone, Marybeth was determined Danny would grow up to bring pride to the MacKinder name.

She leaned down and kissed his cheek, then left the room to go into Delores' room and check on Stanley. It was a rare moment when all four children slept and the house was quiet. Delores had gone marketing. Aaron and Sam had left for Oregon City to see about filing papers on some land there. They had promised to be back by the end of the week for a spring dance being held by the businessmen of Portland, an event they had been told nearly everyone for miles around attended. Marybeth was not so sure she wanted to go, but Florence and Delores had both convinced her it would be good for her, especially since one of their older neighbor ladies had offered to mind the children. It was just one more thing to help pass the time until Cap returned with Josh. Florence had volunteered herself and Delores and Marybeth to contribute home-baked cakes as part of the refreshments.

"It sounds like fun," Delores had said just that morning.

"All the women bring food, and the men roast a side of beef, and there are games and contests before the dance. Everyone goes; I was talking to a banker's wife just yesterday about it." She herself had gone out that morning to buy baking supplies.

Marybeth sighed, wondering what she should wear, but really caring little how she looked to anyone but Josh. Someone knocked at the door then, and Marybeth supposed it was Delores with her arms full of packages. She went to the door and opened it, then froze in place for a moment, her eyes wide with shock and disbelief.

"Hello, Marybeth."

She stared at John MacKinder, who at the moment seemed even bigger and more menacing than she remembered, standing there in a wolfskin coat and sporting a beard. He literally smelled of danger, and she forced herself to overcome her shock and fear. She tried to slam the door so she could bolt it, but he caught it with a big, strong hand and slammed it backward.

Marybeth backed away. "You're alive!"

John grinned bitterly. "You disappointed, Marybeth? I suppose with my mother and father dead, you thought you were finally free of the MacKinders."

She backed farther away, realizing what the news of their deaths would mean to him. "I am sorry about that, John, I truly am. It was an accident, like so many other sicknesses and accidents on that wagon train."

He stepped inside, looking around the room. "Where is Danny?"

"He's taking a nap."

"Get him. I have built a cabin farther up in the hills, and I will find a job. My father wanted nothing more than to keep Danny in this family, and I am going to see that it's done."

"What are you talking about?" Her heart pounded with fear and dread. "How did you find me? And where have you been all winter?"

"I found a place to live—with an old miner." He grinned again. "Don't you understand by now that you can't get rid of me, Marybeth? You should have known I would survive up there and come here to find my parents—and you and Danny. Now I am here, and Josh Rivers is dead."

She backed away even further. "How do you know that?"

A strange, guilty look moved through his eyes. "I asked around."

"No one knows for certain that he's dead. Cap has gone to find out. He could still be alive."

"Makes no difference. He's not Catholic, and you are not his legal wife. You and Danny are coming with me where you have always belonged. You have no Josh Rivers or anyone else to defend you now, woman. You are coming with me, and when I am through with you, you will wonder why you ever refused me." His eyes moved over her as though she stood there stark naked. She breathed deeply for control, told herself she could be just as determined as John MacKinder. She had to call on the courage Josh had helped her find. Josh could come back any time. She couldn't go off with this man, not now and not ever!

"I am not going anywhere with you. Whether you want to consider it legal or not, I *am* married to Joshua Rivers, and I've had twin babies by him, John. Josh will be coming back any day now, and I believe he'll be well and able to take care of his family."

"Get your things together," John hissed, his fists clenching. "And bring just Danny. I'll not be taking on the responsibility of the Rivers bastards!"

Her eyes widened with disbelief. "You're crazy! You've completely lost your mind."

He only smiled. "If I have, it's because of the want of you. I've done everything I could do to make sure you would be mine, Marybeth. And my father wanted nothing more than to keep Danny in the family. That is the way it is going to be."

"What do you mean—you've done everything you could do to make sure I was yours?" She thought about how Josh was shot: Devon's remark that the Indians couldn't possibly have got hold of repeating rifles yet. They all thought John's had been stolen and that he was surely dead. Yet here he stood.

"Why are you so sure Josh is dead," she asked, moving

around the table, trying to keep away from him. "Is it because it was *you* who shot him?"

He only grinned, and her heart filled with anguish. Her problems with the MacKinders had caused Josh so much pain and suffering. "It *was* you, wasn't it? You followed the wagon train! You saw the Indian attack and you took advantage of it!"

"You belong with *me*!" His voice was raised now. She could see the MacKinder temper rising, knew how unpredictable that temper could be. Dear God, if only Josh were here. What could she do alone against this madman? It sickened her to even look at him. His huge physique seemed to fill the whole room.

"What about Dan," she asked, suddenly realizing for the first time the lengths to which he would go to have her for himself. Back in Ireland, before she married Dan, she remembered the vicious fist fights he and Dan used to have over her. "You said you did everything you could to make sure I was yours ... Was it really an accident when Dan fell into that molten steel?"

His eyes suddenly flickered, but his fists were still clenched. "Maybe you understand now. I love you; I always have. And you are coming with me! You and Danny are the only family I have left."

"*Love* me! After all the hell you have put me through? You call that *love*? What makes you think I could ever return that love, knowing you—my God, John, *you killed your own brother, didn't you? You killed Dan*!" Her mind reeled with the impact of this hideous nightmare. He had killed Dan, and tried to kill Josh! His determination to have her had twisted his mind, and she knew that if she didn't think of something fast, he would drag her and Danny off with him and make sure no one ever found them.

Danny came toddling out of his room then, awakened by the loud voices. He rubbed his eyes and looked up at the huge man in the room. "Hi," he said, giving John a sweet smile. The boy obviously didn't remember him; and being afraid of no one, he toddled closer to John.

"No, Danny, stay back," Marybeth screamed at him.

John grinned. "Well, now, look at you, Danny, getting so big—walking, too!" He reached out his arms. "Come to

Uncle John."

Marybeth rushed over, stepping between Danny and John. "Danny, go back to your room," she said sharply.

John grasped her arms painfully, jerking her close. "You'll not keep yourself or that boy from me," he growled. He tried to kiss her, but she jerked her face away. His lips moved along her neck, but then he pushed her away and landed a hard open-handed slap to the right side of her face, sending her sprawling. He walked over and knelt over her then, jerking her to a sitting position and shoving her against the wall.

Marybeth could hardly see him at first. Everything seemed to be spinning. She felt his lips pressing against hers then, tasted the blood in her mouth. His rough beard scratched at her chin, and a big hand moved over her breast, then up to her face, which he grasped then in both big, powerful hands.

"Give it up, Marybeth. You know I'm the only man you ever really wanted. You know I can satisfy you better than any other. You get your things and come with me now. Do like I say so I don't have to hurt you any more. You don't want me to have to do that in front of Danny, do you? If you push me too far, I'll have to drag you into that bedroom and let Danny watch his mommy being hurt. I don't want that any more than you do, Marybeth."

He kept hold of her face in one hand, and she felt his other hand jerk at the bodice of her dress. His hand slid inside it. "I'd rather make you feel good, Marybeth, than hurt you. Every woman gives in once her man makes her feel good. You've just never given me that chance, Marybeth."

She struggled to keep her senses about her. The man was crazy. She realized that now. She opened her eyes to meet his dark ones. "I'll go get my things," she said quietly. "We ... can't do anything here. Delores could come home any minute."

John grinned, bending down to kiss her once more and squeezing her breast. She could hardly believe he could talk about killing his own brother one minute, be beating on her the next, and then actually believe she would want to go with him and let him make love to her. But he seemed to think she

meant it. He let go of her and helped her up. Danny stared at
them both with puckered lips, not quite sure if his mommy was
happy or sad.

Marybeth pulled the front of her dress back over herself
and licked at blood at the corner of her mouth. Her face hurt
fiercely, and white welts that matched John's finger marks were
swelling on her cheek. "I have to change and dress Danny," she
told him, taking the boy's hand.

"Just hurry it up," John told her.

She led Danny into the bedroom and laid him on the bed,
then took a scarf from a drawer and tied it around his waist and
to a bedpost so the boy could not get away and possibly get hurt.
She turned and glanced at Aaron's rifle that sat in the corner of
the room, left there for her and Delores' protection when he
was away. She took a deep breath for courage and picked it up,
carrying it to the bedroom door. She cocked it and pointed it at
John, who looked at her in surprise.

"How could you think I would really go off with you? How
could you think I would let a murderer raise Danny, or that I
would really desert my new babies? You get out of here, John
MacKinder, before I *kill* you!"

His eyes looked as wild as a stalking bear. "You would not
have the courage to shoot me," he said.

"You would be surprised at what I would do to anyone who
would try to kill the man I love—to anyone who would threaten
my babies! Get out of here—*now*!"

She held the gun steadily, but he did not move.

"You bitch," he growled. "No woman points a gun at
John MacKinder! No woman gives me orders! You lied to me!
Bitch! *Bitch!* I never knew a woman like you! I hope Josh is dead,
and I hope he died *slowly!*"

He started toward her, and Marybeth pulled the trigger.

His body whirled and crashed into a wall. Marybeth stood
frozen, hardly believing what she had just done. She watched
him get to his knees, then to his feet. She remembered Cap
telling a story once about a bear that he had shot over and over
before it would finally die. She knew that was the way it was for

John MacKinder, and she prayed he would just leave. She wasn't sure she had enough courage or hatred in her to keep shooting at him like he was some kind of animal; yet she realized that was exactly what he was.

She cocked the rifle again, keeping it steady on him as he turned to face her, holding his arm. Blood poured over his hand and began dripping to the floor. "You ... shot me," he exclaimed, as though he could not believe it.

"The next one will be right in your middle," she told him calmly, inwardly realizing she had shot wildly the first time and could not really guarantee where the next bullet would go. She only prayed he would believe her. "Maybe it will settle in your belly, John MacKinder, and put you through the horrible suffering Josh went through. If you don't want that for yourself, you'd better get out now!"

He stood there shaking, holding his arm. "I will be back, only the next time I will not announce myself," he hissed.

Delores suddenly appeared at the door, her eyes widening at what she saw. She dropped her packages and ran and John stumbled toward the door. He looked at Marybeth once more in disbelief. "You'll pay for this!" He ran out, and moments later Marybeth heard a horse ride off. Delores came running back with two men from the nearby blacksmith shop, one of them carrying a heavy hammer. They found Marybeth still holding the rifle, still staring at the doorway, trembling. Blood had dried at the corner of her mouth, and her right cheek was turning blue. She turned eyes filled with horror to Delores.

"He ... killed Dan ... his own brother," she gasped. "And he ... he shot Josh. It was John, Delores; it was John."

# Thirty

Marybeth pulled up the sides of her hair and pinned it, placing the little flowers in it that Aaron had brought for her and Delores. Today was the spring celebration and dance, but Marybeth did not feel like celebrating anything. Cap had been gone nearly six weeks, and had still not returned.

It had been a week since John invaded the house and threatened her. The local sheriff had hired men to watch the house until Aaron and Sam returned. Marybeth had hardly slept since that day, her nights filled with terrible visions of John coming back, beating her, killing her babies, raping her. Her nerves were nearly shattered, and she was afraid now that if Cap returned without Josh, she would lose her mind completely. She had prayed and prayed for forgiveness for shooting John, but she reasoned God surely understood why she had to do it. She could not forget the horror she felt when at first she thought she had actually killed him. She could not have lived with such a thing, yet she knew that if he returned to threaten her or the babies, she would do it again.

She adjusted her yellow dress, which she had carefully pressed, and remembered the first time she had worn it for Josh. It seemed like such a long time ago now. She struggled against tears, retying the sash and realizing she at least had lost considerable weight and had her waistline back. But it was due mostly to her loss of appetite since finding out John MacKinder still lived and intended to make trouble for her.

She applied a soft cream to her face, lightly patting some cornstarch on her cheek to hide the faint bruise that still showed there. She splashed her neck and wrists with rosewater. She really didn't care what anyone else thought of how she looked, but Josh could return any day now, and she took great care to look her best in case he came. Today she would go to the spring celebration only because Aaron had insisted it was not safe for her to remain behind alone.

She walked into the main room, and Aaron and Delores both exclaimed over how beautiful she looked.

"Thank you, but I feel foolish going to the dance at all," she told them. "For one thing, everyone in town must be buzzing with gossip about me shooting John MacKinder. And what about the babies? They've got to be fed."

"We'll take the babies with us in the wagon," Aaron told her. "I'll carry Stanley, and we'll put a string of rawhide around Danny's waist and let him walk. It will keep him from straying. You will enjoy it, Marybeth. It will be good for you to get out."

"The only gossip is about John, Marybeth," Delores assured her. "Aaron says some men remembered John coming into a tavern about three weeks ago and challenging several men to arm wrestling. That must be when he first got into town. He must have asked around to find out where you were. They all know he's a brute and he's half crazy. No one blames you for what happened."

Marybeth sighed. "The fact remains that he could come back." She looked at Aaron. "I'm going to take a room at the boarding house, Aaron. I won't subject you all to that man's insanity. If he comes back, I know you'll try to defend me, and he'd kill you. I can't let it come to that."

"You let me worry about that. You are not going anywhere until Cap returns and we know what has happened to Josh. If Josh does not return, you will go with us to the valley and live with us there. John will not know where you have gone."

"He found me here. He can find me anywhere, and he is determined enough to do it." She closed her eyes and hung her head. "Sometimes I wish that bullet had struck his heart. It's a horrible thing to say, but I'll never be free of him until he's dead." She looked at Aaron with tear-filled eyes. "If Josh doesn't make it back, you go on to the valley without me. It's time the two of you settled into the home you've been dreaming of—

and led your own lives. The same goes for Sam and Florence. They've had more heartache in their lives than anyone should be expected to suffer. Now they have a whole new family. I'll not subject their children to witnessing the kind of violence and language John MacKinder is capable of using. Somehow I'll find a way to fight him. Maybe the sheriff will keep men on watch."

"Do you really think we would leave you here alone?" Delores asked. "Not only is there your safety to consider, but what about the fact that you have three children to provide for?"

"I cannot let Aaron do it. I have a little money left. I am thinking that if Cap comes back alone, perhaps I will have him take me back east. Maybe I could get some kind of work—as a governess or something. Or perhaps I could try San Francisco. Sam was saying there are some very wealthy people in San Francisco. I'm sure I could find a job working for one of them. If no one is told where I am going, John would probably never find me in a city like that. Everyone could tell him I went back east. That would send him away and I would be rid of him."

"Marybeth, we won't let you—"

"I've made up my mind, Aaron! I'll not be a burden to you and Delores any longer. You have been so kind and generous, but you have many years ahead of you, and you have had little privacy since clear back on the trail when I first started traveling with you. I know you mean well, and that you would do exactly what you have offered to do. I simply will not accept the offer. It is bad enough that John MacKinder has interfered with everyone's lives as much as he has. I have got to find a way to be rid of him, as well as a way to fend for myself."

Aaron sighed, looking at Delores. Neither of them liked the resignation in Marybeth's voice. She was losing her spirit, losing her hope. "Let's not talk about it today," Aaron said. "I want you to come with us, where you will be safer, and I think it will be good for you to get out, Marybeth. Sam and I took the cakes over this morning. There will be lots of food and dancing and laughter."

Delores walked over to Marybeth and put an arm around her shoulders. "Come. Let's get the babies ready. You just fed both of them, didn't you?"

"Yes. They'll probably fall asleep in the wagon."

"Aaron, get the wagon, and we'll put the babies in it."

Marybeth walked into the bedroom with Delores while Danny toddled after Aaron. Marybeth touched Delores' arm. "I don't know what I would have done all this time without your friendship," she said. "And it's because I love you both that I simply can't go on like this, Delores. Please, if you really care about me in return, you'll go on to the valley without me. I would feel much better about it."

Delores's eyes teared, and the two women embraced.

The day was filled with pie-eating contests, sack races, baking contests and the like. Marybeth and Delores enjoyed viewing handmade quilts and doilies, and Marybeth entered Danny in a toddlers' race. She stretched out her arms to him, as all the other mothers did to entice their children, and he ran to her as fast as his fat little legs could carry him, his mouth open in laughter, six baby teeth showing as he headed for his Mama. He landed in her arms full of giggles, and Marybeth lifted him and hugged him tightly, wondering how anything so sweet and loving could come from a MacKinder. She realized Dan and John both must have been this way once, and her heart went out to Ella at what the woman had missed in life. In spite of her own terrible predicament, at least she had had Josh for a while, and Danny's precious laughter gave her the courage she needed to make sure he would not be raised by a man like John MacKinder.

Danny got a little wooden horse for coming in second; a baby three months older had beat him. She thought how Mac or John would have bragged about how some day no one would beat Danny MacKinder at anything, and she vowed that no matter how big and strong her son became, she would never goad him into competition or allow him to lord his size and strength over others.

Aaron kept a rein on Danny then while Delores and Marybeth went into a tent that had been set up for mothers breastfeeding babies. Women smiled and exclaimed over Marybeth's beautiful twins, asking her how in the world she kept up with them. They were the center of attention, and those women who knew about Marybeth's situation told her they hoped her husband would return soon.

"I don't think there are many of us here in Portland who do not have a horror story to tell about our trips west," one woman put in. "It is something we would all rather not think about."

"Aren't you the one who shot at an intruder recently?" another woman asked Marybeth.

Marybeth laid Emma in the wagon and picked up Joe to feed him. "Yes," she answered, unable to face the woman.

"Someone said he was a brother-in-law or something?"

Marybeth moved Joe under the blanket with which she covered herself, putting him to the opposite breast from the one Emma had fed on. "It's a long story," she told the woman. "The man spent the winter in the mountains. I think it affected his mind."

Talk inside the tent quieted for a moment, and Marybeth reddened, feeling their stares.

"I think you must be a very brave and strong young woman," one of them finally put in. "Out here alone, not knowing if your husband is dead or alive, giving birth to twins without him. We don't mean to pry, Mrs. Rivers. It's just that all of us have had to face death and disease and losing things precious to us. I suppose if we can find someone who is worse off than we are, we think it will make us feel better about our own losses. The fact remains we have all suffered in one way or another. We truly do hope your husband makes it here and is healthy again. And we hope the man who gave you trouble won't return."

Marybeth fought tears of embarrassment and frustration. "Thank you," she answered, glancing at Delores, who gave her a reassuring smile. Marybeth felt suddenly out of place, totally alone. Not even Delores' friendship could help. She felt like the only remaining fish in a dried-up lake, flopping and struggling to find water where there was none. Josh was her water.

She finished feeding Joe and laid him into the wagon, and

she and Delores went back outside to watch a horse race with Aaron. Sam and Florence joined them, and they all went to watch their son Billy, and twelve-year-old Ruth Billings in a cake-eating contest. Sam and Florence already had visited a judge and had paperwork in progress to legally adopt the three Billings children, who had adjusted well to their parents' death, thanks to Florence's tender, loving care. Everyone roared with laughter at the sight of the young boys and girls with faces covered with cake and frosting. Billy won, and everyone cheered while the judges presented him with a blue ribbon.

While everyone was laughing and patting Billy on the back and helping clean up his and Ruth's faces, Marybeth glanced up the street to see what other events were taking place. It was then she saw them. They were riding down the street, scanning the crowds as though looking for someone. At first she stood frozen in place, afraid to believe what she was seeing, afraid it was only a dream. He sat on his horse so naturally, looking so strong and sure, just as she had remembered him. Marybeth grasped Delores's arm and squeezed so tightly it startled Delores, who looked up to follow Marybeth's eyes, afraid at first she had seen John MacKinder.

"Josh! It's Josh!" Delores exclaimed. "Look, everybody, it's Josh and Cap!"

They all turned to stare. "By God, it *is* him," Aaron shouted. "My God, he's riding a horse! Would you look at that? Go on, Marybeth," he said then, taking the wagon handle from her. "We'll watch the babies."

Delores saw the tears on Marybeth's cheeks. She gave Marybeth a little nudge as Josh came riding toward them, all grins. "Go on, Marybeth. It's really him. *Go to him.*"

Suddenly Marybeth could not hear the crowd around her. She heard no voices, no laughter, no whinnying horses, no children's squeals. She moved through the crowd on rubbery legs, her eyes glued to one man who came closer, riding a handsome Appaloosa, smiling the warm smile she had remembered. So much thinner he was! But there was no mistaking him, and no mistaking the fact that he was riding a horse on his own.

"Marybeth," he called out. She watched him dismount as Cap grinned in the background. She stared at Josh as he walked toward her as though he were an apparition.

"Josh," she whispered. She ran toward him then, and in one quick moment she was swept up in his arms. Oh, the glory of it! His arms were still strong, his scent so familiar when she buried her face against his neck. She felt him lift her feet off the ground and whirl her around. Was this the same man she had left near death back at Fort Hall eight months ago? She could not let go of him. She could only cling to him and weep, crying his name over and over, mingled with the words "Thank God," and "Thank you, blessed Virgin Mary."

She sensed they were surrounded by people now, felt him let go of her with one hand so he could shake hands with the others, but still she would not let go of him. She clung to him, her face buried against his chest as she heard him saying something about coming as fast as he could. "I still have to put on more weight, but I'm feeling good," he was telling Aaron. She felt Florence and Delores hugging both of them together.

"You're just in time to come to the valley with us," Aaron was saying. "I found the best piece of land a man could ask for."

"I can't believe this," Sam said. "My God, Josh, we never really thought you'd make it, certainly not looking this healthy, and standing on your own feet like this."

He kept a firm arm around Marybeth as he explained about his determination not to come to Oregon unless he could ride his own horse. For the next several minutes there was general commotion and conversation, back-slapping, tears and laughter. "We went to the house, but nobody was there," Josh was saying. "Talk about being disappointed. I picked a heck of a day to come back. What's going on?"

"Spring celebrations. There's a dance tonight, but I have a feeling you and Marybeth won't be there," Sam said.

A rush of old desires and passion swept through Marybeth at the meaning of the words, and she felt Josh press her closer as the man laughed. "Where are my babies? What's this about twins?" He was bending down and kissing her tear-streaked cheeks now. Were those really his lips? "My God, woman, I said I wanted a family, but I didn't mean I wanted an instant brood."

There was more laughter, but Marybeth still could not speak. "Here are your babies," Delores was saying. Josh reluctantly let go of Marybeth, but kept hold of her hand as he knelt down to study the sleeping twins. He reached out to touch their tiny, velvety cheeks. "How old are they?"

"Six weeks," Delores answered.

"Hell, I don't—" His voice broke, and he kept his head bent as he wiped at his eyes. "I don't know which is which," he said jokingly.

Marybeth knelt down beside him. "The one closest to you is your son, Joseph. The other one is your daughter, Emma."

Josh looked at her. "Cap told me what you named them. That was really nice, Marybeth." Their eyes held, and he put a hand to her face. "God, I can't believe I'm really looking at you—touching you."

She broke into uncontrolled sobbing again as she hugged him tightly around the neck. "Oh, Josh! Josh! You're alive and ... walking. You're really here!"

Aaron leaned down to them. "We have a lot to talk about, Josh. We can do that tomorrow. Why don't you take Marybeth and the babies back to the house for now. We'll watch after Danny and we'll all stay over at Sam's place tonight and leave the two of you alone."

Josh rose, pulling Marybeth up with him. "I'd appreciate it, Aaron. Sorry to surprise you this way, but there was no way of telling when we'd get here."

"Did you really think we would mind? This is the best surprise any of us could have asked for. We're just damn glad to see you, especially looking as good as you do. I guess all of our prayers worked."

"Hell, I was only about half way to Fort Hall when I run into him," Cap put in. "He was already this side of the mountains."

Marybeth let go of Josh just long enough to give Cap a tearful hug. "Thank you, Cap. You saved his life. He'd be dead if it wasn't for you."

Cap patted her back. "Well, at the time I wasn't sure if I'd saved him or killed him. I'm as relieved as everybody else."

"Let's go back to the house," Josh was saying. Was it really and truly his voice, his arm around her? She took the wagon handle and he took hold of his horse's rein but kept one arm around her as they headed back toward the Svensson's house. A few people stared, some of the women commenting it must be the long-lost husband.

"How wonderful for her," Marybeth heard someone say.

Yes, how wonderful. She was so afraid she would wake up from this wonderful dream. They left the crowds and he kissed her hair. "You look more beautiful than I even remembered," he told her.

"I got fat as a buffalo before the twins were born," she answered, stopping to take a handkerchief from a pocket of her dress. She blew her nose and looked up at him. "I still haven't … lost all the weight."

"You look beautiful." He wiped at his own eyes with his shirtsleeve and looked her over. Her own eyes fell to his middle.

"Are you really all healed, Josh? Does everything work right—you can eat and all?"

"I've been eating regularly for quite a while now. It's a long story, and as long as I'm healing, I don't want to even talk about it, Marybeth. It's something I'd rather forget for a while, if that's possible." He touched her face. "I just want to feel you in my arms again, be a husband to you again, take you to the valley and settle like we dreamed about doing." He leaned down and kissed her lightly. "We've got some catching up to do."

She knew she should tell him about John, but not now. She didn't want to spoil the moment. All that mattered was that he was here, alive, well, walking, holding her. She reddened, feeling suddenly awkward. They had been apart for months, loving each other desperately but now feeling almost like strangers. He put an arm back around her and they walked together to the house. Josh tied his horse and they went inside.

"I want to get a good look at the babies," he said, pulling the wagon to a chair and sitting down. He pulled the blankets away and looked down at tiny arms and legs, miniature fingers and toes. "My God, Marybeth, they're beautiful—so perfect." He met her eyes, his own filled with tears. "I'm so damn sorry I wasn't here when they were born. Are you all right now? No problems?"

She reddened a little. "I just get tired from the constant feedings and running after Danny. But I'm … I'm healed, and I feel good."

He sighed, covering the babies. "I can't wait till they wake up so I can hold them."

"You can hold them now if you want."

He met her eyes. "I'd rather they didn't wake up just yet." He rose, moving around the wagon and pulling her into his arms. "Thank you, Marybeth, for my son and daughter. You're a hell of a woman. When I think of what you must have gone through—being here with three children and no husband. I don't want you to worry about another thing. I'm here now and I'm going to be all right. The only thing that kept me going was the thought of coming for you. I was so afraid for you."

"Oh, Josh, I can hardly believe you're really here. I prayed and prayed. Oh, it feels so good to have your arms around me again. Surely God *does* mean for us to be together, just like you said. There isn't a woman in the world who could be happier than I am at this moment."

"And no man happier than I am."

She looked up at him, and their lips met for the first time. He kissed her gently, hesitantly at first, as though unsure how she would react after being so long apart. But it took only that first kiss to reawaken all the passion and need they both had hungered for for so long. Desperate happiness and aching memories enveloped them as his kiss drew deeper and he felt his needs awakening, telling him he could still be a husband to her. She reached up around his neck, and he moved his hands along her ribs, moving his thumbs over the sides of her full breasts.

He left her lips, holding her so tightly she could hardly breathe. "God, Marybeth, maybe it's too sudden for you—"

"No," she whispered. "I need to know as much as you do."

"Are you sure? Are you healed enough?"

"I'm sure."

"I don't even know if I can do this," he said, his voice gruff with desire, his hands tangling in her hair.

"I have no doubt that you can," she answered, her voice quivering with excitement and desire. Josh! He was really here, holding her, kissing her, loving her, protecting her. He pulled away, kissing her eyes. "I'll bolt the door," he said. "We have a lot to talk about, Marybeth, but I won't even be able to think straight until I can be a husband to you again. It's all I've thought about for weeks." He ran a hand over her hair and walked over to lock the door. Their eyes held as he walked back to her and he put an arm around her, leading her into the bedroom. He pulled the wagon along behind them into the bedroom, then closed the door.

Marybeth sat down on the bed, feeling suddenly shy, worried her body had changed and he wouldn't like what he saw. He sat down beside her, putting an arm around her. "I've got a nasty scar you might not want to look at."

"Do you really think I would care about a scar?" She met his warm, brown eyes. "I still have a soft belly from the babies."

He grinned. "I don't think either one of us cares how the other one looks, do we?"

She smiled tearfully. "I ... feel a little strange, almost like our wedding night—nervous."

He kissed her lightly. "I feel the same way this time." Their eyes held, and he met her lips and laid her back on the bed. It was all either of them needed. Suddenly they could not get enough of each other. He pulled her dress open and moved his lips to her breasts, gently kissing them. She reached up and unbuttoned his shirt when he sat up to pull her dress farther down. He sat still while she opened it and studied the scars— one from the original wound and he other from when Cap had cut into him to relieve the infection.

She leaned up and kissed them. "My poor Josh," she whispered. "I pray I never have to see you suffer that way again."

He touched her hair, taking the combs from the sides and

letting it fall over her soft shoulders and full breasts. "I can't believe I'm here with you, looking at you this way, touching you," he told her.

He laid her back again, and their need was too great for preliminaries. He took time only to pull off his boots and pants, leaving on his half-buttoned shirt. He pushed up her dress and she moved to help him pull off her shoes and stockings and bloomers. He moved on top of her then, and in the next moment he was pressing himself against her thigh. "God, Marybeth," he groaned. "I don't want to disappoint you."

He moved inside her, and he was anything but a disappointment. His hands slid under her bare hips and he pushed deep and hard, groaning her name, moving eagerly and rhythmically as he realized he could still be a man and had the strength and energy for this. She took him in raptured glory, in the happiest moment she had ever experienced.

It was all too wonderful, too intense. Quickly his life spilled into her. They both lay there spent and weak. Finally he raised up and took off his clothes, then helped her with her dress. They said nothing as he pulled back the covers and they crawled under them together, pressing damp, naked bodies together.

"I just want to hold you for a while," he told her. It was only minutes before she was again swimming in his kisses, overwhelmed by his tender touch. She opened herself to him, and when he moved inside her for a second time, they both cried with the realization that this was real. He was alive and still a man, here to love and protect her. *Protect her.* She thought about John again, then quickly shoved the thought away. Not now. Not in this most beautiful moment of her entire life. She would not let John MacKinder rob her of this moment. Tomorrow was soon enough to mention his name.

# Thirty-One

Marybeth stirred awake, vaguely remembering getting up during the night to feed the babies while her husband slept an exhausted sleep. The ride to get to her and their intense lovemaking into the night had been hard on his still-recovering body. Was it all real? She opened her eyes to see him still lying beside her, and when she met his eyes, he was watching her.

"It *is* real," she whispered.

He reached out and touched her hair, looking her over lovingly. "It's just as hard for me to believe as it is for you." He kissed her eyes and turned on his back to stretch. Her heart ached at how thin he was, at the puckered scars on his side and back. "I could eat one hell of a breakfast," he said.

She smiled, moving a hand over his ribs. "You *need* one. You've got to get more meat back on these bones."

"Don't worry. Now that I'm settled in one place and will be eating your cooking, I'll put it back on fast enough." He reached out for her and she settled into his shoulder. "I'm thinking of living right here until next spring, Marybeth. I don't think I'm ready to go out chopping down trees and building fences and rustling up wild horses. I don't want to do anything to risk the health I've managed to get back. I'm thinking if I could get a job around here that isn't too strenuous, after another year I'd be strong as ever, and the children would be bigger and stronger too. With them so tiny, and you so worn out from feeding them all the time—I don't know, I just hate to expose any of you to living out of a wagon again while we're building a house. I could go with Sam and Aaron and see the property, stake out the boundaries and such, but one more year won't make a hell of a lot of difference. What do you think?"

"I think it's a very good idea. I don't care where we live, Josh, as long as I am with you."

"Well, Aaron and Delores will be moving out of here soon. As long as the cabin is here, we might as well use it. I'll make things right with Aaron. I still have some money left, but maybe I can save a little more working here in Portland for the winter."

She raised up on one elbow and leaned down to kiss his chest. "I just want you to get as well and strong as the Josh I married. I don't ever want anything bad to happen to you again. From now on—"

A strange look came into his eyes as he studied her face. The morning sun, filtering through a crack in the shutters, hit her right cheek brightly. He frowned, touching her cheek. "What is this?"

Her smile faded, and she felt her chest tighten. How she had dreaded telling him, wished it could be avoided! He would be so angry. He might do something foolish, something that would put him in danger all over again. Yet she knew for his own safety she would have to tell him. How she hated John MacKinder for always spoiling her happiness!

"Looks like a bruise," he was saying. "I didn't even notice it yesterday. You fall or something?"

She closed her eyes and laid her head down on his chest. "No." She swallowed. "Josh..." She sat up then, scooting against the head of the bed and pulling a blanket over herself. "John MacKinder isn't dead. He's—living someplace up in the hills, around Portland."

He slowly sat up, turning and moving up beside her. "*He* did that to you?"

Already she could feel the terrible anger. She met his eyes, which a moment before were soft and loving, now blazed with hatred. "When! What happened, Marybeth!"

She closed her eyes, and the tears came. "Oh, Josh, I don't want you to get hurt again. You can't get into a fight with him— not now! He would kill you!"

He placed his hands gently at either side of her face. "You let *me* worry about that. First tell me what happened, Marybeth!"

She jerked in a sob and told him about John's invasion and threats. "When I said I wasn't going with him … he hit me and—tore open my dress."

"Jesus," he swore, turning and clenching his fists.

"I let him think I would … go with him. I came in here, and I got the rifle and pointed it at him, and told him to get out. He … wouldn't leave, Josh. He didn't think … I'd use it. He started toward me—and I shot him."

He turned back to her, his eyes full of shock and pity. "*Shot* him!"

She sniffed. "I hit his arm. I guess he was so surprised he ran off. That was—about nine days ago. He hasn't been back. The sheriff had a couple of men watch the house after that—till Aaron and Sam got back. Oh, Josh, I was so afraid he'd come while Aaron was here … and Aaron would get hurt or killed. And now I'm afraid for you. He's crazy, Josh. He's worse than ever. He wanted me to leave my babies. And he … Josh, he as much as admitted he killed Dan—his own brother! Dan fell into a vat of molten steel. I think John pushed him."

Josh's eyes widened in disbelief. "His own brother?"

She leaned forward and hugged him. "Oh, Josh, I think he's the one who shot you. I'm so sorry. I should have just stayed with him. It would have saved you so much suffering."

He moved his arms around her, pulling her close and kissing her hair. "I wouldn't have had it any other way. And I already figured out myself it must have been John who did this. I had a lot of time to think when I was laid up, Marybeth. The way that Indian raid went, it didn't make sense me being the only one shot with a repeater; being shot in the back made even more sense. John MacKinder would be low enough to do that." He petted her hair. "My biggest fear while I was laid up was that he'd show up here and give you trouble. Don't cry, Marybeth. You just worry about taking care of my babies. I'll take care of John MacKinder."

"But how? Josh, you don't dare get in another fight with him. That's just what he would want. A few blows to your wounds, and he'd kill you."

He gently pushed her away. "You forget that he doesn't even know I'm here. What did you tell him about me?"

She wiped her eyes. "Just that I didn't know if you were dead or alive. I told him Cap had gone to see."

Josh got up and pulled on his longjohns. "What did he say after you shot him?"

"He said I'd pay. He said it was my fault his parents were dead." She met his eyes. "Did Cap tell you about Ella and Mac?"

Josh nodded. "That's when I got really alarmed. I knew if John was alive and found out he'd blame you—both of us." He buttoned his underwear and walked to the window, opening the shutters to the sunshine and looking out. "That means he'll be back. He's probably just nursing that arm." He looked at her with hard eyes. "You get washed and dressed. And I'd sure like it if you could rustle up some breakfast." He put a hand to his flat belly. "You wore me out last night, woman."

"Josh, what are you going to do?"

He reached for his shirt. "I'm not sure yet. First I'm going to get Cap over here and see what he thinks. One thing is sure. When a man deliberately does to another man what John MacKinder did to me, he's got to pay." He buttoned his shirt rapidly, anger in every movement. "I won't forget the hell I went through as long as I live. And any man who would kill his own brother doesn't deserve to still be walking around. Dan MacKinder might not have been any better than John, but a brother is a brother." He met her eyes. "He must have wanted you awful bad—bad enough that he's bound to come back and try again, especially after getting shot. I can imagine what he thinks of a woman chasing him out with a gun. He won't get over that one for a while. He figures you need to be taught a lesson." He pulled on his pants. "And when he comes for you, he's going to get a lesson of his own."

"Josh, I'd die if anything happened to you now."

He saw the terror in her eyes as he buttoned his pants. He put on a leather vest. "Nothing is going to happen to me. You don't think God pulled me through all that for nothing, do you? Hell, he wanted me to live so I could get my revenge."

He went to the wash basin and poured water into it, splashing his face and drying it.

"God doesn't think in terms of revenge," Marybeth told him.

"Doesn't He? I'm not so sure. What about the great flood? And what about when Moses parted the Red Sea, and all those Egyptians or whoever they were rode in after him and were drowned?"

She smiled and watched him dampen a rag and dip it in a can of baking soda sitting near the wash basin, watched him scrubb his teeth with the baking soda and pour water into a tin cup to rinse his mouth. "How do you know those Bible stories?" she asked.

He took a drink of water and went to the mirror to study his beard. "My ma used to read to us from the Bible all the time. Remember I told you that? She used it to practice her own reading—named all of us after Bible characters: Joshua, Luke, Matthew, Rachael." He ran a brush through his hair. "You just get dressed and make some breakfast. I'm going next door to talk to Aaron. Make enough breakfast for everybody. I'll bring them back here, and I'll shave after breakfast." He leaned down and grasped her face, kissing her lips tenderly. "Don't you worry about a thing. I've got the edge this time. That bastard snuck up on me when I thought he was dead. Now I have the chance to do the same to him."

"Josh Rivers, you're actually looking forward to it."

The hard look of vengeance came back into his eyes. "You bet I'm looking forward to it! For one thing, I'm relieved to know what happened to him, instead of always having to wonder about him. Now I know he's alive, and what he intends to do. I'm one step ahead of him, Marybeth. And when I'm through, that man will never bother either one of us again."

He bent down and pulled on his boots, then grabbed his hat from the bedpost. He hesitated at the doorway and looked back at her. "I love you, Marybeth. Last night was … it meant even more to me than even our wedding night. Things are going to be good for us from now on."

He went out. Marybeth got up and went to the window, keeping a blanket around herself and watching him walk to the Gentry cabin. He had the same masculine gait; the old, cocky confidence of the Josh Rivers she had married. Oh, how she loved him, and how she feared for him. How cruel and unbearable it would be to finally have him back, only to lose him again.

Josh paced nervously, puffing on a cigar. "I wish Cap would get back with Stone," he grumbled.

"Josh, what do you have planned?" Marybeth asked. "I don't like any of this."

"And I don't like knowing a man who wants me dead is on the loose and could back-shoot me again. I'm going to flush that bastard out and get this over with. I'm not waiting for him to make the first move."

Marybeth glanced at Delores, seeing the worry in her eyes also. Both women kneaded dough for bread, while Aaron sat at the table repairing a bridle. "You just let us know what we can do, Josh."

Josh went to a window. "The last thing I'll do is put any of you in any danger. If my plan works, this little confrontation will take place far away from here, away from friends and children. All you and Sam need to do is stay right here an extra few days and lie for me if John MacKinder shows up. I wasn't sure what to do till Cap said he found Bill Stone working over at the sawmill, and I won't know if my plan will even work if Stone doesn't want to cooperate." He puffed the cigar a moment longer, pacing again. His tension could be sensed by everyone. Even Danny sat quietly in a corner watching "Zosh" walk around the room like a caged wildcat. "Something had better happen pretty soon. I'm going crazy hiding in this cabin," Josh complained.

Someone knocked at the door, and Josh quickly opened it. Cap stood outside with Bill Stone. Stone's eyes widened at the sight of Josh. He started to exclaim his name when Josh grabbed his arm and yanked the man inside. Cap followed, closing the door.

Bill jerked his arm away from Josh's grasp and stared at the man. "You're alive!"

"You bet I'm alive," Josh answered.

Bill looked around the room, meeting Marybeth's eyes before turning back to Josh. "What the hell is going on here? What do you want from me?"

"Do you know where John MacKinder is holed up?"

Bill frowned, then stepped back, fear coming into his eyes. "Look, I'm not going to get mixed up in whatever you want with John MacKinder! The man is crazy! I want no part of it."

"You've seen him then? Talked to him?"

Bill glanced at Marybeth again.

"Come on, Stone, we need to know," Cap put in, stepping closer to the man. Aaron rose from his chair, and Bill Stone found himself surrounded by three threatening men. He swallowed before talking.

"Look, I heard he was in town one night—arm wrestled a bunch of men over at the Sierra Tavern. I was sure he was dead, so I wanted to see if it was really him. Besides, I figured he needed to know about his folks being dead. So I looked him up. He … he stayed the night there with a … prostitute."

The women reddened and busied themselves putting bread dough into pans. Marybeth felt she had to keep busy or go crazy with worry over what could happen to Josh. Bill swallowed nervously again before continuing.

"I found him, and I told him about his folks. He got mighty angry. You know how he is. He … he asked about Marybeth."

In an instant Josh slammed Bill against the wall. "And I suppose you told him where he could find her, you bastard!"

"Josh, watch yourself," Cap put in, stepping over and grasping his arm. "Let go of him."

"I'd like to *kill* him," Josh growled. "He knew John would try to hurt her—her over here alone, hardly healed from having her babies—"

Aaron grasped his other arm. "You won't get anything more out of him this way, Josh. Don't go and get *yourself* hurt."

Bill just stared at him in wide-eyed terror. Josh let go of him, but his eyes were so full of murder Bill could almost feel a gun at his head. "Look," he said, panting now with fear. "You … you know how that man is—especially when he's angry. He'd have beat the hell out of me if I would have told anyone first. I'm sorry if he came over here and made trouble."

"You could have warned Marybeth!"

"Well, I … I figured she had her friends around her. I didn't know Aaron and Sam would be gone. He must have snooped around and waited till they left. All I know is afterward he came to my cabin, out behind the sawmill. I had told him I was living there—offered to let him stay there if he needed a place. Anyway, he came to me after the thing with Marybeth—wanted me to patch up his arm. He was afraid to go to a regular doctor; figured maybe the law would be onto him. He was madder than anybody I ever saw in my life. I was afraid to refuse to help him, so I bandaged up his arm for him. He told me he was staying in some kind of shack higher up in the hills … kept talking about how he was going to get Marybeth one way or another—her and the boy. Said he wanted to take them up to that shack to live with him. He kept saying that if he could just…" He glanced at Marybeth again, then back to Josh. "Well … you know—he figured if he could get her in his bed, she'd want to stay with him. You know how he is about women. He's got one opinion of all of them."

Marybeth turned away and sat down in a chair, staring at the fireplace, unable to look any of them in the eye. Josh slammed his fist against a can of saddle soap and sent it flying. He began pacing again, while Bill just watched him, unsure of his own safety.

"Josh, I knew the law would be in on it by then. I figured Marybeth was reasonably safe. John went back to his shack to heal."

"And he said he'd be back, didn't he? He said he'd make Marybeth pay, and you just let him go, and never told the law or Marybeth or anyone that you knew where he was staying."

Bill stepped away from the wall, breaking out in a sweat

from fear. "What the hell good would it have done? He didn't kill her or anything like that. He'd have been arrested for nothing more than disturbing the peace. He'd have served a few days and got out again, and then he'd come after *me* for telling the law where they could find him!"

Josh turned, fists clenched. "I intend to fix it so *nobody*—not even you—has to worry about what that man is going to do any more. But I need your help, Stone, and after the danger you let my wife be put in, you *owe* it to her to help us!"

"I don't have to do anything of the kind! I want no part of any more dealings with John MacKinder, you hear? You can't make me do it."

"Can't I? You'll help us, or I'll have John MacKinder riding your ass so close your butt will feel on fire! Cap's got a good nose for tracking, Stone. He'll find that shack *without* your help, and he'll go and get the sheriff. They'll arrest John and put him in jail for a while, just like you said. Cap will make sure John thinks that *you're* the one who told the law where he could be found. Then he'll come after you, just like you said he'd do."

Bill looked at Cap, who just grinned and nodded. He looked back at Josh, almost ready to cry. "Listen, I traveled all the way out here with the MacKinders. Mac—he was a hard man, bullheaded, sometimes flat-out mean. But him and me, we got along all right. And he wasn't a murderer or a rapist or anything like that. John, he's different, especially since he spent the winter in the mountains. He's a killer, Josh. Hell, he as much as admitted being the one to shoot you."

"You think I didn't already figure that out?"

"All I'm saying is, I don't want to get on the wrong side of him."

Josh stepped closer. "If my plan works, you won't have to worry about him at *all* any more."

"But what if it doesn't?"

The room fell chillingly silent for a moment. Josh glanced at Cap. "If it doesn't, we'll probably *all* be dead. But I've got a wife and three children to protect. Don't you think I'll make damn sure it *does* work?"

Bill closed his eyes and took a deep breath. "What is it you want out of me?"

Josh's eyes glittered. "It's real simple, Bill—no danger to you at all." He walked over to the table and picked up his cigar, relighting it. "All you have to do is go find John—make out like you're being a loyal friend by telling him something you know he'd want to know about. You go find him, and you tell him you've heard Marybeth has decided to go back east."

Marybeth turned and looked at him in surprise, as did Delores and Aaron. Only Cap knew what Josh's plan was.

"That's it?" Bill frowned. "I don't understand."

"You don't have to understand. The less you know, the less danger there is to you. You tell John you figured he'd want to know. Tell him Marybeth has learned I died up at Fort Hall, that she figures there's nothing left here for her and that Cap has agreed to take her back east. You ran into Cap in town, after he got back from going to find out about me. You tell John you got all your information straight from Cap—that they're leaving in, oh, let's say one week from today. That should give you time to find him. Next Saturday. Remember that. Cap will be taking the regular route—same one he used to come into Oregon. Marybeth figures she can find work easier back east; figures it would be better for the babies to live in more civilized places. You got all that?" Bill nodded. "You think you can find where he's living?"

The man nodded again. "He described it pretty good."

Josh stepped closer, taking his six-gun from a holster that hung on the wall near Bill. Bill stared at the gun wide-eyed as Josh pulled back the hammer and slowly pressed the barrel of the gun against Bill's throat. "One more thing," he said, keeping the cigar between his teeth. "If anything goes wrong—if MacKinder finds out I'm still alive and comes after me here, for instance—or if something happens to Marybeth, I'll know who told him, won't I?"

Bill swallowed. "Yes," he answered gruffly.

"And you'll be a dead man, I promise. If I get killed, it's Cap who'll come after you. He's a good friend. He'll do it—for me and Marybeth. Don't you cross me, Bill, or you'll be found with a big hole from under your chin clean up through your brain and out the top of your head. Understood?"

"Yes, sir. I just … I don't understand what you've got planned," he whispered.

Josh slowly put back the gun hammer. "I told you, you don't have to know. I don't *want* you to know. You just get going and find the man and deliver the message. How about repeating it to me?"

Bill wiped sweat from his forehead. "I … I ran into Cap in town and found out you died. Cap said Marybeth has decided to go back east to find work, and where it would be safer for the babies. Cap's taking her—leaving next Saturday."

Josh grinned and nodded. "Just don't act so goddamn nervous when you tell him. Remember, you don't have to *be* nervous. You're doing him a favor. He'll be grateful. You don't have one reason to be afraid of him." He puffed the cigar again. "One more thing—this is between just the people in this room and nobody else. No matter what happens, you don't say one word to the law, understood?"

Bill nodded. "I understand. If anybody's got a right to pay a man back for what's been done to him, you do. When it was a family thing … back in the beginning … I figured it was their affair. I stayed out of it. But John, he got kind of crazy about it."

"I'll tell you how crazy he got. Just so you don't feel like too much of a traitor to him, you ought to know he killed his own brother so Marybeth would be left a widow—figured he could move in and take over after that. He told Marybeth in so many words. Leastways, he didn't deny it."

Bill lowered his eyes and shook his head. "I kind of suspected. I just didn't want to believe he could really do a thing like that. Dan, he was a big bully just like John, but the way he died—it was awful. For a man to do that to his own brother…" He sighed and looked around the room at all of them. "Whatever you've got in mind, you just make sure you do *your* job right. I don't want that man coming for me."

Josh's eyes glowed with the smell of victory. "He won't be

coming for you. I *guarantee* it. Now get going. It might take you a couple of days to find him."

Bill nodded and hurried to the door, looking around when he stepped outside, then hurrying away.

"Josh, what on Earth do you have planned?" Aaron frowned at him. "If you send Marybeth out there in a wagon, she'll be in danger."

Josh just grinned. "Marybeth won't *be* with the wagon. Cap will lead a wagon east, all right, and there will be a woman sitting on the seat of the wagon. You can bet John will be waiting for them, ready to ride down and steal Marybeth and Danny away. But Marybeth will be right here. She'll hide out in the Gentry cabin, in case John comes here first to see if she's left. You'll tell him she has, that I'm dead and Marybeth has gone back east. You'll even beg John to leave her alone. That will just make him more determined to go after her."

He patted his thinner waistline. "I'll bet I could fit into a woman's clothes, thin as I am right now—at least a loose skirt and a shirt. With a big slat bonnet on my head, who's going to know from a distance it's not a woman sitting on the wagon seat?"

They all stared at him for a moment, as Marybeth slowly rose. Aaron grinned, then burst into hearty laughter. "Oh, I sure would like to be there to see the look on his face!"

Josh glanced at Marybeth. She was not laughing; not even smiling. He saw only fear in her eyes. She knew the danger involved. He walked over to her, and she fell into his arms. "It's got to be done, Marybeth. He's a back-shooter. As long as he's alive, we can't go anywhere to live without wondering when he'll sneak up on us. I'd rather flush him out and face him head on. It's going to work, and at last we'll be free and able to live our lives the way we planned."

She couldn't find her voice for the moment. She clung to him, relishing the feel of his arms around her; she had had him back for such a short time. But she understood why he had to do what he had planned. She pulled away from him, wiping at her eyes. "Let's go see ... if we can find something for you to wear," she told him then.

He laughed lightly. "That's the spirit." He gave her the teasing wink she had come to love. "I want something pretty—maybe with flowers." Everyone laughed as he followed her into the bedroom. Josh shut the door and grabbed her close, kissing her hungrily, both of them remembering the horror of being apart and never wanting that to happen again. He pressed her head against his chest. "It will work, Marybeth. I promise it will work. I've never broken a promise to you yet, and I'm not about to start now."

# Thirty-Two

The wagon bounced and jostled over Barlow's Road, alongside the raging Columbia. Orville Dunne had agreed to help Cap and Josh in their plan. He was someone John MacKinder would not recognize, appearing as simply a hired hand to help lead the oxen while Cap rode ahead.

Josh sat on the wagon seat, wearing a blue skirt and flowered blouse. From a distance, no one could tell the inside seams of the blouse's sleeves and bodice had been ripped open so it would fit over Josh's arms and chest. Since Florence Gentry was bigger through the ribs than Marybeth, Josh wore one of her camisoles, which had been stuffed with stockings and pieces of cloth to give Josh the full bosom of Marybeth. Getting him ready had helped ease some of the tension over the danger of his mission. He doubted anyone had seen a more comical vision than he was when he finished his disguise. When he put on the slat bonnet, everyone laughed until the tears came; everyone but Marybeth, who only watched with fear and concern in her eyes.

He thought about her now, about their night of lovemaking before he left, made more intense by the realization that they could again be separated. But he had made up his mind to take any risk necessary to keep her from ever again being threatened by John MacKinder, let alone the fact that his own life would be in constant danger. He had been through too much to let anything stop him now from having a happy life with Marybeth and his new family.

They had been traveling for three days now. Josh carried a bundle in his arm that was wrapped to look like a baby, but inside his six-gun lay hidden. Occasionally he would climb into the back of the wagon and get some sleep by day, since he spent his nights sitting awake inside the wagon, sure that if John made his move, it would be at night. He knew it could be any time now. The man would wait until they were well away from Portland. He searched the wild, brush-covered hillsides constantly, watching for any strange movement, hoping neither Cap nor Orv would get hurt.

It was late afternoon when the sun caught a rifle barrel in the hills and caused a flash that Josh caught out of the corner of his eye. "Orv," he called out quietly.

"I seen it. Let's just keep goin'. I reckon' Cap seen it, too."

Josh kept his eye out for any more movement as they traveled on, making camp along the riverbank for the night. Cap and Orville made a fire and cooked the meal.

"Marybeth ain't feelin' too good," Cap told Orville, loud enough for anyone nearby to hear. "She's stayin' in the wagon with the babies tonight. Danny's already fell asleep."

Orville nodded. "She'd better try to eat."

Cap shook his head in seeming sorrow. "I ain't been able to get her to eat enough to keep a bird alive, ever since she found out about Josh. I feel so sorry for her, but I don't know how to help her."

"It's a real shame, that's what—her with them new babies and all."

They turned their talk to general trail talk. Cap mentioned he hoped to join up with some supply trains headed east so Marybeth would be safer. "I don't like travelin' alone like this."

Both men ate, all the while keeping their eyes and ears open for odd sounds and sights. Night settled in, and they set up their bedrolls. Josh waited inside, gun in hand. They had all seen the glint of the rifle barrel. None of them doubted this was the night John MacKinder would make his move.

Wolves howled in the distance, and he thought about their journey west, all the hardships they had endured to stay alive and be together. Marybeth had put up with the MacKinders long enough. It was time for the hell to be over and the happiness to begin.

After nearly two hours Josh heard a horse whinney, and

immediately his thoughts left him. He straightened, his hand clasping the six-gun. His ears strained to hear a faint rustling sound outside, and he waited for the right time and the right move.

"All right, up with you—both of you!" It was John MacKinder's voice.

"What the hell?" Orville jumped up. "Who the hell are you?"

"Name's John MacKinder," John said proudly. "Walk into the firelight and away from your guns. Come on, now. Get up Cap. Remember me, you old buzzard? Thought I was dead, didn't you?"

Cap rubbed his eyes and stood up. "What the hell are you doing here, MacKinder?"

"I've still got friends left, no thanks to you. And one of them told me Marybeth was going back east. But this is as far as she goes, Cap. She's coming with me. And you ... I ought to shoot you for what you did to me! In fact, I intend to. I just want Marybeth out here first. I want her to see what happens to people who try to keep her from me!"

"You already showed her that when you shot Josh Rivers. *You* did it, didn't you? Marybeth said you even killed your own brother, back in New York."

John grinned. "Sure I did. I killed both of them, and now there's nobody left to come between me and Marybeth." He held his rifle steadily on both men. "Once a man starts killing, Cap, it gets easier, just like it's going to be easy to kill you. People will think it was outlaws or Indians, and they rode off with the woman."

Orville backed away as though frightened. "Look, Mister, I don't even know you! Let me go. I won't say anything."

"Sure you won't. You stay right where you are. Marybeth! Get out here," John shouted then. "I know you're in there! You can't run away from me, woman, you should know that. Get Danny and get out here."

Josh made a whimpering sound.

"I mean it! Get out here or I'll come in there and kill those damn Rivers babies like a couple of weak pups in a litter."

Josh opened the back canvas, keeping his head down and making whimpering sounds as he climbed out. The minute his feet hit the ground, he raised his head and his six-gun, cocking it and aiming it at John. "Put down that rifle, MacKinder."

John stood frozen in place for a moment. He backed up slightly, turning to look at the tall figure in the dress. The voice sounded familiar, and John's blood ran cold when he realized whose it was. "Josh Rivers," he almost gasped.

"That's right; and I'm not too happy about the hell you put me through the last few months, MacKinder. You're going to hang for it. You've bragged in front of too many people about trying to kill me—and about killing your brother."

John kept hold of his rifle, standing still, trying to think. "How ... did Bill do this?"

"Doesn't matter. I just wanted to get you away from Marybeth first, and I wanted to hear you say with your own mouth that you shot me and killed your brother. Now drop that rifle. It wouldn't take more than a breath for me to pull this trigger, after what you did to me! There's nothing I want more right now than to open a hole in that head of yours! I'm just not the *murderer* you are!"

For a moment there was only the sound of crickets, and John's heavy breathing as he stood there undecided. If he gave up now, Josh Rivers would have defeated him again, Rivers and Marybeth both!

"You better do like he says," Cap told the man. "A man's got to pay his dues, MacKinder."

"No!" John suddenly roared the word, whirling with the rifle. Josh's gun went off and John felt a horrible sting at the side of his head as he turned. He fired his rifle and heard Josh cry out. By then Cap and Orv had both ducked out of the firelight. John fired into the darkness. Someone fired back at him, and he cried out at pain in his right thigh. As he turned and limped into the brush, he heard someone following.

Josh ripped off the skirt and blouse as he kept his eyes riveted on the big dark figure that ran into the wild brush along the riverbank, lit up by a bright, full moon.

"Josh, don't go after him alone," he heard Cap yelling.

He was not about to lose sight of John. He cursed himself for being stupid enough to want to do this by the law. Men like John MacKinder didn't understand or deserve justice. He grimaced at the pain in his left shoulder, remembering the burning agony of a bullet wound all too well.

He saw John jump down over the riverbank, and he watched quietly, noticing the man did not go out along the river. He was apparently crouched in the brush just under him. Josh pulled a knife from his boot and quickly slashed at the strings of the camisole, throwing it off along with the material stuffed into it. He could feel the blood trickling under his own shirt which he had worn under the camisole. He shoved the knife back into its sheath and picked up his gun, keeping his eyes on the riverbank. There still was no sign of John MacKinder.

"Come on out of there, John," he yelled. "I know I hit you. Give it up!"

John leaped out of his shelter and began firing wildly in the direction of Josh's voice. Josh ducked aside, rolling behind the trunk of a big fir tree. He fired twice more, hitting John again. The way he spun around, Josh guessed it was in the upper left chest. His emotions were mixed as the man dropped, then got to his knees, then his feet again. John MacKinder was not going to go down easily. In one sense Josh enjoyed the realization that the man was suffering; yet he didn't like shooting any man over and over. Again he asked him to give up. Again John fired at him.

"Josh, where the hell are you?" He heard Cap running through the brush.

"Stay back there, Cap. It's all right!"

John fired at him again and Josh fired back, and again John went down. Josh had one shot left in his gun. He watched John for several seconds. This time he did not move.

"Josh!"

"I'm all right, Cap." He moved carefully down the riverbank, keeping his eyes on John MacKinder. It seemed a shame that a man—any man—would have thrown his life away as MacKinder had. He slowly approached him. John lay on his side. Suddenly he curled up. Josh stayed back. "We'll get you some help, John."

The man coughed. "MacKinders ... don't take ... help." He coughed again. "You ... stole her ... stole her."

"I didn't steal anyone. I love her and she loves me. You've created all your own problems, MacKinder."

"She ... belonged ... to me—Danny ... belonged to me. I was ... the right one. You ... damn you ... *damn you*!" He turned, pointing the rifle at Josh. Josh jumped sideways as the rifle went off, and he fired his own last bullet. As if by design, it struck John MacKinder in the head. Even then the man sat staring at him for a moment, looking as though he might actually get up and shoot again. Finally he slumped back, stiffening, his eyes staring. There was a moment of quiet, with just the sound of the flowing river and an owl hooting somewhere nearby.

"So, it's finally done," Josh muttered. "I suppose it was leading to this all along, wasn't it, MacKinder?" He had no feelings of victory or vengeance; he only felt an odd sadness, mingled with tremendous relief.

"Josh! Goddamn it, where are you?"

Josh turned and called up to Cap. "Down here."

The man came crashing down the riverbank. "Jesus, I must have heard ten shots at least. You all right?" He stopped near John's body. He and Josh looked at each other in the moonlight. "He dead, Josh?"

Josh sighed. "It took four hits. The poor bastard wouldn't stay down. Kept turning and firing at me again."

Cap put a hand to the dark stain on Josh's shirt. "Damn it, you've been hit yourself. This is the last thing you needed."

"I think it went clean through, up by my neck. It's a far cry from being gut-shot. I'll be all right."

"You come up to the campsite and let me fix you up. Marybeth is gonna be real upset about this."

"She'll be more upset about John being dead. I hate to tell her, Cap."

"Did you really think she didn't expect this? We all knew you'd never bring him back alive. John MacKinder wouldn't have accepted that kind of defeat. We knew it, and so did Marybeth. Now come let me tend to that wound before you stand here and bleed to death. Orv and I will come back and bury him. We'll mark the grave as an emigrant—died from a shooting accident. There ain't all that much law out here yet, Josh. No sense stirring up trouble neither you nor Marybeth needs right now. This was a personal thing, and there ain't a man alive who'd blame you for what's happened."

Josh leaned down and closed John's eyes. "What about Danny? How can I tell him when he's older that I killed off his last relative? When he finds out what the MacKinders were like—"

"Josh." Cap leaned down and touched his shoulder. "Marybeth said she wanted Danny to grow up to bring pride to the MacKinder name. All that boy ever has to know is that his pa was killed in an accident back in New York, and the rest of the family died on their way out here. There is no reason on God's Earth to tell him any more than that. If you tell him things that make him proud to be a MacKinder, then he'll just build on that. Marybeth is proud to be Irish, and she'll instill that in Danny. It won't hurt that boy if you lie to him a little about the MacKinders."

Josh rose. "I suppose not. But *I* have to live with it."

"You have to live with the fact that you saved Marybeth from a living hell, and made sure Danny wasn't raised by a man like John. You did right, Josh; you did right. Come on now. Come back to camp with me."

Josh turned and followed him back, feeling suddenly weak and spent. He sat down near the fire so Cap could see better, and Orv quickly heated some water.

"You've got to learn to dodge bullets better than this, boy," Orville told him.

Josh grinned a little, then winced as he moved his arm back so that Cap could pull off his shirt. His arm and hand and chest were covered with drying blood. "Looks like the bleeding's slowed," Cap said. "You're right. It went clean through. You lucked out this time—just missed your shoulder bones, looks to me like." Josh grunted with pain as the man felt around the wound, struggling against memories of a lot worse wound and not feeling quite so bad about killing John MacKinder.

"You think she'll be all right, Cap? I don't want her blaming herself for any of this. There's nobody to blame but MacKinder himself."

"She'll be all right. She's one strong woman, Josh. Before them babies was born, she was already talkin' about ways she could provide for her children if you was dead—for all of you if you was crippled. She's a survivor—a good woman to have out here. What you both need to do is put all this behind you now and get down to the kind of livin' you planned on out here." Cap began washing the blood from Josh.

"Yeah, it is pretty country, isn't it? I just realized I've got to write my sister and tell her I got here all right—tell her about Marybeth. I think I'll leave out all the bad stuff. No sense worrying her with it. Hell, maybe I can convince her and my brother-in-law and my brother Luke to come out here. They'd love it, and Rachael would love Marybeth. They're a lot alike in spirit."

"Well, I'd sure like to meet any sister of yours."

Josh closed his eyes and breathed deeply against the pain. He realized most of what he loved about Marybeth *was* her spirit—her willingness to stand up against great odds to have the man she loved. His mother had done that, and so had his sister. Now they were free to love and be happy. There would be no more terror and threats for his Marybeth.

"Let's head back tonight, after we bury John," he told Cap. "Hell, there's a bright moon. I don't want Marybeth to worry any longer than necessary."

"What you really mean is you can't wait to get back to her."

Josh grinned. "Yeah. You're right." He thought of how good it was going to feel to hold her against him and know they were truly free to love. They had both survived a living hell. God surely did mean for them to be together. "I think I'll have her teach me about those crazy beads of hers, Cap. I swear they have some kind of power."

## May, 1853 ...

Josh drove the wagon to the crest of a hill that overlooked his land in the valley. "Well, here we are," he told Marybeth. "You sure you don't mind living out of this thing for a week or two till we get a cabin built? With Sam and Aaron to help, it shouldn't take too long."

She grasped his arm and rested her head on his shoulder. Danny, now two and a half years old, and the twins, a year old and already walking, romped in the back of the wagon, squealing and laughing.

"Oh, Josh, you know I don't mind," Marybeth answered, looking out over the sweeping valley. A sparkling stream ran through the middle of it. "All that matters is that we're here, alive, together." She straightened and drank in the view. Today there was a scent of ocean air on the wind. Her eyes teared. "Josh, it's prettier than I even imagined it. Just think, we have this beautiful land and we're near our friends. Oh, I hope your sister comes out like she wrote she was thinking of doing. But I wouldn't want some of the bad things to happen to them on the way that happened to so many of the others we traveled with."

"Hell, she's got the Rivers spirit. She'd be all right."

She met his eyes, those soft, brown eyes that always held so much love for her. He was strong now, had his old weight back. Both of them were stronger, rested; best of all they were free of the pain of the past. "I love you so much, Josh."

He kissed her lightly. "And I love you. Let's go home." He picked up the reins and got the mules underway. "Watch the babies," he said then. He gave out a loud, Texas "Yahoo!" and whipped the mules into a faster run toward the valley, and Marybeth laughed, hanging onto the wagon seat and realizing this was the last time she would have to bounce around in a wagon and use one for a home. Soon they would have that home they had talked about for so long. Far off in the distance she could see Aaron and Delores waving at them from their cabin to the south.

She looked back at the children. Danny, as big as most children at least a year older than he, had his arms around Joe and Emma, hanging onto them, his dark eyes sparkling with laughter. In his face and build she could see the MacKinder blood, but this MacKinder was going to bring pride to the name. She and Josh would make sure of it.

# More from Rosanne Bittner

### Tennessee Bride

Raised in the hills of Tennessee, Emma Simms dreams of the day she'll escape her life of poverty to start over in the excitement of Knoxville But when her mother dies and she's left with no one but her stepfather, Luke Simms, her dream abruptly becomes a nightmare. Luke plans to send Emma to Knoxville alright—straight to a notorious brothel.

River Joe, the mysterious Cherokee-raised frontiersman, knew from the first time he set eyes on the beautiful Emma that he had to have her as his own. And one glimpse at the handsome, buckskin-clad stranger ignites the flame of dangerous desire in Emma's heart.

Their passion could consume them both, but their love could very well save her life.

### Texas Bride

A man who must choose between his love or his life in this dazzling tale, named a Romantic Times Book Reviews All-Time Favorite.

Rachel Rivers is the most beautiful woman that Brand Selby has ever met. From the moment he laid eyes on the proper schoolteacher and watched her tremble beneath his longing gaze, he knew he wanted nothing more than to win her heart.

But Rachel lives in a land where hatred for the Indian runs deep, and where she is courted by Texas Ranger Jason Brown, Brand's sworn enemy. But the fate of Rachel and Brand's love has already been sealed, and not even the prospect of Rachel being cast out from her own kind, nor the threat of Brand's own demise, can extinguish the flames of desire in their hearts.

### Full Circle

The last thing sheltered missionary Evelyn Gibbons wants upon arriving at the South Dakota reservation is to fall in love. Yet, from the moment she clashes with Black Hawk, the complicated man of the Sioux, she knows he's everything she could ever want, and everything she can never have.

Living in the hills with his young son, Black Hawk reveres the ways of his people and is determined to preserve Sioux traditions. But when he meets Evelyn, a woman from the society he most abhors, not even his own prejudices can smother the flame of desire that burns for her.

But in the midst of their unlikely romance is a storm tide of treachery and hate that threatens to destroy their love, and their lives.

### Until Tomorrow

Addy wants nothing more than to leave her small Illinois home for the gold-rich hills of Colorado, where a teaching job awaits. But her plans are thwarted when a band of outlaws rob the very bank in which she is withdrawing her savings, taking her hostage in the process. Rogue and ruthless, her captives sweep her off to the country with evil intent, but one man stands in the way.

Ex-Confederate soldier Parker Cole doesn't understand his own fierce determination to protect the beautiful captive from his fellow bandits. Touched by her courage and spirit, he vows to prove his love to her, following Addy to a mining boomtown filled with dreamers and desperados. Fearless though he may be, Parker must summon all of his courage to beat out the line of rich and powerful suitors in the pursuit of the greatest treasure—Addy's heart.